THE Darkest Magic

THE *Darkest Magic*

A BOOK OF *Spirits* AND *Thieves* #2

MORGAN RHODES

razOr
bill

An Imprint of Penguin Random House LLC

An Imprint of Penguin Random House

Penguin.com

ISBN: 978-1-59514-761-5

Printed in the United States of America

1 3 5 7 9 10 8 6 4 2

Design by Anthony Elder

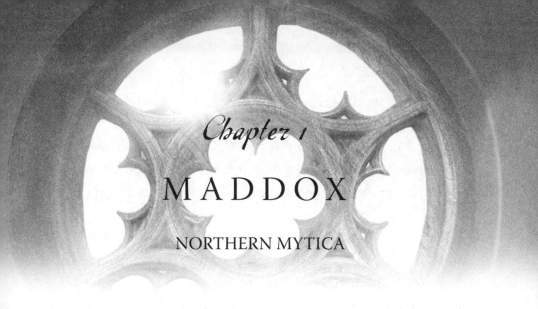

Chapter 1

MADDOX

NORTHERN MYTICA

Each step he took was torture.

It was as if a curse from a vengeful goddess had turned his flesh to fire. Still, he knew he had to be brave—to bear it as long as possible.

Maddox's companion eyed him with curiosity as they strode along the dirt road that cut through the village of Silvereve.

"It's the boots, isn't it?" Barnabas said.

Maddox's jaw stiffened. "I don't know what you're talking about."

"You're limping. And I'm sure I just heard you whimper." Barnabas frowned. "You should have let me take care of stealing the boots. I would have found ones that properly fit you. But no. You wanted to do it *yourself*."

Perhaps Maddox hadn't hidden his error as well as he'd hoped. "I didn't whimper."

Barnabas grinned, white teeth glinting in the moonlight. "Admit you're a terrible thief. Go on. Don't be embarrassed."

Maddox gritted his teeth. Perhaps he couldn't blame *every* difficulty he faced on the goddess. "Very well, if that's what you want to hear. I'm a terrible thief, and I desperately need new boots."

"We'll get you some tonight. Promise. A fine leather pair fit for a royal prince." Just then, a burst of boisterous voices sounded from the center of the village, which was lit up with torches and lanterns. Barnabas turned to look. "I thought you said Silvereve was a quiet place."

It usually was, which was why Maddox now took a long, hard look at the stone-sided shops and landmarks that made up the otherwise familiar town square to be certain they hadn't taken a wrong turn and ended up in another world altogether. He could barely focus thanks to all the shouts and laughter, singing and hollering.

It was so loud, and he was concentrating so hard, that he didn't notice the man with a large round belly, bright red cheeks, and ear-to-ear smile who had approached.

"Welcome, friends!" he boomed, slapping Barnabas on his back and handing him a tall green bottle. "Wine flows freely tonight. Drink up!"

Barnabas tossed a skeptical glance at the bottle in his grasp, then fixed a crooked grin on his face. "Thanks, *friend*. What inspires such generosity on this otherwise mundane evening?"

The man's bloodshot eyes bugged out. "Haven't you heard? Only today, Her Radiance announced that she has extended her anniversary celebrations from a mere season to a full year! Not only that, but in gratitude to her loyal subjects, wine touched by her magic will flow like water throughout the celebration."

"Really now." Barnabas's smile faltered, and the friendly light in his eyes became cold and hard. "A full year? Well, that's our radiant goddess for you. So generous and kind to us all."

"She is, my good sir." The man slapped Barnabas on his back

again. "She certainly is. Praise her name: Valoria, goddess of earth and water! And wine!"

The drunk man turned away, and Barnabas tossed the bottle away from him as if it had been overflowing with maggots.

"*Touched by her magic*," Maddox repeated with disgust. "The wine has been *tainted* by her magic, is more like it."

A year of celebrations in honor of that creature of darkness. The thought made Maddox sick to his stomach.

"Precisely what I was thinking," Barnabas said. "As much as I enjoy a good bottle of wine, I'll make sure not to touch one again until next year. Come. Let's fetch your mother and be gone from this place."

After they found Damaris and ensured her safety, their plan was to capture and interrogate Valoria's scribe, who'd spent the past several months by the goddess's side.

His job, according to Barnabas's witch friend, Camilla, was to rewrite the history of Mytica and fill it with lies that would fool generations to come. Among the dozens of historical records the scribe had already altered was the account of King Thaddeus's truly heroic reign, as well as the very existence of the rightful heiress, a young girl named Princess Cassia, whose throne Valoria had stolen when she'd murdered the king.

Camilla was certain that this scribe would know Valoria's weaknesses.

Everyone had a mortal weakness. Even an immortal goddess.

They continued on their route to the cottage where Maddox had been raised, the revelers in the village echoing all the way. Maddox tried to concentrate on anything other than Valoria—or his abused feet. So he decided to focus on his companion.

Barnabas was as tall as Maddox. The thief had let his dark hair grow out long and wild, and now he had it tied back from his face with a scrap of black leather. A short, thick beard covered half of his tanned face. This was a man who could skillfully play the part of the fool when circumstances called for it, but apart from the sparkle in his dark brown eyes, the man looked every bit as dangerous as Maddox knew he was.

And he had even more reasons to hate Valoria than Maddox did.

That hate grew stronger with every step he took. It gave him strength and purpose as they neared his home.

They finally arrived at the cottage to find it empty and dark, with no fire burning in the hearth.

"Don't panic," Barnabas said, which only made Maddox worry more—if Barnabas knew to calm him preemptively, that meant he was concerned for the safety of Damaris Corso as well.

"I'm trying my best not to."

"Good," Barnabas said. "Likely, she's in the midst of the celebrations."

Maddox shook his head. "Not likely," he said. "She despises the goddess. Always has."

"Ah, but these festivities give her the chance to pretend she feels the opposite. You know as well as I that right now it's much safer to blend in with the rest of the ignorant fools in this kingdom than to call attention to your reasonable beliefs. We'll find her, I promise we will."

Barnabas's assurance gave him some relief, but now they needed a plan. They'd continue searching for information in the main market area and ask those they passed for help in their search.

To Maddox, every inch of this section of Silvereve was haunted with ghosts. Right now he was haunted by memories of a mother who worked hard from dawn to dusk to support her only son, to keep the dangerous secret that he could see spirits, could coax the dead from their graves without even trying. If Damaris had one fault, it was that she had been vastly overprotective, keeping Maddox at home most of the time and scaring away potential friends who were curious about the strange, pale boy with the dark, haunted eyes. There were times he'd resented it, wanting to be as normal as any of the others. But that wasn't what he was thinking about now. Instead, he thought about how she would hold him when he had nightmares, promising that he was safe. How she'd read his favorite books to him, make crisp biscuits topped with melted sugar—his favorite—when he was scared.

She'd taught him to read and had inspired his love of books—the kinds of books that Valoria had recently banned. The goddess claimed her decision to allow only approved publications containing what she deemed to be useful, practical information—rather than fantastical tales that did nothing but rot the minds of the young and make them believe in nonsense—would improve the intelligence and overall lives of her citizens.

Thirteen years he'd lived here, rarely straying farther than a couple of miles away to visit the neighboring village of Blackthorn with his mother. But then came Livius, who had discovered Maddox's abilities and decided to use them for his own gain, stealing him from his home and his mother with the lie that they were only going to Blackthorn for the day. Maddox hadn't known he wouldn't see her again for nearly a year.

"You will do exactly as I say," Livius had hissed at Maddox after they'd left Silvereve. *"Otherwise, when you next return here, you will find your mother dead. And you'll have only yourself to blame."*

It was easy to frighten a thirteen-year-old with barely any experience in the world. He'd believed in Livius's threats, and so he'd done exactly as Livius said: traveled with him across Northern

Mytica convincing nobles that their villas were besieged by evil spirits and that only the witch-boy and his guardian could help them—for a price, of course.

Every now and then, Maddox did have to deal with a real spirit. But those encounters were rare, and he soon learned that nobles were remarkably easy to fool.

All his life, Maddox had hated this dark magic that drew these frightening, shadowy spirits to him.

But recently, all that had changed.

Because not all spirits were the same, he'd discovered. He'd come to know one that was beautiful, helpful, and kind: a spirit girl named Becca, who claimed to be from another world.

Sadly, Becca had returned to that world long before he was ready to say farewell. Now it seemed their handful of days together had been only a dream.

But she wasn't a dream, he told himself firmly now. *She was real— as real as I am. And one day I will see her again.*

Maddox held on to this hope, refusing to think about how truly impossible it was.

At last they reached the crowded village square. Hundreds of men and women strode past them, laughing and drinking from bottles and flasks. Maddox and Barnabas scanned the area for any sign of Damaris but saw nothing. When Maddox tried to stop revelers and ask if they knew her, all he received were drunken shakes of heads and incoherent mumbling.

His worry over his mother's safety grew with every moment that passed.

Maddox caught the shoulder of a man with a red face and stringy black hair. "Pardon," he said, "but can you tell me if you know of a woman named Damaris Corso?"

"Damaris Corso, you say?" The man then let out a loud crack of a laugh. "I know her."

"Excellent!" Maddox tried to smile, keeping his hand on the man's shoulder to keep him and his foul-smelling breath from getting too close. "Do you happen to know where we might find her? We have an urgent matter to discuss, and she's not at her cottage."

"No, I don't suppose she would be. She's keeping everyone's bellies full at the Serpent's Tongue. Lovely thing, she is. Got to grab a handful of her skirt earlier this evening before she managed to slip away from me."

"Did you?" Barnabas said low and evenly while Maddox clenched his fists at his sides, outraged by the man's claim.

The drunken man winked. "Give me time and I'll get all I want from that woman."

"I'm sure." Barnabas nodded, then slugged the man in his face. He dropped like a bag full of hammers to the ground, grunting and grabbing his nose, which was now gushing blood.

If Barnabas hadn't hit him first, Maddox was sure he would have.

"What"—the drunk sputtered—"what was that for, you arse?"

Barnabas glowered down at him. "You insult my sister, I break your nose. It's a fair price to pay, I think."

Maddox blinked. *Sister?*

"Your sister"—the man clumsily got back to his feet, his eyes blazing with fury—"isn't much more than a common whore."

This time, Barnabas punched the man with enough force to knock him unconscious. Then he swept his gaze over him from head to foot.

"Nice boots." Barnabas nodded at them. "I think they're your size, Maddox."

Maddox just stared at him. "Your *sister*?"

Barnabas's expression turned tense. He dropped to his knees and hastily untied the boots. "Yes. Haven't I mentioned that?"

"I think I'd remember if you did."

"Yes, well, I have now. It's true. Damaris is my sister, therefore one of the very few people in this world I trust—despite her unfortunate decision to hand you over to Livius."

"She didn't exactly hand me over."

"Regardless, that's a matter I'll make sure to discuss with her."

Maddox's mind was still reeling. "Your *sister*," he said again.

"You already said that," Barnabas said.

This was truly unbelievable. Why wouldn't he have mentioned something so important before now? "How many siblings do you have?" Maddox asked.

"Only two—that I'm aware of. Damaris and Cyrus."

Maddox remembered Cyrus. He was a rebel who had found work as one of Valoria's guards, a position that gave him access to information and sometimes allowed him to help fellow rebels who had been arrested.

"And before you chastise me for keeping secrets," Barnabas said as he threw the pair of heavy black boots at Maddox, "know that this is simply what I must do. Out of necessity, to survive. I keep secrets. I trust very few in this world, and that's not going to change any time soon."

Maddox eased off of his blustering, but only by a fraction. "Don't you trust me?"

"I do. Of course. I just—" Barnabas groaned. "I keep secrets from everyone. You're not the only one. So," he said, clearly trying to change the subject, "what's the Serpent's Tongue, anyway?"

"A tavern. It's not far from here."

Barnabas nodded. "Lead the way."

The newly stolen boots fit Maddox perfectly, as if they'd been made especially for him. But Maddox wasn't ready to gush with gratitude just yet. He was deeply annoyed that Barnabas had waited until tonight to reveal that Damaris was his sister—and that he'd only done so in reaction to the taunts of a drunken man.

It was especially tough considering that Maddox was still coming to terms with the new knowledge that the only mother he'd ever known wasn't connected to him by blood. His birth mother had been an immortal who'd fallen in love with a mortal man.

His family tree was getting more crooked and confusing with each day that passed.

It didn't take long for them to reach their destination. Maddox had never ventured inside the Serpent's Tongue before, but he'd passed by it many times and would recognize its exterior anywhere. Carved above the heavy wooden front doors was the head of a snake, its mouth open in a hiss, the points of its sharp fangs only an arm's reach above the heads of patrons entering the dark and crowded establishment.

Tonight, at an hour when many would have otherwise already taken to their beds, the tavern was packed from wall to wall, long wooden tables loaded to capacity with both locals and visitors participating in the celebrations.

"Do you see her?" Barnabas asked.

Maddox scanned the multitude of sweaty faces, all seemingly drunk and happy. "No."

"Let's take a seat."

"Where?" Maddox asked, gesturing at the completely full taproom. "They're all taken."

Suddenly and with little effort, Barnabas shoved two men off the wooden bench to their left. "What were you saying?" he asked as he sat down.

"Nothing useful, apparently." Maddox continued to search the crowd. Nearby, a woman smoking a cigarillo sent a cloud of rancid smoke into Maddox's eyes, making them start to water.

He rubbed them and kept looking, his gaze moving past face after face. Despite living here all his life, no one looked familiar. And no one looked at him as if they might recognize him.

A fat man spun a laughing woman around in a circle to the music of a fiddler standing on top of a table. Some others were clapping in time to a song that Maddox didn't recognize. Three men pounded on their table, shaking it, to garner the attention of a barmaid.

"More wine!" they called.

The barmaid appeared, elbowing her way through the crowd. She smiled and nodded and promised that she would be back as soon as possible. One man slapped her on her bottom, and she spun around and scolded him, but she was laughing as she turned from the table and locked gazes with Maddox.

"Mother," he whispered, his heart swelling. He raised his hand in greeting and found that his cheeks already hurt from how widely he was smiling.

Even though she looked different tonight in her tight white bodice that showed far more of her bosom than Maddox was used to, and a long black skirt that hugged her hips, he would recognize her anywhere. Her smile, her laugh, the kindness in her eyes— even when dealing with thirsty heathens, it would seem.

Damaris Corso quickly weaved her way through the crowd toward him and threw her arms around him, hugging him close to her.

"My sweet boy! I've missed you so much!"

"I've missed you too," he said, his throat tight with both happiness and relief at finding her. He cast a look over her shoulder at Barnabas, still seated, who nodded his approval. "When you weren't at home, I thought . . . well, I didn't know what to think. And now, you're here and . . . you're a . . . a . . ."

"A barmaid. Yes, it's true." She sighed, but her smile didn't falter as she kissed both of his cheeks. "With all these celebrations, it's the easiest way to earn my coin." Her eyes were kind, but it wasn't until now that Maddox saw how tired they were, and he felt guilty for feeling any shame over his mother's new occupation. "Oh, I'm so glad you've come home!"

Yes, it was possible that his heart might burst. "Me too," he said, smiling so as not to shed a tear.

Then, Damaris's joyful expression shadowed. "Where is Livius?" she asked in a low voice.

"Not here, thankfully," replied Barnabas.

She turned her surprised gaze to Barnabas as he rose from his seat and drew back the hood of his cloak so she could fully see his face.

Damaris's mouth fell open. She appeared to grapple for the right words. "You . . ." was all she managed.

Barnabas nodded. "Yes, it's me. How've you been, sister?"

In one lightning-fast motion, she slapped him, hard, across his left cheek.

Barnabas winced, stroking his face gingerly. "I suppose I deserved that."

"Sixteen years! Sixteen years without a single word from you! I thought you were dead!" Then she grabbed him into a tight hug. "I've missed you so much, you horrible thing!"

Barnabas grasped her shoulders and gave her a grin. "The feeling is mutual, Dam. Now we need to get out of here."

"What? I can't leave. Do you see how many people are in here? On a night like tonight I can earn enough to live on for at least a month! Go back to my cottage, stay as long as you like, and when this place closes up I'll come home. Then we can catch up on all that has happened."

A man with a shaved head in a red tunic climbed on top of a nearby table and raised his tankard high in the air. "To our radiant goddess Valoria!" he slurred. "May she reign for a thousand years! And a deadly curse upon the dark goddess of the South! We would rather spit than speak her name!"

A deafening cheer followed this toast, and patrons pounded on the tables to show their approval. Maddox watched all of this uneasily. What would they do if they knew the horrible truth about their beloved goddess?

"More wine for everyone!" the drunken man called out.

"I can't talk long," Damaris said, gesturing at the eager patrons rushing to the front with their goblets and mugs. "But I promise to return as soon as I can."

Maddox grabbed her wrist as she turned away. "I know, Mother. I know everything."

Her face blanched, and her gaze found his again. "As soon as I saw Barnabas . . ." she sighed. "If he found you, I knew it had to mean . . ." She swallowed hard. "You know *everything*?"

He nodded solemnly.

"So you know that Barnabas is . . . is . . ."

"My father," he finished, still struggling to believe it was true. "And that you're not really my mother, even though you . . . you *are*. I've been thinking about this for days on end. You will always be my mother. You kept me safe my whole life, with no one to help you, even though you've always known who I am. *What* I am.

I love you for that—I'll always love you for that."

Damaris drew in a shaky breath, her eyes brimming with tears as she pulled him close and stroked the hair on the back of his head. "I wanted to tell you, Maddox, but it was never the right time. I wanted to assure you that your . . . abilities . . . came from a good place. Not from evil. Never evil." Maddox didn't want to let her go, but when he finally released her, she sniffed and rubbed her hand under her nose. "When Livius arrived, I thought that if he knew at least part of the truth, then perhaps he could help me protect you. I trusted him, foolishly. I was so stupid. I'm sorry. I'm so sorry for all the misery that man caused both of us."

Maddox grasped her hands and squeezed them. "It's all in the past. Really. That part of our lives is over. But I must urge you to come with us now."

There was no time to tell her everything. That Livius was dead, killed from a poisonous bite from Valoria's pet cobra. That Maddox and Barnabas had attempted to exile Valoria to another world but had only met with failure and the promise of a goddess's wrath. That now the plan was to capture and interrogate Valoria's scribe.

Damaris's brows drew together. "What is this? Barnabas, what's going on?"

Grim lines had settled into Barnabas's expression. "Maddox isn't the only one who knows the truth now, Dam."

She stifled her gasp with the back of her hand. "Valoria."

He nodded. "We need to get you somewhere safe. It's no secret that Maddox has been with you all these years. Now that she knows who he is, it's not beyond her to use your safety against him. She wants his magic for herself. For him to be at her disposal at all times."

"She can't have it," Maddox gritted out.

Damaris was quiet for a long moment, until finally she nodded firmly. "Very well," she said. "Let's go."

Without another word, the three of them made their way through the crowd toward the exit. Thanks to his good boots and knowledge that his mother was safe, Maddox now walked without any pain in either his feet or his heart.

"Not staying for another round?" The man in red who'd toasted to the goddess on top of the table now stood between them and the door.

"Afraid not, friend," Barnabas said. "I guess that means more for the rest of you."

"For the rest of *them*," he said, gesturing at the drunken crowd with a jerk of his chin. "I stay away from inebriants myself. They cloud the mind. Don't you agree, Barnabas?"

Barnabas drew the dagger from the sheath at his belt. "Who are you?"

"My name is Goran."

"How do you know my name, Goran?"

Goran glanced at Maddox, whose heart had started racing in his chest. "And you're Maddox, are you? I wasn't expecting more than a mere boy, but look at you. Practically a man."

"Let us pass," Maddox growled as Damaris gripped his arm.

Goran glanced at the weapon in Barnabas's hand. "Not a good idea to wave that about, Barnabas. Some innocent person in here could get hurt."

"I'm not planning to hurt any of them," Barnabas said. "Only the person who prevents us from leaving."

"Perhaps you wouldn't like to hurt anyone. I, on the other hand, would kill everyone in here without blinking an eye."

Barnabas narrowed his eyes. "What are you? An assassin?"

"I was. But I've recently been specially chosen to follow a worthier path."

Barnabas cocked his head. "Let me guess. By Valoria?"

Goran smiled. "Her Radiance told me what happened. Did you really think this could end any other way? The boy comes with me tonight. If you try to stop me, I will kill you and everyone else in here."

"That would be a mighty feat for even the most skilled assassin."

"You thought this would be that easy?" Maddox snarled at the bald man. "That you'd just take me out of here and walk away and all is well?"

Goran raised a brow. "I've heard about your magic, boy. I know that as soon as we leave here, you will try to kill me. Therefore, I'll be sure you're not conscious for the journey."

Maddox glanced around anxiously. No one else in the tavern seemed aware that there was a life-or-death negotiation going on in their midst. His stomach churned, but the amused expression on Barnabas's face helped to keep him calm.

"Valoria has sent a single assassin after us," Barnabas said, casually shifting his dagger back and forth between his hands. "Well, damn. It seems as if we're defeated."

"You speak mockingly," said Goran. "You shouldn't."

"Oh yes, you're right. I'm incredibly intimidated." Barnabas inched close to Goran and stared him straight in his eyes. "Get out of our way, or I'll send you back to your radiant goddess in pieces."

"There's no need for violent threats," Damaris hissed, her hold on Maddox's arm growing stronger. "There is a peaceful solution to be found here."

Maddox almost smiled at that. His mother was always searching for peaceful solutions. How often had he found a large spider on his bed, only to watch his mother carefully scoop the creature up in a cooking pot to set it free while he'd been searching for something to kill it with.

"Every creature deserves a chance at life," she'd tell him. *"Even the ugly, eight-legged ones."*

But an assassin working for Valoria could surely do things much uglier than any spider could.

Maddox examined Goran closely. He had tattoos on his neck and muscular forearms, some sort of writing in black and gold. Maddox couldn't read the language, although it seemed oddly familiar to him. He pulled his gaze away when he felt the assassin notice him looking.

"My tattoos," Goran said, holding out his arms. "The ink is so fresh it's barely dried. They are gifts from the goddess herself. She told me that if she had her dagger, she could have made the marks deeper, more permanent than she was able to with her earth magic alone. Though these will work just fine."

Among all the items she greedily sought, the one the goddess prized the most highly was a golden dagger. This dagger, she believed, had the power to turn mortals into slaves if it was used to carve special symbols into their flesh.

For a while now, Maddox had suspected that these symbols were words written in the language of the immortals—the same language and symbols that filled the magical book that had sent Becca Hatcher's spirit to Mytica.

"How fancy," Barnabas said drily. "But your little drawings change nothing. And you're still standing in our way. I suggest you move."

He raised his dagger to Goran's throat, but the assassin didn't even flinch.

"When you return to your goddess with your tail between your legs," Barnabas said, "kindly tell her she can kiss my arse."

Goran moved with supernatural speed, grabbing the dagger out of Barnabas's grip. Barnabas looked down at his empty hand with shock. He didn't have time to so much as look up before Goran picked Barnabas up and threw him across the room, as if it took no more effort than tossing a small rock into a river. Barnabas hit the wall hard and landed on a table, sending plates and goblets flying in all directions. Damaris shrieked and let go of Maddox's arm. Everyone in the tavern fell silent and turned with surprise toward the violence.

Maddox didn't wait another moment. He clenched his hands into fists and summoned his death magic. Enough to harm, but not to kill. It was like a shadow rising within him, filling his limbs with dark strength, and he focused this mere taste of his magic on his foe.

"Yes," Goran grunted. "I feel it. Like a hand thrusting through my chest to grip my heart. It's just as the goddess warned."

From the corner of Maddox's eye, he saw Barnabas push himself to his feet and draw closer.

Goran staggered forward one step. His next step was much smoother. And then he took another.

No one had ever been able to push back against Maddox's magic like this before.

This was no normal man.

"Maddox, be careful," Barnabas warned.

"Not so strong, really," Goran said through clenched teeth. "Is that all you have in you, boy?"

The earth magic in Goran's marks, Maddox thought. Could that be what was dulling the effect of the magic?

"No, not all," Maddox bit the words out.

Maddox drew more magic to the surface. It was a cold sensation running through his veins, his limbs, but perspiration began to drip down his forehead at the effort. He hadn't needed this much before, and he wondered how much of it he had. Would it be enough?

He clenched his teeth and fisted his hands, his muscles tensing down his arms enough that he began to shake from the effort of trying to stop this man from drawing closer to him.

"Enough of this," Damaris said. "Maddox, stop!" She moved to stand in front of him. She held her hand up, palm out and facing Goran. "I won't allow anyone to be hurt here tonight. Leave here now. Tell the goddess that if she wants Maddox, then she can come here and face us herself."

"Step back from him," Barnabas hissed at her.

She kept her attention fully fixed on the assassin. "No, Barnabas, let me handle this. You've done enough."

Goran stopped, an arm's reach away from Maddox and Damaris. A smile curled up the corners of his mouth. "You mean what you say, don't you? You wish to find a peaceful solution to this."

Damaris raised her chin. "I do."

"I don't have many weaknesses, especially not now," he said, looking down at his fresh marks, "but one of them is for brave women who stand up for what they believe. Who protect what they love. I admire that more than I can say."

Amazed, Maddox watched this exchange. Would his mother be able to stop this assassin, using only words as her weapons?

Damaris nodded firmly. "Good."

Goran's smile widened. "Luckily, I learned to ignore my weaknesses long ago."

The silver blade caught the flickering lantern light as Goran slashed Barnabas's dagger forward, cutting Damaris's throat in a single, deep line.

"Mama, no!" Maddox caught her as she dropped to the floor,

her hands flying up in vain to try to block the flow of blood. She sought Maddox's gaze, her eyes full of pain and regret. Barnabas was there too, next to his sister and clutching her hand.

Goran glared down at him. "Come with me now, boy, and no one else has to die here."

Maddox tore his gaze away from his dying mother to send a wave of cold death toward this murderer. Goran's eyes widened in pain as he dropped the bloody dagger and clutched at his throat. He staggered backward, his face convulsing and turning red.

"What—?" he gasped. "Your power . . . it's so much . . . stronger. . . ."

He fell to his knees as Maddox twisted the magic like a black knife, and blood began to pour from the assassin's nose.

The tavern had transformed from a den of wine-soaked revelry to a pit of chaos. The patrons had realized their lives were in peril, and they flooded toward the exit, blocking Maddox from the killer. By the time they cleared out, Goran was nowhere to be seen.

The assassin had escaped.

"Damn it," Barnabas said, his voice pained and shaky. "Damn it all. And damn Valoria for this!"

Hot tears streaked down Maddox's cheeks. Damaris weakly clutched his arm.

"I'm sorry," Maddox choked out. "Mama, I'm so sorry. Forgive me."

He gazed down at Damaris for as long as he could. Apart from the pain in his mother's tear-filled eyes, there was only love. Peace.

And then her gaze went blank, her expression still and lifeless.

Maddox pulled his mother's limp body against him and sobbed against her shoulder. The sheer force of his anguish reached outward, and his magic shattered every window in the tavern.

Chapter 2

CRYSTAL

Toronto—Present Day

Becca had started to twitch, her expression growing tense, her forehead furrowing, and little pained gasps escaped her lips.

Little sisters were a lot like kittens. It was pretty easy to tell when one was having a nightmare.

"No, please, no," Becca whimpered. "No, don't!"

Crys sat up and shook her. "Hey. Wakey, wakey!"

Becca drew in a quick breath. Her eyelashes fluttered. She blinked a few times, her expression slowly turning into one of recognition as she registered Crys sitting on the side of her bed.

She frowned. "Were you watching me sleep again?"

"You make it sound so creepy."

"It *is* creepy."

"I'd rather think of it as watching over my kid sister so she isn't yanked into a faraway fantasy world again. Like a guardian angel."

Becca's frown didn't fade as she sat up, stretched, and glanced at the clock. "Is that really the time?"

"Yup."

"It's *noon*?"

"Well done. And here I thought that after a whole week away

from school you'd forget everything you ever learned. Oh wait, that's just what Mom thinks will happen."

From the corner of her eye, Crys saw Charlie, their black-and-white kitten, saunter into the room and sit down at her feet. He looked up at her and mewed, which she translated to mean: "Please pick me up."

Crys reached down and did as requested, placing Charlie on top of the white duvet cover.

As Becca absently scratched his back, Charlie got down on his haunches and raised his tail high in the air, purring happily. "I had a horrible dream," she said.

"I could tell. What about?"

"I was there again. In Mytica."

Mytica. The name of the fantasy land Becca claimed her spirit visited while, here in the real world, her body had been trapped in a coma. She kept telling Crys and their mother about it like it was real, like it all really happened. And Crys listened, allowing her to talk about it as much as she needed to.

She tried really hard to believe her sister, but seriously? Another world?

Crys would admit, albeit reluctantly, that she'd recently come to believe that magic books and evil sorcerers were real, but she still had her limits.

Anyway, playing along with this Mytica place was easy compared to what Becca had just gone through. The important thing was that Becca was safe. She believed her story was true, and the last thing Crys wanted to do was make fun of her for it. There were still plenty of things that were fair game for Crys to mock, but this was serious.

"Go on," Crys said after a few moments of silence. "What about Mythica?"

"*Myt*-i-ca," Becca corrected. "Not *Myth*-i-ca."

"Yeah, that's what I said! What happened in the dream?"

A pained, faraway look filled Becca's dark blue eyes, which were much more serious than any other fifteen-year-old Crys had ever known. But Becca had always been the more serious sister. She was also the one who liked to correct her older sister's grammar and pronunciation way too frequently.

"I was watching. The whole time. I wasn't part of it, but I could hear noises coming from this tavern. I could smell, like, sweat and smoke and other nasty things."

"Nice," Crys said, trying unsuccessfully to make Becca smile.

"Maddox's mother . . ." Becca inhaled sharply, her eyes growing glossy. "She's dead. Her . . . her throat . . . that man cut it. Oh God. Poor Maddox!"

"Whoa, wait a minute. Calm down. It was just a dream, remember? Only a dream. Maddox is fine."

Maddox. Aka Becca's boyfriend from another world. Whenever she talked about him, she got this dreamy look in those serious eyes—which was new for her. As far as Crys knew, or at least as far as Becca had ever shared with her, she'd never crushed this hard on anyone before now.

Dream Boy was the first.

Then again, Crys and Becca hadn't exactly been super close for the last few years.

The thought of all the time they'd wasted dug a painful hole deep inside of Crys. No, the time that *she'd* wasted, being a brat and a lousy sister ever since their father had left them to join Markus King's secret Hawkspear Society. She'd hated Daniel Hatcher for turning his back on them, and what had she done? Taken it out on her mother and sister, the two family members who hadn't left.

But Crys had always been her dad's shadow. They used to share everything—a love of photography, sushi, books, and foreign films. He even used to talk politics with her, and Crys couldn't think of any other kid whose father trusted her knowledge and opinions enough to engage in any kind of serious debate. But all of that was two years ago, before he left everything and everyone behind just to please Markus. Crys had only reconnected with him to find out the truth about Hawkspear, about her father's role in it. And about just how deeply entwined her entire family history was with that of an immortal "death god." This was what Markus liked others to believe he was so that they'd allow him to carve magical marks into their forearms with his golden dagger, believing it brought good health and not realizing that the main reason Markus did it was to ensure their unwavering loyalty and obedience.

Now Becca kept saying that Markus had stolen that same golden dagger from Mytica, from an evil goddess who desperately wanted it back.

Damn. Crys wished she could believe Becca's story completely. And it wasn't that she didn't trust her sister or thought she was going crazy. But Crys had always had a difficult time believing or trusting anything that she hadn't seen or experienced for herself.

Which now unfortunately included knowing where her father was or whether he was safe. The last she'd seen of him, he was helping her and Becca escape from Markus with the Bronze Codex, the book that would allegedly restore Markus's fading magical mojo.

Crys also had the book to thank for the fact that they weren't at home above the bookshop right now and instead were crashing at a borrowed penthouse in Yorkville. The place belonged to one of Crys's aunt Jackie's associates, a British guy named Angus Baltha-zar, who had previously helped Jackie steal priceless artifacts—like the Bronze Codex—in Europe. After their near-death experience at Hawkspear, Jackie had called Angus at his London flat to see if they could stay at his house in Toronto and wait out the trouble.

Though he'd had absolutely no problem with them staying and had even asked the condo's security team to watch over them, Crys wasn't ready to call him a hero—not yet. She didn't really trust anybody except her own family, but all the same she had decided to hold off on judging Angus until she met him. Which would be soon—Jackie had just told them yesterday that he was en route to the place now to lend a hand. Jackie said Angus was an expert in all areas of magic, which was why she'd gone to him for any helpful insight he could offer on the Bronze Codex and how to use it to stop Markus once and for all.

They'd been holed up in the huge apartment for a week, under strict orders not to leave for fear that Markus would be lurking nearby, ready to snatch the sisters up and use them to blackmail Jackie and Julia into handing over the Codex. Julia had gotten them out of school with some lame story about them having to take an unexpected family trip. Crys had to laugh at that—she now had enough family time to last her a couple of lifetimes. As nice and ritzy as this place was, she was itching to get out and breathe some fresh air again. Gigantic balconies on the fiftieth floor totally didn't count.

Still, cabin fever aside, she knew enough to take their current situation seriously. Possibly even more seriously than Becca did, which was saying something. Because Becca hadn't seen all that Markus was capable of, how he could get people to do what he wanted. How his marked society members followed his every order without stopping for a second to question his motivations.

Markus may have had his entire following convinced that he

was a good man who wanted to make the world better, safer, more peaceful. But Crys saw him for what he really was: a power hungry freak who was beyond ancient, yet had the face and body of a young male model. And he wouldn't think twice about killing anyone who got in the way of what he wanted most.

If he ever found out what Crys's father had done . . .

Becca put her hand on Crys's shoulder. "What's wrong?"

"Hmm? Oh, nothing."

"You're not as good of a liar as you think."

"Fine. I'm worried about Dad," Crys admitted, her voice now hoarse.

"I know," Becca said in her most comforting tone. "But he can take care of himself. He's been doing that for years."

"I'd still feel better if he were here with us."

"You know Mom and Jackie would never be okay with that. He's still under Markus's control, right? He helped us, but who knows how much pain and resistance he had to go through to defy Markus just that one time. He's still dangerous to us."

"The logical mind of Becca Hatcher." Crys nodded, swallowing past the lump in her throat. "Present and accounted for."

She knew what Becca said was true, but she couldn't get it out of her mind. What her dad had risked. What he'd done to save them . . .

"Let's try to think about something else," Becca said in an upbeat manner, though her expression was still haunted by her nightmare. "Like . . . Angus's library." She slipped out of bed and pulled on a fuzzy blue bathrobe. "Let's go check it out again."

The only thing that was almost as fancy as—and definitely more interesting than—Angus Balthazar's penthouse was his personal library.

Angus had tons of rare and impressive early editions in his library—Jane Austen, Charles Dickens, even a signed UK first edition of *Harry Potter and the Philosopher's Stone*, which Crys personally coveted. But he also had many unusual titles in his collection, most of which shared an undeniable theme: magic.

There were big tomes on witchcraft, Satanism, paganism, voodoo, séances, hauntings, exorcisms. Handwritten grimoires in dozens of different languages. Journals of real people accused of being witches in England and the States, who were sentenced for crimes that no one could really prove.

She explored the library with Becca for a few minutes, but her buzzing head became so distracted that she had to take a seat on one of the oversized leather armchairs in the center of the room. Becca kept searching the shelves until a title caught her eye. She took the big volume and sat on the floor, cross-legged, in front of Crys.

Then, with a jolt of tension to her gut, she thought back to that day—that horrible day when Becca's interest was piqued by a different book, the Codex, which had arrived at the Speckled Muse wrapped in brown paper and string, mailed from England by Jackie herself. The book looked old, ancient, and was handwritten in a weird language Crys hadn't recognized. She'd been unimpressed, but Becca was immediately taken with it. She'd grabbed hold of it, flipped though the pages . . . and then something had grabbed her, *literally* grabbed her, and she fell into a coma for over a week.

Well, to Crys it was a coma. To Becca, the Codex was a ticket to a magical place filled of witches, thieves, and beautiful boys.

Crys's heartbeat quickly doubled, slamming against her ribcage. Her chest grew tight, and suddenly it became hard to breathe. It felt a whole lot like a panic attack—and she hadn't had one of those since her father first left.

She tried to keep the thoughts at bay, but they stormed and whirled in her mind like a furious tornado.

Becca isn't my sister. She's my cousin.

Becca is Aunt Jackie's daughter, not my mother's. And her real father isn't my father—it's Markus King.

Half-immortal. Half-magic. And she has no damn idea.

Crys lurched to her feet. Becca looked up at her with surprise. "What's wrong?"

"Nothing," Crys said quickly. "Nothing, really. You . . . you keep looking at the books. I'm going to go see what Mom and Jackie and Dr. Vega are up to downstairs."

She was out of the library before Becca had a chance to respond.

Downstairs was a living room, a large study, and a kitchen that put the one they had in their small apartment above the bookshop to shame. Crys headed directly to the study, which was piled high with everything from Dr. Vega's office at the university. Inside, she found Jackie sitting next to Dr. Vega, both of them bent over a thick manila file folder.

Dr. Uriah Vega, a renowned language expert and professor at the University of Toronto, was an old friend of Jackie's. He had been trying valiantly to decipher the book. A week ago, he'd been beaten within an inch of his life by Markus's minions, so he'd been invited to stay with Crys's family as he healed and recovered his strength.

"Where's Mom?" Crys asked.

Jackie looked up from the papers. "She went to the convenience store downstairs. For supplies."

Her aunt was tall, blond, and beautiful. Just like Becca. The dark circles that had taken up residence under her eyes for the last couple of days marred her looks only a little.

"Good morning, Ms. Hatcher," Dr. Vega said. He gave Crys a bright smile despite the fading bruises and bandages on his face. "You're looking quite *determined* today."

"I think I am. Jackie, can I speak to you privately please?"

"Of course." Jackie's smile was strained as she followed Crys to the kitchen.

Crys reached into the fridge to grab a can of Diet Coke.

"What is it?" Jackie asked.

"You need to tell Becca the truth," Crys said. She liked to think of her characteristic bluntness as a personal virtue that saved everyone valuable time.

Jackie's expression was suddenly pinched, and Crys knew her aunt knew exactly what she was talking about. "Not yet," Jackie said.

"Why not?"

"Because I'm not ready."

"Not ready to . . . what? Face the truth? Admit to your past mistakes and live with the consequences? Take responsibility for your daughter? Let me know if I'm getting warmer."

"Lower your voice," Jackie hissed. "She might hear you."

"Good, I hope she does." Crys hesitated then. Her bluntness was usually a good thing—in her opinion—but even she knew that sometimes she could be too harsh. And she didn't want to chase after a butterfly with a baseball bat, especially not now. "Look," she said. "I don't mean to be a bitch. Well, *mostly* I don't. But I'm sick of waiting around for something to happen, for life to go back to normal around here. Or is normal life just an impossible wish at this point?"

Jackie twisted a long piece of blond hair around her index finger. "I promise that I have a plan."

"Oh? And what is it?"

"I understand that you're anxious and want answers, but, Crys, it's only been a week. And Dr. Vega is still working with the book."

"I know. Okay? I know that." Crys started pacing back and forth, not even taking a sip of her pop, instead trying to focus on the feel of the surface condensation on the can to help cool her off a bit. Her frustration had a tendency to grow so intense that it just exploded, like fireworks. Or a bomb. People anywhere near her might get hurt, including herself. "You've been avoiding her," she said finally.

"No, I haven't."

"Yes, you have."

Jackie sighed. "I hate that you know the truth about me now. I hate that anyone knows it."

"Which part of the truth? That you were madly in love with Markus King? That you still are?"

Her eyes went wide. "Is that what you think? That my life is some kind of romance novel come to life? That I was just some cliché of a naive teenage girl falling for a powerful immortal? That I'm *still* that cliché?"

"Yes, actually. You should write it all down. You could make millions. Those kinds of stories sell like crazy."

"How wrong you are. How horribly wrong."

Crys flinched at Jackie's reaction, but she quickly regained her sharp composure. She felt she was close to a truth that hadn't yet been shared. "When you called him that night, when he had Becca and me, it was like he forgot everything except you," she said. "He probably forgot his own name. He handed the Codex over to Dad like it was a box of tissues, like it wasn't important to him at all. If you have that effect on him, all these years later . . . There's obviously something still there."

Jackie's cheeks flushed bright pink—but not from embarrass-ment. A look of sheer outrage clouded her face. "That man mur-dered my grandmother. He murdered my parents. He stole our family's fortune. And you think I still have a *thing* for him?"

Like a threatening storm cloud that had decided to show mercy, Crys lost her bluster. "I'm not saying it isn't complicated," she said quietly.

"He marked me, Crys. I was sixteen years old, and he carved symbols into my flesh with a knife to make sure that I did any-thing he told me to. I looked at him with awe, this handsome man who made time for *me*. Thousands of years separated us, but he looked no more than five years older than me. He took me into his confidence. And yes, I believed I loved him. Hell, maybe I did, for a time. But our . . . relationship wasn't natural—it was forged out of magic. Out of coercion. Do you see how messed up that is?" She thrust her forearm, bare and clear of any scars or blemishes, toward Crys. Crys knew how Markus's magic worked, that he could heal the dagger's marks as soon as he made them, leaving no trace behind. "I had no choice but to do as he said," Jackie went on. "Whether I truly believed at the time that I actually wanted him, that I actually loved him, makes no difference. I was under his in-fluence, and he used me. For that, I can never forgive him. For that, I'll always hate him."

"I'm sorry," Crys said. It was all she could say—even though she did want to congratulate Jackie for making her feel like a com-plete ass in record time.

"So am I. Believe me. But I'm not sorry that Becca exists. If there's one good thing that came out of that twisted relationship, it was her. But he can never know that she's his daughter. For her own safety."

"Agreed." Crys worked all of this over in her head as she took a shaky sip of her drink. "I know it's not easy for you to talk about, but . . . Jackie, he was *visibly* distracted when he learned you were on the phone. He still has feelings for you."

"Perhaps," Jackie admitted reluctantly, but in a tone that told Crys she wasn't surprised. "And perhaps I can use those feelings against him. If I need to."

"What did you say to him on that phone call?"

Jackie blinked, regarding Crys with her arms crossed tightly over her chest.

"Jackie, please," Crys said after a short silence.

"I told him that I know his magic is fading. That he needs the book, this book he's been obsessing over for years. He thinks it will make him the god his society believes he is. I told him that if he comes anywhere near me or my family, I would tear the pages from it one by one and burn them all. I didn't know he had it in his possession at the time."

"Oh," Crys said. She was looking at her aunt with growing awe. "I imagined that conversation going a totally different way."

"I'm sure you did." Her aunt's expression remained uncharacteristically grim. "Luckily, the book is with us now."

Julia Hatcher entered the kitchen carrying two plastic bags, interrupting them. "What's going on in here?" she said, eyeing her sister and daughter warily.

"The usual," Jackie said. "Your daughter is grilling me to make sure my loyalties lie with the family instead of my true and everlasting love, Markus King."

Julia nodded. "Good for her."

"Oh, shut up."

Julia's cell phone rang, and she scrambled to pull it out of her pocket.

"Hello?" After a pause, she glanced at Jackie and Crys. "I'll be right back," she said, leaving the room.

Crys began to put out the contents of the shopping bags. Three bags of potato chips, a large package of M&Ms, a variety of frozen meals, and two plastic containers of sushi. She eyed the sushi with equal parts disgust and gratitude.

Her mother was trying to make her happy. With convenience-store sushi, but still.

"So you really had no choice back then," Crys said quietly to Jackie. "You *had* to do what he said, like . . . like some kind of puppet."

"It didn't feel like that," Jackie said without a pause. "At the time, when I was doing those things, it felt like I had free will. Like I *wanted* to be doing them. But looking back at it . . . I know I didn't."

Absently, Crys pressed her hand against her ribs, still bound with bandages and sore from where one of Markus's minions had kicked and beaten her, all while Farrell looked on without stopping him.

Ugh. The absolute last person in the world Crys wanted to spend any time thinking about was Farrell Grayson. He was a rich kid from a family of Hawkspear members, known for his misdeeds and arrests more than anything else. He wasn't a nice guy even before he was a society member, even before he received his marks. But now he was really bad news. He'd recently tried to get close to Crys—but only because Markus had ordered him to. Crys had been poking around the society, trying to find out secrets about Markus and her father in case it might help save Becca.

And, unfortunately for her, before she found out that every time his lips moved it was either because there was a cigarette between them or he was lying, she'd really started to like Farrell.

Crys was ashamed at how easily he'd been able to manipulate her, which was why she'd kept the details of their brief association mostly to herself. But even now, if she were honest, she still found herself wanting to make excuses for everything Farrell did and all he lied about. She'd catch herself blaming what he'd done on his marks—after all, they were the same marks Jackie once had, before her aunt became pregnant with Markus's half-immortal child, when they'd become null and void.

But despite all that, Crys always came back to the one sure thing she knew about Farrell: Some of the things he'd done were unforgiveable.

"I'm going out on the balcony," Jackie said, thankfully pulling Crys out of her unwanted memories. "I need some air."

Crys offered her a bag of potato chips. "Hungry?"

"No." But she grabbed them anyway and left the kitchen just as Julia returned.

"I found something, Crys," Julia said. "You've been hiding things from me."

Her stomach sank. What was she in trouble for now?

"What?"

"This." Julia pulled a crumpled piece of paper from her pocket. Crys recognized it immediately: the flyer advertising a photography show at a nearby gallery, which she'd thrown away when she'd cleaned out her purse earlier that morning. "Andrea Stone. She's your favorite photographer, isn't she?"

Andrea Stone was known for her portraits. She traveled the world to find her subjects, none of them models or professionals. Real people with interesting faces, wrinkles, moles, warts, and all. Her work had been featured more than a dozen times on the cover of *National Geographic*, and Crys had every issue in her personal collection.

Favorite photographer was putting it mildly. *Primary inspiration* and *idol*? That was more like it.

"I'm surprised you know that," Crys said quietly, taking the flyer from her.

"Maybe I know more about you than you think I do."

"That's kind of scary."

Julia grinned. "The show is ending soon."

"I know. But unfortunately I can't go. It's just that I'd much rather stay here and play Monopoly or stare blankly at the walls for hours on end."

"Nope. Think again. You're going, and I'm coming with you. Tomorrow."

Crys snapped her head up and met her mom's gaze. "I'm sorry, I must have you confused with someone else. I thought you were my overprotective mother who loves rules and would never risk my safety for something as silly as the chance to view the life-changing work of my one true career role model."

"I am your overprotective mother, and I'm taking you to this photography show."

Crys's heart skipped a beat. For the first time in quite a while, a genuine, goofy grin broke out on her face. But it fell almost as quickly as it arrived. "What about Markus?" she said. "Aren't you afraid he might find us?"

Julia sighed. "I believe that Markus is able to find us whenever he likes, wherever we are."

That was a deeply unsettling thought. "Are you serious?"

"Unfortunately, yes. Still, the security is better here than back at the shop—for now, anyway. But I swear to God, if he decides to show his ancient face and ruin something I damn well know you've been looking forward to, I will personally claw his eyes out."

Crys regarded her mother with nothing short of shock. "I think that's the most badass thing you've ever said."

"From you, I'll take that as the highest compliment. Our stay here is only temporary. It was never a safe haven, that's not why we came here. We have the book, and Jackie is ready to destroy it if necessary. Markus knows that. He's weak. Dying. He wouldn't dare make a move against us unless he already had the book in his hands."

"You're sure about that?"

"Cautious now, are we?" Julia said, a smile reappearing on her face and her eyes sparkling with mischief. "Come on, let's break out of this dump and go to the show tomorrow. What do you say?"

Crys could barely believe this was really happening. "Um. I say *hell yes!*"

"Jackie!" Dr. Vega shouted from the study. "Julia! Come here immediately. The book—THE BOOK!"

Her excitement about the show disappearing all at once, Crys pulled Jackie off the balcony, and both of them rushed after Julia to the study.

"What's wrong?" Jackie demanded. "What happened?"

Dr. Vega looked up at them, his wide eyes magnified behind his thick, round glasses. "The book is changing."

"What do you mean, *changing*?"

"Right as I studied this page, the text . . . shifted. It *changed*. Right before my eyes!" He shuffled through a stack of photocopies, picking one and jabbing his finger at it. "Look! Here is a photocopy of this very page."

They drew closer. Crys looked from the photocopy to the leather-bound Codex, which lay open on the desk. At the center of both the photocopy and the original page was an illustration of a plant bearing purple flowers. But the text—both the format and the individual words—now varied wildly between the two, and at the very top of the book page, where there was once nothing but black-and-white writing, was a new illustration of a sun.

"Um. Is the sun . . . glowing?" Crys whispered as the black ink shifted to a golden shade, and light began to emanate from the parchment as if illuminated from within the fibers of the paper itself.

"What's going on?"

Crys's gaze shot to the doorway, where Becca now stood, still wrapped in her fuzzy blue bathrobe.

Her eyes were full and glowing with the same golden light.

Chapter 3

BECCA

One of Angus's many books was a dream encyclopedia. Becca leafed through it, hoping to find some answers about her recent nightmares. She'd wanted to dream about Maddox since she'd returned from Mytica, but the nightmare Crys had woken her from had been too real, too violent, too horrible. Her hands still shook from it.

But then she felt it—something else entirely.

It was a sensation deep inside of her, an urgency she couldn't ignore. Something was drawing her out of the library, down the stairs, and before she knew it she stood at the doorway to the study without even knowing why she was there.

"What's going on?" she asked, but even to herself, her voice sounded dreamy and faraway.

Her family and Dr. Vega all looked at her, expressions of surprise on their faces.

She wasn't sure if they answered her or not, because suddenly all she could see was the book.

The Bronze Codex.

She hadn't seen it since the night she woke up back in Toronto,

Markus King, her father, and Crys standing over her. She'd been so out of it then that she hadn't been able to register much. All she could do was blindly obey when Crys told her to run.

Since then, everyone had been treating her with kid gloves. And it didn't take psychic abilities for her to get the funny feeling that she was the main topic of hushed conversation in their temporary lodging. Her family and Dr. Vega spoke in whispers, and whenever Becca entered a room, they'd go quiet and look guilty. She tried very hard not to let it bother her, but how could it not?

Becca Hatcher: the crazy girl who claimed her spirit went on vacation to another world. Was that how they saw her?

Brain fuzzy, gaze locked on the leather-bound book, she stood there in the threshold for what felt like a very long time.

It's calling to me, she thought suddenly. *It wanted me to come here.*

"Becca?" came the sound of her name, but it was soft, like an echo underwater.

Did anyone else even realize how beautiful the Codex was? From the moment the book had arrived at the Speckled Muse, she'd felt an inexplicable but nonetheless immediate connection with it. She couldn't read its language—not in the traditional sense, at least. She didn't know what it was that day, of course, but she'd still felt oddly—*how to explain it?*—*protective* of it.

That feeling had never entirely gone away, but right now it was stronger than ever before.

That book belonged to her, no one else.

"Becca, I'm seriously going to slap you if you don't say something."

"Don't say that, Crys."

"Mom, look at her. She's, like, possessed or something."

"Becca, honey." Becca barely felt her aunt touch her shoulder, but the pressure was enough to make her raise her chin and see Jackie at her side, peering at her warily. "Are you all right?"

"Fine," Becca murmured. "But you should know, there's a spirit trapped in the hawk."

"Okay, now she's seriously talking crazy," Crys said.

Ignoring her sister, she focused on a memory of Maddox using his magic to pull a dark and violent spirit away from her. He'd trapped that spirit in a piece of metal—the bronze hawk on the cover of the Codex.

With the spirit trapped inside of it, the metal had given off an aura so bone-chillingly cold it felt as if it could freeze her very soul.

But today the book ushered in a warming sensation. An aura that felt welcoming. *Sparkly*, even, like a pleasant shiver down one's spine. The sensation shifted to an image: somewhere that was big, vast, and endless, sprawling over miles. Hundreds, thousands of miles.

Rolling meadows of green grass, jewel-like flowers of every shade and size, and a city made from crystal that sparkled like diamonds under the sun . . .

In three swift, thudding motions, Dr. Vega slammed the Codex shut, dropped it in a desk drawer, and locked it with a key.

She felt a cold pain hit her, as if an elastic band had suddenly snapped inside her brain, and she gasped. After the pain cleared, her mind finally did the same, and she looked up at her family with a wide, wondering gaze.

"Thank God." Crys sighed. Her face was pale and drawn. "No more glowy eyes. I don't like the glowy eyes at all. It's not a good look for you."

"My eyes were glowing?" Becca asked, her throat thick.

"Like lightbulbs from hell."

The haze was gone, but something else had replaced it—an intense need to see the book again. To touch it, to hold it. It was like an itch that needed to be scratched.

Julia hushed Crys and helped Becca into a nearby chair. She pushed the blond hair off of her daughter's forehead and smiled at her.

"Well, that was rather dramatic, wasn't it?" Julia glanced over at Jackie. "What do you make of it?"

Jackie just watched them, her expression troubled, her arms crossed tightly over her chest. "I wish like hell I knew."

"Perhaps we should ask Becca herself," suggested Dr. Vega.

"I don't know if that's a good idea," Jackie replied.

Becca glared at her. She couldn't help it. She loathed when people talked about her—or worse, spoke *for* her—as if she weren't even there.

She'd only met Dr. Vega yesterday, but she liked him quite a lot. She knew how Crys felt about him—that he was abrupt, scatterbrained, and perhaps a little too eccentric—but Becca thought he was kind of funny. He wanted to learn much more about her experience with the book, but Jackie and Julia—*and* Crys—had told him she still needed some time to recover before he could grill her about it. She appreciated that Dr. Vega didn't look at her like she was just a fifteen-year-old kid; the couple of times he'd talked to her so far, she'd felt respected. Like a peer.

Then again, maybe it was more like a lab rat. She thought of him slamming the Codex in the desk drawer just moments ago. Perhaps it was too soon to tell whose side Dr. Vega was on.

"I do think it's a good idea," Becca said to Jackie. "I want to help if I can. The more you learn about that book, the better you'll be able to figure out why it has these effects on me, right? And why it doesn't seem to have any effect on anyone else."

"You are exactly right," Dr. Vega said, giving her a toothy grin. He pushed his glasses up higher on his nose, then reached for a pen and notebook. "Excellent. Let's begin."

Julia shook her head. "I don't know. Are you sure you feel up to this, Becca?"

Her mother was actually giving her a choice in the matter. That was new. And appreciated. "Yes. Seriously, Mom, I want to help."

Jackie and Julia shared a concerned look.

"All right," Julia said. "But promise you'll stop if it gets to be too much, okay?"

"Promise." Becca shifted in her seat. "Where should I start, Dr. Vega? At the beginning, when my spirit left my body and went to another world? Or start from just a couple of minutes ago when that book turned me into a zombie?"

Vega raised his bushy brows. "Is that what it felt like to you? That you were a zombie?"

She thought back. "All I know is that I was upstairs in the library, reading, and then, suddenly, I was here. Like my legs were thinking for themselves. So *zombie* might be the wrong word, but . . . it also feels pretty accurate." Becca paused, not sure if putting this strange experience into words made her feel more relieved or more nervous. She looked up at Crys. "You said my eyes were glowing?"

"Yeah," said Crys, and Becca was both surprised and grateful that she didn't follow that up with a snarky joke this time.

Dr. Vega scribbled something down in his notebook, then sent a cautious glance at Julia and Jackie, both of whom stared at Becca with a perturbed look in their eyes. "May we continue?" he said.

Julia twisted her hands. "Yes. Please do. We all need to know more."

He nodded solemnly. "All right, Becca. I have previously hypothesized that this book is the gateway to another world. And from what little I know of your experience, you can confirm that. Yes?"

"Well, yes"—Dr. Vega beamed—"and no." And just like that, the doctor's face fell again. Becca went on. "When I was . . . away, I learned that the book contained magic spells from a race of immortal beings."

The statement would have been met with disbelief anywhere else, but here it was different.

"Like Markus," Julia said under her breath uneasily. Jackie remained silent.

"Immortal beings who dwell in another world called . . ." Vega flipped through his previous notes excitedly. Becca was about to help him out when the professor looked up, eyes wide. "Mytica."

Becca nodded. "I got the impression that most of the immortals live in *another* world, an entirely different one set apart from where I was. There were only two immortals in Mytica while I was there. The people thought of them as goddesses."

Vega scribbled away furiously. "And both of those goddesses—did they practice magic?"

"Well, I only saw one of them." She remembered the horrible demon with the face of an angel. "Valoria. It's said she has the powers of earth and water. The one I never saw is the goddess of the South. Cleiona. She does magic with fire and air."

Vega's eyes grew wider, full of amazement. "Elemental magic, yes. How absolutely fascinating! You saw some of this magic at work?"

Becca nodded. "Valoria . . . she could control snakes. She could turn people into plants." She shivered. "She could . . . she could summon this kind of mud, and it would pull you right down to your death. And . . . and when Maddox was *this close* to defeating her, she turned herself into a funnel of water and escaped. I was there. I saw it."

"Maddox? And Maddox is . . . ?"

Becca chewed her bottom lip. "He's . . . a boy. From Mytica. He's about sixteen years old and he also has magic, but it's not like the goddesses'. It was . . . uh . . . *death magic* is what they called it. His father called him a *necromancer*, which is why he could see and talk to me. He was the only one who could. His father is a regular man, but his mother is an immortal."

Becca took a sidelong peek and saw Jackie and Julia exchange a grave look. She wondered if they believed her now, or if, like Crys, they thought her story was nothing more than a vivid dream brought on by a coma.

It happened, she assured herself. *It was real. Maddox was real.*

He is *real.*

Shaking off any concerns about whether or not her family believed her, she continued. "Valoria had the Bronze Codex there. Except they called it something else—the Book of the Immortals. Valoria needed Maddox's magic to work a spell that would open a gateway to our world, where another immortal had been exiled. She wanted to get to our world so she could get to this man, who had stolen a golden dagger from her that she wanted back."

"Markus," Jackie breathed. "The dagger. *His* dagger. That's where it came from."

Becca nodded. "Markus is immortal, so he can read the language the book is written in. Which means he also knows how to use the magic in it."

Once again, the conclusion seemed too simple, too plain: The Bronze Codex was simply a book of spells. Why, then, did this little feeling that it was so much more than that keep gnawing at Becca deep inside?

"Well," Crys said, nodding, and Becca knew that her vacation from sarcasm was over. "I think it was really *swell* of your new boyfriend to toss the book into our world. It's kind of cute, really. Like Toronto is his own private garbage can for hazardous magical materials. And there's a spirit trapped in it too? Awesome!"

Becca glared at her. "As if you even believe anything I've said."

Crys shrugged, a bit sheepishly. "Hey, I saw some stuff too. While you were gone. I believe it's all *possible*."

"Really? You don't even believe in tarot cards."

"Oh, I'm sorry. Have we moved on to a broader discussion of paranormal hocus-pocus in general? What's next on the list? Ouija boards?"

Becca kept her mouth shut. She knew exactly which button Crys was trying to press: A few years ago, on Halloween, they'd found an old Ouija board in the attic and decided to ask it questions at midnight.

A believer in the supernatural from the beginning, Becca had asked if the bookstore really was haunted and what the spirits wanted. Crys had secretly moved the planchette to spell out *K-I-L-L*, and Becca freaked out. So much that she'd locked herself in the bathroom for an hour.

At the time, and because it had been such a "Becca" thing to do, Crys had found it hilarious.

"All right, all right," Dr. Vega said. "That's enough. Becca, this is all so fascinating. Now, can you tell me: In Mytica, who, exactly, has access to elemental magic? Is it just these two goddesses, or are there others?"

"Um, well, no, actually." Becca shot a quick glare at Crys before turning to Dr. Vega and pressing on. "There are also witches that can use elemental magic. But they have a much weaker hold on it."

"Witches! My goodness." He jotted down more notes, shaking his head as his pen flew across the page. "Fascinating. It's all so, so *fascinating*. I wish my father could be here to hear this! Finally, his life's work is coming to fruition. We're finally getting some answers about this book."

"All we really know about it is it's dangerous," Jackie snapped. She got up and moved toward the desk. "Too dangerous to be here—especially near Becca. Give me the book, Uriah."

"Jackie . . ."

"*I'm* the one who stole it and sent it here. I take full responsibility for that thing being here in the first place. For everything it did to Becca. Give it to me. Please."

He hesitated for a long, tense moment before relenting. He unlocked the drawer, opened it, and gave one last pleading look to Jackie before pulling out the book. Becca inhaled sharply. While she'd felt its strange pull while it had been locked away, now that she could see it, that magnetic sensation had ramped way up. She forced herself to stay in place and not immediately go to it.

"Are my eyes . . . ?" she asked, her heart pounding hard.

"Still normal," Crys confirmed steadily.

"Good."

Jackie held the book and stared down at it as if she despised it every bit as much as Markus himself. "We're only putting ourselves in danger by keeping this book near us. And damned if I'm ever going to let Markus get his greedy hands on it again."

Without a moment of hesitation, she opened the book and tore out the first page.

Red hot agony sliced down Becca's arm. A painful scream wrenched from her throat. She fell, hard, to her knees.

"Jackie, stop!" Crys cried out. "Please! Becca! Look at her!"

Crimson blood poured from the jagged wound that had been angrily scrawled down her forearm.

Jackie gasped, a hollow look of horror overtaking her features. She dropped the torn page and staggered backward, stopping only when her back hit the study wall. She covered her mouth with her hand. "Oh, Becca. I'm so sorry! I had no idea!"

Crys scrambled for some tissues and pressed a wad of them up against Becca's arm. Dr. Vega dove to the floor, retrieved the torn page, and placed it carefully back into the book before closing the cover. He unlocked the desk drawer once again and moved to put the book away.

"Wait," Becca managed. "Don't put it away yet."

Dr. Vega drew his brows tightly together. He looked to Jackie, still cowering against the wall, then back at Becca, concern in his eyes. "I think it's best we do, Becca. If we're to draw conclusions about what just happened, it seems that if the book gets damaged . . ."

"Becca does too," Crys said.

There it was. All the proof Becca needed to understand that gnawing feeling in her gut. This was definitely so much more than a simple spell book.

"I want to see it up close," Becca said weakly.

No one said a word as Becca approached the desk, one step at a time, slowly and cautiously.

"Still no glowy eyes," Crys said, and Becca was once again grateful for her unceasing effort to keep things light.

"I feel fine," Becca assured the room. "Not weird. Not yet, anyway." She stood over the book and looked down at it. She studied the fading pebbled texture of the old brown leather cover, the well-made but not particularly handsome bronze hawk.

Plain and simple. The perfect camouflage, she thought. *What are you? And what do you want with me?*

She reached for the book.

"Becca . . . ," Crys began.

"No," Julia said. "Let her."

"But she might—"

"Shut up, Crys," Becca growled.

"Wow. Um, rude much?"

Becca shut her eyes and gave herself a moment to ignore everyone and everything around her. Summoning every last shred of courage she had, she brushed her fingertips over the worn leather. Smooth, cool. Nothing earth-shattering so far.

She let out a little sigh of relief.

Click. Then she heard a familiar—and not entirely welcome— sound. *Click, click.* She looked up with annoyance.

"Crys, are you seriously taking pictures right now?"

"I'm documenting a historically significant moment."

"Video would be much more helpful," Dr. Vega suggested.

"On it," Crys replied.

Her sister and her stupid camera—a gift from Farrell Grayson, which she refused to throw away despite hating the guy. So what if it was *expensive* and *necessary for her future career*? If it comes from your mortal enemy, it has to go.

Becca inhaled sharply. That warm, sparkling sensation that had crept in and clouded her thoughts back up in the library began coursing through her, this time almost completely concentrated in her arm.

She looked down. The wound on her forearm had completely healed.

"Oh my God," Crys whispered. She moved the camera closer. "Are you all seeing this?"

Becca's breathing quickened to match her heart rate as she turned back the cover of the Codex and opened it to the first page—the one that Jackie had ripped out. It had reattached itself and was now securely in the binding as if nothing had ever happened.

"That," Becca murmured, "is some serious magic."

She closed the book, feeling deeply weary all of a sudden, and absently brushed her fingers over the bronze hawk.

In an instant, a funnel of darkness streamed out of the hawk's talons, rising up to the ceiling where it swirled and gathered into a pitch-black whirlpool.

Helpless, Becca stared up in stark horror.

"Becca, what are you seeing?" Dr. Vega asked.

She could only reply in stuttering fragments. "The—the spirit. The one that was t-trapped. It—it's out!"

"What?" Crys put the camera down and was at Becca's side again. "Where?"

"There." Becca pointed at the ceiling.

Crys looked up. "I don't see anything. Mom?"

"Nothing," Julia confirmed. She pressed her hand softly against Becca's back. "What's it doing, honey?"

Becca's throat had practically closed. She couldn't speak. The thought of that creature, the one that had tried to devour her in Mytica, free and on the loose . . . here . . . it was too much. She was going to pass out.

No, she told herself firmly. *Remember—you were only a flimsy shell of yourself in Mytica, but you're so much more than just your spirit now.*

She told herself that this thing had no power over her here. That it was as harmless as a shadow.

Then, as if the thing had heard her thoughts, it grew completely still. It stopped swirling and slithered down the wall until it reached the floor. It remained there, in the far corner, as a small, wispy patch of darkness.

"What's happening?" Crys asked, her voice pitchy. "Is it gone?"

"It's . . . not doing anything," Becca said. "It looks like just a shadow now. It's fine. I—I'm fine."

"Becca, I have more questions about all of this," Dr. Vega said.

"No," Jackie said firmly. "That's more than enough for one day."

Becca couldn't have agreed more. She left the room first to let the adults talk among themselves, trying very hard not to notice that the shadow was following her.

Chapter 4

FARRELL

It was shocking how easily Farrell's mood could swing from heavenly to hellish. Lately all kinds of things were getting to him, but tonight his newly acquired superhuman sense of hearing was to blame.

For the last week he'd been practicing singling out specific conversations occurring between small groups of people in crowds, and he'd become remarkably good at it. Just now he'd blocked out all extraneous noise and chatter so he could clearly hear the two attractive girls sitting in the far corner of Karma, his third-favorite Toronto bar, who probably thought that they were well out of earshot of tonight's conversation topic.

"What do you think?" the brunette said to the blonde.

"Of what?"

The brunette gave a subtle nod in Farrell's direction. "Mr. Trust Fund over there. Think you have a chance?"

The blonde swept an appraising glance over Farrell and smirked. "I heard he's dating Felicity Seaton."

Interesting, he thought. They knew who he was. That would definitely save some time.

"Technically, maybe. On paper. But from what I've read, Farrell Grayson isn't exactly into monogamous relationships—especially with someone as dull as that second-tier socialite."

He couldn't say she was wrong, exactly. His mother had thought Felicity, a pretty enough girl from a good enough—read: *acceptable*—family would be the perfect girlfriend to help her delinquent son regain the good reputation he'd worked so hard to sully.

Farrell had spoken to Felicity just a couple of hours ago, to tell her that he wasn't feeling well, which was why he'd been able to come here solo on a Saturday night. Also, it wasn't exactly her kind of bar. She preferred much more upscale nightclubs, the kind that had bouncers out front and a hefty cover charge. He'd appeased her—thrilled her, really—by promising to take her somewhere special tomorrow, just the two of them.

As for tonight, getting to know both the brunette and the blonde much better was his top priority.

He would start with champagne—they looked like the champagne type. Farrell moved to signal to the bartender, but the girls' continuing conversation distracted him.

"Trust fund, huh?" the blonde said, her voice twisting with interest. "Can you put a number on that?"

"I heard a rumor that Grandmother Grayson left her entire fortune to Farrell. No one else got even a cent. Unfortunately, he has to wait until he's twenty-one to get his hands on it."

"That can't be too much longer, can it?" the blonde replied with a smile. "It's just too bad he's not *nearly* as hot as his brother. I'd be all over that one."

The brunette snorted. "Do you mean the sixteen-year-old? Little young, don't you think? Then again, I *hope* you mean the kid brother and not the older one who killed himself last year."

"I'm not exactly into necrophilia." The blonde rolled her eyes and snuck what she clearly thought was a furtive glance at Farrell. "You know, maybe it's just that ugly mole on his face that throws me off. Otherwise, Mr. Trust Fund is good looking enough."

There it was—the moment when Farrell's mood took a sudden dive into the fiery pit below. His cheek twitched, and he forced himself not to touch the birthmark under his right eye.

He glared at the bartender and tapped his glass. "Another."

The bartender refilled his double vodka. Farrell swished it around in the glass before taking it all down in two swallows, closing his eyes to better concentrate on the familiar burn coursing all the way down his throat.

"Hi there." He turned to see the blonde standing next to him, hand on her hip, smile on her lips. "I'm Brittany. Why don't I buy the next round?"

He glanced at her. "Pretty desperate opener, don't you think?"

Her smile fell. "Excuse me?"

"I'm all for gender equality, but *Why don't I buy the next round?* Pathetic. Bye now."

She stared at him for a moment, eyes narrowed then widened in shock, before she turned around and returned to her friend in the corner.

"Grumpy, are we? Is some meaningless girl's opinion really enough to dent that fragile ego of yours? Or are you just having a bad night?"

Farrell's subconscious had been talking up a storm lately, and unfortunately it had chosen the familiar voice of his dead brother, Connor.

He pushed a twenty-dollar bill toward the bartender, who poured him another drink.

"Don't make the same mistake I did, kid," not-Connor said. *"Plaster on a*

charming smile whether you mean it or not. Make them know you don't care."

"I don't," he mumbled.

"Remember, you want a girl who wants you for more than your bank account or your looks. She should value your shining personality and kind heart."

Farrell couldn't help but chuckle at that. He raised his glass. "To Connor Grayson, long may that dumbass's gift for sarcasm haunt me."

But his dead brother's advice did help bring him back to the present. He'd come here to have fun, and that was what he was going to have. He got up and went to a nearby table and, despite the many protests hollered by its occupants, climbed on top of it.

"May I have your attention!" Farrell called out. "All of you, look at me. Over here. Come on. Focus, people."

It only took a few moments before the sight of him standing on a table, waving his drink around and shouting, brought the room to a standstill.

"Someone lower the music, please?" He waited until the booming pulse of the speakers eased off to a quarter of the volume. "Much better."

He could hear people whispering, many asking each other who this whack job was. It didn't take long for the response to filter around the bar, that he was Farrell Grayson, the middle son of Edward Grayson, one of the wealthiest men on the continent.

With the mention of his name came the recognition of Farrell's reputation as the black sheep of his family, and he could only imagine what they expected of him as he stood before them in the middle of the club. Likely they were expecting a drunken tantrum or some other form of public embarrassment. But behavior like that had no place within his brand new philosophy.

Kill 'em with kindness. Just like Connor suggested. He'd lost his composure with the blonde, but he'd recently decided to believe in the chance for new beginnings. He paused to let the whispers hush, took a deep breath, and smiled.

"Today is my birthday," he said. "You're all now looking at a wise and ancient man of twenty years."

"Happy birthday!" someone shouted.

Farrell raised his glass and smirked at the crowd. "In celebration of this milestone, the next round is on me. Drink up, everyone!"

The crowd cheered, the music returned to full volume, and everyone started moving toward the bar. A group of guys congregated around Farrell and started to sing "Happy Birthday." Farrell found his smile again—he'd lost it at some point as he watched the revelry unfold around him—and he got down from the table.

Now back on ground level, a hint of a familiar face caught his eye. He turned sharply, his breath catching in his chest.

Markus?

Was he here now, watching him? Waiting for him to slip up?

The tall blond guy moved past the crowd that was blocking him, and Farrell realized it was just some random guy, with only a passing resemblance to Markus King.

He hadn't seen Markus in several days. After the drama of the previous weekend, Farrell had chosen not to go in search of his new boss and instead let Markus seek him out.

In the meantime, he was in the habit of checking his phone every few minutes. He flashed the screen on now and was greeted by nothing but the time and a text from Felicity telling him she hoped he was feeling better. He rolled his eyes and clicked his phone off again.

"So it's your birthday, huh?"

Farrell snapped his gaze up to look at the speaker. It was Adam, his light brown hair neat and glowing like a halo, making him seem the angel to Farrell's mussy, dark-haired devil. His little brother had come from out of nowhere and was now standing right in front of him. He swore that the kid had grown at least half a foot over the last year, making them both the same height, dead-on six feet. They also had the same taste for expensive clothes and custom-made leather shoes.

"That rousing chorus of 'Happy Birthday' would suggest as much," Farrell replied drily.

"Your birthday isn't until November."

"Really? What's today's date?"

"April eighth."

"Wow. I was way off, wasn't I?"

A guy in a too-shiny dress shirt passed by and raised his glass at him, giving a big grin that Farrell returned. Who said that you can't buy friends?

Farrell kept the smile on his face as he turned to regard his younger brother. "How'd you get in here, anyway? Did you finally get a fake ID?"

Adam shook his head. "Hundred-dollar bill."

"Nice move."

"I learned from the best."

"Let's try to think of something other than bribery as our go-to example of lessons I've taught you."

Adam crossed his arms. "What's with the fake smile?"

"Fake? What's fake?" He pointed at his face. "This baby is the product of nothing but pure, unadulterated happiness. Life is good. There's nothing to frown about. Maybe you should remember that from time to time." He knew he was playing his part convincingly, but his cheeks were starting to cramp up from the effort. "Anyway, great to see you. I wish you could stay, but I'm sure you have to be going home by now. Bye-bye then."

"No. I'm going to stay here and keep an eye on you."

"Excuse me?" Farrell said, swapping out his smile for a raised eyebrow and a curled lip. "What makes you think I need an under-age babysitter?"

"How many marks do you have now?" Adam asked evenly, not skipping a beat. "Did Markus give you the third one yet?"

"Does it matter?"

"I don't know. Does it matter that an immortal god of death put you under three increasingly intense obedience spells so that you'd be reborn as his mindless minion? Yeah, I'd say that matters."

Farrell drained his drink. He put the empty glass down rough-ly on the nearest tabletop, then grabbed his brother by the arm, tightly, and dragged him into the hallway leading to the restrooms.

"You know the rule, Adam," he growled.

"What happens at the Hawkspear Society stays at the Hawk-spear Society." Adam said in a mocking, singsong voice. He had the audacity to look proud of himself for successfully wiping away Farrell's faux-happy exterior.

"Not exactly how the rule is phrased, but that's the general meaning of it."

"Yeah, well, screw that."

Farrell all but scowled at his meddling little brother. Adam had quickly become the single thorn in the beautiful bed of roses that Farrell had recently fallen into.

"If Markus ever finds out what you did—" Farrell hissed.

"What?" Adam challenged. "He'll kill me?"

"Yes," Farrell said without a moment's hesitation. "And I'll help him."

"No, you won't." Adam's expression soured. "You think you're so tough now. You think you're untouchable like him, that the rules don't apply to you. I don't care how many times he carves into you, you're my brother, and that's never going to change."

They looked at each other for several long moments, Farrell staring his brother down with icy eyes and Adam responding with a stern but pleading gaze.

"Go home, Adam," Farrell said finally, unable to take another moment of his brother's puppy-dog eyes. "I can handle myself just fine. I'm the same as I've ever been; the marks just make me better. Stronger, smarter. They're a gift from a god—literally."

Adam just stood there, his expression unchanging.

"You're not leaving, are you?" Farrell said.

"Nope."

"Tell me." Farrell leaned casually against the wall and crossed his arms in front of his chest. "Have you spoken to your best friends, the Hatchers, recently?"

Adam winced slightly and then recomposed himself. "If I had, I wouldn't exactly tell you, would I?"

"Aw, how cute." He lowered his voice. "You know what Markus is capable of. What his *magic* is capable of. He can find anyone and anything he wants, in this city or anywhere else. There is no hiding from him. Remember that."

Adam shrugged. "If that's true, why hasn't he gone after them?"

"How do you know he hasn't?"

Adam screwed up his face in the most sarcastic look possible. "I think the whole world would know it if he tracked them down and got the Codex back."

Farrell pressed his lips together in aggravated frustration. "He's going to get that Codex. He'll pry it from their hot little hands."

"But he already had it, didn't he? And then he just handed it over to Daniel Hatcher? I don't know. If I had something that important, I wouldn't let go of it."

"He trusted Daniel."

"But that was a mistake, wasn't it?" Adam blinked, his expression turning from solemn to bold. "Did Markus kill him for helping his daughters escape?"

"I seem to remember you helping him out with that, but you're still breathing, aren't you?"

"Yeah, but I have you to thank for that. Daniel wasn't so lucky."

Farrell scoffed. "Keep believing that if you want to." He wasn't going to admit what he and Adam both knew to be true: that Crys and Becca's father was dead for betraying Markus.

And he certainly wasn't going to admit the part that Adam didn't know: that it was Farrell who'd killed Daniel Hatcher.

Connor's voice chimed in his mind again. "*You should feel no regret*," it said. Farrell closed his eyes. "*He chose his fate. He knew the punishment for betraying Markus. You chose to do as Markus said because you're loyal, and you've earned your place in the society. Keep it up, and soon you will reap even more benefits.*"

Connor's voice calmed him, filled him with a coolness that steadied his mind against his brother's meddling.

"I need a cigarette," Farrell said, forcing himself to sound casual. He reached into his jeans pocket to fish out a pack. "Look, Adam. Stay, go. Do whatever you want, I don't care. But if you follow me outside, I swear to everything you hold dear: I *will* blow smoke in your face."

Adam scowled, not taking Farrell's version of an olive branch. "You haven't heard a thing I've said tonight, have you?"

This conversation was over. "Goodnight, little brother."

Farrell turned and went out the nearest exit to join a handful of club patrons smoking in a haphazard huddle. He lit his cigarette, then leaned against the cement wall.

He tried to relax, but the thousand questions zipping through his mind had other plans.

What *was* Markus waiting for? Why didn't he just narrow in on the Hatchers, storm in, and take what was his?

And why the hell would he have handed the Codex over to Daniel as if it were nothing more than a used comic book just because he got a phone call from Jackie Hatcher?

Why did Farrell's left forearm still burn like he'd survived a five-alarm fire, even though a whole week had passed since Markus had made the third mark?

The moment Farrell plunged a knife into Daniel Hatcher's chest . . . why didn't he feel any guilt? Why was he not even a little bit sorry, especially since he'd never killed anyone before?

And why were the girls who came to this club so damned superficial? It was a *birthmark*, not an oozing sore.

"Don't!"

Farrell turned his head toward the voice, thankful to be distracted from his reeling mind. It was a girl on the other side of the smoking patio, berating the guy she was with. "Just don't, okay?"

Farrell narrowed his eyes to get a closer look at the girl with platinum blond hair and black-rimmed glasses that reminded him unsettlingly of Crys Hatcher.

The girl's muscle-head companion grabbed her arm and wrenched her back toward him. "You think you can just walk away from me?" he growled. "Behave yourself, you stupid little bitch."

"Let go of me," she snarled.

"Apologize, and maybe I'll consider it."

"*Apologize?* For what? I hate you. *You're* the one who should apologize!"

He let go of her arm, only to smack her across the face, hard.

Before he knew what he was doing or exactly why, Farrell was upon him. He grabbed hold of the guy and threw him against the wall. He put his right hand around his throat and squeezed, then with his left hand took a drag from his cigarette.

"I agree with her. I think *you* need to apologize," Farrell said.

"Let . . . go . . . of . . . me," the guy gasped, clawing at Farrell's arm.

"Not. Going. To. Happen. First, you're going to apologize to the lady. After that, maybe I won't choose to tear out your windpipe. Sound fair?"

The girl stared at them, eyes wide. "What are you doing?" she said frantically.

"Me?" Farrell glanced at her. "I'm being chivalrous, what does it look like?"

"Let go of him!"

"He hasn't apologized yet. He knows the deal: He apologizes, and I don't kill him. Simple as that."

Her worried gaze flicked between the two them. "Why are you doing this?"

"Violence against women is one of my hot button issues."

"Fine," she breathed out. "Apologize, Larry. Do it!"

Larry's face was bright red from Farrell's hold on him, but his eyes were filled with fury as he spit with as much force as he could manage. It landed on Farrell's cheek with a cold *splat*.

"Now that was just rude and disgusting. Luckily, I'm immune to all germs." Farrell raised his shoulder to wipe off the saliva, then tightened his grip on Larry's neck. Effortlessly, he lifted him a couple of inches off the ground. "Shall we try again?"

Now Larry was turning purple. "Fine . . . I . . . I'm . . . sorry."

"And it will never happen . . . ? Go on, finish the sentence for me."

"Never . . . happen . . . again."

"Good." Farrell let him go, and he dropped down to the ground in a heaving heap. The girl quickly scrambled to help Larry to his feet, and Farrell watched as they both scurried away, beyond the patio and out into the Toronto streets. "Yeah, you're welcome," Farrell called after them. "Anytime, really."

Ignoring the small group of witnesses staring at him, he flicked his cigarette away and went back inside the club. He went to the restroom, stood in front of a mirror, and regarded his reflection. His heart pounded slowly, but so loudly he could hear it.

"Ugly bastard," he told himself.

"*If you want to change something,*" Connor's voice told him, "*do it. You are the master of your destiny. No one else.*"

"You said it, brother."

Farrell drew a small folding knife out of his pocket and flipped it open. Leaning closer to the mirror, he pulled the skin beneath his right eye taut. Slowly and carefully, he sliced off his birthmark.

He should have done this long ago.

Chapter 5

MADDOX

Maddox had always had a knack for memorization, but for whatever reason, he could never remember the names of trees. He could recite stories from his favorite books nearly word for word, but when it came to remembering specifics within larger categories—such as trees, rivers, or villages—he'd always struggled. His mother used to tell him it was because he didn't care deeply enough about those things to take the time to learn.

But now he wanted to know.

A *willowbark* tree. Yes, that was it. He was standing before the largest willowbark tree he'd ever seen, where his mother had been buried. The tree was next to the river where she'd taught him how to swim when he was so young he had only barely begun to walk.

Maddox knelt down by her grave, the dirt still fresh, and placed a silverlily he'd picked from his mother's garden on top of it. They were her favorite flower.

He wasn't sure exactly how long he'd been there, only that the day had turned to dusk and the sky had begun to darken.

"Maddox, my sweet." Camilla, Barnabas's witch friend, placed her hand on his arm. "Can you hear me?"

"Give him another moment," Barnabas said.

That moment passed. Then another, and another.

"It's night, Barnabas. He needs to sleep," Camilla said.

"Very well." Barnabas let out a long sigh. "Maddox, come on. It's time to go."

Maddox nodded shallowly. He tried to push himself up from the hard ground, but he faltered on legs that had gone numb. Camilla was at his side in an instant, smiling at him comfortingly as she helped him to his feet.

"Up you go," she said. "We'll get you into a nice warm bed. Tomorrow will be a better day, I promise."

There had been three tomorrows since his mother had been killed, and none had been better than the last. In that time, Barnabas had sent word to Camilla to join them in Silvereve. She'd arrived quickly, although Maddox had been too wrapped up in grief to register her presence. Camilla and her sister, Sienna, had tried to help Barnabas and Maddox in their confrontation with Valoria. Sienna had spent years working her way into the goddess's circle of trust, all for the chance to use her own secrets to vanquish her.

But their plan hadn't worked. Valoria was still out there, still after Maddox and the infinite power she believed he could offer her, still ready to kill any innocent who stood in her way.

Finally they returned to his mother's house, and Camilla personally put Maddox to bed. He was so tired, more exhausted than he'd ever been before, but his body was fighting sleep. As he was lying there with his eyes closed, he could hear Barnabas and Camilla talking, most likely thinking he was asleep.

"You barely go near him," Camilla whispered in an accusatory tone. "What's wrong with you? You should be *comforting* the boy. He just lost his mother."

"And I lost my sister," Barnabas said. "That doesn't change the fact that Maddox is—that we *all* are—in grave danger. I've no other choice but to be strong right now."

"He hasn't been hardened like you have. He hasn't been through the same struggles. Traveling around with that nasty con man was nothing compared to what you've seen. You know this, and yet you're still cold."

"Camilla, I don't know how to behave with him. Ever, and especially now. I don't know how to be a father, all right?"

"You've had sixteen years to learn."

"And yet I still fail."

"Fine. Then don't be a father to him. Be a *friend*."

"I'll try my best."

"Of course you will. I have no doubt."

Barnabas didn't know how to be a father. Maddox took some solace in this since he didn't really know how to be a son to anyone but Damaris.

But he also would try his best to be Barnabas's friend.

Slowly, finally, sleep found him.

—◆◆◆—

The next morning, it was time to bid farewell to Maddox's village and his mother's grave. He had no idea if he'd ever return. As soon as he woke up, he steeled himself against this day and promised himself he wouldn't shed a tear—not today or any day after. He'd given in to crying too many times over the last few days and knew Barnabas must have thought him weak for it. He swore he'd never cry again.

He wasn't a child anymore, was no longer innocent. Innocent children didn't think of nothing but vengeance.

"I'm ready to go," Maddox announced, his voice strong and steady, but it had a dull edge to it that even he could hear.

Camilla was at the stove cooking *kaana*, a familiar breakfast dish created from mashed yellow beans. When she heard Maddox, she turned around and fixed a bright smile on him. Maddox had to suppress his instinctual flinch at seeing her now, the first time he'd been truly lucid since she'd arrived.

Poor Camilla—she was kind and smart and a gifted witch, but she had not been blessed with the beauty her sister, Sienna, had. Her eyes were lopsided, the few teeth she had were widely spaced and crooked, and her chin was a village of warts, black hairs springing forth from the majority.

Maddox smiled back at her.

"Hungry, my boy?" she asked.

"I suppose so."

She brought him a bowl and spoon and patted him on the back. "There you go."

"Thank you." He stared down at the bowl of *kaana*.

Barnabas sat down in the chair across from him, eyeing him warily. "Camilla and I can go in search of Valoria's scribe. You don't have to join us for this part of the journey. I understand if you're not feeling quite up to it."

"I'm fine," Maddox said calmly.

"Are you sure?"

"I'm *fine*," he said, louder this time. "What's the plan?"

Barnabas raised his brows. "Well, all right then. The plan is simple. We will go to Valoria's palace, locate the scribe, bespell him with Camilla's scented oils, and remove him from the palace to question him at our leisure. He'll tell us how to most effectively bring an end to the goddess's reign, and then all will be well and right in the land."

Maddox glanced at Camilla, who was back at her station at the stove. "Scented oils?"

She stirred a second pot that was simmering next to the *kaana*. "I just need to infuse this with some air magic and a few other useful ingredients I picked up on my way here. Then it'll be potent enough to knock out any man or woman for at least half a day with just one whiff."

"Your skills impress me more every time I see you," Barnabas told her.

Maddox eyed the brew warily. "A half a day, huh?"

"Any longer would need much more simmer time," Camilla said. "I'll pour a little of this in a vial, and we'll be ready to leave. Nothing to worry about."

He appreciated that this witch, who was brewing a knockout potion to aid in a kidnapping, was assuring him that all was well. Then again, both she and Barnabas had been treating him like a fragile object, ready to shatter at any moment. But he wasn't fragile; he was strong. Every moment, every day, getting stronger.

Maddox knew he would be a major asset in this journey. And he knew he would soon avenge the death of his mother. The deaths of both of his mothers: Damaris and Eva too.

—∞—

Maddox remained mostly silent and introspective for the first day of their three-day journey by foot to the palace. On the second day, Camilla managed to coax conversation from him, telling him she wanted to know more about Damaris.

"Was she a good cook?" Camilla asked as they ventured out that misty morning from a small inn that had served them a barely palatable breakfast of burnt eggs and runny *kaana*.

He nodded. "The best cook. She made a lamb stew that was so phenomenal she could have sold the recipe for a couple years' worth of coin. She always managed to get bread—still warm, with a crisp crust, but soft in the middle, and it melted in your mouth—for us every day, no matter how rough our circumstances. Sometimes we ate it for breakfast with honey."

"I'm getting hungry just hearing about it," Camilla said kindly. "She was a very good mum, it seems."

Maddox nodded. He let a peaceful silence settle between them before he worked up the courage to ask a question that had been on his mind for a while. "I've been wondering a lot about . . . well, about what my birth mother was like. Did you know her?"

"Eva?" Camilla asked. She cast a cautious glance toward Barnabas, who walked about five paces ahead of them—certainly close enough to overhear. He didn't turn around or slow his steps, so Camilla turned back to Maddox and lowered her voice to just above a whisper. "I never met her personally. But I have heard many stories. It hasn't been all that long, really, since she . . . passed."

"Valoria and Cleiona killed her," said Maddox matter-of-factly. "Yet Valoria denies she had anything to do with her murder. Is Cleiona solely to blame?"

"Don't you dare say that name again," Barnabas growled.

"What name?" Maddox asked. "Eva?"

"No. The name of the southern goddess."

"Why not?"

Barnabas groaned. "Camilla?"

Camilla cleared her throat. "Well, there are rumors, you know. She is the goddess of fire and air, and some say that with air magic as powerful as hers, she can hear the sound of her name no matter where, when, or by whom it's spoken. This is how she comes to know her enemies."

Maddox had never heard this rumor before. Then again, it was forbidden to publically discuss the southern goddess in the North.

"All right then. I'll never say her name again," he agreed. "But please tell me more about what really happened to Eva."

Camilla sighed, but not unkindly. "No one knows exactly *who* was responsible for killing her. But it is rumored that, at almost the exact moment of her death, she uttered a prophecy."

"What prophecy?" Maddox prompted when Camilla went silent.

A moment passed before Camilla continued. "She allegedly foretold that, in a thousand years' time, her magic would be reborn in the form of a mortal sorceress. It's said that Eva was by far the most powerful immortal of them all—a truth I'm sure Valoria's scribe would like to scrub from history—and for that reason she was the envy of many of her kind. When she found herself with child—a *half-mortal* child—some say that the pregnancy made her . . . vulnerable."

All this information—whether it be rumor or truth—had made Maddox's head start to spin.

"I should have protected her," Barnabas growled.

"How?" Camilla's voice turned harsh. "With your bow and arrow?" She scoffed. "You weren't much more than a child yourself at the time, Barnabas. And you did what you could. You must stop blaming yourself."

"Never. She'd lived thousands of years before she met me. If it wasn't for me, she'd still be alive."

"You don't know that."

"I do. I know it as well as I know I'm the greatest hunter Myt-ica has ever seen."

Maddox had heard this lofty claim enough times to know not to argue with it.

Barnabas turned to Camilla, his expression tense, his fists clenched. "All of this talk of the past reminds me. Do you still have it?"

Camilla raised her chin. "Yes," she said, her tone empty of the confusion that had suddenly gripped Maddox.

"Right now? On your person?"

"I always keep it with me. Just as you asked me to."

"Show me."

She blinked. "Are you sure?"

He nodded. "I want to carry it with me now."

"My hope was that all those years of traveling overseas would help you find some peace. But it seems that isn't the case."

"There can be no peace as long as those two monsters rule this land." Barnabas stopped, turned to Camilla, and held out his hand, palm up. "Please."

"Very well," she sighed. She tucked her hand underneath the neckline of her blouse and, after a moment's fishing, pulled out a gold necklace strung with some kind of charm or pendant. She unfastened the delicate chain, removed it from around her neck, and placed the necklace in his outstretched palm.

It was only exposed for a moment before his father closed his fist around it, but that was long enough for Maddox to catch a glimpse of the pendant, which looked like a brilliant purple stone in some kind of golden setting.

"What is that?" he asked.

Barnabas tucked the necklace away in one of his many well-hidden pockets. "A ring that once belonged to Eva."

Maddox's heart skipped a beat. "May I see it?"

"No." Barnabas's jaw tensed, and he glanced at Maddox. "Apologies—I don't meant to sound so harsh, but . . . not now. Perhaps someday, but not now. All right?"

A hundred questions about Eva and Barnabas appeared on the tip of Maddox's tongue, but the fresh look of grief on Barnabas's face at seeing her ring again for the first time in ages made him back down.

"All right."

"Thank you, Camilla," Barnabas said.

"You won't be thanking me when the nightmares begin again."

Barnabas arched an eyebrow. "Oh, I'm sure there's some kind of a potion to cure that."

"There is," Camilla said. "It's called 'wine,' and it's being administered free of charge all across this kingdom for the rest of the year." She winked at him, then returned her attention to Maddox. "Never mind old Barnabas. He gets morose when he reminisces. Back to the more important matter at hand: your birth mother. She was a brave woman. Legend says that she survived many battles and hardships, including the wrath of her twin brother and the destruction of her original world, and was only made stronger for it."

"*Wrathful twin brother?*" Maddox said. "Are *any* of the immortals actually kind and peaceful?"

"More legends," Barnabas said with a dismissive wave of his hand. "What brother? She never mentioned any wrathful twin to me. Let alone anything to suggest that immortals have ever had another home besides a massive crystal city in another world where, I assume, they are to this day."

"Granted, I know very little about your relationship with her,

Barnabas, but my impression was that all that passion you two shared didn't leave much time for long conversations about life and family."

"We had plenty of time to talk," Barnabas said against a tense jaw.

"*Anyway*, Maddox, to answer your question: It would seem there are very few immortals who are kind and peaceful, which is said to be the fault of Eva's twin. For every ounce of beauty and goodness that Eva was blessed with, legend says that her brother was cursed with just as much of the very opposite. He was a demon, who, with no weapon other than his dangerous, mystical words, brought destruction and chaos everywhere he went. Some say he was created from ice and darkness and that whatever he touched turned to endless winter."

"*Ice and darkness.*" Barnabas rolled his eyes. "Sure."

"So where is this horrible immortal sorcerer now?" Maddox asked tentatively.

"The immortals rose up against him and killed him. It was the last thing about which they were all in agreement."

"How do you know all of this?" Maddox asked.

"Witch legends," Barnabas bit out. "Passed through generations of those who feel they're connected to the immortals by blood and magic."

Camilla grinned. "True enough. But that doesn't make these legends wrong."

"It doesn't make them right either."

"The goddesses are immortals . . . ," Maddox said quietly. "Does that mean they're as powerful as the ones who live in the crystal city?"

"No," Barnabas said. "The goddesses stole the magic they possess. They're nothing more than common thieves."

Maddox took a moment to consider this. "The same stolen magic Valoria used to mark that assassin, so he could resist my magic."

A solemn silence settled between the three for a moment as they continued to make their way away from the village where they'd spent the night with two more days of travel ahead. Maddox looked up at the clear sky, shielding his eyes from the sun, and watched a bird soaring overhead. *An eagle or a hawk,* he thought.

"Yes, that seems to be the case," Barnabas finally said, his tone troubled. "I was not aware that she had that ability."

"But it wasn't enough. He chose to run away rather than stay and fight me. He knew he wasn't strong enough to survive my magic, let alone stop me. I'm going to find him. And when I do . . ." Maddox set his jaw into a tense block of pure resolution. "I'm going to kill him."

Barnabas stopped, turned, and grabbed Maddox by his shoulders. Anger flashed in his eyes, taking Maddox by surprise.

"You are going to kill no one," he growled. "Do you hear me?"

Maddox glared up at him. "Why shouldn't I?"

"Have you ever killed anyone? Ever used your *magic* to kill anyone? Pushed, shoved, choked, made unconscious, yes—you've done all that very well. But killed?"

Maddox's chest tightened. "No. Not yet."

"You are not a murderer, Maddox. You must never kill. Not ever."

Barnabas had never made less sense. "How can you say that? You told me yourself what my magic made me—I'm a necromancer. My magic is *death* magic. Killing is one of the few things it lets me do."

Barnabas's expression grew haunted. "When I first found you, you were nothing like what I expected. I'd expected you to be . . . darker. Empty. Because wielding dark magic blackens the soul."

Maddox was about to laugh; just the idea of a soul made "black" by a certain kind of magic was preposterous to him, but Camilla spoke before he could even crack a grin.

"It's true, boy," she said. "I've seen it happen to witches far less powerful than you, who've foolishly tried to strengthen their naturally given powers with blood magic. No matter how good your heart is, that kind of dark power will turn it black, cold, and shriveled."

The urge to laugh had passed entirely. Maddox thought back to when he'd used his magic, to when he'd really channeled it for the first time to strike unconscious a guard who'd been about to ex-ecute an accused witch. The most vivid thing he could remember about it—other than his victim's dull and lifeless appearance—was the sensation of a cold darkness rising up inside of him.

Even now, he wasn't sure if he'd been scared of it or if he'd liked it.

"So, what then?" Maddox said in the most biting tone he'd used in days. "We just let Goran get away with it?"

"No," Barnabas said. "Just like you, I plan to find him. And when I do, I'll kill him myself. Don't worry, I have no death magic to corrupt my already shadowy soul."

"Then the matter is settled," Camilla said, her kind smile re-turning. "Now, let's focus on finding the goddess's scribe so we can torture some information out of him, shall we?"

———

When they finally reached the palace, they found they were among at least a thousand other visitors, all milling about in the royal square.

The massive palace—a monstrous masterpiece of black granite set into the rocky cliffs—cast a jagged shadow over the crowd.

Maddox nudged a tall man jockeying for space beside him. "What's going on?" he asked.

The crowd began to cheer.

"The goddess is about to make a speech," the tall man said, nodding his head up toward a balcony chiseled high into the granite palace.

Maddox drew his hood closer around his face and looked up at the forbidding palace from their position at the back of the crowd. He had barely a moment to register the vast impressiveness of the craftsmanship when a flash of crimson appeared against the backdrop of blackest granite. It was the goddess, gliding out onto the balcony in a brilliant red gown. Her shining ebony hair cascaded over her shoulders, falling down well past her waist in waves. Even from a distance, Maddox could see the sharp and vivid boundaries of her dark red lips and emerald green eyes.

Unsmilingly, she raised her hand. The crowd went silent.

Maddox chanced a look at Barnabas, who glared up at the goddess with hatred in his eyes.

Valoria began to speak. "Much gratitude for your presence today, my citizens," she intoned, her voice smooth yet menacing, like honey poisoned with venom. "I grow stronger through the presence of each and every one of you."

The crowd chimed with respectful hollers of appreciation. She smiled, and Maddox wondered if he was the only one who thought it looked more like a grimace than a grin.

Valoria waited for the crowd to hush before going on. "I'm sure most of you have heard by now that I've decided to extend the commemorative celebrations until the end of the year."

The crowd broke out in cheers, this time more joyful than reverent.

Valoria's smile slipped. A flash of annoyance flickered over her lovely face. Suddenly, the ground began to tremble, the shaking quickly evolving into a rippling earthquake. The violent waves of stone and earth made their way across the square, knocking hundreds of people off their feet and injuring several others.

Camilla grasped hold of Maddox's arm to remain on her feet. Barnabas simply glared up at the goddess, his fists clenched at his sides. He then sent a quick, concerned glance at Maddox. "You all right?"

Maddox nodded. "For now."

The brunt of the quake passed, but the ground still shook with a buzzing tremor.

"Silence!" the goddess commanded. "I've more to say."

The battered crowd—now moaning and sobbing instead of cheering—went silent in an instant.

The ground went still, and Valoria's smile returned. "My decision to extend the celebrations is in gratitude to you all for your loyalty to me these past fifteen years. Today is a special day, for it is the day that I shall finally bless my kingdom with an official name."

Valoria gazed down at her cowering, injured people. "Two words can express the way I rule this land: *strength* and *wisdom*. *Limo* and *rossa*, in the language of my people. And so this is why I have chosen to use my reign and my power to rename Northern Mytica . . ." Valoria paused here, allowing a sense of drama to hover over the square. Then, with a smile more insidious than Maddox had seen on her yet, she delivered her pronouncement. *"Limeros."*

The crowd below was motionless, silent. Maddox looked about to gauge their reactions, but all they did was stare, waiting.

"You no longer have to remain silent," she announced with an arched brow.

The crowd erupted in a forced, whining cheer, while Barnabas just narrowed his eyes with even more hatred.

Maddox scrunched up his nose. "Strength and wisdom? That's what *Limeros* means?"

Barnabas sneered. "For a woman who forces chastity on her people and values only abnegation and piety, she truly is the vainest person I've ever known." He let out a groan as the people once again policed themselves into silence. "Oh my. It seems as though she's not done yet."

Indeed, the goddess was still on the balcony, poised to go on. "I spoke about the importance of loyalty," she said, pacing the balcony as if to make sure everyone below her knew she was talking to them. "Indeed, there is truly nothing I value higher. Without trusted mortals at my side, without devotees who unquestioningly obey the commands that keep our kingdom fed, clothed, and housed— why, I could not rule at all. Over the last several days, some events have transpired that have tested this theory and proved that it has never been more true. It has recently come to my attention that one of the mortals I've come to trust more than anyone else is planning to betray me. His plot to rise up against me and in effect our entire kingdom has come to me in a clear vision of prophecy. As a suspected traitor, he shall be beheaded here today."

Barnabas and Maddox shared a furtive look. Of all the things they'd prepared to do today, witnessing a public beheading was not one of them.

"Before the execution begins, I have another announcement to make. In light of this and other suspicions of betrayal, I have called for the immediate arrest of any and all witches who are breaking the law by practicing magic in this kingdom. It has come to my attention that there are many more of these women than any of us previously thought, and we cannot tolerate their poisoning presence. Therefore, I am offering a reward for information that leads to the arrest of suspected witches and those accused of helping to house or protect these evildoers."

Maddox shot a concerned look at Camilla, who gazed back at him with a smile. Her face was calm and resolute, but Maddox knew he saw alarm in her eyes.

"Now," Valoria said. "Bring out the prisoner."

Quiet commotion rustled through the crowd as three men—two uniformed guards flanking a restrained man wearing fine but soiled clothing—emerged from the palace. The two guards walked the restrained man to an execution platform constructed underneath the balcony, where a masked man waited before a heavy black block.

"Oh no," Camilla murmured.

"Goddess," the man cried out, straining his neck as the guards forced him to his knees behind the execution block. "My radiant, beautiful goddess! Please, don't do this! I did not betray you—not now, not in the past, not in the future. I swear it—it must have been someone else you saw in your vision! I am nothing more than your humble servant. Please, forgive me for this crime—a crime that no one has yet committed!"

Valoria regarded the man coldly. "My decision is final," she said, then nodded at the masked executioner. "Remove his head."

The masked man took up his ax with a steady heave. The man continued to plea, and as the ax began to fall, Maddox looked away. Finally, mercifully, the man ceased his desperate cries.

The body was quickly carried away, but the man's head was

mounted upon a tall spike on the platform: a warning for all to see.

Some looked up at it with solemn expressions, others with fear.

Barnabas winced, then turned to Camilla, speaking in a whisper. "Camilla, who was that? Did you recognize him?"

"Yes," Camilla said. She sighed heavily. "That, I'm very sorry to say, was the goddess's scribe."

Chapter 6

CRYSTAL

They were only a block away from the art gallery when Crys stopped and grabbed her mother's arm. "You're sure about this?"

"Crys, we've already discussed this."

"I know. But . . . you're still sure that you're sure?"

Julia raised an eyebrow. "When did you become the cautious one? Haven't you been dying to go to this show? *And* to get out of that apartment?"

Crys looked around at where they were, surrounded by tall buildings, sleek steel and glass everywhere, in the city's upscale Yorkville neighborhood. The sidewalks were busy with people shopping, heading in and out of restaurants, enjoying their weekends. Nearby, a driver was valiantly trying to parallel park in one of the only available spots, which was far too small for his client's Mercedes SUV.

"Of course." Crys frowned. "You're right. When *did* I become the cautious one?"

Julia grinned. "The question of the day."

"But what if—"

"Crys," Julia cut her daughter off. "We're not going to wear sandwich boards advertising who we are and where we'll be for the next hour. We're going to a photography show at a small art gallery, and then we're going straight back to the apartment. No lurking around in dark alleyways, I promise."

Crys exhaled shakily and forced herself to nod. "Fine. In and out. I'm not even going to try to meet Andrea and ask for her career advice, which is exactly what I'm dying to do."

"That is entirely your prerogative."

Why was her mother looking so . . . fierce today? She was dressed in a fitted black pencil skirt, a matching blazer, and heels, and looked ready to take on the world. While Becca's spirit was off in another world, Julia had temporarily lost that shiny aura of confidence Crys had always loved in her. She was just starting to get it back, which is why it really bothered Crys to see it slip and falter after Becca's little *incident* with the book yesterday. But Becca had made a quick recovery, and Dr. Vega had locked up the book to keep Becca away from it.

The thought of the book sending her sister's spirit away again sent a shiver of dread coursing through her limbs. If that ever happened again, there was no guarantee she'd come back.

"If it helps," Julia said as Crys continued to scan their surroundings with paranoia, "I did bring this along to give us a sense of protection."

She slipped her hand into her purse, and there it was: a glimpse of the handgun that was normally kept locked away in a safe in the bookshop. Crys remembered the day her father bought it five years ago, after a string of burglaries on their street. She also remembered the loud argument they had about it, Julia berating him about how unsafe it was for them to keep a gun in the same house as their daughters, and Daniel countering that the only reason he'd bought the gun was to protect his daughters and keep them safe.

"Great," Crys mumbled, looking at the gun now as that shiver of dread made a swift return appearance. "My mother's packing heat. I'm sure that has exactly what it takes to take down an immortal death god."

"No matter what he might tell anyone, Markus King is no god," Julia said with a sneer. "He's nothing more than a fading fraud, and to hear Jackie tell it, he's not far from a well-deserved death. That's why he hasn't dared show his face yet, even though that book is the puzzle piece he's been dying to get his hands on for who knows how long. Looks like someone's afraid we might have more power than he originally thought."

That didn't sound much like the ruthless, sociopathic man who terrorized Crys and her sister mere days ago. "Markus is afraid?"

"Sure seems like it. Either that or maybe he's deluded enough to think that Jackie is still madly in love with him and that he can charm her into just handing over the book."

"Yeah. Good luck with that, right?" Crys grimaced, not able to concentrate on anything other than the glint of the gun, which was still visible in Julia's open purse. "Put that thing away, would you?"

She closed her purse, then hooked her arm through her daughter's. "Come on. Let's try to go ten minutes without thinking or talking about that evil creep. Teach me more about photography and why you love it so much, okay?"

Crys fought off one last urge to scurry back to the relative safety of the penthouse before she finally nodded. "Okay."

As soon as they walked through the glass front doors and entered the gallery, Crys was hit with a palpable sense of excitement.

The place was as busy and buzzing as she'd expected—probably more so—and she stopped to take a deep breath of gratitude beneath the sign announcing the title of the show: "The Passion of Andrea Stone." The main exhibit space was open and airy, with high ceilings and crisp white walls that showed off fifty framed photos, each one chosen carefully by a curator as representative of various stages in Andrea's career. The first photo in the exhibit was a self-portrait of Andrea looking down, her frizzy, graying hair in a massive bun, her face set in a serious expression, and her chin resolute.

Crys read the little placard next to the portrait. *"Photography isn't a job, it's a true calling. A passion one cannot ignore."*

Someone in the gallery let out a loud, ringing laugh, causing Crys to turn and look across the crowd. There, in person and only twenty feet away, was Andrea Stone, the photographer herself, standing at the center of a group of people, dressed head to toe in all black, no makeup except for her trademark slash of bright red lipstick.

"Oh my God," Crys said out loud. Julia heard her and turned to look as well.

"Not terribly glamorous, is she?"

Crys shrugged. "I think she looks super glam."

"If you say so. I will admit that she looks wise, though." Her mother nodded up at the self-portrait. "It's all in her eyes. You can tell that she's seen a lot, experienced a lot, and not all of it was good. I know exactly how that is."

Crys touched her mother's arm, finally tearing her gaze away from Andrea. "You can talk to me, you know. About anything you want."

A shadow crossed over Julia's expression. "I know you're worried about Becca. As worried as I am."

Crys nodded. "I have a million questions about what she is," she said in a lowered voice. "I can barely sleep thinking about them all, but . . . but then I wake up, and I see her, and I know she's my sister, no matter what. She's *his* daughter, but she's not like him a bit."

All of a sudden, Julia looked very tired. "I feel the same way."

"You can talk to me about other stuff too," Crys said. "Not just about Becca. Like . . . what it was like back when you were in the society. About what you went through with the marks and dealing with all of the craziness that came with them. Even how you feel about . . . Dad."

Her mother gave her a weak smile. "It's still all so painful to think about those days, especially when it comes to your father. But . . . I know you love him. I do too—in a different way, mind you, but still. The fact that he helped you—you and Becca"—she shook her head—"that was so brave. I didn't think he'd be willing to help, even though it was his own children who were in danger."

Crys's throat closed up at the reminder of her father and what he'd risked. "We have to help him get away from Markus," she said. "I asked him to come with us that night, but after giving us the book and helping us escape, he went back to that freak. He's not safe with Markus, Mom. And the fact I haven't heard from him in a week, not even a text . . . I'm so worried about him." Her voice caught, and she forced herself to take a deep breath. She didn't want to break down in the middle of the gallery.

Julia grabbed hold of her hand and squeezed it. "Have you tried to get in touch with him?"

Crys shook her head. "No. I'm afraid if I call or text and Markus sees the message . . ."

"That your father will be punished."

"Yes."

"I'll tell you something about your father, Crystal. He's smart. And resourceful. And he's a damn good liar when he needs to be. When we were younger and still together, whenever he got himself into tight situations, he always managed to wiggle out of them. My father wasn't exactly a great fan of me dating someone who . . . well, someone who wasn't part of our social circle. But in two meetings, Daniel had convinced Dad that he was the perfect match for me because he lied through his teeth about his family. He did so well that my father even personally invited him to the family Christmas party, which, trust me, he *never* did for any of my other boyfriends. I admired Daniel for the way he made all of that up just to get in my father's good graces—just to get me—and, well, I guess I hated him a little for it too. And it's that same ability that makes me believe that, right now, he's doing and saying whatever he has to in order to survive. If he's not getting in touch with you, there's a reason for it. And once things settle down a little, I swear to you that we will do whatever it takes to bring him back to us."

Crys stared at her, shocked and wondering if she'd heard her mother correctly. "Are you serious?"

Julia nodded, her eyes glossy. "I sure am."

"Thank you," Crys said, resisting the urge to hug her mother in front of all of these sophisticated, decidedly unsentimental art enthusiasts. "Thank you for listening to me."

"I admit, I haven't been so great at that lately."

Crys managed a shaky grin. "Ditto."

Julia's cell phone started to ring. She fished it out of her jacket pocket and glanced at the screen.

"Give me a sec, Crys. I need to take this."

"Okay." Any other day and Crys would have chastised her

mother for being rude and answering a call in the middle of an important cultural event, but she was still riding high from the news about her father, so she let it go. "I'll be over here drooling at literally every single piece."

Julia nodded, then turned and walked away a few paces. "Yes?" she said into the phone. "Yes, I can talk now. Go ahead."

Crys distractedly wondered who had called her mother. Maybe Dr. Vega with news about the book, but Julia's tone was a little too formal to be talking to him. Maybe it was Angus Balthazar, the penthouse owner extraordinaire who was supposed to be able to help them with all things magical. She wasn't sure how convinced she was of his unparalleled expertise, but she had to admit: The guy had a great apartment.

Still, there was one thing about Angus that kept nagging at her: He was a thief. More than that, he was a thief who was so accomplished and successful that he could afford a lavish, professionally decorated home. So why was Jackie so ready to trust him with something as precious and valuable—and dangerous—as the Codex? What was to stop him from stealing it and selling it to the highest bidder, no matter how close he and Jackie were?

Stop thinking so much, Crys told herself. Of all the people involved—her well-connected aunt with the somewhat sketchy past, her former-society-member mother, and her half-immortal-and-touched-by-magic sister—she was the least qualified to question any aspect of the situation. She was merely related to these people.

Nothing special.

It was something she'd never admit to anyone else, but this thought—that she was an ordinary nobody in a family full of extraordinary somebodies—had become a recurring one lately, and conjuring it now gave her an unpleasant twisting feeling in her gut. Becca had been through a laundry list of madness, and after witnessing what happened yesterday, even the most skeptical bones in Crys's body were starting to believe her story.

Becca was special. Important. Probably magical. Potentially powerful, Crys supposed, even if Becca herself didn't realize it yet. Her sister was a secret that needed to be kept.

And Crys . . . well, she was just taking up space and getting in the way.

No. She refused to feel weirdly envious that she hadn't been the one to get jerked out of her world and sent on a roller coaster ride to another world. Crys liked it when her world made sense. She actually enjoyed planning for—well, daydreaming about, mostly—a solid future. It was funny, really. She hadn't even known that about herself until recently.

I am Crystal Hatcher, she thought. *And I love it when things are boring and predictable.*

She guessed that made her boring and predictable too, but she was pleased to find she didn't even care.

She tried to clear her head and focus only on the photo in front of her: a black-and-white image of a perfectly ordinary person. According to the museum label, the subject was an old woman who was raised in Montana on a horse farm where she'd lived all her life, through summers of blazing sunshine and winters that ranged from bitterly cold to devastatingly harsh. Each of her eighty-some years showed in the depth of her expression and the wrinkles, sunspots, and smile lines on her face. Her eyes told a story that could fill many books. By physical description alone, she appeared to be perfectly normal, yet that didn't keep her from being—or Andrea from capturing her in such a way that she appeared—magical in her own way.

Crys knew her father would have loved this show, especially since he was the one who'd introduced her to photography in the first place. Her heart ached as she wished he were here to share it with her too.

"Call me crazy, but this? This *has* to be fate."

In an instant, Crys's blood to ice. Every single shred of substance—words, thoughts, images, memories—fell out of her mind as she shut her eyes and braced herself against the sound of Farrell Grayson's voice.

Fate indeed.

As her heart violently played bongos against her rib cage, Crys struggled to remind herself that they were in public. Which was a good thing—nothing bad could happen here. Nobody was going to get hurt.

Which was too bad, since she really, really wanted to hurt him.

"Look at her," Farrell continued, speaking in a mock-lofty tone. "So enraptured by this photo that the rest of the world fades away, becomes meaningless. She's truly a sight to behold."

"I swear to God," Crys growled, "if you take another step closer to me I'm going to start screaming."

"Well, that would be rather embarrassing. For you, of course."

Crys finally willed herself to focus enough to cast a glare in his direction. He leaned against the wall, right next to the photo of the old woman, studying Crys as if she were a piece in the exhibit as well. That half smile she'd come to loathe was firmly fixed on his lips.

"Stalking me, are you?" she said. "Are you on your own this time? Or are you here under order from your lord and master?"

"*Me*, stalking *you*?" He raised his brow. "And here I thought it was the other way around."

Crys scoffed. "Ha! As if it's a coincidence that you came to this exact show at the exact same time I'm here."

"Vanity, thy name is Crystal Hatcher," Farrell said, shaking his head and gazing around the room. "Actually, I'm here for a friend. And with a friend."

"Sure you are." Crys scanned the crowd, searching for her mother, but she was nowhere to be seen. *Damn.* She knew coming here had been a mistake. "Get away from me."

"Are you a fan of this photographer? Or do you just stop by all the shows?"

"I said, *Get away from me.* What language do I need to say it in for you to understand?" Farrell ignited within her such an odd mix of emotions—fear and hatred, blended with about three times as much sheer annoyance. But she didn't underestimate how dangerous he was.

And where was her mother?

Farrell took his eyes off Crys and set his gaze somewhere behind her. "Andrea!" he called. "Andrea, stop for a sec. I have someone I want to introduce you to."

Slowly, her stomach a pit of gravel, Crys turned around. Walking toward them was none other than Andrea Stone.

"This is Crystal Hatcher," Farrell said. "She's quite young but already an accomplished photographer. Crys, this is Andrea Stone."

"May I call you Crys too?" Andrea Stone held out her hand, a smile on her ruby red lips. "It's lovely to meet you."

Crys was frozen. She was in front of her idol, with a chance to say anything she wanted, and she had absolutely no idea how to respond.

Somehow, as if an invisible puppeteer were controlling her muscles, she grasped the hand of her idol.

"I'm such a fan of your work," Crys managed to sputter out, still unable to truly believe that it was Andrea Stone herself standing right in front of her.

"Thank you," Andrea said. She put a hand on Farrell's shoulder. "You're one of Farrell's friends?"

Crys knew that her mouth was moving, but words refused to come out.

"*Close* friends," Farrell replied with a smirk. "In fact, I don't mean to brag, but I was the one who convinced Crys to finally try digital photography. She's a modern girl, but old school in so many ways."

"Oh?" Andrea said. "You worked primarily in film before, then?"

Crys found herself nodding. "It's how I learned. Black-and-white only. With a manual Pentax from the eighties."

"And you develop it yourself?"

She nodded again, which made her wonder if she'd ever stopped. "In the bathtub. My mom hates it."

Andrea grinned. "My mother didn't like it either—I did the same thing when I was your age. Trust me, Crys, if you want to be a photographer, it's best to know every aspect of the art. So many people rely on digital photography now, but my favorite camera is still the one I've had for over forty years. There's a kind of purity in the act of taking a photo and not knowing exactly how it will look until it develops in the chemicals. Sure, you can set up a composition, but with film there's always a surprise with the finished product."

"I totally agree."

Andrea grasped Crys's hand again. "Thank you so much for coming to my show."

"Thank you for . . . for being *you*."

With another smile and a squeeze of Crys's hand, Andrea wandered off into the crowd.

"Thank you for being you," Farrell repeated. "That's so adorable I want to frame it."

Crys turned a cold glare on him. "What do you want?"

"Other than to introduce you to a woman I've known since before I could walk who also happens to be your idol? Hmm, well, I do always love a nice glass of complimentary champagne. I think they've got some over there in the corner."

"Stop playing dumb. I honestly wouldn't care if you introduced me to the Queen of England—I'd still scream my head off if it meant getting rid of you."

"Crys, Crys, Crys. I know that things were a bit unfriendly and angsty when we last parted ways, but that doesn't mean we can't patch our burgeoning friendship back together."

"Where's Markus?" she asked bluntly, her stomach churning. "And where is my mother? Are you just trying to distract me so he can get to her?"

"Markus isn't here. Actually, I haven't seen him since the night two little blond mice escaped a maze and scurried off into the darkness." Finally, his smug expression eased off, his dark eyebrows drawing together. "Even I'll admit that was a rough night. And I know you were just trying to protect your sister."

She laughed, but it came out humorless and sounded more like a cough. "Do you? Well, that changes everything between us, doesn't it?"

"How is Becca?"

"None of your damn business."

"Fair enough. And what about the Codex? Is Aunt Jackie keeping it nice and safe in your hiding spot you all think is so safe and secure?"

Crys didn't reply; she wouldn't give him the satisfaction of thinking he'd rattled her. Her mother already told her that hiding wasn't an option, that Markus could find them wherever they went, so why should she care or be surprised that Farrell might know the truth?

"I'm going to tell you something, Crys. As a friend," he continued. "When the time comes—and it will come—that Markus shows up for the book, do yourself a big favor and give it to him. He hasn't just forgotten about it, if that's what you're hoping."

"Where's my father?" Crys asked, making a conscious choice not to indulge anything Farrell said.

And perhaps her method was working: This time, Farrell was the one not to respond immediately. He cocked his head. "Worried about him, are you?"

"What happened to him that night?"

"You mean the night he betrayed Markus, gave you the book, and let you escape?"

"Actually," Crys said, "it was mainly your brother Adam who helped us escape. Call me crazy, but I don't think Markus would like very much to hear that one of his youngest followers disrespected him like that, would he? I'm going to go ahead and assume you didn't tell on him. But, then again, maybe I'm wrong. Maybe you are that much of a monster. How is your little brother doing these days anyway?"

Farrell's smile went cold at the edges. "Adam's just fine, thanks."

Crys narrowed her eyes. "Where's my father?"

"All I know is that he's not in Toronto anymore. And that if you've been expecting to hear from him anytime soon, don't hold your breath. Markus wouldn't be happy if he were to find out you two had been in touch—unless it was for you to hand over the Codex to him to give it back to its rightful owner, that is."

She felt a weight sink down on her chest. Part of her had hoped that Farrell might know something that would ease her mind about her father. What a laugh. "My father stuck a needle in your neck," she said. "Why would he be talking to you about where he is and what his plans are? I'm sure you're not exactly best buds."

"Never were. Actually, I didn't even know he existed until very recently. Until I met you, as a matter of fact. We're connected in so many ways, Crys. We're tangled together like an intricate web."

"A web of lies, maybe."

"So clever." His gaze grew serious again as his gaze moved over her. "You have new glasses, just like the ones that broke."

Crys pushed them up the bridge of her nose. "I had a second pair."

She expected him to make a comment about how ugly they were, but he didn't.

"I want you to know that I'm sorry I didn't stop Lucas from hurting you," he said instead. "There. I said it."

Crys stared at him, totally bemused. "Oh my God. An apology for letting your fellow minion kick the crap out of me. Well, in that case, all is forgiven."

"Wow. I'm standing here, trying to be earnest, and you hit me with the sarcasm stick. You're cruel." He managed the edge of a smile as he studied her even closer. "I can't help but notice your strawberry scent is gone. What was it again? Some kind of soap? You should buy more. I miss it."

She could never tell when he was mocking her, but right now she was going to err on the side of caution. "And your grotesque birthmark is gone. I *don't* miss that."

He brushed his fingers over his right cheek, his eyes narrowing slightly. "Had it removed. Been meaning to do that for, oh, nineteen years or so."

Too bad. She'd actually liked it. It made him look different and more interesting than the average insanely gorgeous rich kid, not that she'd admit that in a million years.

"I'm not here to mess with your head, Crys," he said, leaning in just a little. "But those pesky grains of sand are slipping through the hourglass, and soon Markus will be finished licking his wounds and come back for more. And when that happens, I won't be able to protect you if you get in the way."

Every sentence he spoke was a surprise. "Protect me?" Crys said. "I'd be shocked if the thought of doing that even crossed your mind."

"You think I'm an evil bastard, that Markus has messed with my head and poisoned me with magic, but you're wrong. I'll be the first to admit I'm a jerk, that I've hurt people, but I swear I mean no harm to brave girls who just want to protect their families."

Was he being serious now? He sounded sincere enough. He'd even temporarily lost his trademark smirk.

Crys found herself speechless again.

Had Adam been right? Was the real Farrell Grayson still in there, somewhere that Markus's magic couldn't touch?

"Farrell?" A female voice cut between them. "Who is this?"

Crys watched Farrell tear his gaze away, and finally she remembered how to breathe.

A blond girl approached them and stood next to Farrell. She was tall, thin, and impeccably dressed. The only feature that marred her model-like looks was her sharp nose, down which she stared at Crys.

"Felicity Seaton," Farrell finally said with an introductory flick of his hand, "this is Crys Hatcher."

"A friend of yours?" Felicity asked crisply.

"Ex-girlfriend," he replied. The smirk had returned, right on schedule.

Crys met Felicity's sour look full-on. "I'm not his ex. He's lying. He does that a lot. We went on, what? One or two substandard dates?"

"I'll always have memories of eating sushi with you."

Felicity forced a smile. "I despise raw fish."

"Not all sushi is raw . . . ," Crys began to explain, but then decided she didn't care enough to expend the energy.

"Actually, Crys and I are in a book club together now. She borrowed a book from a friend of mine, and he really, really wants it back."

Every muscle in Crys's body grew tense.

"How quaint," Felicity replied, and Crys could practically feel the chill emanating off of her icy tone.

"Don't worry," Crys told her. "I'm no competition to you or . . . whatever this is between you two. Actually, I hate Farrell. Besides, he much prefers girls from Hawkspear than ones from the real world."

"Hawkspear?" Felicity repeated, frowning. "What is that? Some kind of sorority?"

Crys stared at her, surprise filling her eyes.

Farrell took Felicity by her elbow and began directing her toward the refreshment table. "Marvelous to see you again, Crys," he said as he hurried away. "I'm sure our paths will cross again very soon."

"Only in my nightmares," she replied, smiling for having succeeded in making him nervous.

As soon as they had disappeared into the crowd, Crys turned to search the room for her mother. She actively stifled all the anxiety and fear for her mother's safety that Farrell's presence stirred, and she sighed in relief when she spotted her near the entryway. She was only now finishing her oh-so-important phone call as Crys scurried over and made her put down her full glass of white wine.

They left the gallery as fast as they could.

Chapter 7

BECCA

The spirit was watching her.

Or at least what Becca *thought* was a spirit. The spirit she'd seen Maddox summon back in Mytica had had a more human shape than whatever it was she saw down in the study. Maddox's spirit was also shrouded in darkness, but it did have legs, arms, a head, and a torso—all things her inky black blob lacked.

It had been a whole day now since that dark being had escaped from the bronze hawk. Where Becca went, it followed, staying in the corners. Not coming any closer to her, but never leaving her line of sight.

It was like a scary puppy.

"What do you want?" she demanded of it now, but like always, she received no response.

Her fear had faded a little since it first appeared, and now she was left with nothing but questions. Questions a blob of darkness didn't seem all that interested in answering.

If it wasn't a spirit, then what was it? A dark little raincloud that had come down from the sky to be her roommate?

The thought reminded her of the powers Maddox had given to

her: a tiny cloud of his death magic that had mixed with the book's gateway magic. It had been enough to bring her spirit back home and reunite it with her body.

The shadow crept a few inches toward her. She took a step backward, and it crept toward her again, even closer this time. She leaped away from it, but then, taking the form of a thick black ribbon of smoke, the shadow slithered along the floor, giving her a wide berth, and moved toward the door. It appeared to hesitate, swirling around in a circle for a moment before leaving the room entirely. Becca waited, holding her breath, until it appeared again, peeking around the edge of the door frame.

Becca glanced at Charlie, who was curled up on her bed, fast asleep and snoring. The kitten was no help at all.

"What?" she asked the shadow, as if it might actually answer her this time. "Do you want me to . . . follow you?"

It waited in place until Becca drew closer. She walked across the room, slowly, until she followed her instinct and trailed after it at a faster clip.

"Well, if I wasn't certifiable before, I definitely am now," she told herself, feeling strangely giddy rather than scared, as if she were close to laughing. "They're going to put me in a straitjacket for talking to shadows."

The inky presence led her downstairs. The curtains were partially drawn over the glass doors leading to the balcony where Jackie and Dr. Vega were now standing. Jackie was smoking a cigarette, which Becca knew her aunt only did when stressed out.

The shadow paused when she paused, and then slithered right into the study. She glanced in through the open door to see it swirling on the floor right in front of the desk.

"I have a funny feeling I know exactly what you're trying to show me," she whispered. "But Dr. Vega locked you-know-what up so I wouldn't touch it again."

It started swirling more quickly now.

Becca hissed out a breath and glanced toward the balcony again, where Jackie and Dr. Vega still stood looking very engaged in conversation. She knew Crys and her mother were at the photo show, which meant she had eyes on all the penthouse guests and didn't have to worry about anyone interrupting her. Finally, she moved toward the desk and tried the top drawer. "See? Just like I said. It's locked, and I have no idea where the key is."

The shadowy ribbon curled around the desk leg, snaked up toward the drawer, and disappeared through a crack. It reappeared, pouring out of the keyhole, and returned to the ground.

Becca watched, mouth slightly ajar, and then tried the drawer again. She was not exactly surprised to find that it now slid open easily.

And there it was. The bronze hawk glinted under the desk lamp's meager light. Regarding it now was like staring at the sun— she knew very well she shouldn't do it, that it wasn't good for her, but she couldn't seem to tear her gaze away.

Before she realized what she was doing, she had grasped the Codex and pulled it out of the drawer. Upon contact, that strange but pleasant shiver moved up her arms, but this time no other magical sensation followed.

They all wanted to keep her away from it, but the book refused to let that happen.

It needs me, Becca said to herself.

She frowned. What a bizarre thought.

"But for what?" she mused aloud. Tentatively, after taking a deep breath, she opened the cover. This was the first chance she'd had to really look at the Codex without interruption. She knew Jackie would be furious if she caught her, so she had to be quick about it.

It wasn't as if she had a choice, though. This wasn't a decision. It was a *compulsion*.

She turned the pages swiftly but delicately, and once again she was instantly enchanted by the fragile, almost weightless, feel of the paper. The pages were filled with beautiful, indecipherable black-and-gold writing and colorful illustrations rendered with a fine hand.

"As if being a book of otherworldly spells isn't enough, now it seems you and your shadowy little friend over there are trying to tell me you're something more than that. So then what *are* you?"

Just then, Becca saw the words on the page start to move. Her breath caught in her chest.

No—they weren't *moving*, exactly. They were *changing*. They were transforming into other words, rewriting themselves before her very eyes. Then, an illustration of a small rabbit-like animal turned on profile started shifting as well, until the creature was turned forward to face Becca, its beady little eyes staring right at her.

She heard a hissing sound behind her and started. She turned to the doorway to see Charlie, his back arched, slinking his way inside the room. She followed the cat's gaze downward until she saw the shadow there at her feet. It had curled itself around her ankle.

Becca let out a harsh gasp of surprise, and then—

A rabbit-like animal, just like the illustration in the book, appeared in the room. It was right in front of her, sitting in a green field and chewing on a plant that looked like a bright pink clover. Beyond the field, sparkling under a bright sun, was the same majestic crystal city she'd seen the last time she'd touched the book.

The animal took off like a shot. Becca spun around to see what had startled it, and her eyes widened with horror.

In the distance, the ground was crumbling. It was falling away into an endless abyss, leaving nothing in its wake. The devastation grew closer and closer to her until the ground just in front of where she was standing began to fall away into a vast, dark emptiness.

Before Becca could scream, the view in front of her changed. It shifted and whirled all around her in a blur of colors and textures and motion until finally she was able to get a sense of her new surroundings. Instead of the dim study, she now stood in the middle of a crowd gathered in the shadow of a tall black palace.

"That, I'm very sorry to say, was the goddess's scribe," said a strangely familiar voice. Becca turned toward it to find the source.

She could barely believe what was right in front of her. It was Camilla, the Mytican witch who'd helped Maddox and Barnabas in their attempt to defeat Valoria.

"Curse it," said another voice. "So now what do we do?"

Maddox.

Becca shot her disbelieving gaze to the dark-haired boy with the warm, bottomless brown eyes, who saw her, heard her, *helped* her, when no one else could. She stared at him, stunned.

"Maddox," Becca managed to say through a choked voice. "Maddox, it's me!"

Maddox turned, and Becca's heart leaped. But he'd turned to look at Barnabas, whose handsome, short-bearded face was the same as Becca remembered.

The older man looked grim as he gazed back at Maddox. "Give me a moment to think."

"Think about what?" Maddox said. "That source of yours, the only one who knew how to bring an end to Her Radiance, is now nothing more than a head mounted upon a spike! What's there to think about?"

Becca looked up, toward the palace, and what she saw there turned her stomach. Stuck on the top of a spike on a balcony was the severed head of a youngish man.

"This is such a horrible place," she whispered, closing her eyes and shuddering. "It's like a horror movie here, everywhere you turn."

"We'll begin our search for the princess anyway," Barnabas said. "Proof of King Thaddeus's heir's existence will draw new interest to the rebel cause."

"And with no proof to back this discovery up, all we'll get are more rebels killed," Camilla added, nervously twisting a glass vial filled with liquid that she wore on a thin leather rope around her neck. "My, Barnabas, what an excellent plan. Come now. I know you're smarter than that."

"And what would you suggest?" he countered. "Should we go ahead and demand information from a severed head?"

"Yes," Maddox said a moment later. "I think that's exactly what we should do."

Suddenly, a voice cried out, so loud that it rang in Becca's ears, forcing her to close her eyes and cower right there in the village square.

"God damn it, Becca!" It was her aunt Jackie. "What are you doing in here?"

Like the blinking of a television changing channels, Maddox, Barnabas, and Camilla flickered away. Becca was back in the study, where she realized with dismay that her aunt was now holding the Bronze Codex, staring at Becca with outrage blazing in her blue eyes.

Becca could barely catch her breath. For a moment she thought that she'd actually returned to Mytica, but now she saw that she hadn't even taken a single step away from the desk.

The shadow had unwound itself from her ankle and retreated to the corner of the room, where it looked like nothing more than a spot of inky blackness.

"Answer me, damn it!" Jackie slammed the book down on the desk.

"Don't do that!" Becca snarled, her own fury suddenly exploding from deep within. She was sick and tired of being told what to do and reprimanded when she didn't do it. "Don't hurt it, or you'll be sorry!"

Jackie drew in a shaky breath. "What's gotten into you? Why would you risk even *touching* this thing again? You know how dangerous it is—especially to you!"

Dr. Vega entered the room, pushing his glasses up higher on his nose. "Oh dear," he said, taking in the scene in front of him. "What happened?"

Jackie shot him a steely look. "Oh, nothing. Just happened to find my niece messing with fate to find her boyfriend from another world."

Becca gaped at her. "You think that's why I—?" She was so angry she could barely form words. "You're unbelievable, you know that? This has nothing to do with that! Maybe I want to know *why* that book is so dangerous to me! Why does it affect me and nobody else?"

Crys and her mother appeared at the doorway, worried expressions on both of their faces.

"What's going on in here?" Julia said.

"Becca can't seem to stay away from this thing." Jackie flung her hand toward the Codex, the gesture filled with equal parts fear and annoyance. "It's like she's *addicted* to it or something."

"Seriously?" Becca said, Jackie's flippant explanation only infuriating her further. "You have no idea what it really is, do you? No idea at all."

"And you do?" Dr. Vega asked, snatching up a pen and notepad from the desktop. "Please, tell me all about what you've experienced. Your testimony might be all I need to figure this conundrum out."

"You *can't* figure it out," Becca growled. "None of you can. This kind of magic is so far beyond the brain capacity of mere mortals . . . that I . . . I literally can't even explain it to you."

"Whoa, Becca," Crys said, approaching Becca warily and peering at her with concern. "Are you okay? You're talking seriously crazy."

"Maybe I'm the only one who's sane around here." She heard the words leave her mouth, but she had no idea why she said them or if she believed them. In truth, she didn't know much more about what the book really was than Dr. Vega and Jackie, and she certainly didn't know enough to make such a lofty, pompous statement. All she had was a hunch that the Codex was something more than the book of spells that everyone believed it was.

"Let me see that thing," Julia said as she reached for the book. Without hesitation, Jackie hefted it up off the desk and gave it to her. "Thank you." Julia looked down at the Codex and frowned. "I can't tell you how sick I am of this damn thing. From the moment I first learned it existed it's caused nothing but problems." She turned and left the room.

Jackie trailed after her. "Where are you going with it?"

Julia stopped in the hallway and said, "I'm going to give it to Markus."

Becca's eyes widened with shock. She was the first to follow Jackie out the door, but soon Vega and Crys followed.

They all chased after Julia, who walked steadily toward the front door.

"Did you say you were going somewhere with the book?" Becca

asked hoarsely as Julia grabbed her coat and purse. "To take it to *Markus*?"

"Markus needs this. So badly that he's willing to *kill* for it. Has been for the last twenty years. So let's let him have it. Why would we want something like this anywhere near us? Maybe then he'll leave us alone for good."

"Mom, have you lost your mind?" Crys said.

"Not even a touch. In fact, I'm finally thinking straight. I'm finally doing what needs to be done."

"You're not taking that book out of this house," Jackie snapped.

"Yes, I am."

"No. I won't let you."

Julia pulled a gun out of her purse. She pointed it at Jackie, who stopped in her tracks. "If you try to stop me, I swear I'll kill you."

"Mom!" Becca shouted. "What are you doing?"

Julia turned the gun on Becca, whose heart leaped into her throat as she stared down the barrel.

"I'll kill you too," Julia said, an eerie calmness in her voice.

The moment was frozen in place, like a horrifying snapshot, right in front of Becca's eyes.

"Mom," Crys said, her tone stern but gentle as she dared to break the silence. "This isn't you. Please, don't do this. You don't want to hurt Becca. You don't want to hurt any of us."

The gun began to tremble in Julia's grip, her entire body shivering while her eyes grew wider and wider.

"Mom!" Crys yelled, making Becca jump. "Drop the gun now!"

Finally, shaking, Julia dropped the book and the gun. She put her hands up and staggered backward until she hit the wall.

"Oh my God," Julia said through a quaking voice. "What am I doing? What have I . . . Becca . . . sweetheart. I'm so sorry!"

Carefully, as if approaching a wild animal she didn't want to startle, Jackie picked up the book and handed it to Dr. Vega, who took it in his trembling hands. She picked up the gun and checked the cartridge.

"It's loaded," she confirmed grimly.

"It's for—for protection," Julia said. "We need something to defend ourselves against Markus and his people." Julia slid limply down the wall and to the ground, where she drew her knees up against her chest. "I'm so sorry. Why did I do that? I don't want Markus to have the book! And I'd never want to hurt any of you!"

"Mom, think back," Crys said. "When we were at the gallery. Who called you?"

Julia shot her tear-filled gaze to Crys. "I . . . I don't remember."

"She was on the phone," Crys said, turning to Jackie. "She answered a call and then walked away for privacy. She left me alone long enough for Farrell Grayson to find and corner me. We had a very unpleasant conversation, but he didn't try anything. He didn't tell me anything *real* or actually helpful, but I definitely got the impression that Markus is biding his time, waiting for the right moment to strike."

Jackie swore under her breath. "Jules, let me see your phone."

Julia fumbled in her purse and pulled out her phone. Jackie took it and scrolled through the call list. "You've gotten several calls over the last couple of days from a blocked number. You don't remember who it was?"

Julia shook her head, her complexion pale and her expression bleak. "If I don't remember . . . if I just tried to murder my own family so I could take the book to Markus . . . Oh my God, Jackie—my marks. I never thought their effect was that strong, not even when I first got them, but he . . . he must still have some sort of power over me!"

"That son of a bitch," Jackie muttered. "Don't worry, sis, I'll figure this out. That might not even be what's happening, so don't make yourself sick."

Julia nodded erratically. "But until you figure it out, what happens? No one's safe around me."

"Angus's arriving today. He's the magic expert, remember? He'll be able to help."

"The expert at stealing magic, you mean."

"Honestly, at this point? I don't care one way or the other. There's no one else on the planet who's better equipped to help with this kind of problem. He's smart. As smart as you are, Uriah." Jackie glanced at the professor. "Your specialty is ancient languages. Angus's is magic. Real magic. And maybe it was his career as a thief rather than time spent at university that earned him that knowledge, but that doesn't make it any less valid to me right now. If this really is the dagger's spell working on you, then Uriah and Angus have got to be able to put their heads together and find something in that Codex that can break it. And if this *is* what's going on and we *do* help you, sis, that means we have the information we need to help everyone else in the Hawkspear Society escape that evil scumbag once and for all."

Becca watched the scene unfold in front of her, stunned, for the first time feeling solely responsible for every bit of drama the book—and the act of her touching it—had caused.

But no. Deep down she had a feeling that all of this would have happened with or without her.

All she knew for sure was that Markus King could never, ever get his hands on the book again.

Chapter 8

FARRELL

Another night, another bar. Farrell was starting to question the utter lack of motivation he was experiencing this week. Even for him it seemed oddly unnatural.

He sat in a lonely booth in a lonely pub and raised his glass of vodka on the rocks. "To bleached-blond girls with ice blue eyes and miserable, judgmental scowls, especially the ones who hate my guts," he said. "Yeah, I'll drink to that."

"You'll drink to anything," Connor's voice said.

"True." Farrell downed his drink in one gulp.

"You need to stop obsessing about her."

"Obsessing? Me? That's ridiculous." A passing waitress sent him a confused glance, and Farrell flicked his hand at her. "Don't worry about me. Just having a conversation with my dead brother, that's all."

"Uh ... okay," she said, then stopped reluctantly. "Another drink?"

"Absolutely." He placed his empty glass on her tray. "Keep them coming."

"Rough night talking to ... a ghost?"

"Not a ghost." Farrell leaned heavily on his hand as he gazed up at the fuzzy image of the waitress. He'd never been to this generic bar before tonight, and at the moment he couldn't even recall the name of it. The waitress was older, heavyset, and looked mean enough to take a bite out of someone if they gave her a hard time. "He's my conscience," Farrell went on. "My compass—albeit imaginary—that tells me what to do and what not to do. And since I seem utterly devoid of focus at the moment, it's helpful."

"Like an angel on your shoulder."

"Actually, more like a devil."

"If you say so." She gave him an unfriendly scowl before she strode back to the bar.

He watched, annoyed, and annoyed that he was so annoyed tonight. What did he have to be annoyed about?

Everything.

Nothing.

His phone buzzed. He pulled it out to see a message from his very much alive younger brother, Adam.

Where are you?

Farrell ignored the message, switched the phone to Do Not Disturb, and tried to summon his inner cheerleader. He needed to figure out what he wanted to do next.

He'd been gifted with good looks, perfect health, newly ramped-up senses, plenty of leisure time, a substantial allowance to be followed by an enormous inheritance in less than two years, and a gift for being charming even when he wasn't really feeling it. He had the world at his fingertips. How had he ended up all alone tonight at some random dive bar, without even a hot cocktail waitress to flirt with?

"Chin up, kid," Connor told him. *"All is well. A couple more drinks and you'll be feeling just fine."*

"Who murdered you?" Farrell mumbled. Not too long ago, this was the one question that drove him not only to find answers, but to find meaning in his lifestyle and daily activities. But recently that drive had faded. Why was that?

"I wasn't murdered," Connor said. *"I committed suicide. I was depressed after Mallory dumped me, so I killed myself. You know what a tortured artist I was, always taking everything so seriously. You know I wasn't murdered. You're the one who found me."*

It was a blood-streaked memory, which Farrell preferred to repress whenever possible.

He shook his head. "Smash some windows, raise some hell, mope for a year, and treat everyone around you like crap—I can understand that. But slit your wrists? At home, in your childhood bed? It just wasn't like you."

"People are capable of extreme acts of despair when they're depressed."

"You didn't seem particularly depressed to me."

Actually, around the time of his death, Connor had seemed just the opposite. Six months earlier Markus had taken him on as part of his inner circle, a fact revealed to Farrell only recently, when Markus chose him to take his brother's place. But when it was still Connor in there, life for him seemed perfect. So what changed? Sure, there was Mallory. Farrell didn't know too much about their relationship, but from what he could gather, Connor's girlfriend of three years had dumped him for being cruel and unemotional. Farrell was more certain than ever that his cold behavior was probably a side effect of the second and third dagger marks. He knew exactly how his brother must have felt carrying around those invisible scars that made the world so black and white that it was difficult to suffer fools any longer. That feeling was why imaginary Connor had suggested that Farrell try to beat people with the charm stick rather than say whatever withering comment came into his mind.

The darker the thought, the more vital it was to cage it. Trapped in his mind, it could be observed and appreciated but couldn't bite anyone with its razor-sharp teeth. Plus, he was a better help to Markus if he didn't draw too much attention to himself.

The waitress brought Farrell his next drink. He studied it for a long time, willing himself not to finish it all in one go, then took a modest sip from the glass. Why was he relying on booze to make himself feel good? Just being the new *him* should have been more than enough.

The world was his to lose, and all the power and respect he'd ever wanted were practically already in his grasp. He could have anything he asked for.

"Except Crystal Hatcher," Connor commented.

"As if I give a damn about her. All she is to me is a pain in my ass."

"She's under your skin."

"Yeah. Like a splinter." He took a larger sip of his drink. "I killed her father and feel no remorse about it."

"True. And you promised Markus you'd have no problem killing her too if she causes him any more problems. Remember that?"

Farrell tightened his grip on his glass. "I remember."

"The only reason you want her is because she doesn't want you. She sees you for what you really are, and your fake charm won't work on her. Well, who the hell cares? You have Felicity at your beck and call, and if you don't want her then just choose any other girl in this city. Crys isn't worth your time or energy. Get over her."

"I should have grabbed her and taken her to Markus when I saw her at the gallery."

"But you didn't."

With one steady motion, Farrell drained his glass.

Seeing her there, out in the open, was as big of a surprise to him as it must have been to her. There she was, nothing more than a means to getting the Bronze Codex for Markus, exposed and vulnerable.

Yet he let her slip away.

It was a choice of weakness.

Surely the others in Markus's circle—whose identities he still didn't know—wouldn't have failed him like that.

A chill rippled down his right arm. He glanced to his right and received a shock so cold he almost dropped his glass. Walking straight toward him Markus King. The real Markus this time, definitely not some sort of illusion.

Tonight Markus didn't shine with the golden light of the young, vibrant man he appeared to be—despite the fact that he was ancient. Tonight, there was no glow. There were circles under his eyes so dark and heavy that it was as if he hadn't had a moment's rest since the last time Farrell had seen him. His posture was slightly hunched as he walked, and his hair appeared lank, its normally radiant shade faded to a dull blond color. His tan and golden skin was now ashy and pale, and even his eyes, usually an intense shade of dark blue, seemed muted somehow.

"From your shocked expression, I take it that I look as bad as I feel," Markus said, breaking Farrell out of his trancelike stare.

"Possibly a bit worse," Farrell admitted.

Markus glanced around the bar with distaste. "So this is where you spend your free time? Filthy establishments where you can drink to excess?"

Farrell raised his glass. "Yes. And I seem to have a lot of free time. Please, join me."

Markus slid into the other side of the booth.

Markus was silent for a few moments while Farrell was bursting with questions. He tried to be nonchalant, to wait for Markus to speak, but he couldn't fake any charm or cool this time. "What's wrong with you?" he blurted.

Markus managed a small smile, the corners of his mouth lifting slightly. "I'm dying."

Farrell's stomach flipped. "Don't say that."

"Why not? It's true."

"You're not dying. You just need that damn book."

Markus began to laugh, a chilling sound low in his throat. "Yes, I damn well do."

More proof that Farrell truly had failed him by walking away from Crys Hatcher. "I'll get it. I promise. It's the least I can do after all you've done for me."

"Jackie Hatcher won't let you get within twenty feet of that book. Or her daughter."

"She's *your* daughter, too," Farrell said.

A shadow crossed over Markus's already dark expression. "Yes."

The waitress returned to the table and turned to Markus. "What can I get you?"

Markus glanced at Farrell's glass. "I'll have whatever he's drinking."

"I'll need to see an ID first, honey."

Markus turned a blank stare up at her before he started to laugh in that scary, hollow way again. She waited patiently, her hand out.

"I'm thousands of years old," he told her.

She smirked. "And I'm sure you have a driver's license to prove it. Come on now. No ID, no drink. Don't think you're the first college kid to try."

"How about a ginger ale?" Farrell suggested. "It's a delicious alternative to alcohol."

"Fine," Markus sighed, and the waitress disappeared.

"I despise carbonated beverages," Markus mumbled. "I despise so much about this world. All I've ever wanted for this place is to make it better—to make it like my world was so long ago, before everything fell into chaos. Yet I am opposed at every turn."

Farrell watched him with growing dismay. Who was this broken man across from him? He was nothing like the powerful, enigmatic, and ruthless leader he'd come to know over the last three years.

"*She* could have helped me, you know," Markus continued. "*She* had the book. But she thinks I killed her family—her grandmother, her parents. I always thought she'd come back to me, but it's been years and—nothing. Not a word until last week, when Jackie came back into my life to tell me she hated me, that I shouldn't come anywhere near her or her family. But I need to see her. So I invited her to the masquerade ball."

Farrell grimaced, then quickly recomposed himself. *What was Markus thinking?* He tried to hide his surprise, however, and instead chose to focus on how much he was dreading the upcoming masquerade ball, an annual charity event organized by a group of women, including his mother, from the society. Tickets were expensive and almost impossible to get, snapped up immediately by Toronto's elite, which baffled Farrell, considering how deadly boring the ball always was.

Markus went on. "It would have been the perfect place for us to speak—both public and anonymous. I need her to give me a chance to mend our mistakes and clear up all the misunderstandings that occurred between us in the past."

"*Would have been* the perfect place?" Farrell said. "I assume she declined the invitation then?"

"She might change her mind."

"You really think so?"

The waitress returned with the ginger ale and fresh vodka for Farrell.

Markus waited for her to depart before responding. "If there's one thing she knows about me it's that I'm not a fool. I've now seen my daughter in the flesh. I know Becca is mine."

"And . . . you want to . . . be a father to her?"

There was that haunted laugh again, raising the hair on Farrell's arms.

"Jackie knows that that girl is as valuable to me as the Codex is. The magic that lies dormant within her . . . it's magic I can use. That I can take."

"And that would help you survive."

"Yes."

Was this really happening? Was this man—this immortal— really admitting all of this to him?

"*Well, look at that,*" Connor whispered. "*Seems like there's no one else in this world that he trusts. Only you. You can use that to your advantage. If you help him, listen to him, be there for him, he'll give you anything you want. If he can take magic from someone else, maybe he can give it away too. To you.*"

Yes, Farrell liked the idea of that very much. He wanted whatever he could get to make himself more powerful.

"So what's the plan?" Farrell asked. "What are the odds she'll come to the ball?"

"Knowing Jackie as I do, I believe the odds are high," Markus said, and Farrell responded with a furrowed brow. "A chance to see me, face to face, in public, where she can hide behind a mask and have her say without any repercussions? It's an opportunity she'd be a fool to pass up." He was silent for a moment. "I need you there."

Well, there goes my chance at backing out of this thing at the last min-ute, Farrell thought. "Of course I'll back you up in case she tries something."

"No, that's not why I need you there. If I'm preoccupied with Jackie, I'll need you to watch everyone else. I believe we have a traitor in our ranks. Someone—possibly even a member of my circle—who wishes to destroy the Hawkspear Society from the inside. If Daniel was a turncoat, there could be others. Will you help me find this traitor?"

Farrell found that he was suddenly speechless.

It was Adam who was the traitor. Adam, who was unaffected by the Hawkspear marks. Adam, who had already defied Markus and helped Daniel. Adam, who was too young and stupid to realize where his actions could lead.

"It would help if I knew who else was in the circle," Farrell fi-nally said. "Are you ever going to tell me who the others are? There are three others, right?"

"No, only two now. And I will tell you, just not yet. I want you to watch everyone with unbiased eyes and report back to me what you see, if anything. You will do this?"

"Of course I will," Farrell said immediately.

"Good." Markus pushed his glass away. "Now let's go."

"Where are we going?"

"I need to spill blood tonight."

"You . . . *need* to?" asked Farrell, this time certain that he was unable to hide the surprise he felt.

Markus regarded him calmly. "Spilling blood brings about blood magic. Blood magic gives me enough strength to make it through another night, another week, another month."

"How often do you do this?"

"Whenever I feel the need."

Farrell practically heard the *click* of a large piece of a very complex puzzle settling into place. "So this is the real reason why we hold executions at the society?"

Four times a year, Markus brought a criminal to trial at the society. A jury of Hawkspear members would sentence death by execution upon the guilty citizen, and Markus would stab them in the heart with his golden dagger. A swift death, followed by a wave of rapturous magic that swept over the entire society. *Addictive* magic.

"No, that's not the reason. You know very well why we host the executions." With that, Markus stood up to go. "Come on now. We have work to do."

The two left the bar and walked out into the nighttime streets of Toronto. Farrell wasn't sure what to think about learning Markus's secret to permanent life, but he wasn't about to argue or ask questions. Not when they were on the hunt for Markus's next victim.

"There." Markus nodded at a man twenty feet ahead of them on the sidewalk. "He's a killer, walking among innocents, seeking another victim."

"Him?" Farrell asked in a whisper. "How do you know? We can't even see his face."

"I can sense it. I can feel the evil emanating from his very soul."

Farrell considered this for a moment. "I killed someone. What's emanating from my soul?"

Markus cast him a sidelong look. "Loyalty belonging to someone I can trust to do what needs to be done for the good of the world, even if it is distasteful. The certainty I feel about your loyalty is unlike anything I've encountered since Jonathan was alive."

Jonathan Kendall—Crys and Becca's great-grandfather and the cofounder of the Hawkspear Society. It was the most meaningful compliment Farrell had ever been paid.

He narrowed his gaze at their target. "What do you need me to do?"

"For now, just keep following him. We need to get him somewhere private."

They trailed the man down that same central road for fifteen minutes, until he stopped at the intersection of a small street. He turned left, and Markus and Farrell followed, finding themselves on a dark, narrow road, vacant except for the three of them.

Markus nodded at Farrell. "Go. Hold him in place. My strength—it won't be enough tonight without help."

Without a single question or thought, Farrell quickened his steps. He caught up and started walking next to the man, who looked up at him with a frown.

"Nice evening," Farrell said.

"I suppo—"

Farrell grabbed the man's arm. He wrenched it behind his back, and the man yelped out in pain. Quickly, without much effort at all, Farrell had both of his arms pinned securely.

"What the hell are you doing?" the man cried out.

"Shut up," Farrell growled. "You know you deserve this. You know what you've done."

"What have I done? I haven't done anything! Do you want my wallet? My phone? You can have them—anything!"

A shadow crossed over them as Markus approached. He drew the golden dagger from beneath his coat. The man struggled even more at the sight of it, but Farrell easily held him in place.

"You are guilty of murder," Markus told him flatly. "And so I must sentence you to death. This world will be a better place without you in it."

"*What?* What are you talking about? Murder? I haven't murdered—"

Markus plunged the dagger into the man's chest. His body went rigid, pushing back against Farrell, but without another word, not one more useless plea or argument, he slid down to the sidewalk.

And instantly, a wash of golden power hit Farrell with the force of a tsunami.

Pure pleasure flowed into him and saturated every limb, every cell of his body. So this was what it was like when he didn't have to share it with two hundred other people.

"Do you feel it?" Markus asked.

"Yes." Farrell had felt this magic before, but not until tonight had it made him feel like a god.

The wave of power began to fade, and Farrell gasped for breath. He shook his head and tried to focus on Markus. "Do you feel any better now?"

Markus looked down grimly at the man's dead body. "No. It's not enough anymore. I'm not strong enough to face Jackie, to do what needs to be done to acquire the Codex—permanently this time. And the girl . . ."

If Markus failed, if he died, all of this would be over. Half of Farrell was concerned for Markus's fate—and the fate of the world he wanted to help. But the other half was concerned purely for his own future, which was now tied up with Markus's. The stronger Markus was, the stronger Farrell would be.

"What can I do?" he asked.

Markus looked up from the corpse. They'd need to dispose

of it quickly, Farrell thought. "There is something," Markus said. "Something I've never tried before."

"Tell me."

"To gain my daughter's dormant magic, I will need to give her a very special mark. But all of life is composed of magic—elemental magic. You have some of this magic within you to share, especially now that you are so strong."

Farrell blinked, trying to sort all of this out in his mind. "So . . . you can give me another mark—a mark that lets me share my strength with you?"

"Yes. I would understand if you weren't willing. This could take a toll on you."

Farrell almost laughed aloud. "I have you and that dagger to thank for the strength I have. Of course I'm willing to do whatever it takes to help you." Without another word, Farrell undid the button at his left cuff and pulled up his shirtsleeve to bare his arm.

Markus's jaw was tense as he took the golden blade and wiped the man's blood on a handkerchief. "I knew you were the one, Farrell. The one who could truly help me. Thank you for this."

Farrell gritted his teeth as the tip of the blade sank into his flesh, still sensitive from the last time. He watched Markus carve the symbol, which was much more intricate than the previous ones. It was composed of loops and wavy lines, almost as if Markus were writing words in script, but it was in a language Farrell had ever seen before.

"The language from the Codex," Connor offered in his mind.

Yes, that was it. That's what Markus was etching into his arm— a language of magic, whose twists and turns were far more painful than even the most complex tattoo. He watched his blood drip to the ground, forming black puddles in the moonlight, and the pain was so strong and the mark so intricate that he thought Markus would never finish.

Finally, though, Markus was finished. He looked up, his forehead shining with perspiration and his hands smeared with Farrell's blood. "Yes," he said, looking at the finished mark. "I think that will do it."

Farrell watched through a veil of pain as the foreign words etched into his arm began to glow with a golden light that seemed to come from within him. Markus reached over and covered Farrell's forearm with both of his hands and, shuddering with the effort, summoned the little magic he had left to heal the wound.

When it was done, Farrell wiped the blood away, surprised to see that he could still plainly see the words—lightly, as if they were a scar from a years-old wound.

Markus looked exhausted and disappointed. "I'm sorry," he said. "It's the best I could do."

"It's fine." Farrell closed his eyes. He stood still and silent, trying to sense whether anything had changed within him, but he felt the same as before—strong, awake, alive.

Farrell opened his eyes to find Markus looking at him in a dead-on stare. His eyes appeared to glow softly, golden. "You will be greatly rewarded for this, I promise you," he said.

Farrell was counting on it.

Chapter 9

MADDOX

After the beheading, Maddox couldn't shake the strange feeling that someone was watching him. The feeling was fleeting, only lasting a moment or two, but long enough to notice the hawk that had come down to land in the center of the crowd in the palace square and that then took flight again the second he'd glanced at it.

Was it the hawk he felt watching him?

Perhaps Valoria was right: Listening to too many fantastical tales did numb the mortal mind. Such ludicrous theories as being watched by a hawk were the work of an overactive imagination.

But was it ludicrous? As soon as the hawk left, whispers of the name *Becca* began to stir in Maddox's mind. Still, this kind of thing had been happening a lot lately, anytime he witnessed something that reminded him of his friend. Becca would have hated to witness this execution. In fact, she'd once told him that she hated everything about Mytica . . . except for Maddox himself.

She'd liked him when he hadn't liked himself. She'd believed in him when he'd doubted every decision he made. She'd quickly become the best friend he'd ever had.

"And what would you suggest?" Barnabas asked Camilla. "Should we go ahead and demand information from a severed head?"

"Yes," Maddox said, suddenly drawn out of his memories of the spirit girl. "I think that's exactly what we should do."

Both Barnabas and Camilla shot him a startled look, as if they'd forgotten he was even there.

"The head doesn't look very receptive to such a suggestion," Camilla said gently, placing a hand on Maddox's shoulder. She turned to Barnabas. "Perhaps we should leave and find ourselves a nice meal somewhere."

"I'm a necromancer," Maddox explained. "I vividly recall raising skeletons from their graves not so long ago."

"That's true," Barnabas replied, studying him with a serious look. "Do you believe you could use that kind of magic on purpose, not by accident?"

"I'm not sure," he said honestly. "But I could try."

Barnabas looked up at the crowd around them, then drew Maddox and Camilla off to the side of the square, away from the ears of any curious passersby. "Even if you *did* raise those dead, all you rose were a bunch of shuffling, mindless corpses who didn't seem very open to conversations about revolutionary actions."

"Those corpses had all been long dead," Camilla said. "Some of them for centuries, I'm sure. The scribe only just died. He's still"— she grimaced—"*fresh*. That could make all the difference."

"I don't know . . ."

"Don't discount the potential of this without careful consideration," Camilla said. Her lopsided eyes were narrowed and curious. "I know you're afraid that if he goes too far, dark magic will consume him. But he's strong and capable. He's already shown us that. And if this doesn't work, we're no worse off than we are now. At the very least, it will be a great test of what is and isn't possible."

Barnabas's expression grew tense. With a furrowed brow, he studied Maddox for so long it seemed as if the man might never speak again.

"If you really won't agree to this," Camilla said, "then there's always my plan."

"Not a chance," Barnabas said through gritted teeth.

"What plan?" Maddox asked.

Camilla raised a patchy eyebrow. "To go to the South and seek audience with Cleiona. Her infamous hatred for Valoria could prove useful to us."

"You said her name," Maddox pointed out.

"Yes, and perhaps she'll hear me and agree to help. Save ourselves a trip to the South."

"No," Barnabas said firmly. "As much as I despise Valoria, you'll never get me to agree to beg that *other* one. Not for anything. Ever. Those two are equally vile and equally in need of being destroyed."

"Well then." The witch spread her hands. "It seems you have limited choices, doesn't it?"

Barnabas fell silent again, face reddening and jaw clenched. "Very well, Maddox," he said finally. "You can try to coax answers out of the head. But the moment I feel it's too much, that it's getting too dark, you will stop. Do you hear me?"

Maddox just looked at him, barely repressing a smile.

"What?" Barnabas demanded.

"You sound a little like a . . . a *parent*. If I were anyone else, would you be so protective?"

Barnabas grimaced and then swore under his breath. "I do, don't I? Telling you what to do and what not to do. My apologies."

"No, it's fine. I just meant . . ." What *had* he meant? He hadn't expected Barnabas to suddenly take on a fatherly role; it was coming as quite a surprise. "It's fine," he said. "This time, I suppose."

"This"—Camilla clasped both of their arms, grinning widely—"is adorable. Shall we all embrace?"

Barnabas shot her a dry look. "Not when we have to find a way to steal a freshly severed head in front of a large crowd."

Camilla winked. "I can help with that."

They waited until night had fallen like a dark blanket over the kingdom. The first part of Camilla's plan to steal the head was for Barnabas to cause a distraction that would draw the attention of the guards and any citizens milling about at that late hour. As soon as it was time, Barnabas set off for the square just in front of the palace, playing the part of a dangerously drunk reveler on the verge of causing great destruction. Just as Camilla had promised, a group of guards heard his racket and rushed over to investigate. While they were preoccupied with Barnabas, Camilla summoned a gust of wind that, miraculously, was strong enough to dislodge the scribe's head from the spike. Off it flew, and landed directly into the canvas sack that Maddox was waiting with below.

As the head sunk heavily into the sack, all Maddox could think of were the times he went to the market with his mother. She would pick ripe melons and gourds, then toss them over her shoulder without a glance, knowing that Maddox was ready with a basket to catch them. He'd never dropped a single one.

Swiftly, they left the square and made their way to the nearest stretch of forest, where they'd made camp the night before. Camilla started a fire with flint from her pocket, while Barnabas hunted for a rabbit for their dinner.

Maddox sat on a fallen log and stared at the sack.

What had he been thinking suggesting such a horrific thing? Accidentally raising a full graveyard of corpses from their resting places was strange and unnatural enough, but doing it to a severed head? On purpose?

Doubt, that familiar yet unwanted friend, came to sit next to him.

Soon Barnabas returned with the game. "Do we even know what his name is?" Maddox asked hoarsely as he approached.

Camilla nodded as she poked at the half-cooked rabbit on the spit. "It's Alcander Verus," she said.

"*Alcander Verus*," Maddox repeated, nodding.

"If you're having second thoughts . . . ," Barnabas began, but then stopped himself. "Well, I've been wondering whether there's another way to find out that wicked creature's weaknesses, but I've come up blank. What we need are the answers that live in that head."

Maddox nodded. "No need to worry about sounding like a father now. Or are you so sure that I'll fail that you find yourself less concerned about how I'll fare against the dark magic?"

"What troubles me most, my young friend, is that I don't think you'll fail." There was a sense of gravity and worry to his words that Maddox couldn't ignore—and that made him certain he wasn't joking.

Playing with life and death wasn't a game.

And his power, should he be able to harness it, would be impossible to fully comprehend.

"If this works," Maddox said so softly he doubted the others could hear him, "I could bring my mother back to life."

Barnabas said nothing, but Maddox heard his breath catch in his throat.

Camilla came to sit next to Maddox and gently took his hand in hers.

"Look at me, sweetling."

Maddox forced himself to meet her troubled gaze.

"I know you miss your mum," she said. "As much as I miss my own, I'm sure. It's a shame Damaris is gone. But she's gone to a place beyond here, a wonderful place of peace and light. She's had some time now to settle into that place of paradise, and to attempt to wrench her out of there now . . ." Camilla shook her head. "You'd be bringing back something else. Something as dark and twisted as the spirits you've faced."

"But how do you know that for sure?" he said, his voice breaking. "That paradise beyond this world—isn't that just another old legend?"

"Many legends only become legends because the stories are true. Death is nothing to tamper with, even if you have the means within you to switch life for death. Even this"—she glanced at the sack—"is a dangerous use of your magic."

He was hit with a sinking feeling in his chest, because he knew deep in his heart that Camilla was right. For a moment, just one wonderful, hope-filled moment, Maddox had thought it might really be possible to bring his mother back to life.

Maddox allowed a second wave of grief to tear through him, bearing the pain silently and stiffly, before it receded like a cold tide on an icy shore.

"The rabbit is nearly ready," Camilla said softly. "First we'll eat, then we'll discuss this more."

"No," Maddox said. "No more discussion. I want to do it now." Camilla nodded quietly and gazed at him with serious but supportive eyes.

Summoning as much bravery as he could, Maddox untied the canvas sack. He reached in slowly, his fingertips grazing a patch of dry hair and a cold scalp. His skin crawled, and he pulled his hand back a bit. Bracing himself again, he reached in further. He got a strong grasp on a handful of hair and pulled the head out. He held it up. There it was, the scribe's head dangling before him, its expression slack, its eyes open and glazed. Staring.

"How do you feel so far?" Barnabas asked.

"Like I'm going to be sick."

"Understandable."

Repressing a retch that rose in his throat, Maddox placed the head down on the ground, where the firelight flickered warmly against its grayish complexion.

Maddox breathed in, inhaling a mix of mossy forest and roasting rabbit, and tried to find his focus. He'd found that his magic tended to work best when he was angry or frightened or whenever his emotions were otherwise elevated. Right now he didn't feel much of anything. Sickened, uncertain, sad, and numb didn't seem to be the right ingredients.

But the magic was still within him. It *was* him. And there were many roads to take to access it.

He forced himself to think of Goran, ending his mother's life in a crimson trail of blood. He let his hatred for that cowardly assassin, his need for vengeance, flow through him in a fiery rage.

There it was: a quiver, a chill, racing through him, and then a shadow creeping into the periphery of his vision. As soon as he spotted the shadow, he let his hatred for Goran guide him toward the magic, drawing it into a ball of darkness, molding it into the shape his strange instincts told him he needed.

His racing thoughts grew quiet, and a somber stillness slid

through him like thick, icy sludge, filling his veins, his heart, his mind.

For a moment, there was only his magic; everything else in the universe ceased to exist. He took this magic, which he'd condensed by now into a swirling, smoky ball, in his hands and pushed it toward the scribe's head.

Wake up, Alcander Verus, Maddox thought in an echoing monotone filled with all the power and strength he didn't normally feel. *Wake up and talk to us. Tell us what we need to know.*

The ball of shadows burst into dozens of spidery wisps. As they separated, they flew right into the corpse head, entering through its eyes, nostrils, mouth, and ears. And then they disappeared.

All was still and quiet. Maddox watched, trying to will the head to reanimate but not trying to scare the effect away by hoping too hard. So he watched.

And watched.

And then watched some more.

"Maddox?" Barnabas asked after quite some time.

Maddox tore his gaze away from the head to glance at him. "What?"

Barnabas didn't reply right away, but he shared a concerned look with Camilla, his jaw tight.

"How do you feel?" Camilla asked Maddox evenly.

"Fine."

"Are you sure?"

"Am I sure?" Maddox frowned. "Of course I'm sure. But I need to try again."

"No," Barnabas said. "That's enough for tonight. More than enough, I—"

The muffled sound of a grunt rose up in between them, causing Barnabas to stop midsentence.

Maddox craned his neck, eyeing the dark forest around them. "What was that?"

Camilla's eyes grew wide as she stared at a spot on the ground. "The head . . ."

Maddox shot his gaze back to the severed head. "Did it just grunt?"

"I—I think so."

Barnabas drew closer, crouching down next the head. "I don't know. Perhaps there's just a warlog nearby, digging up night grubs."

Then, in a quick fit of motion, the scribe's eyelids fluttered.

Maddox stopped breathing.

The eyes shot wide open and began darting from side to side.

And then the head began to scream.

Barnabas jumped up from the ground, staggering back from the head and covering his ears. "Make him stop, will you?"

"You're asking me?" Maddox shouted, also on his feet now. "I haven't any idea how!"

"Oh my! Do something! Maddox, stop him!" Camilla's lopsided gaze darted all around, her hand clamped over her mouth in shock.

"Why do you think I can do something?" Letting out a long, shaky breath, Maddox tried to summon his composure. "Hey! Head, listen to me. Listen to me! Stop screaming!"

The head stopped screaming.

Barnabas nodded in relief. "Well done."

"Wh-wh-what?" it sputtered, eyes still darting and clearly struggling to understand why its neck wasn't doing its job of turning. "Wh-what's going on? Where am I? Who are you?"

Twisting her hands in front of her, Camilla took a step closer to it. "Greetings, Alcander. My name is Camilla. This is Barnabas and his son, Maddox."

Its eyes widened. "I . . . know those names. You're the rebels who attempted to trick the goddess! The rebels who put thoughts of traitors in her radiant and glorious mind!" The head cleared its throat and took on a very smug expression. "You are all hereby arrested in the name of Valoria, goddess of earth and water. Oh, this is wonderful! How well I will be rewarded when she learns I have apprehended you all."

"So far delusional thinking seems to be the main side effect of your resurrection spell, Maddox," Barnabas said with a nod. "Interesting."

"Resurrection spell?" Alcander repeated. "What in the goddess's blessed realm are you talking about?"

"Do you remember what happened to you?" Maddox asked, though he was barely able to focus on anything the head was saying because—*it had worked!*

The head was *awake*. It was *talking*. It might be delusional, but it definitely wasn't dead.

Alcander frowned. "What do you mean, boy?"

Maddox grimaced. "I mean . . . um, how do you, ah, feel right now?"

"Why, I feel just fine. Certainly, I'll admit to being a bit rattled—I've just had a rather horrid nightmare. But those are quite normal for me, I'm afraid, due to my large and active brain. I'm always creating stories, you see. After all, I'm a scribe—the goddess's *personal* scribe."

"Yes, we know," Barnabas said, his arms crossed over his chest. "Tell me: What was your nightmare about?"

Alcander scowled at him. "You're rather rude for someone who's just been arrested for treason! But I suppose we do need something to talk about during our journey back to the palace. In this terrible dream, Her Radiance had been fooled into thinking I was planning to betray her." He paused and glanced at Camilla. "I assured her I would never, ever do such a thing, but she didn't believe me. Before I knew it, the guards had their filthy hands on me and were hauling me out to be executed in front of a most bloodthirsty crowd."

Alcander fell silent.

"Oh my, that does sound like a horribly frightening nightmare," Barnabas said, clearly taunting the poor scribe. "What happened next?"

"Well . . ." Alcander frowned deeply. "Next, one of the guards took me to the execution block. There was a man who wore a black hood and carried an ax—the executioner. And then they forced me down to the block . . . and the executioner stood over me . . . and then he . . . and then he chopped my head off!"

Barnabas nodded. "I'm sorry to be the one to tell you, but . . . that wasn't a dream."

Alcander just looked back at Barnabas, blinking with confusion. He looked next to Camilla, and then his gaze finally fell on Maddox, who returned his befuddled expression with a squeamish one.

"It's true," Maddox told him. "I'm sorry."

"The executioner chopped off my head," Alcander said flatly.

"Yes."

"Bah!" Alcander scoffed. "What absolute nonsense!"

Alcander began to laugh, on and on until tears began to stream from his squinting eyes. Then he looked down.

And he started to scream again.

"Oh!" he cried, eyes to the sky. He was still crying, but not out of laughter anymore. "Oh, radiant goddess—I am dead. I'm dead! It wasn't a nightmare—this is real! How could you *do* this? To *me*? Your most loyal and trusted and obedient servant?"

"Because she's evil," Barnabas said bluntly. "And guess what? You're going to help us destroy her. She did suspect you of being a traitor. Said she saw it in a vision. Ha! What a laugh. Eva was the only immortal who was capable of having visions of the future. Valoria can do nothing more than sleep and hope for dreams."

Alcander blinked rapidly, his anxious whimpering slowing to a stop. "Wh-what did you say? That I'm going to . . . help you?"

"You know her," Maddox said. "You know her weaknesses."

"I don't know anything about her. You think what she tells me is the truth? Like your father just said, the woman is full of lies. There's no way to tell what is real and what is not. Oh, I hate her. I hate her so much I could kill her with the force of my anger!"

"Now that's a much more helpful way to talk," Camilla said, nodding.

"No, it's not," Barnabas replied sourly. "He just admitted he knows nothing that can help us. This was a waste of Maddox's magic. Let's throw the head into the fire and be done with it."

"Wait!" Alcander exclaimed. "Wait just a moment now. Let's not be hasty, good sir! Did I say I don't know *anything*? I know plenty. I worked closely—intimately—with the goddess for a very long time. I was her closest friend and confidant. Clearly, you have sought me out with"—he looked at Maddox this time, a shadow of fear sliding behind his eyes—"your rather impressive necromancy. Yes, the goddess told me about you and what you could do. What she wanted you for."

"And what's that?" Maddox asked, his throat tight.

"To use you as a weapon, of course."

It wasn't a surprise, but all the same, the thought of it made Maddox's stomach churn.

"She can't have him," Barnabas growled. He grabbed Alcander by his hair and picked him up. "We're done here."

"No! Please! I want to live!"

Barnabas scoffed. "Don't misunderstand your current situation. You're not *alive*. You're a severed head that can talk."

"You're wrong! I *am* alive. I *feel* alive! I am clearly a bit . . . *lacking* at the moment." He paused, and then his eyes filled up with tears once again. "Oh, goddess, why?" he wailed. "My body! I miss my body! But I do know where it would have been buried."

Barnabas glared at him. "And tell me: How does that help us?"

"When I prove useful to you—when I've earned redemption in your eyes by helping, as you've requested, put an end to Valoria— the boy will use his magic to reunite me with my body."

"But I—" Maddox began to protest.

Barnabas put up his hand. "Is that so?" he said. "All right then. Give me a piece of information that we would find useful, and perhaps we can negotiate the terms of your continued existence."

"Very well," Alcander said nervously. His eyes moved rapidly from side to side as if he were scanning the interior of his mind. "Yes, I have it! Rebels are famous for being secretive, of course. But you can always count on a certain type of rebel who is willing to give up information for coin. There are traitors on *both* sides."

Barnabas kept glaring, his brow furrowed more deeply now. "Go on."

"I know that your goal is to locate the heiress to the throne. Valoria has known about this plan for longer than you might think. When she first got word about it, she began seeking information about Princess Cassia. And she found her."

"I don't believe you," Barnabas snarled.

"It's true!"

"Tell me more."

"Agree to the deal and I will."

Barnabas held the head over the fire. "Tell. Me. More," he repeated.

Alcander shrieked. "Fine. Fine! Three years ago, the family that took in Princess Cassia was killed, but the princess escaped. She hasn't been seen or heard from since. But I know where she is!"

Barnabas pulled him away from the flames, but only a few inches. "Where?"

"I will personally lead you there."

Barnabas grimaced and went to shove him back over the fire again, but Maddox caught his arm.

"No," Maddox said. "Don't hurt him anymore. He's suffered enough."

"Seems we disagree on that."

"He says he'll help us find Princess Cassia. His word is good enough for me."

"Is it? Well, consider me far less trusting than you." He went silent for a moment. "Still, if what he says is true . . ."

"It is!" Alcander insisted.

"What do you want me to do, Barnabas?" Camilla asked.

Barnabas cast a look at the witch, his brow drawn in thought. "I'm going to need you and Sienna to keep close to the palace while we're gone and stay alert to any information the rebels can use."

Camilla nodded gravely. "Of course."

Barnabas looked back to Alcander, his fist still gripping him by the hair. "You have one week to prove your usefulness to us. One week—or you go into the fire and stay there. For good this time. Agreed?"

Alcander's frightened face flooded with relief. "Agreed."

Chapter 10

BECCA

She dreamed she had golden feathers.

And sharp talons that gripped the lowest branch of a tree.

Her eyesight was incredible—she easily spotted a mouse-like creature slipping through the grass no fewer than twenty feet away and a little black beetle crawling up the trunk of a neighboring tree.

Curious to learn more about what it was like to be a bird, she tried to move her wings, but they didn't work. She huffed and strained with effort, but nothing she did could make them budge. She was stuck on the tree branch. All she could do was observe.

She craned her flexible neck toward the water, and her heart leaped at what she saw: a young man kneeling next to a river.

Maddox.

He was shirtless, wearing nothing but wet trousers as he washed his beige canvas tunic in the water. His feet were bare; a pair of leather boots sat on the shore nearby. Maddox might only have been a year older than Becca, but he certainly didn't seem like a boy. He looked taller than she remembered, with broader shoulders and lean, defined muscles.

Perhaps he'd always been this way, but she hadn't totally noticed until now, which was the first time she'd allowed herself to sit back and simply gawk at him. Well, the first time she took her time with it, anyway.

He scrubbed the worn material and then held the sodden garment up to inspect it.

"A bit better," he said, and Becca learned that her sense of hearing was also much improved.

"Hard to get blood stains out, isn't it?" It was Barnabas, emerging from the forest where Becca had previously spotted the small rodent.

Maddox sent him a glare. "Yes, it certainly is," he said coldly.

"What? You're cross with me? I was trying to feed you."

"By tossing a dead warlog at me without warning?"

Barnabas scoffed. "Oh, please. It's not as if I asked you to bring it back to life so I could kill it again. I was only excited to provide you with something other than berries and leaves to eat." Barnabas paused, absently scratching his dark beard while Maddox still stared at him coolly. "The meat's almost cooked. I promise it tastes almost exactly like rabbit. Come back to the camp when you're done washing up. I'm tired of listening to Alcander and his incessant chattering all by myself. That scribe loves to talk."

"I'll be there in a moment," Maddox said, his tone no less cool than the expression on his face. He wrung out his shirt as Barnabas departed, then flapped it in the air to shake off the excess water. "Berries and leaves," he muttered to himself. "I'm more than capable of finding something better than that out here. I'm not completely helpless."

Maddox had turned to face Becca, who found herself mesmerized by the increasingly dreamy view of the shirtless boy before her. It took her a moment to raise her gaze up to his face, but when she did she was just as glad. When dry, his black hair tended to be a bit shaggy, and he wore it pushed forward so it hid part of his face. Now, his damp hair was pushed back, and Becca took a moment to appreciate the warmth of his deep brown eyes, the pale scattering of freckles on his nose, and his lips . . .

Maddox Corso had very nice lips.

Suddenly, as if somehow sensing he was being watched, Maddox turned his head and looked up, locking his gaze right on Becca, whose branch was only four feet above him. Her heart jumped in her chest as Maddox cocked his head to the side.

"Greetings, pretty hawk," he said. "You know, you remind me of a hawk I saw the other day. Your eyes are the same deep shade of blue . . ." He frowned and shook his head. "But that's impossible."

Maddox, it's me! Can you see me?

He ran his hand through his dark wet hair, still frowning up at her for a long moment more. "It's impossible," he said, almost sadly. "It couldn't be you."

Look closer. See me. I'm here!

His frown deepened. He took another step closer to her. "Becca?"

Her heart leaped into her throat. *Yes! It's me!*

He said nothing for a long, breathless moment, then he put his head down and shook it. "Clearly, I've gone insane. Talking to blue-eyed birds. Farewell, pretty hawk."

She tried to speak, to squawk, to flap her wings—but she was frozen. She couldn't do anything but watch as Maddox tore his gaze from hers, gathered up his belongings from the riverbank, and disappeared into the forest.

Disappointment wrenched through every inch of her. To be so close to him yet not be able to communicate—it broke her heart.

A rustling in some bushes below caught her attention, and she turned her hawk-eyed stare in that direction. The next moment, a girl emerged. She had long, dark blond hair and wore a dirty blue dress. She stepped closer to the river and kept her careful stare on the path Maddox had taken into the woods.

In her left hand was a dagger.

Panic gripped Becca. Once again she tried to flap her wings, to get to Maddox in time to warn him about the girl, but she couldn't get anything to budge. She was stuck there, forced to watch helplessly as the girl with the dagger disappeared down Maddox's path.

Finally, what felt like hours later, the hawk spread its wings and took off into the air, flying across the river and away from Maddox. Becca lurched awake to see Crys standing above her, shaking her.

"Time to get up, Sleeping Beauty," her sister said in a voice decidedly devoid of cheer. "The alleged answer to all of our magical woes has finally arrived."

Chapter 11

CRYSTAL

The first time Crys saw the man, she was making a quick trip downstairs to the convenience store in the condominium lobby, trying to make the most depressing decision in the world, between a wilted-looking cheese sandwich and a truly heinous tray of prepackaged California rolls.

She noticed him right away. He wore a black suit with a white shirt and mirrored aviator sunglasses. He had a receding hairline and a short salt-and-pepper beard that was neatly trimmed. What little hair he had was the same color as his beard. But it was the bright red bow tie that originally caught her eye.

Crys watched as the curious man took a large bag of jelly beans off the display and slipped it into the inner pocket of his jacket. Suddenly, he looked up, and there was no doubt he saw Crys watching.

Crap.

Crys was about to turn away, but then stopped. The man grinned at her, then put his index finger over his lips in a gesture of *shh*.

Then, just like that, he turned on his heels and left the store.

Crys just stood there, appalled at the way that richly dressed man just stole something without a second thought and then casually sauntered out. She thought about telling someone, but when Crys approached the counter to pay for her sushi, the clerk was talking on her cell phone and didn't even notice the customer standing right in front of her.

"Here," Crys said coldly as she slapped a ten-dollar bill on the counter, took her sad lunch, and left.

As Crys pushed through the exit, she saw Mr. Bow Tie leaning against the wall outside the store.

"Were you tempted to tattle on me?" he asked in a crisp British accent.

Reluctantly, Crys stopped and turned to him. "Don't know what you're talking about."

"Sure, sure," he said. "Of course, Crystal, dear. Now why don't we go up and see your auntie?"

Crys stared at him. "You're Angus Balthazar."

"At your service," he said, bowing his head.

Crys had just watched the man Jackie was counting on shoplift a bag of jelly beans.

Perfect.

Just to be sure she wasn't about to escort a psychopath up into her family's safe house, Crys asked Angus to show her his ID and house keys. Graciously, he complied and supplied both items—though Crys had to wonder about the validity of an ID that belonged to a thief who most likely had at least a dozen counterfeits on hand.

"After you," Angus said as they walked into the building.

Jackie was at the door when they arrived. She greeted him, grasping his hands. "Angus, you're here. I'm glad to see you."

"Sorry it took me so long, love. I assume you're enjoying the place?"

"Very much. Thank you so much for sharing it."

"Not that you gave me much choice." He pulled off his sunglasses and tossed them, carelessly, onto the nearest end table. "Why do I get the feeling that you'd have found a way to break in if I said no?"

"You really think my aunt would be stupid enough to try to break into a place like this?" Crys said with barely a fraction of the jauntiness that seemed to be Angus's trademark.

"Let me think about that," Angus said, scratching his stubbled chin. "Yes, I think she would try something like that. In a heartbeat, actually. Do you know even half of what your dear auntie is capable of, little girl?"

"Angus . . . " Jackie said under her breath, a smile frozen on her lips.

"You don't want your niece to know, do you?" Angus said teasingly. "I suppose I can see how her young mind might be scandalized to know that her Aunt Jacqueline is a skilled thief who has long belonged to an international organization of criminals specializing in procuring and reselling unusual objects and artifacts said to possess certain . . . powers."

Crys watched Jackie's face grow pale as Angus spoke, and she looked slightly queasy.

Crys took that to mean that Angus was telling the truth.

"*Powers?*" Crys repeated, trying to show Angus that his little performance hadn't fazed her.

"Yes," Angus said. "And you'd be surprised how many people there are in this world who are willing to pay a great deal of money to get their hands on such items."

"Angus," Jackie snapped. "That's more than enough."

"It's fine," Crys said, although her stomach churned to hear Jackie all but confirm everything Angus claimed. She already knew her aunt had a shady side, and recent events gave her imagination a lot to work with in terms of getting a fuller picture of Jackie's career. But to hear all this—major crimes and dealings with potentially dangerous people—coming from someone like Angus, no less . . . perhaps it *did* corrupt her a little. "Please," Crys went on, still working hard to keep a cool, nonchalant exterior. "I already knew some stuff about what Jackie does. Your life sounds like something from a movie, Jackie—a woman leading a life of danger and intrigue and magic. I mean, Dr. Vega already told me about how you stole the Codex from a private library."

"Dr. *Uriah* Vega?" Angus said. His face lit up with a rather predatory grin. "Where is our little Rosetta stone? Has he cracked the code yet?"

"He's working on it," Jackie said, her arms crossed tightly over her chest. The kind and welcoming expression she wore when she first saw Angus was now a faint memory.

"He should give up already. Why waste his valuable brain cells on an impossible task? Take me to it. I need to see it."

Crys grew tense at the idea of letting this candy-stealer within fifty feet of the Codex.

"First, I need to fill you in on a few things," Jackie said.

"Fill away," he said, then nodded at Crys. "Perhaps we can speak in private and away from the child."

"*Child?*" Crys glared at him. "I'm not a child."

"Are you under twenty-five?"

"Well . . . yeah."

"Then, trust me, you're still a child." He flicked his hand at her dismissively. "Why don't you go watch some reality TV while the grown-ups discuss business."

Who did this jerk think he was? "I'm not going anywhere."

A shadow crossed over his expression, and Crys swore she saw a something dark and dangerous flash in his eyes. "Oh?" he said quietly.

"Angus, it's fine," Jackie said. "She can stay. She's part of this, and so is her sister." Jackie nodded at Crys. "Go get Becca."

Crys went, but only after tearing herself away from the staring contest she'd unintentionally initiated with the jelly bean thief.

She woke a disoriented Becca up from her nap and, noticing the troubled look in her eyes, made a mental note to check in with her as soon as they were done with Angus. They went downstairs to find that Jackie and Angus had gone into the study to talk to Dr. Vega.

"Oh, goodie," Angus drawled. "She's back."

Crys granted him a small scowl but then shook it off. She couldn't let him rattle her—not with Becca here.

And certainly not while they were all in the same room with the Codex, which was laid out on top of the desk.

At the sight of it, Becca inhaled sharply.

"Careful," Dr. Vega said as he watched her move toward it, as if powered by a remote control.

Crys grabbed hold of her hand to keep her from getting any closer to it. Bad things happened when Becca was anywhere near that stupid book.

Angus raised a dark eyebrow at Becca. "You. What's your name?"

"Becca," she replied.

"This book . . . its magic affects you."

"Jackie told you?"

"No. Just an educated guess." He gave her a less than genuine smile. "But how absolutely interesting to know I'm right. Now, the enigmatic Markus King needs this mysterious little tome so he can keep on living forever. Julia's marks have somehow been reinvigorated and are back to binding her to his will. And young Becca here seems to be right in the middle and knee deep in all of this muck. Fascinating."

"I'm not sure that's the word I would use," Jackie said. "Angus, just tell me. Can you help us? Help Julia?"

"First of all, your sister should not be anywhere near this thing, Jackie," Angus warned, rapping his knuckles against the book's cover. "Right now, even when she's away from the book, she's like a stick of dynamite, ready to explode at any second."

"That bad, huh?" Julia said.

Crys swiveled on her heels and found herself facing her mother, standing in the doorway, her face pale and haunted.

"Mom," Crys began.

After the incident with the gun the day before, Julia had locked herself in her bedroom and hadn't opened the door since, except to take in the plates of food Jackie brought her. Meanwhile, Jackie had locked the gun away in a cabinet in her room.

Julia shook her head. "It's okay, Crys. He's right. I refuse to help that monster, but I don't know if I can control myself. I'd rather die than hurt any member of my family. The lock on my door secures only from the inside—I can get out whenever I want. Without a way to break this spell, that's not going to be good enough."

"Well, that's the question," Crys said, her voice raw. She hated seeing her mother so upset.

"I'm guessing this is the sister," Angus said.

"Yes." Jackie grimaced. "Angus Balthazar, this is Julia Hatcher."

"So pleased to finally meet you in person," Julia said tightly.

"Yes, of course you are. I'm the one who might be able to get you out of this gigantic mess. Now—let's talk possibilities. I prefer the one I've already discussed with you over the phone, Jackie."

Jackie cringed. "Angus, I don't think we need to talk about that right—"

"The dagger Markus King uses to carve this obedience spell into everyone needs to be destroyed," Angus said calmly and evenly. "And Markus needs to die."

Jackie shook her head. "I always forget how horribly blunt you are."

"Indeed," Dr. Vega agreed tightly.

"That's not the tone you took when we first hatched our plan. Remember? You said you could assassinate him at the charity ball?"

"Please, stop talking now," Jackie said weakly.

"What?" Becca gasped. "You—you're going to *kill* him? How could you agree to something like that?"

Jackie looked at her bleakly. "*I* didn't say I was going to do it. Angus did. It wasn't my plan."

"When was all this discussed?" Julia said. "Were you going to tell me?"

"Yes, of course I was going to."

"Julia," chimed in Angus, his tone infuriatingly lighthearted, "how exactly did you think you'd ever be completely free of those marks? Did you think that, with time and patience and maybe a vigorous scrubbing every other day, they'd simply just go away? Jackie tells me those invisible marks that keep you under Markus King's command are created by magic. A combination of Markus's magic and all the power hiding within his dagger. So the solution to your problem should be obvious: Destroy the source of the spell—in this case, that's both Markus and the blade—and the spell, in turn, is destroyed."

"Why not try destroying the dagger first and then seeing what happens?" Becca offered. Angus shot her a *mind-your-own-business-little-girl* look that was so harsh it made Becca flinch.

"An excellent idea," Dr. Vega said.

"Pacifists," Angus said with disgust. "Let me tell you a secret, both of you. Some people need to be killed. Their absence allows the rest of the world to work much better."

"I hate this," Julia said. "I hate *all* of this. Markus King is pure evil and needs to be stopped. But, Jackie, for you to suggest that you could stop him—*kill* him—yourself . . . Are you sure?"

"If she isn't," Angus said, "I'm happy to do the deed. Of course, such a high-profile job that requires specific talents does come with a steep price—but I will give you the friends-and-family rate."

"You," Dr. Vega said, his eyes wide behind his wire-rimmed glasses, "are a very scary man."

"Thank you," Angus said dismissively.

"Markus is dangerous—and magical, which makes him even more so," Dr. Vega continued. "No one knows how much he might be capable of. I've never before heard of a person who has such abilities."

"Well, that makes one of us. In fact, word has traveled through the grapevine that Markus is not the only magician in Toronto right now."

"What are you talking about?" Jackie snapped.

Angus shrugged. "Could just be a rumor. But it also could be fact. Don't know. I just pass along information when I see fit."

Julia shook her head, while Crys and Becca looked on with disbelief.

"What kind of magic?" Julia asked. "Elemental, like Markus?"

"I'm afraid I couldn't say. All I know is that several of my associates refuse to come within a thousand miles of this city at the moment. They're calling him the Whisperer."

"*The Whisperer?*" Crys frowned. "What a stupid name."

"Yes, well, one could argue that *Crys* isn't the smartest-sounding moniker out there."

She couldn't stop herself—she gave him the finger.

Angus laughed. "I like you." He winked at her. "You're sassy."

What a *complete* sleazebag. Another reason not to believe a single word that came out of his mouth.

"I wonder if Markus knows about this man," Julia said. "And what it might mean."

"It means we'll get distracted if we focus on it," Jackie replied. "And right now I don't care about any rumor that doesn't directly relate to Markus himself."

"Angus, you didn't answer my question," Becca said. "What if the obedience magic is all in the dagger and not in Markus? Markus may be the only one who knows how to use the dagger, but if you destroy it, wouldn't *that* be the thing that would make the marks—and necessarily Markus too—null and void?"

"It's possible," Angus admitted.

Crys couldn't help but be surprised that this strange man was actually acknowledging this. Becca looked just as shocked.

"Then we need that dagger," Dr. Vega said. "Rather desperately."

"Jackie's already on that, aren't you, love?" Angus nodded at her. "She plans to accomplish a great deal at the ball tomorrow night."

Julia frowned at her sister. "Jackie? What's he talking about?"

Jackie twisted a section of her pale blond hair around her

finger. "I didn't tell you because I didn't want to worry you. I was going to handle it on my own. Markus invited me to the society's charity ball tomorrow night. A masquerade. I turned down the invitation, of course. But I've thought about it some more, and now I realize that going to the ball is the easiest—maybe the only—way to get to him."

"And kill him," Angus added.

"Wait a second," said Crys. None of this made any sense to her. "Markus is immortal. He might be getting weak—might even actually be *dying* on his own because his magic is fading away—but do you honestly think that you can kill him? Without any magic? Why not at *least* wait it out to see if his lack of magic kills him first?"

"The dagger," Angus supplied helpfully when Jackie didn't respond. "Magic knives can kill magic men."

"Oh yeah?" challenged Crys. "And you have proof of that?"

"What? You don't believe me?"

Crys turned and stared at Jackie, needing to full-on ignore the loathsome, if somewhat informative, Angus before she devolved into a tornado of expletives. "So, what, Jackie? Your plan is to romance the dagger away from him and then shove it in his heart?"

"This conversation is officially over," Jackie said, pointing at the door. "Crys, Becca, go upstairs."

"Finally, someone's talking some sense around here," Angus said.

Crys was so furious that she could hardly see straight. To think, she'd once idolized Jackie Kendall, had wanted so much to be like her in every way. Jackie, who'd dropped out of high school to go off and have wild adventures in Europe. That's all Crys had ever wanted—to be a free spirit who made her own rules, went where she wanted, when she wanted.

But now she knew the truth about her aunt.

Jackie had been a teenage mother who couldn't handle the responsibility, so she'd dumped her baby on her more responsible older sister. All her life, all she'd done was blame others for her mistakes and then leave them for someone else to clean up. She'd turned into someone who thought that stealing and killing were perfectly good answers to any problem that might arise.

All this time, it was Julia that Crys should have been trying to emulate. Julia, her own mother, who was smart, capable, brave, strong, and fierce. It was her mother who'd been so patient with Crys all these years, who'd helped her through all of her ups and downs, and it was Crys who never acted like she appreciated it. And now it was her mother who needed her help.

She turned to Julia. "Mom, what should we do?"

"Look after Becca. Keep her safe. And try very hard to stay out of your aunt's way while I'm gone, okay?"

She blinked. "What do you mean, while you're gone?"

"Jackie's already arranged for me to leave here today with Angus. He knows a place I can stay, away from the book, where I won't be a burden to anyone and where I won't be able to follow any of Markus's orders to bring him the Codex."

Crys's chest tightened. "Mom, no. Please. We didn't even discuss this."

Jackie's arms were crossed tightly over her chest. "Because I knew you'd disagree. It has to be this way, Crys. Not forever, but for right now."

"Mom!"

Julia shook her head. "Please, honey, don't worry. I'll be fine. Let Jackie do whatever she feels she needs to do to make everything right again, okay?" She grabbed Crys into a tight hug. "Everything I've ever done has been to protect you girls, and I'll be damned if I'll let Markus break my streak. I trust you, Crys. I know you'll do the right thing."

Hot tears streamed down Crys's cheeks as her mother let go of her and turned to embrace Becca. Julia's decision to take herself out of the equation was a complete surprise to Crys, even despite just yesterday witnessing her mother waving a gun around for those few horrifying moments—an image that would stay etched in Crys's memory forever.

"Time to go then, Julia," said Angus, Crys hating his voice even more now that it was the thing that pulled her mother away from her daughters.

Everyone followed Julia out of the study and toward the door. Silently, Dr. Vega brought up the rear, his expression somber.

Crys's heart sunk even further to see that Julia had already packed a bag, which was waiting for her just outside the study door. She grabbed it and straightened her shoulders as Angus opened the door to the hallway.

"You have my number," Jackie called after them. "Don't hesitate to call for any reason, okay?"

"Got it," Angus replied, then smirked. "Uriah, keep at that translation. I have absolute faith that it's only a matter of time before you'll crack it."

"I appreciate your confidence," Dr. Vega said coolly with a nod.

"I love all of you," Julia said. "Don't ever doubt it okay?"

Crys wanted to say something, to protest again. But she knew no one would listen to her, and anyway she couldn't find the words.

And then they were gone.

Crys spun around to face Jackie, her hands clenched into fists.

"Don't," Jackie said, shaking her head. "Don't start with me. I'm not in the mood."

"I couldn't care less what kind of mood you're in. This is *my* family you're destroying—"

"Crys." Becca grabbed her arm. "Come on, let's go upstairs."

Reluctantly, with one last sneer at Jackie, Crys allowed Becca to lead her away and up the stairs.

There was so much Crys wanted to say to her aunt. She wanted to remind her that this was all her fault. That all of Jackie's bad decisions had led up to this one horrible moment.

"This is ridiculous," Crys snarled. She was upstairs now, pacing back and forth in Angus's library, forcing Charlie to dodge around her quick steps on the floor. "Mom's gone, who the hell knows where. Angus is as trustworthy as a bag of lying snakes, and Jackie is almost definitely going to get herself killed tomorrow night if she goes to that ball."

At the mention of Jackie, Becca snapped her gaze to Crys's and locked her in a skeptical glare.

Crys looked back at her sister. "What? You think she has a snowball's chance in hell against Markus?"

"Honestly?" said Becca. "No." She bit her bottom lip and gently pet Charlie, who had grown tired of making way for Crys and was now sitting on Becca's lap.

"Exactly! Yet we're just supposed to let her go on this idiotic mission all alone, while we wait here with Dr. Vega. It's insane."

"That's not what we're going to do," Becca said calmly.

"What do you mean?"

Becca just gazed back at Crys, all of a sudden seeming very serene. Considering how serene Crys *wasn't*, this was making her seriously uneasy.

"I need to talk to Markus myself," Becca said.

Crys was sure she'd heard her wrong, but all she could do was gape while Becca went on talking.

"I don't think killing Markus will do anything to help Mom," she said. "I'm sure that the magic within the marks comes from the dagger—lives inside the dagger—and it's the dagger that needs to be destroyed to break the spell."

"How are you so sure?"

"That goddess from Mytica—Valoria. She wanted the dagger. And maybe even more than the dagger itself, she wanted to make Markus suffer for stealing it. If I were him, I'd want to know about her plans. That she knows what he did and where he is now. Maybe if I tell him, he'll choose to help us."

Crys didn't know what to say. Becca sought her gaze, her blue eyes serious and haunted. "I keep dreaming about Mytica . . . about Maddox," she said. "It has to mean something."

"And you think it means you should walk on up to Markus King and have a friendly heart-to-heart with him?"

"Maybe. Maybe not. But if Markus is going to be at this ball that Jackie's going to . . ."

"Then what, Becca? What are you saying?"

Crys had never seen such determination in her eyes before. "Then we're going too."

Chapter 12

FARRELL

Farrell was all but certain that his mother had been the one to choose the theme of this charity ball, which was already in full swing not half an hour after the official start time. Mrs. Grayson was a fierce lover of Shakespeare and always had season tickets to the Stratford Festival. So even though it was barely spring, Farrell found himself in the midst of Hawkspear's *A Midsummer's Night's Dream* Masquerade Ball to Benefit Literacy.

Thanks to his mother, the usual parade of sparkly masks, Oscar-worthy face paint, outrageous ball gowns, and tailored tuxedos now included countless pairs of glittery fairy wings.

And *countless* almost wasn't an exaggeration—this year, tickets had sold out as soon as the news spread that Markus King himself would be attending in a rare public appearance to make a speech about the power of books and literacy.

Farrell had already decided to stick with club soda tonight, to keep his head clear. Nevertheless, he stuck close to the bar, where he could get a good view of the full room, every square inch of which was pinned, taped, or draped with some sort of fairy-themed decoration.

If there really was a traitor in their midst like Markus believed there was, Farrell swore he'd find them.

He was having a silent laugh at a middle-aged man dressed up as Bottom, the half-man, half-donkey character from the play, when a dark-haired woman approached him. Her ornate mask had peacock feathers and a veritable rainbow of sequins, which in Farrell's opinion made her outlandish emerald green ball gown look incredibly age inappropriate.

"Try not to say that out loud," Connor reminded him. *"Charm, remember? Even with her."*

"Mother, I must tell you again that you look absolutely gorgeous tonight," Farrell said, forcing his most innocent smile on his face.

Isabelle Grayson's expression changed from pinched to calm, as if surprised by the compliment. She then patted her hair, which was swept back in a tight bun, a fancier version of her signature, everyday style.

"Thank you, Farrell," she said. "By the way, look who I found sitting all by her lonesome at our table." Mrs. Grayson turned and gave a ladylike nod of her chin toward the girl who had followed her over to the bar.

Felicity Seaton's grin was five times brighter than the white pearls she wore at her throat. Her pale pink gown shimmered in the dim candlelight, and she wore a fuchsia mask lined with crystals and even more pearls.

"I thought you were getting us drinks," Felicity said.

"I was," Farrell lied, trying to cut her off before she could mention that he'd left the table more than thirty minutes ago. He'd excused himself so that he could make another sweep of the room, taking note of who was seated at which tables and ascertaining whether any ticketed guests were absent. "The line was killer; it's only started to settle down just now." He turned and signaled to the bartender for two glasses of champagne, which he offered to Felicity and his mother. "Ta-da."

"Have you seen Markus yet?" his mother asked eagerly.

"Not yet."

"Do you know when he'll be making his speech?"

"Soon, I'm sure." Dinner had already been served. Society members now picked at their plates.

Farrell leaned against the bar and took yet another look around the large ballroom. His eye landed on Adam, who was speaking with two elderly women Farrell didn't recognize—rich ticket-holders who weren't part of the Hawkspear Society. He was smiling and nodding, surely bored out of his mind by those two old bats, and Farrell couldn't be bothered to focus his excellent ears in on the conversation.

Old ladies loved angelic little Adam.

"Not so fast. Adam could be the one and only traitor Markus suspects," Connor said. *"If that's so, and if Adam's up to more nefarious behavior, would you turn him in?"*

It was a question Farrell was reluctant to ponder. He knew what Markus did with traitors, and when it came to imagining Adam in those scenarios . . . The thought made him wonder if even the new-and-improved Farrell was ruthless enough to hand his kid brother over for a swift trial and certain execution.

"The band is excellent, Mrs. Grayson," Felicity commented.

Farrell tried to mostly block out the string quartet playing classical-style renditions of pop songs for those who ventured onto the dance floor.

"They certainly are," Isabelle agreed. "I selected them myself after hearing them play at a gala in New York."

"An excellent choice. I adore dancing and haven't done nearly enough of it tonight." She looked pointedly at Farrell, who tried very hard not to meet her gaze.

"Yes, you were a student of ballet, weren't you? Your mother has told me how incredibly talented you were. Such a pity you didn't pursue it further."

Felicity frowned apologetically. "It just wasn't my calling. But I certainly hope Farrell will be interested in joining me on the dance floor later."

Kill me now, Farrell thought, draining the last of his club soda in one gulp and wishing more intensely than he had all night that there were vodka in it.

"I'd love to," he lied.

As he turned and placed his glass back on the bar, he spotted his father standing near the podium where Markus would be speaking, talking on his cell phone.

"Good old Dad," Connor commented. *"Always on the clock, even at a party. Wouldn't want any business opportunities to slip past him."*

That may have been Connor's take, but all that seeing his father on the phone made Farrell think of were his mother's recent paranoid suspicions that Edward Grayson was having an affair. Farrell concentrated. He honed in on his father's voice while consciously muting all others, straining himself to see if he could tell who was on the other end of the line.

"Yes, all is well," Farrell heard his father say. "My family is here with me tonight. We won't be leaving for quite some time. Yes. Yes, I understand. I'll let you know when to arrive."

Farrell was so deep in concentration, trying but failing to hear the voice on the other end of the line, that it took him a moment to see Edward flick his gaze up and look at him. When he finally did lock eyes, his father nodded at him, and Farrell nodded back.

Must be Sam, he thought.

Sam was one of the Graysons' chauffeurs. Lately, he was Farrell's exclusive driver—he needed one ever since his DUI rendered his license useless. And since the family chauffeur was on vacation this week, Sam stepped up to fill in. It made perfect sense that his father would need to speak with him in the middle of a party.

His mother still had no real proof of a mistress yet, and the thought that his father might possibly be faithful to his mother landed as a strange relief.

"Oh, excuse me," Felicity said, glancing across the room. "I just spotted a friend. I'll be back soon."

"Take your time," Farrell said under his breath as the girl scurried away, her satin skirt swishing in her wake.

"Farrell, are you sleeping all right?" his mother asked suddenly.

He glanced at her quizzically, as if just remembering she was still standing there. "No worse than usual. Why do you ask?"

"You look absolutely dreadful."

He kept his grimace and sarcastic retorts on the inside as he remembered his pledge to be as amiable as possible, even to his mother. "I guess I've been feeling a little tired the last day or so."

The sleeves of his tuxedo covered up the dagger scars, which still hadn't completely faded—not with Markus's magic or his own accelerated healing ability. It wasn't just that the marks were still visible; they *hurt*. Even the application of light pressure on his forearm caused him searing pain, and trying to fall asleep last night was a challenge that he had failed because of it.

To make matters worse, he also felt a cold, dull ache in the center of his chest. No matter how much ibuprofen or antacid he took, he couldn't shake the overall feeling of unwellness. He could only describe it as something akin to a harsh hangover, one that had lingered far longer than even his worst hangovers ever did.

His mother placed a cool palm on his cheek, surprising him. "You feel fine, darling. That's a relief."

Darling? She hadn't called him that in years. "I am fine."

She studied him, frowning. "I can't believe you had your birthmark removed."

"Glad it's gone," he scoffed. "It was ugly."

"It was part of you."

"It was an *ugly* part of me."

She shook her head. "Without it, you look so much like Connor. I can't believe I never realized the similarities until now."

A familiar shadow of grief slid behind her eyes as she mentioned her deceased eldest son. As if responding to a command, Farrell placed his hand on top of hers.

"What can I say? You gave birth to three very good-looking sons."

This made her smile, just a little. "This is true."

"I think more champagne is in order."

She nodded.

He wanted to be cold and unfeeling toward her, to summon up hatred for this woman who spent so much of her life refusing to offer him any kind words, but tonight he found he didn't have the energy even for apathy.

Seeing her display her grief in front of him, unshielded, made a deep-down part inside of him twinge with sympathy. Because he felt that same grief too.

"*How sweet,*" Connor said. "*Mother and son bonding over little old me. Unsettling, of course, and kind of pathetic, but sweet. Still, you're not exactly doing your job. If you don't find a traitor tonight, Markus will be disappointed in you.*"

Maybe there was no traitor in the society like Markus believed there was. Maybe the treason started and ended with the dearly departed Daniel Hatcher, and Markus was only being paranoid.

And Adam had only been a helper, not an instigator.

Markus could be wrong.

"Ah, you know better than that," Connor said. *"Markus is never wrong. And the second you agreed to get that fourth mark on your arm, you became his best friend forever. Remember, as long as you follow his lead, it's all going to be worth it, kid."*

Farrell really hoped he was right.

"Oh my God," Isabelle gasped, pulling Farrell out of his head. "How dare she show her face here!"

Farrell calmly turned around to see what scandalous wardrobe choice or other minor offense had caused such a dramatic reaction in his mother. But his jaw dropped along with hers when he saw whom she was looking at: Mallory, Connor's ex-girlfriend.

"Farrell . . . ," Isabelle began, her voice breaking. "I can't bear it. It's too much."

He nodded. "I'll handle it."

"Handle what? What's wrong?" Felicity asked as she returned from speaking with her friend, trailing after Farrell as he crossed the room to block Mallory's path.

Farrell tried to ignore her.

"What are you doing here?" Farrell asked Mallory sharply, before she could get out so much as a hello. There was absolutely no reason for him to use any charm with this girl. Felicity was behind him like a shadow, and he could feel her trying to peek around and get a good look at the girl who'd caused the uproar.

Beneath her sparkly mask, Farrell watched Mallory's eyes widen and her pretty face go pale. "Farrell, I . . . I'm here with friends who work with a small independent publisher in the city. They bought a table and offered me a seat."

"How generous of them. Why don't you have a glass of champagne and whatever shrimp or crab cakes are left over on the cold buffet, and then I suggest you leave."

Felicity touched his arm and stared up at him, a flash of horror in her eyes. "Farrell, don't be rude."

"I'm sorry, I should have introduced you. Felicity, this is Mallory. Otherwise known as the reason my brother killed himself."

Mallory went a shade paler. "Don't say that," she said quietly.

"Why not? It's true. He was happy, successful, on his way to becoming a famous artist, but you broke his heart. You may as well have slit his wrists yourself. Hell, maybe you did."

She shook her head, her eyes welling with tears. "I loved him."

"Yeah? You had a really great way of showing it. Now get the hell out of here, or I promise to make you very sorry you even got out of bed this morning."

Mallory took a shaky step back from Farrell. From what he could see behind her mask, her widening eyes had filled with a satisfying amount of fear.

Finally, she turned and fled.

All Farrell could see was fiery red. In mere moments, his mood had shifted from attentive and slightly bored to furious.

Murderous.

Felicity touched his tense arm, and he flinched.

"Don't start," he snarled. "I won't stand for it tonight."

He risked looking right into her eyes, but instead of the outrage or accusation he expected, he saw only patience. "You did the right thing, getting that nasty girl out of here," she said. "And I'm pretty sure you need a drink. I'll go get you a vodka?"

He nodded stiffly. She smiled and headed toward the bar.

"What a helpful and attentive girlfriend you've got there." Farrell nearly jumped at the unexpected sound of Markus's voice. "Excellent choice."

"She is," Farrell replied. "Thanks." He raised a brow at the society leader. "You look . . . much better."

"I *feel* much better. Thanks to you."

Much better was an understatement. The circles under Markus's eyes had been erased, and his hair was back to gleaming. His sickly, pallid skin had been revived with its golden flow, as if it shone from within.

Markus King looked like at least a billion bucks, and it was all thanks to the newest scars on Farrell's arm.

"And how are you?" Markus asked.

"Oh, fine. Only a little worse for the wear. I'd say I'm running on about eighty percent of my recently acquired amazingness. But you're more than welcome to that remaining eighty."

Markus nodded grimly. "It won't be for long, I promise. This is only a temporary solution to my ills."

"If it works—if you start to feel better—then it's all worth it."

Markus took Farrell's hand in both of his in a collegial kind of handshake. "You are a true friend, Farrell. I haven't had one of those for a very long time."

Farrell didn't say it aloud, but he genuinely felt the same way. Instead he just nodded, then made a subtle gesture to the rest of the ballroom. "I've been keeping watch, but I have to say, I haven't seen anything strange."

Markus nodded. "That's good. I would prefer to have my suspicions disproved, of course."

"Of course."

Markus raised a brow and looked out toward the podium. "Well, I suppose it's time for me to get up there. Wish me luck."

"You don't need luck." Farrell grinned. "You're Markus King." Markus returned the smile and crossed over toward Isabelle Grayson, who was already making her way toward him, her teeth bared in a shark-like grin.

Isabelle escorted Markus up to the front of the room as masked faces turned to watch, hushed whispers following him the whole way. Isabelle showed Markus to a seat behind the podium, then stood at the microphone to introduce him.

"Welcome, everyone. I am Isabelle Grayson, one of the organizers of tonight's ball. I hope you are all enjoying yourselves. It is my great honor and privilege to introduce Markus King, whose incredibly generous donation made tonight's event possible. This means that one hundred percent of all proceeds from ticket sales and new donations go directly toward literacy programs and an effort to make art grants available to struggling poets and writers in this talented city. Please, join me in giving a warm welcome to Markus King!"

Farrell had wondered how his mother would introduce a millennia-old god of death. Now he knew: as generically as possible.

Isabelle left the podium to the tune of applause for Markus, who gave Isabelle a kiss on the cheek and a thank you that only Farrell's enhanced hearing could pick up. He stood at the podium and smiled, already perfectly playing the part of the young heir whose passion for reading translated into a philanthropic dedication to literacy.

"It is my honor to be here tonight, Isabelle. To say that books are a vital part of my existence would be a great understatement. I think you could say that without certain books in my life, I might actually die."

Was it Farrell's imagination, or was Markus actually making a joke? The man was full of surprises. And either way, the crowd before him chuckled.

"I am lucky enough to have the funds to help such important charities, and I want to thank you all for delving into your hearts, digging into your pockets, and making tonight so special and so important. Because of your generosity, Isabelle has informed me that we have raised over one hundred and fifty thousand dollars for our chosen charity.

"I'm so inspired by this that I would personally like to match this amount and put it toward providing books, tutors, and special programs to underprivileged children who struggle with learning disabilities. Every one of you has helped to make this world a better place, and for that you have my eternal gratitude."

Markus swept his cool but kind gaze over the crowd as the applause swelled once again. Farrell looked on, his chest swelling with pride in time with the applause. But a moment later, all of that pride and confidence slunk away as he watched Markus, still up at the podium, freeze completely, his regal smile dropping into a grim line.

Farrell turned around, trying to see what could have caught his attention and caused such a chilling reaction. It took only an instant for him to identify the cause: a beautiful blond woman in a short black sequined dress standing at the back of the ballroom, near the entrance. Unlike the other women here, she wore no gaudy jewelry draped around her neck or wrists. No mask to hide her identity or her stunning face. Her lips were bright red and curled up in a half smile.

It seemed as though the whole room noticed at the same time and that the crowd had parted to make room for the creature that had left Markus King dumbstruck and paralyzed.

Jackie Kendall, Farrell thought.

She'd accepted Markus's invitation. He never would have guessed in a million years that she'd actually show up here tonight.

Based on Markus's stunned expression, he must have felt exactly the same way.

Markus left the podium and moved toward her through the crowd. After a moment, the rest of the partygoers went back to enjoying the ball, the band began to play at Isabelle's signal, and conversation rose up again. Many people took to the dance floor, beneath the sparkling lights cast from the chandelier.

Farrell focused his enhanced hearing, muting out every sound but Markus and Jackie's conversation.

"Jackie . . . ," Markus began in a hushed voice as he reached the woman. "You're here. I can't . . . I can't believe you actually came."

"Yes, I'm here," she replied stiffly. "And we need to talk."

"I couldn't agree more." He started to lead her toward the exit, but she stopped him, her hand on his elbow.

"No. I want to stay out in the open. With all these people."

"All right, but let's move off to the side."

Farrell sought to keep them in view—his hearing only seemed to work if his targets were still in sight—but he lost them in the crowd.

So that was the infamous Jackie Kendall. The keeper of the Codex, mother of the secret baby, had arrived. Was this a good development or a bad one?

"Are you kidding?" not-Connor asked him. *"This couldn't be worse. That woman has power over Markus whether he realizes it or not. He's exposed himself here tonight, something he never does. All for the chance that she might stroll in. And when she does, you just let them walk away."*

He was failing Markus by not keeping a close eye on him.

Farrell took one step, ready to follow, and then, a deep frown claiming his face, he stopped. Above the lingering scents of the evening—crème brûlée, fresh coffee and espresso, and imported French perfume—he smelled the unmistakable scent of *strawberries*.

He swiveled on his heels, immediately pinpointing the source of that familiar scent.

"Well. Looks like we have a number of late arrivals tonight," he said to himself.

Past a dancing facade of ornate masks and formal wear, Farrell watched Crystal Hatcher and her sister, Becca, enter the ballroom.

Chapter 13

MADDOX

Unsatisfied after a dinner of half of one small warlog—and still reeling from that truly surreal moment when Maddox mistook a hawk for Becca Hatcher—the ground felt particularly hard on this chilly night. As he lay there unable to sleep, all he could do was wonder what it said about his mental state that for even one instant he'd allowed himself to believe that Becca had been watching him through the eyes of a hawk.

"I don't know how you do this, Barnabas," Maddox grumbled into the darkness, drawing his still-damp tunic closer around him for warmth.

"Do what?" Barnabas replied gruffly.

"Sleep outside all the time."

"Well, pardon me, Lord Maddox. I looked high and low for you, but it seems the forest is fresh out of feather beds and personal attendants eagerly waiting until dawn with silver trays filled with pastries."

Maddox picked up a small rock and hurled it at Barnabas. He heard a yelp of pain, but not from the mouth of his target.

"Sorry, Alcander," Maddox muttered.

"It's quite all right. In the morning it'll be nothing more than a small bruise, young man. All is well. And please—do call me Al. Alcander is so formal—I really only use that name to sign my work."

Maddox nodded. "All right then, Al." Al had made every effort to be pleasant and helpful since, in exchange for his knowledge of Princess Cassia's whereabouts, they'd agreed to keep him . . . well, *alive* didn't seem to be quite the word.

Conscious? Sentient?

Maddox still couldn't believe it had worked. That he'd actually *breathed life* back into a severed head. Thinking about it for too long—especially the part about how it had barely taken any effort for his necromancy to have such a drastic effect—disturbed him on such a deep and basic level that he'd already learned to keep these moments of wonder short.

"Thank the goddess you're a lousy shot," Barnabas said. "Sleep well, then. Don't let the night-maggots bite."

Maddox tensed. "Er, sorry. What's a night-maggot?"

"Oh, you know. Those gigantic worms that come out at night to feast on sixteen-year-old boys who complain about not getting enough dinner."

"Very amusing, Barnabas," Al said, chuckling softly. "I can tell by your imagination and way with words that you would make an excellent scribe yourself."

"No thank you."

With everyone settled in for the night, a surprisingly soothing kind of quiet set into the campsite. Maddox closed his eyes, crossed his arms over his chest, and tried to sleep.

The storm started only minutes later. After a solitary rumble of thunder as the only bit of warning, rain began to slam down upon their campsite in torrents. Their fire was doused in seconds, robbing them of their only flicker of light and warmth in the dark forest.

With grumbles and grunts, Maddox and Barnabas rose and quickly gathered up Al and their scant supplies. Together they stumbled through the forest, and though they were purposely trying to avoid towns on their route, they were grateful that there was one not too far away. When they reached the edge of the forest, Barnabas pointed to a dim grouping of lights about a half mile off.

"There. That's got to be an inn," Barnabas said.

Maddox nodded as they set out for the rest of the miserable trudge.

They entered the first inn they came across, trailing water in their wake. Maddox held tightly to the sopping-wet canvas sack containing Al, taking a quick peek in to make sure he was breathing.

"You all right?" he asked.

"Yes, fine!"

"Tell him not to say anything for a while," Barnabas suggested.

"Don't say anything for a while," Maddox told him.

"I can hear him. And I won't. Do whatever it takes to keep us out of this horrid rain before I drown!"

To the right of the entrance was a set of stairs leading up to the rooms. To their left was a wooden archway leading into a tavern. They entered the busy tavern, taking the first available seat at a heavy wooden table. The delicious scent of roasted pheasant and boiled potatoes drifted under Maddox's nose, making his stomach growl. At least twenty others were also in the tavern, drinking and eating in this shelter from the storm. A fire blazed nearby, its heat helping to take the chill from Maddox's bones.

He never wanted to leave.

A weathered-looking man came over to their table, eyeing

their soaking clothes with either annoyance or pure distaste. "The kitchen's closed for the night."

Maddox tensed and shared a pained look with Barnabas.

Barnabas straightened his shoulders. "I realize it's getting late, but the boy and I need a hot meal and a dry room."

"We're full up tonight. You should have arrived earlier."

"I'm sure you must keep one or two rooms vacant at all times? For emergencies?"

The man blinked. "I don't see any emergencies here."

"I have coin," Barnabas said. "We can pay."

"That may be, but I don't have any rooms to sell you. Apologies, but it's late, and I'm very tired." The man then gave them a cold smile. "Be on your way."

Maddox was determined not to spend the night in the cold, wet, and completely dark forest.

Just then, a shadow moved along the floor and caught his eye. He turned to see what cast it but saw nothing.

Strange.

"Can you suggest another inn, then?" Barnabas persisted.

"I'm afraid we're the only inn in town. Only one within a day's journey, in fact."

As Maddox's hopes were rapidly starting to sink, a plump woman emerged from the kitchen, wiping her greasy fingers on her apron. "What's going on?" she asked.

"These two," the innkeeper told her, "want us to produce rooms that don't exist. Perhaps they think we're witches."

Barnabas gave the woman his most charismatic grin—the one Maddox had seen work wonders on the fairer sex. "Lovely lady," he said in a honeyed tone, "I hope you might have the heart to give us a place to stay while we wait out this fierce storm. Young Maddox, well . . . he's very sickly. If I keep him outside any longer in this rain, I shudder to think of the state I might wake to find him in tomorrow morning."

Barnabas shot Maddox a pointed, urging look.

"Yes," Maddox said, then let out a pathetic-sounding cough. "Very sick."

The woman pursed her lips. "You're not sick. I know sick, and you're not it. We have no place for liars here—in our rooms *or* in our tavern. Be gone with you."

Maddox then spotted the strange shadow again, moving swiftly along the edge of the room.

His gaze was then drawn by a glint of metal. Around her neck, the woman wore a charm Maddox had seen many times before: a crescent moon within a circle stamped upon a round piece of silver.

The shadow crossed his periphery again, and the answer to their problem landed squarely in Maddox's mind.

"How many spirits haunt this inn?" he asked the woman as he gently placed Al's sack down on the seat beside him.

She gasped. "What did you say, boy?"

Barnabas looked at him with alarm in his eyes. "Maddox . . ."

Maddox glanced again toward the corner where the inky darkness now perched. He was surprised he hadn't sensed it the moment they stepped foot in the inn, but he set that aside for now. "There are spirits in this inn. There's one in this tavern with us right now, but that's not the only one that resides here."

His statement had reached the ears of other patrons, who had stopped eating and drinking and were now silent, their wide-eyed gazes fixed on him.

"Did he say *spirits*?" one patron said to a friend.

The woman clasped her hand to her mouth, clearly in shock.

The innkeeper put his arm around her and drew her closer as he studied Maddox intensely.

"How could you know this?" he demanded.

"I can see them," he said simply.

The woman shook her head as she put her hand to her throat and twisted around her charm, meant as a totem to protect against evil spirits. It was really nothing more than a useless scrap of tin made by profit-hungry witches, which Maddox knew because Livius used to sell these charms to anyone superstitious enough to believe his claims.

No mere charm could repel or vanquish a dark spirit.

"I was right!" the woman practically hollered. "All this time, I was right. The creaking sounds, the cold drafts, the horrible sense of despair that follows us around. What are we going to do?" She looked around at the shocked faces. "Don't tell anyone what you've heard here tonight! If word gets out, we're ruined! No one will dare enter these cursed doors!"

Barnabas watched Maddox curiously, not daring to interrupt.

"I can help you," Maddox told them.

"Help us?" the woman said. The pair exchanged a frenzied look. "How?"

"The same gift that allows me to see the spirits also allows me trap them." He stood up and held his hand out to the woman. "Give me your charm, please."

She yanked the charm—chain and all—right off her neck and offered it to him with a shaking hand. "If it will help, take it!"

"Thank you." He squeezed the charm once before placing it in his open, upturned palm. He'd done this many, many times before, and the muscle memory came back to him as if he were with Livius just yesterday.

He picked up Al's sack and handed it to Barnabas. "Best keep you-know-who away from this vanquishing, just in case."

Barnabas nodded. "Good idea."

He got up and moved, with Al, toward the archway, as far away from Maddox as he could get.

Then Maddox walked in a circle around the tavern, knowing that each and every patron watched him intently. He tried not to be distracted by this—or by the half-eaten pheasant on their plates and the ache of his empty stomach.

It didn't matter where the spirits were located, Maddox always started a vanquishing the same way: by looking up. In this case, at the wooden rafters of the tavern's ceiling.

"Dark spirits who reside in this inn: I command you to obey me!" he said. "You are troublesome to these good people, whose greatest want is to help the tired and hungry citizens who come to them in need of food and rest. I command you to obey me. Come to me, dark spirits. *Now.*"

This was a part of the act he was used to with Livius. Really, he didn't have to say anything externally, just in his mind, to summon the spirits.

Maddox concentrated hard, until his magic became a magnetic force, forcing obedience. He now directed his gaze to the floor and held very still as three shadows slithered toward him, winding themselves up his legs, around his arms, their sheer proximity cloaking him in an icy chill. They kept writhing all around him, rising up as if heading for his neck, until they reached the level of Maddox's palm and then dove, disappearing into the silver amulet.

All went quiet for a moment, and Maddox sensed nothing except the sound of rain outside and the scent of delicious food.

"It is done," Maddox said. "The spirits are trapped and will never bother you again." He returned the amulet to the woman, who accepted it from him gingerly. "Bury this deep in the earth as soon as you can and know with certainty that you are now safe from harm."

That part, of course, was a lie. The spirits he'd encountered in his life couldn't harm the living—they could only scare them. But telling that truth to the innkeeper and his wife wouldn't elicit the response he was aiming for.

Silence hung in the air for several tense moments. No one in the tavern spoke a single word, but then the woman's face lit up with a wide smile, causing Maddox to exhale a big sigh of relief. "You are a miracle, young man," she cooed. "A true miracle!" She grasped his face and kissed both of his cheeks.

"Incredible," a man at a nearby table agreed, nodding. "I've never witnessed anything so brave!"

The other patrons also voiced their enthusiasm and awe.

"Alas," Barnabas drew closer to Maddox, holding the sack, muting the cheer surrounding them with his grave tone of voice, "now we must begin our search for a place to lay our weary heads tonight. Come, Maddox. Let's be on our way." Barnabas put his hand on Maddox's shoulder and turned him toward the door.

As they walked, Maddox slowly counted: *one . . . two . . . three . . .*

"Wait!" the innkeeper called out just before Barnabas grasped the door handle. Maddox grinned—he knew they'd never make it past three. "We can't let you go back into that storm. You have more than paid for lodging here tonight, as well as a fine meal."

Barnabas frowned. "That's very kind of you, but I thought you said you had no more rooms."

The innkeeper's cheeks reddened. "We have but one left, and it's yours. You'll have to share it with your son, but it's a very fine space. Please, take a seat again, and my wife will bring you something to eat while I prepare your room."

Barnabas turned to him, now smiling. "You are too kind."

Maddox tried to lose his big grin as he and Barnabas sat back down at their table, people murmuring with awe at what they'd seen tonight.

"I've heard rumors of the witch-boy before," Maddox heard one man whisper. "Figured they were nothing but legend."

Maddox caught Barnabas stealing a glance at the whispering man. "Exactly why I wanted to avoid taverns and inns," he said. "Best to leave here very early in the morning, lest news of this real-life legend starts to spread."

"A legend indeed!" Maddox started at the sound of Al's muffled voice from inside his sack, which Barnabas had placed on the tabletop. "Well done, young man."

"Are you all right?" Maddox asked, nudging the edge of the canvas aside to glance at Al. "My magic . . . did it affect you in any way?"

Al blinked. "No, I don't think so. I didn't even feel a tingle!"

"Good." This was a relief. As gently as possible, he gestured to Al to keep quiet again. He then looked up to regard a surprisingly sour expression on Barnabas's face. "What's wrong? You don't look nearly as thrilled as everyone else does about my performance tonight."

"I'm not."

"Is it because I used my magic in public? Or that you fear this has brought my soul one step closer to being corrupted by darkness?"

"A bit of both, to be honest."

"I feel fine."

"I'm glad to hear it. Next time, however, I'd prefer that we discuss our options before you jump right into spirit-capturing."

Maddox frowned. He couldn't tell whether he was grateful for Barnabas's instinct to protect him or annoyed that he couldn't just do as he pleased without being chastised for it afterward. After all, he knew his limitations, and easy magic like the kind he performed tonight was nothing new for him.

Finally, the innkeeper's wife arrived with two trays, each bearing a veritable feast of the roasted pheasant he'd been craving since smelling it, warm and crusty bread, boiled potatoes, and a bowl each of barley soup. Once all that was placed down, she hurried away and returned again with enough ale for them to drown in. Maddox ate until his stomach hurt, and then he ate a little more. The woman kept returning to refill their mugs, and Maddox had never been more grateful to have a roof over his head.

Maddox was just leaning back in his chair out of fullness when suddenly the tavern door opened. A frigid gust blew in, bringing the wet storm with it. Maddox looked up to see a woman enter through the archway. She was every bit as sodden as he and Barnabas had been when they'd first arrived. Her dark blond hair was slick against her face, her gray cloak dripping onto the wooden slats of the floor as, shivering, she took a seat at a neighboring table.

For a moment Maddox expected someone to follow in after her, but she seemed to be without a companion.

A flash of boldness he'd never felt before took him over. "Miss?" he said. "You're welcome to join us over here, if you'd like the company. That is, if you don't mind, Barnabas."

"Certainly not." Still, Barnabas looked at Maddox with an arched eyebrow. "Please, do join us. Plenty of room."

After a moment of hesitation, the young woman approached their table. Barnabas hopped up to his feet, helped her out of her wet cloak, and pulled out a chair for her.

"There you go," he said once she was settled in her seat. "Now tell me: What is a lovely young lady like yourself doing out on a fearsome night like this?"

She eyed Barnabas's damp clothes and generally disheveled appearance. "I suppose I could ask you the same question."

The innkeeper's wife approached then, refilling their mugs once again. Maddox noticed the young woman watching her, a flash of hunger leaping to her gaze as she eyed their empty plates.

"Can I get you something, miss?" the innkeeper's wife asked.

"Yes, please," she said. "Whatever these fine gentlemen had to eat would be lovely."

"Certainly. It won't be long." The innkeeper's wife scurried away.

"I will warn you," Barnabas said. "We ate quite a bit."

"Luckily, I'm very hungry."

Looking at her now, Maddox couldn't be sure of her age. When he first saw her in the doorway she'd looked like a proper lady, but up close she looked quite young—more of a girl than a woman. Still, though her face was soft-skinned and young-looking, there was something about her grayish-blue eyes that looked world-weary to him.

"I'm Liana," she said.

"I'm Maddox," he said with a smile.

Thankfully, Al remained silent. Maddox took his sack off the table and placed it next to him instead.

"It's a pleasure to meet you, Maddox."

"I'm Barnabas," said Barnabas, holding out his hand for several moments until the girl finally turned from Maddox and took it. "The pleasure is entirely mine. Liana is a beautiful name for a beautiful woman."

Maddox tried not to roll his eyes as Liana regarded both of them silently for a moment.

"I think I know how I can repay you for your kindness in inviting me to sit with you this evening," she said with a twinkle in her eye. "How would you like to know your futures?"

Barnabas let out a groan of disappointment. "A fortune-teller. That explains why you're traveling alone. Maddox, beware of pretty fortune-tellers. They will take you for every coin you have if you give them half a chance."

"Quite the cynic, aren't you?" Liana scowled at him. "May I remind you, it was Maddox who asked me to sit with you. I didn't invite myself."

"She's right," Maddox said, then turned to his invited guest. "Ignore Barnabas. You're welcome to tell my fortune if you'd like, Liana. I'm actually very interested in what lies ahead."

"You're sure?" she said, her pinched expression quickly replaced by a wicked grin. "You might not like what I have to say."

Barnabas waved his hand dismissively. "Let the girl do her performance, Maddox, and pay little mind to what she says. That is, as long as she realizes we're not paying her a single coin for her show."

Once again, Maddox found himself newly surprised by how rude Barnabas could be toward everything and everyone. "Calm yourself, Barnabas. Like she said, she's offering us our fortunes in return for our hospitality."

Liana eyed Barnabas. "You don't trust easily, do you?"

"I trust no one."

"What about your son? You don't trust him either?"

"Maddox has proven the single exception to my rule."

"Very well," Liana said, turning in her seat to face Maddox. "Let me look into your eyes, Maddox."

Al coughed.

Liana frowned. "What was that?"

"Nothing," Maddox said quickly, lightly poking the sack next to him. "Nothing at all."

He then held the pretty girl's gaze, seeing new depth and a range of colors in her eyes. He found himself momentarily lost in their strange mixture of shades, from a soft silvery shade to bright sapphire.

"You're on a journey," Liana said. "In search of something very important."

"Ha," Barnabas scoffed. "That could be said of anyone."

"When it comes to your goals," Liana went on, unfazed, "you and your father are of like minds. And, despite the questionable means you might use, or have already used, on your journey, your intentions are good, and your hearts are pure." Liana paused, her eyes still locked on Maddox's. "Am I close? Is your heart pure, Maddox?"

"I'm not sure sometimes," he said uncertainly. "I hope it is."

"He speaks the truth," Liana said, smiling. "Honesty is a rare gift, and it's one you definitely possess. And so is love. I see it for you, Maddox. I see that you have felt love before. There is a girl whom you've lost, and though it seems an insurmountable task, you hope to find her again."

Maddox swallowed hard and nodded weakly. "Yes. I do hope to find her again. But I don't know how."

"It will happen," Liana said evenly. "One day, perhaps sooner than you think. Perhaps even on this quest you're on with your father." The fortune-teller paused again, this time looking even more deeply into Maddox's eyes. "You seek a hidden treasure, one that might change the course of many people's destinies. Is this right?"

Maddox found himself nodding, very conscious of his full stomach and those several mugs of ale working him into a warm, pleasant mood. "Yes, that's right."

"Who exactly are you, Liana?" Barnabas asked, his tone especially cool.

Maddox looked up at the interruption and started to see that Barnabas had pulled out his dagger.

"What do you think you're doing with that?" Maddox demanded.

"This?" He pressed the blade against Liana's waist, beneath the table and hidden from the rest of the tavern. "There will only be trouble if she doesn't answer my question. Who are you, girl?"

Liana's expression grew strained. "A fellow traveler, that's all."

"Put that away, Barnabas," Maddox hissed.

Barnabas's jaw stiffened. "Ah, there it is. The difference between you and me, my young friend. You haven't lived long enough to see as much deception as I have. You meet a person who acts friendly, and you assume they're a friendly person. But I'm wise enough to see beyond that facade. What I see behind that friendliness is nothing but devious intentions."

"Do you?" Liana said coolly. "Well, then, did you see this coming?"

With a flash of metal, Liana pressed her own dagger against Barnabas's trousers. At a very vulnerable spot.

Maddox cringed.

Barnabas clenched his jaw even tighter. "Clever girl."

"Clever enough to handle a brute like you, at least."

"Between your little fortune-telling act and this weapon of yours at the ready, you must already know exactly who we are."

"What makes you say that? Perhaps I'm simply a girl who's had to learn how to defend herself against violent criminals. Do you make a habit of threatening the lives of women you've only just met?"

Barnabas let out a feeble, choked laugh. "Not usually, but I'll make an exception for you, *fellow traveler.*" He paused to let a sly smile spread across his face. "I never said Maddox was my son."

Now it was Liana's turn to laugh. "Pardon me for assuming that two men of vastly different ages who are also traveling together are related."

"There are many ways for two people to be related, my dear. Why not assume I'm his uncle or his cousin or . . . I don't know, perhaps his older brother?"

Liana cocked her head. "Have I struck a nerve, Barnabas? Are you worried you look old?"

"Thirty-four is hardly *old.*"

"No, you're right. It's *very* old."

Barnabas narrowed his eyes. "I don't think I like you."

"That's fine with me. Now lower your weapon, or say farewell to the thing that makes you a man."

"My sparkling personality?" he said, then grunted in pain as she pressed her blade down harder. "Fine."

He pulled his weapon back. A moment later, she did the same.

"That's better. Perhaps now we can speak a bit more freely," Liana said. "First, perhaps you can share with me why one of your traveling companions is a reanimated severed head?"

Barnabas eyed her with an increasingly wary gaze. "How long have you been following us?"

"Long enough."

Maddox was barely breathing now. "H-how? *Why?*"

Liana, her cheeks now flushed, flicked a glance at him. "Out of pure necessity. I swear I mean you no harm."

Barnabas shifted in his seat and grimaced. "Ugh. I think I'm bleeding."

"Erm, Barnabas?" Al piped up from his hiding place in the sack. "Perhaps you should be more careful when speaking to a lady."

"If I saw one, perhaps I would." Barnabas growled. He grinned darkly as he watched Liana eye the talking canvas sack with equal parts shock and curiosity.

"I *knew* it," she said. "Maddox, your magic is incredible."

Maddox was too stunned to reply, but a small part of him glowed inwardly at the compliment.

"Talk, fortune-teller," Barnabas snarled. "Tell us what you want from us, and then be gone."

Liana sat back in her seat, pulled up her skirt, and returned her dagger to a sheath she wore strapped to her shapely right thigh. "I know what you're planning," she said. "Some of it, anyway. You mean to find Princess Cassia, and from there you wish to remove both goddesses from their thrones." Both Barnabas and Maddox perked up in their seats, ready to argue, but she raised a hand and silenced them. "Please. Don't try to deny it; I already know it's the truth. But you have nothing to fear from me."

Barnabas snorted. "Fear you? Dream on, little girl."

She shot him a pinched and unpleasant smile. "If you don't fear me by now, then you're not nearly as smart as you think you are. You'd be surprised by what a woman can accomplish when she puts her mind to it."

"Oh, I know that much about women. But I'm not convinced about *you*. Or your motivations for trying to sleuth all of this out. What you've just suggested is treason and grounds for execution."

"Of course it is. But some goals are worth dying for."

"Those kinds of goals are rarer than slugs' teeth."

"True. But they do exist, don't they?"

Barnabas studied her for a long, silent moment. "You can't help us."

"Yes, I can."

"How? By telling fake fortunes to passersby, perhaps earning us a few coins? We can just as well do that ourselves."

"I'm thinking something more like this." Liana licked her fingers, snuffed out the candle on the table in front of her, then fixed a concentrated gaze on the wick, her forehead furrowing.

A moment later, the wick caught fire.

Maddox gasped. "You're a witch!"

"Shh." Liana looked around nervously. "I'd rather not let everyone in here learn the truth about me tonight. But yes, I can work some fire magic. Enough, I think, to be useful to you. Add to that my interest in seeing King Thaddeus's heir on her rightful throne, and we have a great deal in common."

"An interesting proposition," Barnabas allowed.

Liana ignored him and instead studied Maddox carefully. "You wield death magic."

Visions of vanquishing spirits and raising a severed head back to life filled Maddox's mind, but he knew better than to answer Liana's question definitively.

Barnabas continued to regard her like she was a lump of horse dung he'd just scraped from the bottom of his shoe.

"It's all right," Liana said after a silence stretched between them. "You don't have to say. I know the truth when I see it. And this"—she reached across the table to poke the canvas sack—"is evidence of the truth."

"Ouch," said Al. "My eye."

Liana turned once again to Maddox and grasped both of his hands. "I can help you," she said. "I *can*. In many more ways than you even realize right now. I know tales—true tales—about the immortals that I know you'll want to hear. Perhaps I can help you learn more about yourself and what your magic can do."

"I also know many of these stories," Al said. Then, despondently: "As related by Valoria, of course, so who's to say how true they are."

"No, this isn't going to work," Barnabas said firmly, standing up from the table. "We're done here, Maddox. It's time to get some sleep. And when we leave in the morning, we'll be going alone—just you, me, and the head."

"No," Maddox said, immediately and just as firmly.

"No?" Barnabas repeated, one eyebrow arched.

It was one of those rare times when a sharp instinct jabbed at his gut. "Liana is coming with us."

Chapter 14

CRYSTAL

In the hours before they'd left Angus's penthouse, Crys had tried, only semi-patiently, to explain the danger to Becca, but it was no use. Becca insisted on going, with or without her.

"You think you can just follow Jackie there?" Crys had tried to reason. "She'll see you."

"No," Becca had said. "Of course not. But we don't need to follow her there. See, there's this thing called 'the Internet,' and it's really good at finding addresses of the only venue in Toronto holding a big charity ball on this exact date."

Smartass.

Crys hadn't protested nearly as much as she should have—especially given the promise she'd made to her mother to keep Becca safe.

And then there was the fact that Crys thought it was possible her father might be at the event tonight, back from wherever Markus had sent him. It had taken every last bit of her strength not to text him for the last week, but she knew it was still way too early for that to be safe.

She and Becca decided to check out Angus's closets, hoping to find something to wear. Sure enough, within a huge walk-in that was bigger than both of their bedrooms at home combined, they found a more than sizable selection of formal wear for both men and women. Thankfully that selection included two dresses, both black, one just about Crys's size and one that was right for Becca's delicate frame. Becca's had a beaded neckline and flowy skirt; Crys's was simple, sleek, and satin. There were shoes to match in the back of the closet, though only Becca was lucky enough to find a pair of pumps that fit her, while Crys was forced to jam her feet into some patent leather stilettos that were one size too small. Why Angus had all of these extravagant women's clothes in his apartment was beyond Crys, and she decided not to think too much about it.

Crys knew she would have to say *something* to Dr. Vega before they left, so they crept down to the study, where he was still pouring over the Codex pages. They stood in the doorway for many moments, but he was so fixated on his work that he didn't even look up.

"He probably won't even know we're gone," Crys whispered to Becca, who gave her a relieved smile. Quietly, they left.

It was a masquerade ball, so on their way, they bought a couple of sequined masks at a cheap little shop near the apartment. Knowing she'd have to don one of these tonight, Crys had put in her contacts and left her glasses next to her bed before they'd left. It would have been kind of hard to pull off a delicate disguise with those things on her face.

Pulling at her too-short hemline and wobbling in the too-small heels, Crys followed the annoyingly poised Becca into the black-tie venue. Only then did she realize there was one vital detail they hadn't considered.

Tickets.

They stood in the lobby of the ballroom while a stern-looking, gray-haired woman wearing what looked like an entire jewelry store's supply of diamonds searched for their names on the guest list. "I'm sorry, but you're simply not here."

"Pardon me?" Crys said, trying to look shocked by this information. "That can't be right. Can you please check again?"

"I can," the woman said impatiently, "but I've already checked twice, and I have a feeling your names aren't bound to magically appear on the third go round. Perhaps if your parents are inside . . . ?"

"Yes," Becca said. "They are. And they're going to be furious that we're late."

Crys suppressed a small grin—she was both impressed and a little taken aback at Becca's quick-thinking gumption. "Our limo broke down on the way here," Crys added. "So we had to wait for another one. A *worse* one—just our luck. Rich-people problems, you know? Such a pain!"

"I'm sure." The woman scanned the girls' outfits, head to toe, and Crys was certain they'd been made. Of course this rich old bat knew the difference between a gown tailor-made for a particular body and a wild vintage frock stolen from an eccentric criminal's closet. "Perhaps you might want to get back into your *limo* and go home. Wherever that may be."

Becca gave Crys a defeated look.

"This is for the best," Crys whispered, grabbing Becca's hand and turning away from the woman. "Sorry, I know that's not what you want to hear. But it's true."

"Gloria?" said a familiar voice, echoing a little ways past the registration table. "Is there a problem out here?"

Crys looked up to see Adam Grayson, recognizable even with

half his face covered by a satin mask the exact same shade of blue as his suit.

Gloria smiled at him, wrinkles fanning out from the corners of her eyes. "These two young ladies aren't on the li—"

"There you are!" Adam said to Becca and Crys, pretending not to hear Gloria. "You missed dinner. Everyone's been asking about you."

"You know us, always fashionably late," Crys offered without missing a beat.

"I certainly do." Adam slid his arm around each girl's waist and winked at Gloria. "I'll handle these two troublemakers, promise," he said to her. "It's my fault they're not on your list in the first place—they're my plus-ones, but I forgot to submit their names. Sorry about that."

Gloria responded with nothing but a silent, sour smile, and before Crys knew it, they were down the hall, through the archway, and in the midst of a buzzing masquerade ball.

Becca looked up at Adam with unshielded relief. "Once again, we have you to thank for helping us out."

"Don't mention it," he said tightly. "Should I ask why you're here tonight? Do I even want to know?"

"If we told you, we'd have to kill you," Crys said, the lameness of her joke hitting her right before the realization of how inappropriate it was in the context of the society. "Um, just kidding, of course."

If Adam was here, it meant the other Graysons were too. She'd figured Farrell's attendance was a given, but the reality of knowing she was in the same room as him was shockingly stomach-churning.

"We're here because I want to talk to Markus," Becca said.

Adam's jaw went slack in a stunned response. "Wow. That sounds like a *really* bad idea."

"I couldn't agree more," Crys said. Just the thought of Becca standing face to face with that man was enough to make her want to buy a couple of one-way tickets to Mexico and leave tonight.

He escorted them into the ballroom. The absolute *last* place they should be: a large room filled with marked members of the Hawkspear Society.

The ballroom was unlike anything Crys had ever seen outside of TV shows about glitzy millionaires plotting, scheming, and working on their rap sheets, all while looking fabulous. She tried not to be distracted by the all the gorgeous gemstone jewelry and designer clutches the women here were sporting.

Adam drew them into an alcove near the bar. His eyes darted around the room, as if he were searching for potential eavesdroppers or threats. "Then how about you reconsider? Like, immediately?"

"Not going to happen," Becca said. "This is important."

"I don't know if anything's that important."

Every cell in Crys's body wanted to scream at Becca that she was insane, that she needed to listen to the advice of Adam Grayson, of all people. But she knew Becca wouldn't listen. For all their differences, her sister was every bit as stubborn as she was.

Crys had her own reasons for wanting to be here, despite how dangerous it was for both of them. She, too, searched the room from their current position. "Adam, is my father here?" she asked, her throat tight.

Adam's jaw grew tense. "I don't think so," he said quietly. "I haven't seen him since . . . that night."

"Do you . . . do you think he's okay?"

"I don't know," he replied after a brief pause. His expression was grimmer than Crys would have liked. "I'll try to find out, though. I promise. Try not to worry, okay?"

She just nodded. But she was worried. Very worried, and she couldn't put it out of her mind any longer.

"So I really can't convince you two to leave?" Adam said.

"Nope," Becca replied simply. "I have to do this. There's no other way."

"You really think you're just going to waltz up to Markus and talk to him?" Adam asked, clearly frustrated now. "And what? Ask him for a truce and then invite him over for tea?"

"I have information that I know will interest him," Becca said.

Adam scoffed. "The only thing you have that he's interested in is that book. His interest in it is so strong that I'm surprised you're even still here in the city with it, let alone that you'd risk coming here tonight. You two are crazy thinking you could sneak in here. Your whole family is crazy!"

Becca scowled at him. "*You're* the one who helped us get in. I'm surprised you even recognized us."

"Sorry, but those little masks aren't exactly the best disguise. You two are kind of impossible to miss."

Don't trust him. The thought entered Crys's mind so clearly, so intrusively, it was as if someone had whispered it directly in her ear. *He's one of them.*

Crys eyed Adam with renewed distrust.

"Where's Markus?" Becca asked.

Adam regarded both of them in turn, frowning. "He was here, but he left with some blond woman after his speech. Not sure if he'll be back, but we can keep watch for him."

Crys and Becca shared a tense look. The blond woman had to be Jackie.

"We're too late," Crys said under her breath.

"No, we don't know that," Becca replied.

Crys gave Adam a skeptical look. "What now? Are you going to alert your little club members that we're here?"

"Crys," Becca hissed. "He's trying to help us."

"She's right, I am," Adam said, his expression tight. "You could try to give me a chance to prove it. Come with me."

He's trying to manipulate you, make you let down your guard. Be very careful with him, or you'll regret it.

Crys winced at the probable truth in that thought. She needed to remember not to trust anyone, especially a Grayson.

Skeptically, and with every inch of her body tense and ready to run if she had to, she followed Adam and Becca toward Adam's table. While they walked, she scanned the ballroom for signs of either safety or danger but instead saw only about five hundred people enjoying themselves. The band was playing a strings cover of an up-tempo soul song to a full dance floor illuminated by sparkling, pink-tinted lights.

Crys searched for her aunt in the sea of masked faces but couldn't find her anywhere. If the blond woman Markus had left the ballroom with was, in fact, Jackie, then she had to be here somewhere. Though *somewhere* could still mean out of eyeshot. Which meant that anything could happen now.

Markus could already be dead.

Or Jackie could have failed and could now be facing the wrath of a murderous immortal.

The thought was so bone-chilling that Crys knew she couldn't focus on it and still keep her eyes on the prize: finding her father and keeping Becca safe.

Crys was willing to give this another ten minutes, and then they had to get out of there, no matter what.

Adam stopped in front of a table with an impeccable view of the whole dance floor. In the middle of it was a centerpiece of roses and lilies, the same as on every other table, only this bouquet seemed a bit bigger and fresher than the rest. The table was mostly empty—everyone was dancing, Crys guessed—but there was a woman sitting there who was impossible to miss. She was beautiful, with jet black hair pulled into a simple yet perfect twist. Behind her feathered mask Crys saw a kohl-lined pair of eyes in a most familiar shade of hazel, eyes that scanned the ballroom floor as if searching for someone.

"This is my mother, Isabelle Grayson," Adam said. "Mom, I'd like you to meet my friends Becca and Crystal."

Crys looked again at Isabelle Grayson's hazel eyes, immediately knowing why they were familiar and dismayed that she so vividly remembered even the smallest details of Farrell's face.

"Lovely to meet you," Mrs. Grayson said distractedly. "With whom are you here? Perhaps I know your family."

"They're here with me," Adam said before either of them could utter a word.

Mrs. Grayson arched an eyebrow, finally giving Adam her full attention. "Oh? Is that so?"

"It is."

"You didn't tell me you'd invited friends."

"Sorry, I totally forgot. Crystal and Becca are very involved in the city's literary scene. I thought they would really enjoy this event."

"And we do," Becca said readily. "It's incredible."

"Involved with literacy, are you? That's lovely. In what way?"

"We work in a bookshop," Crys said. She took a seat—her heels were already killing her—and couldn't help eyeing the mostly untouched platters of tiny fancy cheesecakes and raspberry tarts arranged on the table. Her stomach grumbled. She couldn't remember the last time she ate.

"Booksellers," Mrs. Grayson said. "How wonderful that such a quaint profession is allowed to thrive in our city."

"Actually, Mom, what they do is vitally important to literacy," Adam said. "Without booksellers, no one would be able to buy books to read. Books are kind of the main reason we're here tonight, right, Mom?"

"Yes," Mrs. Grayson replied, her red lips pursed. "How very right you are. I apologize; I'm a bit distracted at the moment."

"Everything all right?" Adam put his hand on his mother's shoulder.

She patted his hand. "Nothing more than an unwelcome ghost from the past, darling. It's fine."

"Becca, sit down," Crys whispered. "Have something to eat."

"I'm not hungry," Becca said, turning around in her chair and scanning the room.

Crys grabbed Becca's hand, squeezed it hard, and pulled her sister down into the seat next to her. The last thing she wanted right now was for Becca to hone in on Markus—or worse, for Markus to hone in on her.

"I'll get you both something to drink," Adam said, rising from his seat.

This kid's seriously too good to be true. It's all an act.

A glass of champagne suddenly appeared on the table directly in front of Crys. Immediately, her neck grew tense, and she chanced a glance up and over her shoulder to see who had placed it there.

Oh no, she thought, as her gaze locked with a pair of unforgettable hazel eyes.

"No need, little brother," Farrell said, his tone as smug as ever. "I've got it covered."

"I'm not thirsty," Crys managed.

She glanced at Becca. From the tightness of her jaw and the poisonous glare in her blue eyes, it was clear that she remembered Farrell from the theater that night. Crys had shared little else with her sister about that snake or the things that had happened between them.

Farrell walked around the table so that he faced Crys and Becca. He looked far too relaxed and confident in his perfectly fitting tuxedo, and Crys imagined that this must be what the devil himself looked like when he got dressed up to go out on the town to devour some souls.

"Don't be silly," Farrell said. "Everyone's always thirsty for champagne."

"Farrell?" Mrs. Grayson said in the least convincing fake-nice voice Crys had ever heard. "Do you know these girls?"

"Oh, sure. Crys and I, we're practically the best of friends. Aren't we, Crys? But I had no idea you were going to be here tonight. And Becca—so glad to see you're feeling better. What a wonderful surprise to see you both."

Becca glared at him. "The feeling isn't mutual."

"Oh—ouch." He pressed his hand against his heart. "That hurts. Come on, Crys—that's expensive bubbly. Drink up."

Crys finally grabbed the champagne by the stem and pulled it toward her. But she refused to take a sip.

"It's not poisoned," he assured her.

"Better safe than sorry," she said.

"Best of friends, you say?" Mrs. Grayson eyed them all with a furrowed brow. "Apparently, Adam invited Crystal and Becca to the ball without telling anyone."

"Hmm. Well, Adam's in the habit of surprising the people he's closest to these days. Aren't you, Adam?"

"I learned from the best," Adam retorted.

"Farrell, where's Felicity?" Mrs. Grayson asked. Clearly she was accustomed to ignoring any tension between her children.

"Somewhere," Farrell replied, clearly untroubled. "I lost track of her a while ago after dealing with that little annoyance of ours, Mother, but I'm sure she'll turn up eventually. She always does. In the meantime . . ."

Crys eyed him warily as he extended his right hand to her.

"What?" she asked sharply.

"Dance with me."

"Hell no."

Mrs. Grayson responded to Crys's rude reply with an audible gasp.

Farrell's smile grew wider. "Oh, come on. Humor me. We're in a beautiful ballroom, and the band is playing beautiful music. You're a beautiful girl, I'm a beautiful guy. Why let all this beauty go to waste? I'm sure Becca wouldn't mind."

"Becca *does* mind," said Becca.

"Then luckily for me, it's Crys's decision."

"No," Crys said again, more firmly.

"Disgraceful," Mrs. Grayson muttered.

"Farrell," Adam growled. "Leave her alone."

"One more try," Farrell said, then he leaned over to hover above Crys's ear. "Dance with me," he whispered, "or I'll go up to the microphone and tell everybody who you and your sister really are. There'll be no more hiding then, will there?"

Her heart pounded as she considered his ultimatum.

She'd never been blackmailed before, and she hated to admit that it was incredibly effective.

Forcing a smile of her own, she took his hand. "Fine. One song."

"That's more like it."

With one last apologetic glance and a reassuring nod sent toward a worried-looking Becca, Crys let Farrell lead her to the crowded dance floor. He entwined his fingers with hers and placed his other hand on the small of her back.

"You smell like strawberries again," he said.

She looked up at him, surprised to discover that at this close vantage point she could see dark circles under his eyes. "And you look like you haven't slept in a couple of days."

"Can you blame me? I've been tossing and turning all night, thinking about you and how to win you back."

With anyone else she'd reply with a polite laugh, but there was nothing remotely funny about this. "Where's my father?" she said bluntly.

"Not here."

"Then where is he?"

"No idea. I'm not his personal assistant."

She wanted to scream. "Is this fun for you? These games you play?"

"So much fun. And what game is it you're playing tonight? Don't tell me you're only here to ask around about your father. I know there's something else that drew you into this sticky little spider web. Or is it just what my mother thinks, that you're here to celebrate literacy because your family owns a local bookshop?"

She tried to look anywhere but up at him, dismayed at being stuck so close to him. "That's the first true thing I've heard you say all night. Yes, we do own a bookshop."

"A famous bookshop that's currently closed until further notice. All those poor readers, hungry for books, but no one to buy them from." Reluctantly, she listened to him talk as he slowly moved her around the dance floor—with far more skill than she might have guessed. "You know, this is the perfect song."

"What song is it?"

"'The Look of Love.'" He smirked. "See? That look you're giving me right now . . . it's sizzling."

"That's probably because I'm trying to burn your eyeballs out of your head with the power of my mind while I wish I'd never met you."

His expression grew more pensive. "Our relationship started off so much better. You were real with me. Believe it or not, that's not something I experience too often. That . . . *realness*. I liked it."

"Everything that comes out of your mouth is a lie."

"Not everything. Eighty-eight percent, tops."

"You blackmailed me to get me onto this dance floor."

"Desperate times call for desperate measures. Maybe I wanted the chance to talk to you without my mother and both of our siblings listening in."

There was a strange weight to his words now that was absent before. Suddenly, that weight grabbed hold of her full attention.

In mere seconds, her heart rate had doubled. "So talk. If you have something important to say, say it. Are you actually going to tell me where my father is? Can you help me? Would you even be *willing* to help me?"

He wouldn't meet her gaze. "Maybe I'm still lying. Maybe the only reason I wanted you to dance with me is to make Felicity jealous."

Crys tried to pull away, but he held on tight.

"Sorry," he said. "That's my defensive-asshole mechanism kicking in. For what it's worth, she means nothing to me."

She glared up at him. "You're not making this any better."

"I guess what I'm trying to tell you is . . . you don't have to be afraid of me."

"Who said I was afraid of you?"

He laughed, but the sound was humorless. "I'm not exactly good at being genuine, so just try to take me at face value tonight. Maybe I deserve your hatred, but that doesn't change the fact that I don't want you to hate me."

This was the point when she should have been pushing him away and storming back to Becca at the table, but something held her in place. Her hands rested lightly on his shoulders, and from a distance, she was sure they looked like any other couple on the dance floor.

She searched his face, his intense eyes—a swirling mix of taupe and emerald—framed with thick black lashes, his dark brows drawn together into a serious expression. Her gaze came to rest on the spot under his right eye where his birthmark used to be.

"Why did you have it removed?" she asked.

He blinked. "It was ugly."

She disagreed, but she wasn't about to admit it out loud. "It healed fast."

"Accelerated healing comes with the territory." His jaw tight-ened. "Actually, I sliced it off myself."

She regarded him with horror. "*What?*"

"I only wish I could cut every ugly part out of myself, but then I guess there'd be nothing left."

For a moment, she found herself utterly speechless. "Farrell, my God, why would you even *tell* me something like that, let alone think or do it?"

"Because sometimes I speak the truth. Don't ask me why I chose to reveal that in particular." His gaze became clouded with confusion and his frown deepened. "No damn idea, really."

It was as if everyone else on the dance floor had vanished and she and he were out there alone. She was staring up at him—his perfect face, perfect hair, gorgeous eyes, tailored tuxedo that felt like the softest silk beneath her touch. And his scent—some musky cologne or aftershave that she hated herself for appreciating even a little.

Was she starting to feel something other than loathing for him? She couldn't be. That would require her to care in some way about the fate of Farrell Grayson, marks or no marks.

All she cared about right now was her family. To hell with everyone else.

You don't really believe that. Farrell needs your help—just like your mother does—with the marks that control him, that make him do such awful things. You know you can't turn your back on someone in that great of need.

"Fine, I'll admit it," she said after another long pause between them. "I did like you when we first met, and I don't think I hid it very well. Was any of that really you?"

"More than you might think."

"I know what the marks do," Crys said, her throat tight. "They *change* you. They mess with your head, with your morals. Markus controls you now—you and everyone in his society."

"Markus doesn't control me. No one is in control of me except me." Farrell had stiffened at the accusation, but he didn't draw back from her.

"Look at me," she said. Finally, he met her gaze, and she searched his eyes for some clue as to what he might really be feeling. "He made you do something you didn't want to do, didn't he?"

His brow furrowed. "Why would you say that?"

"Call it a hunch. Was it . . . something really bad?"

"The worst," he whispered so quietly that she could barely hear him over the crowd.

"Tell me."

After a long pause, he answered. "You know, these eyes of yours—this pale, icy blue that bores right into my soul—they've haunted me since the first day we met."

No one had ever said anything like that to her. Again, he'd rendered her completely speechless.

This is bad, she thought. *Very bad. I can't let him get to me like this.*

And what would be the worst thing to happen if you did?

She didn't have the energy to push the thoughts away this time. When Farrell drew her even closer to him, she didn't immediately pull away.

"Your eyes are just like your father's, aren't they?" He leaned closer to whisper in her ear. "Becca also has her father's eyes—dark blue, like the ocean at dusk."

That was all it took to shock her out of whatever spell she'd fallen under. Her mind snapped back into clear focus as she tried to break away, but he only tightened his hold.

"That's right," Farrell said evenly. "Markus knows the truth. And he needs that book."

"I have no idea what you're talking about," she managed, but already she knew that she'd lost this battle.

"Huh. It seems I'm not the only liar here tonight, am I?"

"Let go of me," she snarled, and she tugged away as hard as she could.

Finally, he released her, just as the song was dying down but before the band had come to a complete stop. She turned and headed right toward the table where she'd left Becca.

But Becca was gone.

Chapter 15

BECCA

The shadow that was invisible to everyone but Becca remained with her, even here at the ball, so far away from the book. Right now it lurked beneath the round dinner table at which she sat, while she tried to feel at ease in her fancy clothes and high heels—a big departure from her usual style, which consisted primarily of jeans, sneakers, and sweaters. She felt like a completely different person tonight.

"What on earth is going on?" Isabelle Grayson muttered under her breath a moment after Farrell and Crys took to the dance floor.

The haughty woman gave Becca a bad vibe from the first moment she saw her, even before Adam introduced them. Even from a seated position, she'd managed to look down her nose at them.

"What do you mean?" Adam asked.

"Farrell and that . . . *girl*. They're not . . . involved, are they?"

"It's just a dance, Mom."

"Doesn't look like just a dance to me." She eyed Becca. "Let me guess: You have your sights set on Farrell's younger brother?"

"Um," Becca stumbled, "I barely know Adam."

Thankfully, a tall willowy blonde approached the table before

Mrs. Grayson could counter. The blonde held two glasses of champagne, one of which she gave to Mrs. Grayson.

"Felicity, darling," Mrs. Grayson said after taking a sip. "Have you heard that my Adam has gone out of his way to bring two young booksellers to this event? Quite a foolish way for him to spend his allowance, don't you think?"

"I suppose it depends on how much he likes the booksellers," Felicity replied, eyeing Becca. "Where is Farrell?"

Mrs. Grayson flicked her hand toward the dance floor. "Having a spin with the other one."

Felicity peered through the crowd with widening eyes. "I know her," she said after a heavy pause. "We met at the photography show on Sunday. She's Farrell's ex-girlfriend."

"Whoa, what?" Becca blurted, horrified at the suggestion. "She's definitely *not* his ex-girlfriend."

Mrs. Grayson straightened her shoulders even more. "I should certainly hope not."

"I think I need more champagne," Felicity said weakly and turned away.

"As do I." Mrs. Grayson made a little huffing noise in the back of her throat. "If you'll excuse me, I see some colleagues I need to say hello to."

She stood up and left them alone at the table, disappearing into the crowd.

"So . . . ," Becca said. "She seems nice?"

Adam snorted. "Sorry about her. She's kind of, uh, how do I put it . . . ?"

"Not super open to adding to her friend group?"

"I was going to say *a major snob*, but that works too."

Becca's heart raced. Every cell in her body wanted to get up, move around, search for Markus, and do what she came here to do before she chickened out.

She knew Crys thought she was crazy. Hell, she probably was. But what was that saying? She'd read it once in a novel about the Civil War, and it had stuck with her ever since: *The enemy of my enemy is my friend.* She knew Markus was no one's friend here, not really. But she also knew for a fact—had seen it with her own eyes—that Valoria was obsessed with seeking vengeance on him for stealing the dagger. And from what little Becca knew about Valoria, she was fairly certain that the immortal didn't have any plans to cease her hunt for Markus, no matter what world she might find him in. She also knew that, Codex or no Codex, Valoria would be after Maddox for his rare magic that could help open the gateway between worlds.

Which only made Becca worry more about Maddox than she already did. It was so strange—the whole time her spirit was in Mytica, all she'd cared about was finding a way to get back home. Now, she felt completely different. She didn't want to go *back* there, of course . . . but she did wish there was a way to communicate with him.

The shadow was no help at all—unless the definition of *help* had been changed to include constant and unnerving distraction.

Please be okay, Maddox, she thought, her heart twisting.

"You still with me?" Adam asked, pulling her away from those clinging thoughts.

"Mostly." Becca gave him a weak smile, then turned her gaze again on Crys and Farrell, who were still dancing. She was surprised that her sister hadn't stormed off the floor yet or kicked him in the groin. She'd even give away her cherished signed copy of *The Fault in Our Stars* to witness that.

"Why would that girl Felicity think that Crys is his ex?" Becca mumbled. "As if that could ever be a possibility. Crys hates your brother."

"Doesn't look like it to me." Becca glared at him, and Adam flinched. "Sorry," he said. "I mean, I totally understand why you hate him. Why *she* hates him. He's made a pretty terrible first impression on both of you. But all of that—the things he's been doing and saying lately—that's not really him. It's those marks."

"So I keep hearing. The marks." She'd really come to hate that previously common word. "Those marks are the reason my father left to be with Markus and Hawkspear instead of with us."

Adam nodded apologetically. "They're powerful. Even just one is enough to trap you and make you completely deny that anything's wrong."

"You don't deny it, though. And you're in the society."

"I'm different from the others, I guess," he said, glancing around nervously.

"And Farrell hasn't sold you out yet?"

"No." He shook his head grimly. "And he won't."

"Don't be so sure."

"Yeah, well, you don't know him like I do. He's actually pretty decent. Well, most of the time. I think all the power and importance he's been feeling recently have messed with his head—along with everything else that's been going on. I'm not surprised. My mother's always treated him like a second-class citizen, always telling him he's a disappointment. He shrugs it off, but I know it hurts him."

"Well, I've met your mother now. And I get the feeling that there's not much in this world that *wouldn't* disappoint her."

Adam smiled slightly, but then worry crossed his expression

again. "My whole life, whenever I've needed him, Farrell's been there for me. More like a friend than a brother. Even more than Connor was."

"Connor?" Becca asked absently. Again she was distracted by Crys and Farrell and was trying very hard to send Crys a mental message: *Come back. He's hot, but he's also Markus's brainwashed minion, remember?*

"My oldest brother. Or he *was* my oldest brother."

She turned immediately back to face him. "I'm so sorry."

"Thanks. He died last year. It was in the news." Adam offered her another small, sad smile. "Our family's kind of famous in this city, you know."

"So I'm learning."

"Yeah. Well, when it happened, Connor was very much in Markus's good graces, just like Farrell is now. That's another reason why I'm worried about him. I know Farrell never believed that Connor killed himself. From the moment they found him, Farrell felt in his gut that he was murdered and that whoever did it wanted to make it look like suicide. I'm starting to wonder if he might be right."

"Oh my God," Becca gasped.

"If it is true, I'd be surprised if it didn't have something to do with Markus. The timing's way too coincidental."

Becca studied Adam Grayson for a long moment, trying to decide whether or not she could trust him. He *had* already helped her and Crys twice now, and it was clear he felt the same way about Markus and his influence that the Hatchers did. She didn't want to give him every detail about what their research had concluded—that they needed to get the dagger as soon as possible to try to put an end to this whole terrible chain of events—but the truth was that she could really use some help from someone on the inside.

Suddenly, something caught Adam's eye, and his gaze shifted to somewhere beyond Becca. His expression darkened.

Becca glanced over her shoulder. There, making his way through the crowd, was Markus King. Her breath caught in her chest. This was her chance, but she felt completely paralyzed.

No, Becca told herself. *No second thoughts.* She knew what she had to do. And right here, in the middle of a huge party, provided the safest environment to do it.

Unless . . .

"How many people here are in the Hawkspear Society?" she asked Adam warily.

Adam thought for a moment, scanning the room. "Less than half, I'd say."

The tight feeling that had built up in her chest eased off by a fraction. "That means more than half of them *aren't* under Markus's spell?"

"What, you're imagining all the Hawkspears will start grabbing at you like zombies if they see you approach their leader at a public event?"

"That's exactly what I was thinking, actually."

She turned back to the crowd to make sure she didn't lose track of Markus, and a familiar flash of blond hair caught her eye. Jackie was trailing only a few paces behind Markus, her gaze fixed on him like a predator on her prey.

Becca stood up, the black shadow slithering out from under the table along with her. She spared it only a short glance before returning her attention to Markus and Jackie.

"Are you even listening to me?" Adam's voice was wary as he

touched her arm. "Markus is dangerous. He kidnapped you a week ago, or did you forget that already?"

"I have to do this."

"You are seriously the most frustrating girl I've ever met." His jaw was set as he also watched Markus. "Is there any way I can talk you out of this?"

"No."

"What you're doing—what you think you're doing . . ." He hesitated. "Do you think there's a chance that it could help free my brother? Free my family from that man?"

The pain in his voice captured her full attention. She met his gaze. "I don't know. It's possible."

Adam responded with only a solemn gaze, but Becca saw enough sadness and empathy in it to keep going.

"Will you help me?" she asked. "I need to get close to him."

Adam was silent for so long that Becca began to worry she'd made a horrible mistake—what if his big speech about morality was all a ploy to get her to trust him when he was the last person she should begin to trust? What if his questions about helping his family were part of the same ploy? She was seriously considering bolting when, finally, Adam nodded firmly.

"Fine," he said. "Let's go."

Becca let out a small sigh of relief. They began making their way across the crowded ballroom.

Valoria claimed that she wanted that dagger to ensure that the mortals she used it on would be loyal, obedient, and trustworthy. She'd used those exact words—*loyalty, obedience, and trust*—but that was a very mild way of saying what she actually had in mind.

What the goddess really wanted was an army of slaves.

Was that what Markus already had in half of these people in

the ballroom tonight, dressed to the nines in their sparkles and masks? Were all these refined members of high society merely slaves required to carry out any evil deed their master commanded of them?

Becca knew how strong and determined Jackie was and that her heart was definitely in the right place. Jackie wanted to save her family and prevent an evil man from doing even more harm, but was she a fool to go after a dangerous immortal who possessed so much power?

Then again, wasn't that almost exactly the same thing that Becca was doing?

All Becca could do was hope that her theory was right: that destroying that dagger would free not just her mother but everyone in Markus's secret society.

With Adam close by her side, she kept Markus and Jackie in her sight. She watched Markus pluck two glasses of champagne from a passing tray while her aunt lurked behind him. Markus turned around, practically facing Jackie now, and Becca almost flinched. But Jackie didn't turn away or act aloof. She just stood there while Markus King handed her a glass of champagne, which she accepted.

Should this have come as such a surprise to Becca? Jackie and Julia were known to Markus, of course. The Kendalls had been a part of the society for generations until the sisters had left it. Jackie must have figured that the best way to get closer to Markus would be to play the *long time, no see* card so she could butter him up and get the dagger.

And kill him.

Becca and Adam followed the pair to the back of the ballroom, opposite the entrance, to an archway that led into a small alcove.

Becca pressed back against the wall and signaled Adam to do the same next to her, making sure that they were out of sight of the pair but still within earshot of their conversation. The ball continued in full view only twenty feet away.

The shadow came to rest next to the nearest empty table, its occupants currently on the adjacent dance floor. She stared at the inky blot of darkness as she strained her ears to hear anything over the sound of the band and the constant din of conversation.

"You spared no expense tonight," Jackie said. "This is wonderful champagne."

"Do you remember your first taste?" Markus replied.

"How could I forget? It's not like every girl gets her first sip of champagne while sitting in the shadow of the Eifel Tower with . . . well, someone like you."

"I'm so glad you came tonight. I wasn't sure you would."

"I wasn't sure I would either. But I'm glad too."

Becca and Adam exchanged a confused look. After seeing that first exchange with the champagne, Becca had certainly been expecting her aunt to flirt, but this discussion seemed *too* friendly. More than flirting. These two had history. Much more than two people merely acquainted through a shared organization should have.

"Honestly, Markus?" Jackie continued. "I'm amazed by your patience all these years."

"With the book, you mean? Or with you?"

"Both, really. I know how furious you must have been to have lost it in the exact same moment you found it."

"I went about things in a foolish way. I know that now, and I apologize. Knowing how much you hated me . . . I felt my choices were limited."

"The thing about hatred is that it almost always fades over

time. Whether you want it to or not—the heart just can't keep up with all that effort."

"I've always believed just the opposite," Markus replied without skipping a beat. Becca could sense a heavy hesitation hanging between them, until Markus spoke again. "I will say it again, my love: I didn't kill your family. It wasn't me."

My love?

Becca was certain she must have heard him wrong. Why would he say something so intimate to Jackie?

Her aunt inhaled sharply. "That is what I was led to believe as a child, yes. But time has taught me that not everything is as it seems. My parents died in a car accident, plain and simple and so tragic because it was so senseless. I was furious at that senselessness, so when the idea was introduced, it was easier to blame you. And I'm sorry for that. And Grandmother . . . I see now that she took her own life."

Becca felt Adam grow tense. She reached out to clutch his hand.

Another Markus-adjacent suicide, and a suspicious car accident too. It could be a coincidence. But Becca didn't really believe in coincidences—especially not when Markus was involved.

Anyway, Becca couldn't really focus on any of that at the moment. Those two words—*my love*—kept echoing in her mind over and over again.

Oh my God, she thought.

They were together when Jackie was in the society. When she hadn't been much older than Becca herself. Is that what that meant? Or was she reading too much into it?

A wave of nausea shot through her like a lightning bolt as she thought of her teenaged aunt falling in love with Markus, an ancient immortal being who treated murder like a day at the office.

She couldn't breathe.

Becca had to find a way to focus, to keep her mind from reeling over this revelation. She closed her eyes and steadied her breath. *Okay. Maybe it's a good thing Markus still has feelings for Jackie,* she thought. Maybe this was even what Jackie was hoping for—and with good reason too. Perhaps his love for her was the only thing that had kept him from muscling his way into Angus's apartment and killing everyone in his path to get to the Codex.

"I have a confession to make, Markus," Jackie said. Becca blinked away all the distracting thoughts from her head and listened, rapt. "I came here tonight to ask something of you. A personal favor."

"What's that?"

"The golden dagger," Jackie said, and Becca's heart leaped into her throat. Jackie continued before Markus could say a word. "I know it's a lot to ask, but I want to see it again. I just want to learn more about it. As I'm sure you already know, I've become involved in an organization that has a special interest in such pieces."

"You assume I've been keeping tabs on you all this time?" Markus's question was innocent enough—he didn't fly into a rage at Jackie's mention of the dagger, as Becca would have expected. But there was a definite change in the tone of his voice, a note of something that wasn't there before.

"I do."

"Well, you assume correctly. And to say I don't approve of your choice of vocation would be to put it mildly. These thieves you've chosen to associate yourself with—you're part of something dangerous."

"There you go again, just as overprotective of me as ever."

"I didn't want you to get hurt. I still don't."

"I know."

"What are you asking of me, Jackie? What do you want to do?

Photograph the dagger? Put it into some kind of database to which your ring of thieves has access?"

"It's not just a ring of thieves, Markus. It's a group of people who are passionate about learning what lies beyond this world. About the possibility of magic within our—everyone's—reach. It's important work that could lead to better ways to protect everyone in this world—which is exactly what you say your society is trying to do."

"Yes, of course. That work does sound very important."

Doubt. That's what now coated Markus's words.

If Becca heard it, Jackie must have as well.

"I do understand if this is something you don't want to share. I know how important that dagger is to the society."

"Do you? Because if you truly understood its importance, you wouldn't ask such a favor of me. Especially given how long we've been apart."

"Forget I mentioned it," Jackie said with a nervous twist of her voice.

"I don't know if that's possible, Jackie. Is this a game to you? Coming here, trying to convince me that you've seen the error of your ways, that all is forgiven? I wanted to trust you. I really did. But I see that nothing's changed between us. That, aside from your improved ability to lie, you haven't changed at all."

Becca's stomach sank. Her aunt had moved too quickly, and it didn't seem like she could recover.

"Really, Markus? You *wanted* to trust me?" Now there was something new in Jackie's tone as well, a bite of iciness that chilled even Becca.

"Of course I did," Markus said. "I knew you would bring me the book eventually, of your own free will, no less. I am not a patient person, but when it comes to you, it seems I have all the patience in the world."

"I see. Funny, though, because if that were true, you never would have started messing with Julia's mind again."

"What are you talking about?"

"I know you've been calling her, tapping back into her society marks to control her."

"I've done nothing of the sort," Markus said, impressing Becca with how genuinely scandalized he seemed. "Her marks were always weak, from the very beginning. I only allowed her to remain in the society because she was your sister, and a Kendall. Your marks, on the other hand, are completely gone. I tried to find you through them so many times, and I never succeeded. I always wondered why."

"I guess they didn't take as well as you always thought," Jackie said, but her voice had grown quiet and timid, the iciness gone now.

"It was the pregnancy," Markus said coolly. "Wasn't it?"

Jackie fell silent. The accusation hung in the air between them as Becca tried to make sense of what Markus just said. Jackie, pregnant? As far as Becca knew, this couldn't be further from the truth.

"See? You don't attempt to deny it because you know it's useless. I know." Markus spoke slowly, his tone calm and even. "Becca is my daughter."

Becca pressed herself hard against the wall so she wouldn't fall when her legs gave out beneath her.

"Markus, I—"

"You've hidden her from me all these years, but now there will be no more hiding, Jackie. She's mine. She belongs to me now."

Becca's mind had gone blank and silent. Behind her eyes was a dark and empty cavern where nothing but the devastation of this moment existed.

"Becca is my daughter."

"Becca." Adam was whispering to her. Dimly, she realized that he had hooked his arm through hers and was helping to keep her vertical.

"I think I'm going to be sick," she managed.

This couldn't be real. It *couldn't*. Markus was lying, and Jackie was just too scared to deny it.

"I want the Codex, and I want the girl," Markus growled. "And I want you out of my sight."

With that, he turned and stormed out of the alcove to enter the main ballroom again. Adam tried to shock Becca into moving on her own, to maneuver in time to get out of Markus's line of sight, but it was too late. The immortal fixed his hawkish eyes on Becca's dazed ones. She stared at him, frozen in place, seeing him as if for the first time.

His dark blue eyes . . . the oval curve of his face . . . the slight dimple in his chin . . .

They were just like hers.

Jackie emerged from the alcove a moment later, a look of fierceness lighting up her face. But when she saw Becca, her hand flew to her mouth, and all that fiery determination was extinguished.

Markus hadn't moved, hadn't taken his attention away from Becca for one moment.

"Becca," Jackie gasped. "What are you doing here?"

Becca tried to speak, to make any sound at all, but she couldn't. Her reeling mind and shattered heart wouldn't let her.

Tears began to stream down Jackie's face. "Damn it, Becca!" she swore loudly. "I told you to stay home, where it's safe."

"Nowhere is safe," Markus said under his breath. "You should know that by now."

Becca wasn't crying—another thing her heart and mind wouldn't let her do—but her body felt as cold as ice. Like one little fall would shatter her into a million pieces.

So this was real. If it were a nightmare, someone—Jackie, Adam, even Markus—would have told her.

The shadow at her feet drew closer to her, weaving back and forth at the floor before her in a slow figure eight. She started to shiver, and Adam took off his suit jacket and put it around her shoulders.

"Why?" Becca finally managed to ask, her voice cracking. "Why didn't you tell me?"

Jackie wiped at her tears and stole an apprehensive glance at Markus. "If you hurt her, I swear I'll kill you."

Markus tore his gaze from Becca and glared harshly at Jackie.

Becca knew he was about to say something atrocious, something that might result in more damage than she could have ever been prepared for. But before he could say or do a single thing, a loud crashing sound rang out across the ballroom. They froze and turned to watch a group of about a dozen people dressed in black come through the entrance on the opposite side. They all wore thick black ski masks—not the kind found on a guest at a masquerade ball.

One of them raised a gun and pointed it at the ceiling. He fired off a shot, and the whole party fell into absolute silence.

Chapter 16

FARRELL

The second the gunshot went off, his forearm lit up with a sharp, burning pain.

"*You have to find Markus,*" not-Connor's voice instructed him. "*He's going to need you.*"

Farrell frowned. His mother and Felicity both looked at him fearfully from across the table.

"*Forget them,*" Connor snapped. "*Markus is more important—you know this already.*"

He stood up and scanned the room, all of his senses ramping up to better help him focus. His vision was clear, his hearing precise.

"*There he is. Go—now!*"

Without a word, he left his mother and Felicity and, keeping his head low, swiftly weaved his way through the crowd. Every single guest was frozen in place as the group of masked and armed intruders entered the ballroom.

Markus stood on the far side of the dance floor, his arms crossed over his chest, his jaw tight. The moment he reached the Hawkspear leader's side, a horrible tightness eased in Farrell's chest, and the burning pain in his arm subsided somewhat.

"What the hell is this, Markus?" Farrell said under his breath as the invaders continued to spread out in the ballroom. Two of them stayed in front of the main doors, guns ready, while a third approached from the reception area and roughly pushed Gloria St. Pierre inside. The old lady cowered in terror.

"I've no idea," Markus said, scanning the room, his eyes darting and mouth set in a tense grimace.

Farrell waited for Markus to follow his flat reply with some sort of explanation or proposed solution, but when neither came, a dark sense of doom descended upon him and settled squarely in his chest.

"Where're Mom and Dad?" Adam asked.

His brother's voice managed to pull him from his intense focus on Markus, and he blinked, as if emerging from a daydream.

"Adam, I . . . ," he began, but then faltered as his gaze shifted to the others standing near Markus. Adam had his arm around Becca, who now wore his dark blue suit jacket over her shoulders. Next to them was another woman: the beautiful blonde who'd captured Markus's full attention at the end of his speech.

Jackie Kendall.

Her eyes were red and glossy but fierce, and the look she gave Farrell was one of disgust and hatred. It was a near match for the look on Becca's face.

Something had happened here between them—something big.

"Somebody needs to call 9-1-1," Adam growled. "I left my phone at the table."

Farrell pulled his phone out of his pocket.

"Don't," Markus said immediately. "I'm curious to see what they want."

Farrell frowned down at the phone. It couldn't find a network connection; he couldn't call anyone even if he wanted to.

"Can you can stop them?" he asked.

"If they give me a reason to."

"Take more of my strength if you need it," Farrell whispered only loud enough for Markus to hear. As much as he dreaded the pain and weakness that would follow another draining of his vitality, he would happily suffer if it meant that Markus could stomp all over these gunmen.

"Hopefully that won't be necessary," Markus replied.

Farrell watched as one of the thugs walked down a line of frozen, whimpering party guests, scanning them closely as if he were appraising items for a pawn shop.

"*A bunch of pathetic thieves,*" not-Connor said. "*They heard about the ball and came here thinking they'd have their pick of the finest jewelry and fattest wallets in the city.*"

Idiots. Farrell couldn't wait to watch Markus destroy them one by one.

"*And you'll be more than happy to help,*" Connor added.

Yes, he certainly would be.

Suddenly, a thirty-something-year-old man, still in his costume mask, bolted toward the exit and tried to run past the two men stationed there. They were ready for him. The bigger gunman grabbed him, while the other hit him over the head with the butt of his gun. He dropped to the ground with a sickening thud.

"Remain calm!" boomed a voice before Farrell could properly react. One of the black-clad gunmen was standing on the other side of the dance floor, at the podium where Markus had given his speech. "Remain calm, and no one will get hurt."

"Who are you?" a man bravely demanded. Farrell strained to see who it was, but he was too far away. "What do you want?"

"End this, Markus," Jackie hissed. "What are you waiting for?"

"Not yet," he replied.

"You can't do anything, can you?" she said tauntingly. "Your magic is too faded, you couldn't even take down one of them."

Farrell eyed Markus with alarm, but Markus stayed silent, his full focus on the podium. He'd never heard anyone speak to Markus with such shocking disrespect.

"What *do* I want?" the gunman said calmly into the microphone. "What a dangerous question. Before we get into all of that, let me introduce myself."

The gunman reached up and removed his mask to reveal a startlingly pale face, jet black hair that fell to his shoulders, and no eyebrows. His eyes were completely black, like shiny buttons, no whites to be seen. The ballroom echoed with gasps, but Farrell wasn't fazed. He assumed the gunman was just wearing special contact lenses, nothing scarier than a Halloween accessory. Farrell noticed he was young—college-aged.

"My name is Damen Winter," the unmasked man said. "It's so lovely to meet you all. You want to know why I came here, what I want. Well, that's simple. It's the same thing I've always wanted, since the beginning of time." Damen paused, clearly trying to build up some dramatic suspense.

Connor's voice inwardly scoffed. *"Goth wannabe. Just some kids playing at being dark and dangerous masterminds."*

"What I want," the goth kid finally continued, "is utter chaos and destruction of this and every other world."

Farrell glanced at Markus, expecting to exchange a look of relief with him. Instead, what he saw made his stomach sink.

Markus's face was locked in an expression of complete and utter shock.

"No," Markus whispered. "It's impossible."

Farrell didn't know what to think. For a moment, he couldn't think. He'd never been more frightened than he was right now, watching Markus King show fear.

"Markus," Farrell whispered, gripping the man's shoulder. "Are you okay?"

"Who is that, Markus?" Jackie whispered, moving closer.

"You want the golden dagger, Jackie?" Markus said, his voice hoarse and hollow. "It seems you've come to the right place. Damen's magic is what created it."

Jackie shook her head, clearly baffled. "You're not making any sense."

"No, I suppose I'm not. Because *this* doesn't make sense. Damen is dead. He's supposed to be dead."

"I have a few questions for you all," Damen continued. Farrell's group went silent again, taut with fear as they focused once more on Damen. "I do hope that you will be truthful with me." He gestured to one of the gunmen, who was standing near the man who'd first shouted up at Damen. The gunman grabbed the man and pulled him to his feet.

Now that he was standing, Farrell recognized the man as a society member. Robert Micelli. He was always complaining about something at Hawkspear meetings—that his charities were being cheated out of funding, that he needed a break on his dues because his business was taking a hit in the bad economy. Whenever Robert took the floor at meetings, Farrell took it as a cue to take out his phone and tune out.

Now, however, Robert Micelli had one hundred percent of Farrell's attention.

The gunman had escorted Robert right up to the edge of the raised platform stage. "Tell me," Damen said to him. "Is Markus King here tonight?"

Robert laughed. "I think anyone with access to a search engine would know that Markus was the keynote speaker at this charity event."

"How charitable of him. Is he still here?"

"I have no idea."

"Then you're worthless to me."

Slowly, while looking directly at Robert, Damen blinked in a purposeful, rhythmic way: a horrible fluttering of white eyelids over glossy black eyes.

Robert clutched his throat. He gasped desperately several times before collapsing to the floor. His wife screamed and lunged toward the podium, falling at her husband's side.

"He's dead!" she cried out. "Oh my God! He's dead!"

Damen gestured to another man in black. This gunman yanked another guest out of her seat—a terrified woman with a purple streak in her short blond hair that exactly matched the color of her gown.

She wasn't a Hawkspear member.

"Tell me, what do you know about Markus King?" Damen asked.

The young woman darted her eyes all around the ballroom, as if seeking answers on the walls and ceiling. "I—I don't know very much about him. I think he's the son of a wealthy man . . . wh-who is involved with lots of charities?"

"You also," Damen said, "are worthless to me."

The woman cried out, her eyes rolling back into her head, and she slipped from the gunman's grasp and fell to the floor.

"Stop this!" Jackie pleaded to Markus in a whisper. "Whatever you have to do, you need to stop him!"

Markus hadn't moved an inch—had barely breathed, as far as Farrell could tell, since Damen first began plucking people off one by one.

"He's like you, isn't he?" Farrell whispered, his throat raw. "A god of death? That's who he is, right?"

Jackie snapped to attention. "Markus still has you all convinced he's a god? You society members are so weak-minded."

"Says the woman who used to sleep with him," Farrell sneered.

She glared at him. "You would too, if he asked you to. You wouldn't have a choice."

Sounds just like something a delusional ex-girlfriend would say, Farrell thought. He only had time to respond with a dismissive smirk before a harsh scream shattered the air around them.

"No!" Becca shrieked.

Farrell whipped his head around. One of Damen's gunmen stood before the podium with a new victim in his grip: Crys.

Damen regarded her calmly, cocking his head to the side. "I certainly hope you'll be of more help than those other two," he said. "Tell me: Who is Markus King?"

Crys trembled, but she kept her chin high and her ice blue eyes focused on the man behind the microphone. "He's the leader of the Hawkspear Society," she said with an impressive amount of forced confidence.

Damen gave her a chilling smile. "Finally, someone who isn't worthless. Tell me, what is the Hawkspear Society?"

"A secret organization founded about sixty years ago. Only the very wealthy are eligible to become members. They host events like this one, but mostly what they do is hold public executions at their meetings. Because Markus tells them it will make the world a better place."

Farrell felt like he was going in and out of consciousness. He wasn't sure if he was happy that Crys was still alive because she had told Damen the truth or if he was ready to kill her himself for outing Markus and the society.

He was leaning heavily toward door number two.

"Just more proof that she's trouble," Connor growled. *"And your fixation with her is a danger to Markus and the society."*

"And how old do you think he is?" Damen asked Crys, his lips curling again into that sinister smile.

"Old. I don't know how old, exactly. But ancient. He's immortal."

The ballroom rose up in gasps again, rumbles of conversation spreading through the horrified guests. Damen held up his hand but was met with only the slightest hush before the talking continued again. He sent an exasperated signal to his gunmen, and another shot was fired into the air. Plaster streamed down from the ceiling, and silence fell again.

"How old do you think *I* am?" Damen asked now.

Crys drew in a shaky breath. "If I didn't know any better, I'd say twenty or so. But since, like you said yourself, I'm no fool, I'm going to go with about the same age as Markus."

Damen let out a wretched little laugh. "Not quite. I'm much, much older than Markus." Crys just stared at him, stunned, as if resigning herself to certain death. "So I'm afraid that's one wrong answer from you."

Every muscle in Farrell's body grew tense. All the rage he'd felt toward Crys for revealing Markus's secrets fell away as he ignited with vengeful energy from within. If Damen made one move to kill her, he was ready to close the distance between him and Crys in a heartbeat.

Instead, Damen only flicked his hand. The gunman released Crys, who staggered away from the podium.

"Crys!" Becca called out to her, and Crys ran across the dance floor to reach her side in moments. The sisters embraced, tears streaming down Becca's cheeks while Crys seemed too shocked to weep. Jackie joined them, enfolding them both in her arms.

"It's okay," Crys said, stroking her sister's hair. "I'm fine."

"Let's continue, shall we?" Damen boomed from the podium again.

As he gestured toward another gunman to find the next victim, Markus's expression was rigid, eyes so furious that Farrell wondered if they might ignite.

"Enough, Damen!" Markus's voice was commanding, loud enough for everyone in the ballroom to hear. He stepped past Farrell to the edge of the dance floor.

Damen looked over and found Markus's gaze instantly. "Ah," he cooed. "There you are."

"Stop this."

"Stop what? Ending little mortal lives that you and I both know are meaningless?"

"You're supposed to be dead."

"Yes, I'm sure that's what you've thought for some time now. Surprise."

"The people here tonight don't deserve this. All this fear and pain. They have nothing to do with you."

"Fear and pain is what reminds them they're alive. That they should actually use the small handful of years they have rather than waste them. You could say I'm doing them a service. Giving them a wakeup call."

"You came here for me, not them. You want me to pay for what I helped the others do. So go ahead. Kill me."

Farrell stared at Markus with horror.

"Kill you?" Damen replied smoothly. "Why, that would be no challenge at all, given your current condition. But you will be coming with me tonight." He stepped down from the podium. Slowly, he made his way through the crowd standing on the dance floor, which silently parted for the monster as he walked through.

Markus was unflinching as Damen came to stand before him. Up close, Farrell came to the horrible conclusion that those black eyes of his weren't due to contact lenses.

"It's been a long time," Markus said.

"Not nearly as long as you think. I've been around. Observing. You've led an entertaining life among these mortals, haven't you?"

"What do you mean, you've been around? You've been here too? All this time?"

"I go where I please."

"Then you would know that the work I do here is for the ultimate good of humanity," Markus said. "My dream is to make this world a peaceful place, a world free of crime and pain."

Damen let out another cold, rattling laugh. "You were always one of the most delusional of our kind, Markus. I've always felt sorry for you. A philosophy like yours has led to nothing but painful disappointment. And I know how cranky you get when you're disappointed. What I don't know, however, is why you were exiled. I'm sure there was a very good reason for it." He paused, smiled. "Perhaps it's time for us to continue this conversation elsewhere. Unless you'd rather we stay so I can find a few more of your friends to help me demonstrate my magic?"

"That won't be necessary."

"My, Markus. You *do* care about these little creatures. How sweet."

"You said you want to leave? Let's leave."

"Yes, we certainly will." Damen glanced at Becca. "And your daughter is coming with us."

"No! Never!" Jackie said immediately, her voice breaking. She put her arm in front of Becca.

Crys clamped her arm around her sister's waist and held her close.

"I won't go anywhere with you," Becca warned, shaking her head. "With either of you!"

"No?" Damen narrowed his eyes and sent a gesture backward toward the ballroom. Suddenly, three people in the crowd clutched their throats and dropped to the ground. "Please reconsider. I'm asking very nicely."

Farrell watched, tense and helpless, as an anguished Becca turned toward her sister and aunt. Crys was crying now, full-on, and shaking her head.

"No, Becca. You can't go with them," Crys managed to choke out.

"I—I have to," Becca said, her voice sounding small but defiant. She slipped Adam's jacket off her shoulders and handed it to Farrell's brother, who took it from her reluctantly, his jaw tight.

"Damn it, Becca, no," Jackie hissed. "I won't allow this."

"More people will die if I don't. I won't let anyone else get hurt."

Farrell was so transfixed on the trio that it took him a moment to register that Markus had his hand in the crook of his elbow and was trying to pull him closer, away from the Hatcher sisters.

"This is Jackie's fault," Markus whispered. "She came here to distract me so Damen could sneak in unnoticed. She's working with him to destroy me."

"What do you want me to do?" Farrell whispered back.

"I want her to suffer deeply for this—for taking me for a fool. I want her to know the pain of losing someone she loves before she takes her last breath. She stole Becca from me all these years, so I will do the same and steal someone important to her. You will kill Crystal and make sure that traitorous bitch knows it was on my order."

And then, before Farrell could reply, Markus was gone. A gunman swept him away and escorted both him and Becca out of the ballroom, Damen leading the pack, while all Farrell could do was watch them go.

After a few moments of stunned silence, utter chaos descended upon the ballroom. People were screaming, running for the exits, stumbling over the bodies of those Damen had killed with his strange magic.

Whatever had previously been blocking the cellular signal was no longer in effect, and now there wasn't a phone in the room that wasn't pressed to someone's ear in a call of distress.

As Farrell looked on, he could feel but one reigning sensation: *clarity*. Yes, Farrell's mind was crystal clear.

A cold wave of darkness began to fill him, ridding him of all the anxiety and fear that had invaded his psyche during the attack. All emotions were washed away, leaving him with a perfect single-mindedness.

Farrell looked at Crys. She was standing with Jackie, gesturing frantically toward the doors. Jackie was shaking her head no.

The stark need to obey Markus's command enveloped him like a cloak of shadows. The edges of his periphery—of the very physical world in which he stood—began to darken.

"*Yes,*" Connor's voice was cool and calm. "*You could do it with your bare hands. Place them around her throat and squeeze. Watch the life fade from her pale blue eyes.*"

"Farrell," Adam said, grabbing his arm. "We need to find Dad and get the hell out of here."

Farrell stared at his brother, not fully seeing him. A harsh, panicked voice started ringing in his ears.

"What's wrong with you, leaving us over there all alone?" It was his mother, standing next to Adam, having reunited with him at some point in the chaos. "Farrell, answer me!"

He was going to kill Crystal Hatcher.

"Farrell!" his mother said again, louder now, and then she slapped him, hard, across his face.

The surprise of the blow and the stinging pain that followed managed to part the shadows around him. He gaped at his mother. "You slapped me."

"You're acting like a fool, standing here in the middle of this war zone! We must go. Now!"

"But I need to . . ."

Wait. What was he thinking? He couldn't kill Crys—she hadn't done anything to deserve it. Even if Markus was right—if her aunt was somehow working with Damen—what did that have to do with Crys?

Crys was innocent. It was a breach of society code to execute someone who hadn't earned their death.

Farrell looked to Crys again. His mother was still screaming at him, pleading with him to get going, but he couldn't look away. It was as if Crys had suddenly become more of a magnetic force for him than she previously was. She met his gaze, and he saw nothing but raw fear in her eyes.

Fear for her sister's life.

He began to tremble. He clenched his fists so tightly that his short fingernails bit into his skin. He peeled the thin mask off his face, only now remembering that he was still wearing it, and threw it to the floor.

He squeezed his eyes shut, trying to block it all out.

What was wrong with Markus, giving him a command like this? Markus hadn't been thinking straight—he was too full of personal pain and misplaced vengeance.

Then, at the sound of her voice, he froze.

"Farrell!"

He forced his eyes open, and there she was, just an arm's reach away from him.

"Listen to me very carefully," he growled through gritted teeth. "Because I'm going to tell you this once and only once." She looked at him earnestly, that fear in her eyes growing even deeper. "You need to stay away from me."

"What I need is to save my sister," Crys said. "You have to help us find out where she's been taken."

"Aren't you listening? Get away from me, or you'll be very sorry."

Whatever she saw in his eyes and heard in his voice made her take a shaky step backward. "Are you trying to scare me?"

"I'm trying to warn you. Go away."

"Farrell," his mother growled. "We're leaving. With or without you."

"Wait!" Crys snapped at Isabelle. "I need answers first. And I know Farrell can get them for me."

Without even realizing what he was doing, he took hold of the front of her dress and drew her closer—so close that all of his senses were completely filled by her. Her warmth, her strawberry smell, her lips. Her vulnerable throat.

"Stay. Away. From. Me," he snarled.

He released her and, forcing himself not to look directly at her again, managed to leave the ballroom without encountering any further obstacles.

Chapter 17

MADDOX

Following Alcander's instructions, they swiftly made their way toward a village just over the border, in Central Mytica.

Liana insisted she be the one to carry Al in his canvas sack. Rather than being squeamish about the head, as Maddox had expected, she was fascinated by its very existence.

What Maddox wasn't quite pleased about was that the witch and the head hadn't stopped arguing since they began their journey.

"Valoria was the first of the immortals created from the magic of the universe, therefore she is the most important," Al said to her now. They'd created a makeshift campsite to rest and eat at before continuing on to the village of Laverte, on the coastline of the Silver Sea.

"Ha!" Liana chirped. "What a laugh. No, I'm afraid it was the sorceress Eva and, some say, her evil twin brother who were the first of their kind."

"Again with the twin brother," Barnabas grumbled. "Eva never told me anything about him."

Liana sat cross-legged on the ground, with Al next to her,

cushioned by the folded canvas sack, and she regarded Barnabas across the campfire burning between them.

"*You* have spoken with Eva," she said, one eyebrow raised skeptically.

"I've done more than just speak to her. But a gentleman doesn't tell tales."

She arched her brow even further. "An immortal—the most important immortal—the most *powerful* immortal of them all—would bother herself with the attentions of a mere mortal?"

Maddox watched Barnabas curiously, eager to hear his response.

"I'll not discuss such personal matters with a common witch," he said with a wicked gleam in his eye. "I'm sure you wouldn't understand."

Gentleman indeed, Maddox thought. His gaze shifted to Liana.

"You're right, I wouldn't know how to grasp a tale as outlandish as that," she said, seemingly unaffected by the rebuff. "Alcander, what else has the radiant goddess shared with you about her history? What does she say about the southern goddess?"

"Please, call me Al. And I assume you're referring to the *inferior* southern goddess?"

"Is that what she calls her, Al?"

"Valoria doesn't sully herself by speaking of her rivals. However, she did once order me to add a specific tale to her official chronicles. I won't bore you with the whole tale, but the central theme of it was that *she*"—he was careful not to speak the dangerous name out loud—"was always jealous of Valoria's beauty. Beauty was not gifted to *her* upon *her* creation, so to make up for it *she* had to use great wafts of air magic to make herself appear attractive."

Maddox nodded. "I have also heard that, uh, *she* is ugly, both in appearance and in spirit."

"I suppose it's possible," Liana allowed. "To possess air magic—to be the *embodiment* of such magic—would offer you endless possibilities."

"The *embodiment*." Barnabas scoffed. "Those two frauds aren't the embodiment of anything, and they're not true goddesses, either—no matter what foolish mortals might choose to believe. They stole their advanced magic right out of the immortals' world."

"*What?*" Al gasped. "You are accusing Her Radiance of being a thief? How dare you!"

"Unbelievable," Barnabas scoffed. "You're still defending her? She cut off your head, remember?"

"Well . . . yes. That is true. But she did so wrongfully. I was her loyal servant, and it's only further proof of my innocence that I still show respect for her in the face of blatant lies and accusations."

Barnabas merely rolled his eyes.

"Tell me more about the magic they stole," Maddox urged.

Barnabas turned to Liana. "Do you know this tale already?" he asked her.

She frowned. "Perhaps a version of it. But I'm fascinated to hear exactly what it is you think you know."

"That reminds me: You haven't told us about your home. Where are you from that you've heard these kinds of tales?" he asked.

"Here and there."

"What is your family name?"

"I'd rather not say."

"When did you learn you were a witch?"

"Quite some time ago."

Barnabas groaned. "How illuminating. I swear, it's impossible to travel with women. Talking to them is like trying to untangle a knotted web of words."

Maddox repressed a smile. He knew Liana was baiting Barnabas, something she'd been doing since they first met. So far, beyond showing annoyance, Barnabas hadn't risen to her sly quips. At first he'd been displeased that Maddox had insisted that she join them, but Maddox was definitely starting to get the feeling that Barnabas had finally seen the value in traveling with a witch—after all, the hardest part of their journey was the gap between Camilla leaving and Liana arriving. Not that Barnabas would ever admit any of that out loud, of course.

"Go on, then, Barnabas," Al said, putting on an overly dramatic tone of diplomacy. "Tell us what you think Her Radiance stole. We can't wait to be educated."

"Al, am I right to assume that you're trying to earn your place in our fire? Or are you angling to have a rag stuffed in your mouth?"

Al blinked prissily. "Neither, if you please."

"Then shut up."

The head replied with only a glare.

"If you really want to know, I'll tell you," Barnabas said. Maddox straightened up and leaned in closer as his father warmed his hands over the fire. "The magic is called the Kindred, a priceless treasure guarded for millennia by Eva and her fellow immortals. Together the Kindred consist of four crystal orbs, each of which contains the essence of the four corners of elemental magic: air, fire, water, and earth. These orbs were both feared and coveted for the very same reason: the unprecedented, world-shattering power contained within their cores. But there was better cause to fear them, in my opinion. For if they fell into the wrong hands, who knows what kinds of disaster and chaos would follow?" He glanced at Liana. "How does this compare with your version so far?"

She shrugged. "I suppose it's about the same."

"Wonderful," Barnabas said, then continued on. "Unfortunately, most of these guardians, these immortals watching over the Kindred, were—and still are—vastly corrupt and greedy. So, sixteen years ago, after much conspiratorial planning, two of them—Valoria and that *other* one—stole the crystal orbs and, in the process . . . murdered Eva." His voice broke upon Eva's name, and he went silent.

Maddox watched him, his hands clasped tightly in his lap. "Barnabas?" he ventured.

Barnabas raised his hand, palm out, to Maddox. "It's fine. The story is nearly over anyway. As I said, this was sixteen years ago. As punishment for their crimes, the other immortals banished Valoria and her cohort—an extreme form of banishment that made it impossible for the goddesses to return to their own kind. They were forced to remain here, in Mytica, with mortals who live for a mere flicker of time compared to one with eternal life. Perhaps that's why they're so cranky and unsatisfied."

"If that's so," Liana said thoughtfully, "if they did steal the Kindred, then why wouldn't they just take the unprecedented, all-powerful magic and leave Mytica? Why not set out for a home that was better suited for them and their greatness? This universe of ours is vast and greatly unexplored, you know."

"That," Barnabas said, "is a mystery to me. One I don't really care to solve. Though, frankly, I'd be happier if they left. Then the throne would be free for the deserving Princess Cassia to occupy."

"Al?" Maddox asked. "Did Valoria ever tell you why she stays in . . . *Limeros*?" It felt strange to speak aloud the new name the goddess had given to Northern Mytica.

"She did not," Al replied. "And I never asked. But I'm certain she has an excellent reason."

"You know what I think?" Barnabas said, his eyes narrowing with suspicion. "I think you know more about her than you're telling us."

"Oh?" Al said haughtily. "And what would I have to gain by withholding information from you?"

"Perhaps you don't trust us to fulfill our end of the bargain to make you whole again when all of this is over."

Al's expression darkened. "Tell me: *Should* I trust a pair of thieves like you? Trust must be earned, Barnabas. And yes, perhaps I know a great deal that you might find valuable. I've no idea which bits of knowledge will interest you and which you'd find useless, but either way, not a word of anything unrelated to finding Princess Cassia will leave my lips until I'm ready."

"I really, truly wish to throw you in the fire," Barnabas growled.

"No," Maddox snapped. "Stop." Barnabas was so smart, so wily, yet his temper often made him act rashly.

"You are a kind boy, Maddox," said Al, relief flooding his tone. "I appreciate you looking after and protecting me from those who wish me harm in my current helpless condition."

Maddox glared at him. "I won't protect you forever. We agreed that you have a week to prove your worth—to find the princess *and* to tell us anything about Valoria that will help end her reign. If you fail, with either or both of these tasks, Barnabas can do whatever he likes with you. With my blessing."

Al regarded him with a fresh look of horror. Oddly, Maddox found this pleasing. Barnabas caught his eye and gave him a wink.

Perhaps he and his father had more in common than he'd thought.

———✠———

After they ate and rested, they continued onward toward the village named Laverte, reaching it just after night had fallen.

"I visited this place before, years ago," Al said from his sack. Liana opened it up a bit wider at the top so they could better hear him. "It was a lovely place—so lovely that I set some of my tales here. Lush vegetation, beautiful and friendly people, well-tended roads. And several vineyards that produced the most outstanding wine. As I always say, one day Central Mytica will be known for its wine."

"I hate to be the one to tell you this," Barnabas said, clearly enjoying the task of delivering his news to Al, "but it seems that Laverte has greatly changed since you were last here."

"What do you mean?" Al practically wailed. "Show me!"

They had certainly not entered the same village that Al had just described. Instead of lush and beautiful, it was dry and stark. Under the moonlight, Maddox could see no greenery, only dirt roads, all of which seemed to lead to a maze of buildings, a sea of gray and brown stones lit by a series of wind-beaten lanterns placed along the road.

The stench of animals and humans alike permeated the air.

It was dilapidated, but it wasn't deserted. As they entered the village center, they crossed paths with several citizens, many of them shabbily dressed, most of them eyeing Maddox's party without a word.

"I can't quite picture Princess Cassia living in a place like this," Maddox said as they passed through a particularly pungent patch of air.

"She's here," Al said. "I know it." But the tone of his voice told Maddox that his previous confidence and enthusiasm had been replaced by worry—likely for his own safety more than anything else.

"Even if she's gone," Liana replied, "we might be able to get a lead on where she went."

"Ah, yes," Barnabas said. "All we need to win the day is optimism."

"Do you have a better plan?" Liana shot back.

"The more dead ends we reach, the more I begin to consider Camilla's vile plan."

"What?" Maddox said, stopping to confront Barnabas more directly. "You really think that seeking audience with Cleiona is possible?"

Barnabas glared at him. "You said her name again."

"Forget that! Are you being serious?"

"Not quite yet, my boy," he said, and Maddox was surprised to see that his strong response seemed to have shaken Barnabas a bit. "But I have to tell you that I am giving it some serious thought. Valoria spreads lies about the southern one. It's obvious, and not only from legend, that they are fierce enemies. If Alcander continues to do nothing but prove what a disappointment he is, then we may have no other choice but to seek the other one out. Besides, I'd be a fool to let my prejudices get in the way of making sound decisions."

"You just wait," Al grumbled. "I have plenty of valuable information in this head of mine."

"Such as?"

"I told you: You'll have to wait."

"Stop," Liana said firmly. "We're wasting time." She covered Al's face completely with the canvas sack, ignoring his protests. "We need to find the busiest tavern in this village and start asking questions."

"Finally, a good suggestion," Barnabas grumbled.

Barnabas led the way, while Maddox, Liana, and Al trailed behind him.

"He hates me," Liana said quietly after a few minutes of silence.

"I'm not so sure about that," Maddox said.

She eyed him. "Oh? Really?"

Watching the two of them quarrel over the last couple of days had actually been quite entertaining to Maddox. By now, he knew Barnabas well enough to know that, had he truly hated the witch, he would have left her behind long ago.

Maddox shrugged. "You give him a hard time, and he lets you. Plus, you're very pretty. Frankly, I think he likes you."

"Unlikely."

"Well, he's too old for you, of course."

Liana fell quiet, but Maddox noticed the way she looked ahead, watching Barnabas with increased interest. "What about you, Maddox?" she said a little while later. "Is there a young lady in your life?"

He'd dreamed about Becca last night, for the first time since she left. In the dream, she was wearing a shockingly short black frock that showed off her very attractive legs. What was stranger than the revealing dress, though, was the glittering mask covering part of her face. She was eager to take him somewhere, to a place Maddox sensed would be filled with danger. He'd wanted desperately to shout at her, to warn her not to go, but his dream self couldn't form words. Still, he kept trying to warn her until the moment Barnabas shoved him awake at the first spark of dawn.

The dream continued to haunt him, refusing to let go.

"There was," Maddox answered Liana. "Well, she was a friend. A good friend." He swallowed hard. "She's gone now, though. A long way away from here."

"I'm sorry."

"Me too. But it was for the best. It couldn't have ended any other way. I realize that now."

"You never know what the future holds," she said half-brightly, half-mysteriously.

Maddox smiled. "Ah, yes. How could I forget you're a fortune-teller?"

"Well, that bit about me being a fortune-teller? That was a lie. Very few people can actually see the future—you should be much more wary of those who claim they can. Barnabas was right to chide you about that. But what I am is an optimist, even at times when it seems that all hope is lost."

Maddox let himself feel a bit of lightness at Liana's words, and the rest of the walk through the village was much more pleasant. It wasn't long before they reached a tavern, which they all agreed was the most popular destination they'd passed. The name of the establishment was carved above the entrance.

Maddox squinted at the sign. "What does that say? Pa-lace? Palacia?"

"*Paelsia*," Liana said, eyeing it uneasily. "It means *beware strangers* in a very old Mytican dialect."

"Oh, now you're an expert in old Mytican dialects?" Barnabas said.

She gave him a smirk. "I have many hidden talents."

They entered the busy tavern, which was full to the brim with men and women so thirsty that Maddox instantly felt sorry for the exhausted-looking barmaids running back and forth with tankards, mugs, and goblets. They stood in the entryway, taking a moment to gather in their surroundings.

Maddox had been in many taverns in his life, but never one like this. There was not a single window. The "floor" consisted of tightly packed hay. Large rocks served as the seats, which were arranged around rough blocks of wood that approximated tables. The walls were carved with words and numbers. As they entered, a man was carving a message into his table with a knife the size of his arm.

The mood of the place was so rowdy it felt like a fight could break out at any moment. Maddox noticed a scowling man who wore a necklace strung with what looked like human teeth. He met Maddox's gaze and gave him a cold grin, showing that he was completely toothless.

Maddox immediately averted his gaze, which fell upon a woman who appeared to have a full mustache. She hissed at him.

"Everyone in here looks like they just murdered somebody," he whispered to Barnabas under his breath.

Barnabas scanned the large room. "Welcome to Central Mytica, home of heathens, thieves, and wanted criminals. Don't be scared, my young friend. Just be careful about whom you speak with. In fact, leave the speaking to me."

"I'm not scared," he replied hastily, offended that Barnabas would assume such a thing, especially after all they'd been through together.

Although, to be honest, it was really just that he'd gotten much better at hiding his fear.

"Glad to hear it," Barnabas said good-naturedly as he led the trio toward the bar. "And you, Liana? A sweet young girl like you probably finds the prospect of being in the center of a tavern full of thugs rather dangerous. Shall I protect you?"

"What a big, strong, brave man you are." She gave him a cold smile that didn't reach her eyes. "I can protect myself, but much gratitude for the offer all the same."

"Suit yourself," he said, his grin fading as he turned to slap his hand down on the wooden slab of a bar. "Three ales, kind sir," he said to the barkeep. "And some information, if you please."

The barkeep gave Barnabas an unpleasant look. "Well, aren't you a polite talker. What do we have here, some sort of lord looking for an adventure, come to slum with our rough lot for a night?"

"If you take me for a lord who would happily bow down before a goddess," Barnabas leaned forward, "you are dead wrong."

The barkeep gave him another sour look and then threw an appraising glance toward Maddox and Liana. Finally, he grabbed three tankards and filled them with golden-brown ale. "Here," he said gruffly, pushing them forward. "And as for your other request, I don't know what kind of information you're looking for, but whatever it is, I'm not going to give it away for free."

"I'm more than happy to pay." Barnabas slid a gold coin across the bar, which Maddox knew was part of the purse he'd stolen from a man in the last village they'd passed through.

The barkeep eyed the sparkling coin greedily. "Talk."

Barnabas leaned forward and lowered his voice. "We're looking for a girl, about sixteen years old. She would have the brightest red hair you've ever seen. A color you wouldn't forget if you were lucky enough to encounter it."

"Bright red hair, you say?" The barkeep narrowed his eyes. "This girl is important to you?"

"Very important."

"Why?"

"That's not relevant to this discussion. But if it helps your memory, I will tell you that the future happiness of all of Mytica relies on me finding her."

"And what do I care about the future happiness of Mytica? As long as those two goddesses sit upon their thrones at either end of it, I don't see how any of us has a say in what goes on in this land."

"Would you say the same thing if I told you there was a way to get them off those thrones? To stop them from making all the rules and punishing anyone who disagrees with them?"

"Perhaps not," the man said, less bite in his voice now. "What business is it of yours where my politics lie?"

Liana, still holding tight to Al's canvas sack, pushed her way up close beside Barnabas and presented the barkeep with a charming smile. "She's my sister," she said sweetly. "The girl we're looking for."

Barnabas turned and stared at her, a slight glimmer of appreciation in his eye.

"Is she now?" The barkeep eyed her skeptically. "Yet your hair isn't red."

"No," she said, reaching up to touch her hair with a bashful grin. "I wasn't lucky enough. She gets that from our mother's side." Liana paused and let her smile drop, her eyes grow big and sad. "She was kidnapped long ago, and it's been my mission for years to find her."

Maddox watched her, both horrified and fascinated at how bold a liar she was. It seemed to come so easily to her.

"And what are you to them, then?" the barkeep said to Barnabas. "Their father?"

Liana laughed.

Barnabas glowered at both of them. "No," he growled with such displeasure that the barkeep knew better than to press him.

"And who's the boy?" the man jutted his chin toward Maddox.

Maddox crossed his arms, still trying to suppress his amusement that the barkeep assumed Barnabas was Liana's father. "Never mind who I am. Do you know this girl or not? We haven't got time to waste here. If you don't know her, we'll continue our search elsewhere."

The barkeep's lips stretched thin, and he reached forward and covered the gold coin with his large mitt of a hand. "I may know something about a redheaded girl." The barkeep looked up and signaled to someone across the tavern.

A mountain of a man walked up to the bar, his scarred and mottled face like something plucked straight from a demon's nightmare. His left eye was covered by a black eye patch.

Maddox watched him approach warily, the bravado he'd felt with the barkeep dissipating like mist at dawn.

"What?" the nightmare mountain man growled.

"These three are seeking a girl. Sixteen, with bright red hair. This one"—he nodded at Liana—"says she's her sister."

"Is that so?"

"The old man here even offered me gold for information. Gold with the northern goddess's face stamped on it."

"Old man?" Barnabas grumbled.

"We're not known for being kind to strangers here," the mountain said. "Especially ones who flash their northern coins around and ask questions about Cassia."

At the mention of the name, Maddox's breath caught in his chest.

"Where is she?" Barnabas demanded, taking a step away from the bar.

The nightmare man was in front of him a moment later, shoving him backward and down to the ground. "You don't move until I say you can."

Barnabas glared up at him from the floor. "Then I see we're going to have a problem."

"I won't. But you will." The thug, lightning-fast for his size, lunged down and, with one hand, picked up Barnabas by his throat. In his other hand he held a long, sharp knife.

Maddox stepped forward. Without any semblance of conscious thought, he summoned his magic.

"No, Maddox!" Barnabas growled. "Just wait."

"Wait until you get killed?"

"They know where Cassia is." Barnabas eyed the thug fearlessly. "Don't you?"

Pulling his blade back, the thug pushed Barnabas toward the door. "All of you. Let's go."

Maddox knew he could knock this guy out without much effort. His emotions were already high—a dizzying mix of anger and fear—so a little concentration was all it would take for his magic to bubble over the edge. In fact, it took a great deal of effort *not* to act, to instead channel his efforts toward keeping calm and waiting.

Barnabas nodded from the door, and the three of them followed the thug out of the tavern. Without a word of explanation, the thug led them to a nearby cottage where six more men, each one more grizzled and hulking than the last, were waiting.

"You still want me to wait?" Maddox whispered to Barnabas as they stood in the threshold, the three of them—and Al—being glared at by the nightmare mountain's six friends.

"For now," Barnabas replied. "But perhaps not much longer."

"Seven is a lot."

"I can help too," Liana said.

"Happy to hear it." Barnabas's expression was grim, his eyes narrowed, as he assessed the group of men surrounding them.

Suddenly, they heard the door behind them open. They turned

to see a short, slim person dressed in a hooded gray cloak enter the cottage and close the door. The nightmare mountain leaned over and whispered something in the person's ear. The person nodded, then drew closer to Maddox and his companions.

"The barkeep told me that you're looking for me." The mysterious person reached up and pushed back the hood of her cloak. A tumble of bright red hair spilled forth, and Maddox let out an audible gasp.

"I knew it," Liana said under her breath. "Al was right."

Barnabas grunted in agreement. "Perhaps I won't throw him in the fire after all."

Wisely, Al remained silent.

Princess Cassia. Maddox regarded her, not even attempting to hide the shock on his face. It was a time to believe in true miracles: Only days into their quest, they'd already found their princess, before Valoria could.

"Your Highness," Barnabas said. He bowed his head. "It's an honor to be in your presence."

The princess laughed. *"Your Highness?* Is that the customary way a father addresses his long-lost daughter?" Barnabas faltered and squirmed as if looking for a response that simply wasn't there. "Yes, they told me who you claimed to be at the tavern. Not a terribly imaginative lie, I'm afraid."

Barnabas groaned. "I never claimed to be your father."

"I'm afraid it was I who came up with the uninventive lie, Your Highness," Liana said. "I claimed to be your sister. It was only assumed that he was your father. Due to his . . . *advanced* age."

"Why are you here? What do you want with me?" Cassia asked.

Barnabas raised his gaze to meet hers, his expression resolute. "First, Your Highness, we are here to ensure your safety and comfort. And second, we need to know if you'll soon be ready to claim your rightful throne."

The princess frowned. "What does it matter? There is a goddess currently sitting upon that throne, the same goddess who murdered my father."

"Not for much longer. I have dedicated my life to ending Valoria's undeserved reign and to returning your family to power."

Princess Cassia regarded him thoughtfully. "Dedicated your life, have you? That's quite unfortunate to hear," she said sadly.

Barnabas looked back at her with confusion. "And why is that, Your Highness?"

"Because your life is about to end." Cassia flicked her gaze to a pair of her nightmare men. "Kill them all," she said coolly. "Start with dear old Dad."

Maddox was just summoning his magic when—

"No!" Al shrieked from his sack. "Don't! You can't!"

Stunned, Maddox's gaze darted between the bloodthirsty princess and the sack in Liana's hands.

The thug froze in place. "Princess?"

But Cassia looked just as shocked as everyone else. "The bag," she ordered. "Bring it to me."

Liana glanced at Barnabas. He nodded, and when the thug reached for the sack, she didn't resist.

"The contents," Cassia said. "Show me."

The thug peeked into the bag and immediately recoiled, a disgusted grimace on his face. Then, closing his one good eye, he reached in and pulled Al out by his hair.

Cassia gasped.

There was a moment of shocked silence. Maddox and Barnabas shared a pained look.

"Your Highness," Al said, dangling pitifully, "I do apologize for my current condition. And for interrupting your royal order of execution. Please forgive me."

She stared at him for another long, horrified moment, then drew slightly closer to get a better look. "This is the work of dark magic," she whispered.

"The darkest magic," the thug agreed.

Cassia shot her gaze to the three of them, first assessing Barnabas and Liana and then ending on Maddox. "I know who you are," she said warningly. "I've heard the legends of the witch-boy—the boy who can summon the dead from their graves. The boy who has the attention and interest of Valoria herself. It's you, isn't it?"

Maddox forced himself not to flinch. This princess was just a girl, he had to remind himself. No older than him. Not a witch, not a monster. She was surrounded by a wall of muscle ready to kill him at the flick of her wrist, but he would not allow himself to be intimidated.

"Yes," he said, raising his chin. "And I advise you to treat us with respect, or you can be sure you will feel my wrath."

She stared at him coolly for several more moments, until finally a smile stretched her lips. "This is good. *Very* good. Welcome to my village, witch-boy."

Chapter 18

CRYSTAL

Watching Becca leave the ballroom was the single worst moment of Crys's life. Even worse than when the Codex sucker punched her sister into a magic-induced coma.

She must have gone temporarily insane to ask Farrell for help. In a matter of moments, he'd made it totally clear that everything he'd said during their dance was a lie. He was too selfish to help anyone but himself.

All Crys remembered after Becca was taken was Jackie grabbing her and pushing her out of the ballroom and into a taxi that took them back to Angus's.

Now the door was clicking shut behind them, and she was surrounded by the familiar furniture of the penthouse.

"Angus, are you screening?" she heard Jackie say, dimly realizing her aunt was on the phone. "This is my second message. You *need* to call me. It's urgent. I have to talk to Julia, got it?"

She hung up and went to the kitchen, leaving Crys standing alone in the foyer. A couple of moments later she returned with two bottles of water and handed one to Crys.

"I know you're freaking out," she said. "So am I. That was rough—very rough—but we can deal with this."

Crys just stared at her, feeling the cold condensation from the plastic bottle against her skin.

Dr. Vega emerged from the study, rubbing his eyes. "Crystal, there you are. I was wondering where you and your sister disap—"

"How *could* you?" Jackie nearly spat at him.

He regarded her with shock. "Wh-what are you talking about?"

"Crys and Becca! How could you let them leave? Follow me there?"

"I . . ." He shook his head, looking to Crys before ducking his head and putting his glasses back on. "I . . . I . . . I'm sorry. I didn't realize they'd left until half an hour ago, when I took a break."

"Seriously, Uriah? You were the *adult* in the house. I left you in charge."

"It's not his fault," Crys said. "We sneaked out."

Jackie ignored her. "Imagine, I'm standing there with Markus King, and suddenly I look up, and there they are, in the middle of the ballroom! And now everything's gone to hell! They have Becca."

"Oh." Dr. Vega's mouth dropped open, his ruddy expression turning pale in an instant. "Oh no. This is horrible. Markus is going to use her to bargain for the Codex."

"No." Then Jackie swore loudly, raking her hands through her long blond hair. "Someone else—some enemy of Markus's—was there. It has to be the man Angus mentioned . . . all those rumors about a new magician or whatever he said. Damn it! I wasn't even listening to him go on about that, and now he won't call me back. And this guy, this *Damen Winter*—somehow he knew about Becca. That she's Markus's daughter."

"She's *what?*" Dr. Vega exclaimed.

Crys must have been shocked into sheer hysteria, because she started to laugh. Vega's cartoonish reaction to this news was far too comical for her to observe straight-faced.

Jackie turned a look of sheer outrage on her. "What are you laughing at?"

"Honestly?" Crys said, barely trying to contain her giddy laughter. "I'm laughing at you. Look at you, blaming everyone but yourself—Becca's *mother*—for what's happened."

Vega's mouth dropped open even further to hear the second half of Jackie's big secret.

Jackie ignored the professor and kept staring at Crys. "You have no idea what you're talking about."

Crys kept laughing, tears now streaming down her cheeks. "This is all so hilarious. You are so full of yourself, you know that? This has all been your fault from the very beginning. Everything bad that's happened to us has happened because of *you.*"

"That's not true."

"No? Let's see. Well, first of all, Becca wouldn't have even *touched* the book in the first place if you hadn't clumsily sent it to the bookshop by regular post."

"I'm sorry, but weren't you the one, Crys, who opened a package that was addressed to your mother?" Jackie countered without missing a beat.

"Please. That's model citizen behavior compared to you. I'm curious: What worse things have you've done over the years than steal a bunch of allegedly magical crap? Because after seeing your little performance with Markus tonight, I know there has to be more. You were so ready to stick a knife into your former lover—maybe you were a hired assassin over in Europe?"

"Wrong. You couldn't be more wrong. You jump to conclusions without any proof, Crystal. That's what you've always done. You're just like your father."

"Thank you. I'll take that as a compliment, actually. At least he gives a damn about his family when it comes down to it. You, though, you just dangle us, like bait, in front of your ex-boyfriend."

"How dare you!"

"You think so damn highly of yourself that you thought you could just put on a tight dress, march into that ball, and make Markus forget his own name. Looks like that was a big fat fail to me. Then again, don't be too hard on yourself. You *are* twice the age you were when he was interested in you. I guess he isn't so into old, used-up hags."

It happened so fast that Crys didn't even register Jackie winding up and backhanding her until her face exploded in pain. She clasped her palm to her burning cheek and stared at her aunt in shock.

Jackie stared back at her, anger blazing in her eyes for a long moment. But gradually the anger faded, replaced by regret. "Crys," she said softly. "I'm sorry. I shouldn't have hit you."

Dr. Vega just watched them, twisting his hands. "Please, both of you. Calm down. We can figure this out, I know we can."

"I need my father," Crys said, swallowing past the lump in her throat. "He can help us." She fished her phone out of her purse and, without thinking twice, composed a text as quickly as she could.

Dad, where are you? I need to talk to you! IMPORTANT!! Call me!!

She pressed Send and waited, hoping for an immediate response. "Damn it, Dad," she snarled at the screen after two minutes passed. "Where are you? You always answer when I need you the most. Come on!"

She began pacing back and forth, hoping with all of her heart and soul that he'd be able to respond from wherever he was. Because contacting him might put him at risk with the society, this was the first time she'd tried reaching out to him in over a week. But her patience was finally at an end, and she knew Markus wasn't going to be around to see the message.

"Crys . . . ," Jackie said gently.

"He's going to answer."

"Honey, I . . . I don't know what to tell you. I don't want to make tonight any harder on you than it's already been."

Crys stared at the screen, willing it to light up, buzz, make a sound. Willing for *something* to happen, anything that would prove that Daniel Hatcher was still out there. That he'd managed to lie his way out of the sure punishment he would have received if Markus knew that he'd helped his daughters escape.

But now, unanswered text message in hand, she found she couldn't do it anymore. She couldn't keep denying the horrible truth she'd known from the moment those elevator doors had closed between them.

"He's dead," she whispered. "Isn't he?"

Her grip came loose, and her phone dropped to the floor. She fell bruisingly hard to her knees.

A painful wail rang out, an almost animal cry of grief. She was numb and stunned, but somehow she knew the cry was coming from her.

"Honey, honey," Jackie was on her knees next to Crys, pulling her niece into a tight hug, rocking her gently back and forth. "I'm sorry, baby. I'm so sorry."

Crys couldn't see anymore; she was blinded by the tears streaming from her eyes. When her father first left Julia for the society, she'd cried so much that when her tears finally dried she promised herself that she'd never cry again.

She'd tried very hard to hold true to that promise, thinking with pride that it made her stronger, tougher.

And maybe it really did. For a little while.

But now . . . it was too much. She couldn't handle—couldn't even fathom—the idea of everything she'd lost.

She used to dream that one day she'd have her family back the way it was—her whole, picture-perfect family that would go out to restaurants together, watch movies on TV and heckle the actors and cheesy fight scenes from the couch. But now she knew that she'd never have that again.

"I'm sorry, Crystal," Dr. Vega said, his voice thick with sympathy. "You haven't deserved any of this. But please, you cannot blame your aunt. She's trying to make it all right again. You have to see that."

"I do," she croaked out. "I do see that. I'm sorry too. Jackie, I'm so sorry."

"Don't even mention it," Jackie whispered. "And we will get her back. I swear we will."

"How?" Crys whispered desperately. "She's with . . . *him*. And that Damen person. He killed those people just by looking at them!" Crys blinked, pulling back from her aunt and wiping her tears. Dr. Vega fetched a box of tissues and offered Crys a wad of at least ten. She frowned as she forced herself to think about the bone-chillingly scary man with the sickly pale skin and black eyes. "What that monster did—could that be called death magic? Becca told me that the boy she met in Mytica could do death magic but that he used his powers to communicate with spirits. Could they be connected?"

"I don't know," said Jackie gravely. "It certainly seemed that Damen is from the same world as Markus. But their magic is very different. There's the dagger, of course, but the magic that comes from Markus himself is elemental—earth magic for healing, and some fire magic."

"He showed me." Crys remembered the afternoon she first met Markus, when she watched with amazement as he summoned a flame to the palm of his hand. "He said he didn't like doing fire magic because it made him feel too much like a Las Vegas magician."

Jackie nodded. "He and Damen clearly have different kinds of magic. And Markus's has faded over the years. This Damen Winter—his magic is strong. He killed those people without even laying a finger on them. And Markus said that the magic in the dagger came from Damen."

"Bottom line: He's a bigger threat than Markus is," Crys said. "And, on top of that, he hates Markus."

"I don't give a damn about what happens to Markus," Jackie said. "All I care about is Becca."

"So what do we do?" Crys asked.

"We need Angus, and we need your mother back to full strength," Jackie said without missing a beat. "Markus says he didn't give Julia the command to bring him the book, but I'd be a fool to just believe him. If we get the dagger, then we wield the power that could break the spell of the marks."

"Yeah, well, if tonight was any indication, doing that will be a lot easier said than done," Crys said. "For all we know, Markus had the dagger on him tonight."

"No, he doesn't carry it unless he plans to use it. He keeps it— or at least he *kept* it—in a box in my grandfather's library." Her expression grew pinched and pensive. "I suppose it's *his* library now, since my grandfather left that mansion and his entire fortune to him in his will."

"I've been in that library. That's where Dad"—Crys's voice broke, and she pushed back a swell of tears—"took me to meet him. I was blindfolded, though, so I couldn't see the way to get there."

"What did he think you were going to do? Go back and break in?"

"Yeah, right."

"Well, that's what I'm going to do," Jackie said resolutely.

"You're going to break into Markus's home?" Dr. Vega peered at her with disbelief.

Her expression was tense. "I sure am. The universe owes me a couple of favors, Uriah. Why can't a smooth and successful breaking-and-entering scheme to steal a magic dagger be one of them?"

"Good." Dr. Vega cleaned his glasses on his sleeve, his brow furrowed. "Get your hands on that dagger and I'm sure I'll be able to properly destroy it—with Angus's help."

Jackie nodded firmly. "I'll go tomorrow morning."

Crys shook her head. "No. We need to go *now*."

"We're both exhausted, starving, and grieving—this is something that requires strength and wits. Wait . . ." She frowned. "I don't remember inviting you along on this mission."

"I'm going," Crys said firmly. "Don't even try to say no."

Jackie stared at Crys for several moments, her eyes worried and her brow furrowed in a combination of concern and fear. "Fine," she finally said. "But after this, we're even, Little Miss Masquerade-Ball-Crasher. And we're going tomorrow."

She wanted to argue, but knew she wouldn't get far. "Fine. But first thing," Crys said resolutely.

"Yes. Then we'll get Julia—if Angus gets off his ass and returns my calls—and free her from Markus's marks. In the mean-time, Uriah, please find everything you can on a Damen Winter—anything that might help us figure out where he might have taken Becca."

"I'm on it," Dr. Vega said, nodding. "Someone as powerful as you say he is will have left a trail of destruction that could lead to useful answers. But, I don't understand: Why did he take Becca?"

"Most likely to give Markus a reason to behave himself and not fight back," Jackie replied. "He must assume that Markus wouldn't risk letting his daughter be harmed."

"Oh God. Becca . . ." The thought of her sister trapped in some unknown location with those two monsters, without any friends or allies nearby to comfort her, made it hard for Crys to breathe, to think.

"I thought Farrell Grayson could help," Crys said, her voice hoarse. "He's so close to Markus now . . ."

Jackie eyed her. "I'm not sure that's a good idea."

Crys picked up her phone from the floor, closing her eyes as she exited the text message window. She scrolled through the ad-dress book, looking for Farrell's number, but it wasn't there.

"Damn. I forgot—I deleted it when I realized he'd been lying to me."

"It's for the best."

Not that Farrell would have helped her, of course. But maybe Adam could talk to him—if anyone could make him see reason, it was his brother. He could convince him that if they found Becca, they'd find his lord and master too.

Suddenly a wash of weariness hit her. Crys was tired. So utterly tired, in a way she'd never been before, she could barely keep her eyes open any longer.

"Don't you dare think about leaving without me in the morning," Crys warned.

"I think I'd be happy going the rest of my life without attracting the further wrath of Crystal Hatcher," Jackie said. She smiled briefly, then looked tenderly at her niece. "I'm sorry, Crys. For all of this. I mean it."

Crys nodded. "I know."

She hugged her aunt again, then she hugged Dr. Vega too. He looked desperately like he needed one after being the sole witness of Crys and Jackie's confrontation tonight.

Tomorrow they would fix this.

—ॐ—

Jackie gently shook her awake. Crys stared at the clock next to her single bed in shock as she realized it was nearly seven o'clock.

"Why didn't you wake me earlier?"

"This is early," Jackie said. "Go get ready."

Crys was out of bed and dressed in less than five minutes. Dr. Vega and Jackie waited for her downstairs.

"I considered taking the tunnels," Jackie said to Crys as she entered the kitchen. "But I don't trust them. It's been a while since I last navigated them, and I don't want to get us lost. We'll take my car."

That was fine with Crys; if she never found herself in the society's underground tunnels again, it would be too soon.

"Did Angus call you back?" Dr. Vega asked as they moved toward the door.

"Not yet."

"But didn't you tell him in the messages why it's so urgent that you talk to him?"

"No. You never know who could be listening in."

There was a firm knock at the door.

Crys and Jackie exchanged a worried look. Dr. Vega went to the door and looked through the peephole. His shoulders tense, he opened the door while Crys looked on, holding her breath.

Two uniformed police officers were standing on the other side.

"We're looking for Jackie Kendall," one officer said, his gaze tracking directly to Jackie, who came to stand next to Dr. Vega.

"I'm Jackie," she said.

He nodded grimly. "We have a warrant for your arrest. We have to take you into custody." The officer pulled out a pair of handcuffs and began to read Jackie her rights.

"Wait—what?" Crys snapped. "What's happening?"

"Looks like my past picked a hell of a time to catch up to me. Markus probably told the police where I was. He's got everyone tied up in his schemes." Jackie gritted her teeth. "Uriah, I'll call you as soon as I can. And Crys—do not do anything crazy without me."

It was the last thing she said before they took her, handcuffed, out of the apartment. The door closed behind them, and Crys just stood there, frozen in utter shock.

She looked at Dr. Vega. "What now?" she asked.

"Whatever Jackie worried you're going to do without her," he said, "I suggest you do it. And as quickly as possible."

It was all the encouragement she needed.

Chapter 19

BECCA

Though she felt more desperate than anything, as Becca let go of Crys in the ballroom, she decided she needed to try to be brave. The look on her sister's face, that naked fear when Becca agreed to leave with Damen and his people . . .

But what other choice did she have?

Now she tried not to think about anything except putting one foot in front of the other. She lost track of Damen when they put her in the back of one of three black limos with a gunman at her side. Markus disappeared into the backseat of another car with two gunmen, and though everything inside of her screamed, needing to know where they were taking her, she didn't ask. Crys probably would have—whenever she was scared, she tended to cover her fear with bravado or sarcasm. They were alike in a lot of ways, but not that one.

When Becca was scared—really and truly scared—she got really quiet.

They didn't blindfold her. At first she was glad for this one small allowance, but the more she thought about it, the less fortunate it seemed. There was no reason to blindfold a kidnapped victim if the kidnappers knew she wasn't ever going to be released.

She couldn't see the driver, only the silent masked man seated next to her.

And she could also see the shadow, which had joined her. It stayed down by her feet, almost touching her but not. The realization made her feel insane, but seeing that frightening yet familiar piece of darkness helped calm her just a little.

Thoughts of what she'd learned at the ball vividly and painfully replayed through her mind during the drive.

Jackie, her aunt—her beloved, fun-loving, fascinating aunt whom she'd adored all her life—was a liar who'd kept the truth from Becca since her birth. Julia, her mother, had been in on it the whole time. And Crys—what did Crys know about the horribly well-kept secret that Becca's life was nothing that she thought it was?

The three of them had been whispering to each other all week, and Becca hadn't known why. She'd assumed they were discussing everything she'd told them about Maddox and Mytica, and perhaps that was partially true. But now she saw that there was more to the truth.

The magical book had affected her, had pulled her into Mytica. She'd wondered what made her so different from anyone else.

Now she wished she didn't know.

It was life-altering information. No, *life-altering* didn't even come close to what it was. The second she heard the truth about her origins, her entire worldview changed. But Becca couldn't process what it meant—not yet.

After what felt like a half an hour, the driver pulled the car to the side of the road. It wasn't a good part of town.

One of the men dressed in black opened the back door. He

was positioned to catch her in case she tried to flee, but she didn't resist and got out on her own. She looked up to see they were parked in front of an old deserted building with chipped and crumbling plaster and a marquee that, in faded letters, read: KING'S PALACE THEATRE. Her masked escort then led her up to the entrance.

The shadow followed her.

Becca hadn't recognized the place on the outside, but as soon as she stepped inside, she knew exactly where she was.

It was Markus's theater, where the Hawkspear Society met and where Becca had found herself when she'd woken from her coma. She had been laid out on a table on the stage, surrounded by people, as if she were some sort of sacrificial offering. It actually had been a ceremony of exchange—Becca for the Bronze Codex.

They entered from the back of the theater, walking first through the shamble of a lobby. As Becca descended the narrow aisle to the main stage, she looked at the rows upon rows of red seats, all of which had been immaculately maintained. Adorning the walls were geometric patterns in once bold, now fading colors, and on several panels there were twenty-foot murals depicting glamorous women wearing sullen expressions, holding instruments and lilies.

Art Deco, she thought randomly, the name of the theater's aesthetic popping into her mind. *That's the style.*

The abandoned exterior of the building was the perfect way to camouflage the headquarters of a secret society.

The masked man guided Becca in farther. She heard footsteps behind her and turned to see Markus walking in after her, two of Damen's henchmen on either side of him, regarding his theater with a stony look in his eyes.

Damen stood at center stage, alone, his hands clasped behind his back, watching them.

Including Becca, seven people were present. She wondered where the rest of Damen's gunmen had gone.

"Why here?" Markus asked.

"Because this is your domain," Damen said simply. "Your kingdom, Markus King. I do like the surname you chose. A bit vain and pompous, perhaps, but that's you."

"And you chose Winter for yours. Frigid and unpleasant to endure."

"I thought you liked winter, Markus?" Damen descended from the stage and moved toward them. "You chose to make Toronto your new home."

"I didn't choose it."

"Yet you've stayed here all these years."

Damen knew a lot about Markus. And by the look on Markus's face, he didn't like it one bit.

Were they alone in here? Perhaps there was someone else in the building, a janitor or maintenance worker? What about Hawkspear members? Did they have access to the theater in between official gatherings?

Becca was bursting with questions, but she stayed silent. Besides, she knew they were probably futile. A psycho mastermind like Damen wouldn't choose a venue that could be compromised by random visitors at any given moment.

"Becca." Damen came to stand right in front of her, stunning her out of her thoughts. "Look at me."

She really, really didn't want to. Still looking down, she clasped her hands together, tightly, until she felt pain. She tried to focus on that pain and nothing else.

She so wanted to be brave. She so wanted to be like Crys, to say something snarky to trick everyone into thinking she wasn't terrified. She'd experienced so much fear in Mytica—even as a spirit, she'd still been faced with the horror of ravenous magic—but it had been nothing like this. That terror descended upon her quickly, and it was over before she knew it.

And in Mytica, Maddox had been by her side every step of the way. They'd helped each other find enough bravery to survive. Here, in this eerily immaculate theater with these demons from another world, Becca had no one to help her find that strength.

The shadow was still with her now, but sadly that didn't count.

"Becca," Damen said again, slower and more deliberately. "Look at me."

But she still didn't look.

"She can resist your magic," Markus said.

"I'm not using magic. Should I, Becca?"

She set her jaw and forced herself to look at him. She met his chilling black and reptilian eyes straight on and couldn't hold back a flinch.

Damen nodded, his pale face expressionless as he walked through the theater, forcing Becca to follow him with her gaze. "It's disturbing to you, isn't it? My appearance?"

She bit her lip, afraid of how he'd retaliate if she agreed or disagreed with him.

"You look very tired," he continued. He reached the foot of stage and climbed its steps up to the hardwood surface. He paced the stage, glancing up at the rafters and lights. "It was a big night for us all. You need to rest."

"*Rest?*" Markus said. "This is hardly a time for rest. Tell us why you brought us here."

"Not yet."

"You think you can just keep me here until you feel ready?"

"Yes, I do. And what will you do about it? Your magic is so faded, it's almost as if it were never there at all. You're not much stronger than a mortal now." He nodded at two of the masked men, who came up on either side of Markus. "You've built a nice little dungeon downstairs," Damen said. "I assume that's where you keep the accused before they face their society trials."

Markus said nothing, so Damen went on talking.

"Fortunately it's empty. Otherwise I would have had to empty it myself. Now, go with my people, Markus. And please don't give me any problems tonight. You know very well that I will make you regret it."

Markus eyed Becca for a few tense moments as she braced herself for what would follow when Markus inevitably disobeyed Damen. But suddenly, to her great surprise, Markus turned away and, without a word, accompanied the two men out of the theater.

Becca held her breath and waited for what might happen next.

"I'm sorry tonight has been so difficult for you, Becca," Damen said as he watched Markus be led out of the room. "You didn't choose that man as your father."

"That man *isn't* my father," Becca spat. "My father is Daniel Hatcher."

Becca puffed out her chest in pride. She sounded strong. Brave. She took some comfort in that. From the corner of her eye, she watched the shadow slither beneath a red seat nearby.

A slight, chilly smile cracked Damen's expressionless face. "Very well," he said dismissively. "As I said before, you need to sleep."

"No, I don't—"

He narrowed his bottomless black eyes. *"Sleep."*

———∞———

That slap of Damen's magic was the last thing she remembered when she woke up on a cot in what looked like a backstage dress-ing room, covered in a soft gray blanket. She sat bolt upright and craned her neck all around. No one else was there.

What time was it? She fumbled for her phone but couldn't find it and didn't remember the last time she'd seen it. The clutch she'd taken to the ball was gone. The only belongings she had were the clothes she was wearing: the fancy black dress with the itchy beaded neckline, tight black shoes, and the silver rose necklace she always wore, which she twisted nervously.

And then there was that dense shadow, which lingered now in the corner.

"I don't know what to do," she said to the shadow. Her throat was raw. "I don't know what you are, but . . . can you help me?"

The shadow simply continued to swirl in the corner.

She sighed and took another look around. All was quiet and still, and though she didn't have a clock, she had the feeling that it might still be the middle of the night. Could it be possible that she was the only one awake in the theater? Quietly, she got up and went to the door. She tried the knob, gasping with surprise to find it unlocked. *Could this actually be happening? Could she just walk away from all of this, right now?* She had only a vague idea where she was in relation to Angus's home, but if she could just get outside, she could find a way to get there. She'd borrow a phone, or she'd even be happy to take her chances on hitchhiking with a random stranger if it got her away from Damen and Markus.

The door creaked as she slowly pushed it open. Trembling, she slipped into the hallway.

But her heart plummeted to see that there was someone wait-ing for her just outside the door. It was one of Damen's men in black, still wearing his mask.

"Damen will be happy to learn you're awake," he said. "Follow me."

She knew she had no choice. Girding herself for the millionth time in the past twenty-four hours, she followed as the man led her through the backstage hallways and out to the stage. On top of the stage was a long wooden table. Damen stood at the end of it.

"Good morning, Becca," he said. He gestured toward the chair opposite him, in front of which was a spread of food. "Please sit. I've arranged breakfast for you."

Though he looked the same as he had last evening—those coal-black eyes were still burning in his face—there was something about him this morning, some invisible sense of danger, that made him even more frightening.

With nothing to do but obey, she walked stiffly toward the table and sat. On the table in front of her were platters of eggs—scrambled, fried, and poached—bacon, ham, sausages, pancakes, French toast, and several glass pitchers of fruit juice.

As if on autopilot, Becca put her napkin in her lap, and Damen took his seat across from her. "I hope it's all right; I didn't know what you like to eat." Becca just stared at him, motionless and si-lent, her silverware untouched next to her plate. "Becca, I would like to apologize for using my magic on you last night."

"Ha!" she said immediately, surprised and a bit horrified at herself, but seemingly unable to stop now that she'd started. "Why apologize? You can get people to do whatever you want them to do, whenever you want them to do it. Why wouldn't you use that magic all the time?"

"Many reasons," he replied coldly.

They were interrupted by a shuffling sound somewhere backstage, and Becca followed Damen's demon eyes to the source. Entering through the curtains was Markus, flanked by two more of Damen's men.

Upon seeing Becca, Damen, and the man in black who'd been chaperoning Becca, Markus groaned. "Why are they still wearing masks?" His escorts led him to his chair, right between Becca and Damen, facing the sea of vacant red seats.

"Why do you think?" Damen asked as Markus sat down.

"Oh, please, Damen," Markus said and sneered. "You think I don't know what you've done? They're wearing masks because you don't want me to see their faces. Faces that I'd recognize, because they belong to Hawkspear members you've enslaved to do your bidding."

Damen smiled sickly in response. "Did you rest well in your dungeon?"

Markus flicked a brief glance at Becca. Her food was still untouched, and she had no plans to change that. "I assume we're here because you mean to put me on trial for my crimes," Markus said, ignoring Damen's taunts.

"Interesting thought. Do you believe you've committed crimes against me?"

"I did nothing to you that you didn't fully deserve."

"You're right, Markus. I did deserve my punishment. All those awful deeds? I was practically begging for it." Damen paused and shifted his chilling gaze to Becca. "I wonder what you'd think of me, Becca, if you knew the truth."

"I don't think anything of you," Becca said as steadily as possible. "I don't even know you."

"You saw what I can do."

No matter how cool Becca hoped she was remaining on the surface, it didn't change the fact that the memory of those bodies slumping to the ballroom floor was still vivid in her mind. It hadn't left her; it was haunting her for more reasons than anyone here in her world could know.

That memory . . . the way Damen had wielded the magic of death . . . reminded her of what Maddox was capable of.

But she tried to shake these bad thoughts away. Maddox would never use his magic like Damen did, so casually, so selfishly. As if a life had no more meaning than an old tissue made to be thrown away.

Damen went on, not waiting for Becca to reply. "You want to be a writer one day, Becca?"

She blinked, the change of subject taking her completely off guard. "How did you know that?"

"That doesn't matter. But I know, and I think it's a wonderful occupation. Perhaps you can tell my story someday."

"Leave the girl alone," Markus growled. "You're scaring her."

Damen turned to Markus. "Scaring her? How? By suggesting she use her talent to tell the true story of someone who has been wrongfully perceived as a villain his whole life, hated by everyone he's ever known? Someone who might have a point of view that should finally be heard?"

"Memories of one's past are tainted," Markus said. "There are no truths to be found in them."

From the corner of her eye, Becca saw her inky shadow slither from its nook on the other side of the stage toward her chair.

Markus glanced down at it, his brow furrowing deeply.

Her breath caught as she realized that he could see the shadow.

The shadow inched closer to Becca's ankle. She tried not to move, tried not to scream, as it wrapped itself around her foot and leg and . . .

The crystal city sparkled beneath a bright blue sky. Dozens of golden hawks circled above the city, all of them squawking, as if panicked. As if calling out a warning.

Becca turned, bracing herself for the abysmal sight she knew she would find behind her. Beyond green fields and rolling valleys, the earth was crumbling away, falling into nothingness.

"Stop this," said a beautiful young woman with long dark hair and wearing golden robes, her voice quavering. "Please, you must stop!"

"Why should I?"

Becca gasped. It was Damen who answered her, only he looked . . . different. His complexion was no longer chalky white but instead glowed with a healthy tan. It shimmered as if dusted with gold. His black hair gleamed, and his eyes—no longer two forbidding black holes—were dark brown and clear, but filled with anguish.

"I'm begging you, Damen," said the woman. "Stop." Standing behind her were others, all in robes, all beautiful and young. A violent chill rushed through Becca when she saw that one of them was Markus. Another was Valoria.

The young woman held the book—the Book of the Immortals, the Bronze Codex—tightly in her arms. "You destroy everything because you're filled with such endless hate. And now you would destroy me too, along with it all?"

"You are the only thing in this universe I love, sister," Damen said. "And yet you are also the one I hate the most. You stand there, with them, rather than by my side. You choose to reject me, to leave me behind? Fine. But this is the price you must pay. Everything you care about—everything all of you care about—I will end it."

A powerful wave of Damen's bitterness, self-hatred, and aching loneliness coursed through Becca as she witnessed this.

Damen was the most powerful being in the world. In the universe.

For this, everyone feared him.

For this, everyone hated him.

His magic was in direct opposition to the magic belonging to these beautiful immortals, who wielded the power of life and creation. His magic was made up of death, destruction, pain, and emptiness.

He didn't belong here with them. He never had.

"You mean to cast me away from this world," Damen said. "To put an end to the pain I cause you all. Well, I will go. But I will leave you with but a shard of this world, only a pitiful fraction of our population. You hurt me, so I annihilate you."

"It doesn't have to be this way," she said desperately, but Becca saw the alarming lack of hope in her eyes.

"It has always been this way, Eva," he said. "Ever since you and I were first created. You were given all that is good, while I was given all that is bad. This"—he paused and gestured to the solemn, petrified group of immortals around him—"*this* has always been my destiny . . ."

Suddenly, the scene shifted to reveal a world on fire beneath a blackened sky. A few dozen immortals, including Valoria and Markus, stood in a circle. Damen was in the middle of the circle, kneeling, bracing himself against the scorched ground. Standing before him was Eva and an immortal Becca didn't recognize, who held a golden dagger in his hand. Eva had a handful of Damen's sleek black hair tight in her grip as she yanked it and forced him to look up at her.

"You've given me no choice, brother," she said, her voice break-ing with choked-down sobs.

She placed her hands on either side of his head. Instantly, his eyes began to glow with bright white light. The immortal at her side took the golden dagger and thrust it into Damen's chest.

Damen screamed. The sound was so wretched it turned Becca's blood to ice, made her want to dive down right into the center of the earth just so that she didn't have to hear it anymore . . .

And then the ruined world faded away. Becca opened her eyes and found herself back on the stage, at the table with the two immortals. Gasping, she stood up so quickly that her chair fell down and skittered backward. The shadow fled and retreated to its corner.

"Is there a problem, Becca?" Damen asked, frowning.

She shook her head. Her heart rate had tripled in the span of seconds.

What was she supposed to say? That a shadow spirit that es-caped from the bronze hawk had just shown her the greatest-hits reel of his horrific past? That it had just confirmed her suspicion that Damen Winter was, by far, the most frightening and danger-ous being in the entire universe?

That he could destroy not only lives but entire *worlds* without a moment of hesitation?

And that a small piece of her, the part that wasn't terrified, felt horribly sorry for him, for all that he'd done and all that he'd lost?

"Is there a problem?" Markus repeated, mockingly, to Damen. "Let's see, Damen. What could the problem be? You've kidnapped this girl! You're subjecting her to great stress without telling ei-ther one of us what you want. Perhaps there's a problem to be found somewhere in there."

"My, what a hypocrite," Damen spat out. "I see that you have not changed one bit. It makes me wonder just whom you betrayed to earn your exile. You were always Eva's favorite."

"What you think you know about my past makes not an iota of difference in this world or any other."

"Perhaps," Damen replied coolly.

"Enough of this, Damen," Markus said, clearly exasperated. "Becca has nothing to do with the vengeance you seek against me."

"I agree."

"So free her."

Becca eyed Markus with curious, skeptical surprise. She had certainly not expected him to suggest such a thing.

"That's not going to happen," Damen said. "I have a use for her."

"What could you possibly want from her? I know it can't be to write your pathetic biography."

"Not quite, though I know my story would be a fascinating read for many. No, Becca is here, Markus, because she is your daughter. Your blood. Your magic."

Becca felt ice in her veins again. "I have no magic," she said, wringing her hands in a nervous tangle in her lap.

"Don't feel bad. It's rare for magic to awaken at an age as young as yours," Damen said. "But your father is an immortal; your mother, a mortal. This combination will always lead to magical, if mortal, offspring. You definitely have it within you. I can sense it. And I know Markus can too."

All of this—all of these bombshells exploding and destroying the life she thought she was living—it was too much for her to digest. She found she didn't even have the breath to ask any questions. She was too dizzy even to see straight.

"No, Damen," Markus said, his voice low and quiet. "Don't think

I don't know what you plan to do. I know, and I'm asking you to stop. Deal with me another way."

"I'd almost forgotten what a fine sense of morality Eva's followers had." Damen shook his head. "Or so they would have others believe."

Becca felt herself losing strength and focus, and she knew that if she let herself go numb completely, she'd be forfeiting everything. She thought of Crys, of Julia and Jackie and Daniel and even little, furry Charlie, and she forced herself to take another breath. She forced herself to be strong. "Tell me," she snarled. "What are you going to do?"

Damen stood up and walked over to Markus. He stood behind his chair, clapped his hands down on Markus's shoulders, and fixed his gaze on Becca. "You asked me why I don't use my magic all the time, Becca. Why I wouldn't want to make everything easier by drawing the truth out of lying tongues, or killing people who cause me even a moment's difficulty. The answer is that it would be incredibly boring. Markus and the rest of his kind destroyed me—*killed* me. Yet I was too strong. So I returned in the form that you see before you now. My eyes—these cold black wounds—are a reminder that I am alone, that this is forever. I see it every time I gaze into my reflection: true immortality. I cannot be killed ever again, not by anything or anyone. One cannot kill death itself.

"My goal is no longer to personally destroy worlds, or lives, or hope. I've discovered it's much more interesting to sit back and watch mortals destroy themselves. They're actually very good at it. Sometimes I do give a little push in the right direction here and there, but it doesn't take nearly as much effort as you might think. Take this world, for example: There's so much potential for growth and sustainability, yet every day, in little ways, humans everywhere choose to accelerate and actively bring about their own destruction and extinction. It's fascinating to observe."

He spoke of fascination, but there was no emotion—no enthusiasm, no shred of reverence—in his tone. All Becca could do was stare at him, horrified that he could so casually speak about—root for—the end of her world.

"It shouldn't be much longer now," he said, finally allowing a cold smile to slide across his lips, "before all the light is snuffed out. And this"—he squeezed Markus's shoulders—"brings us to here and now."

"You want to kill us," Becca said, her voice hollow.

"Haven't you been listening?" he said. "I don't want Markus to die. I want him to suffer. Eternally." Damen bent down and sniffed at Markus's hair. "He is already near death. I can smell it. He's close. And desperate. But if there's one thing that's built into the very lifeblood of all immortals, it's a need—a sheer joy in striving—to survive at any cost necessary. Therefore, I propose an experiment. How desperately does he want to live? Enough to kill a part of himself so that the rest might go on?"

"I won't do it," Markus growled.

Damen snapped his furious gaze to Markus. "You think you're important enough to decide who lives and who dies? Let me make it a little easier for you to decide. Your daughter has within her, buried deep inside, the magic you need to survive. Take it and live. Or leave it and die. I think we both know which option you'll choose."

Damen clamped his hands on either side of Markus's head.

Just like Damen's had in Becca's vision, Markus's eyes began to glow bright white. He gasped in pain as his skin began to go sallow, his cheeks became gaunt, and dark circles formed under his bright eyes. When Damen finally released him, Markus slumped down, head and chest on the table, looking completely and devastatingly drained of energy.

"Take them both to the dungeon downstairs," Damen said to an unnamed masked man as he brushed his hands together. "My guess is it'll be no longer than an hour before he drains her dry."

Two masked men grabbed Becca and pulled her away from the table. She swatted at her untouched breakfast, sending porcelain and cold food flying, as a red hot fire rose inside of her.

"Go to hell," she snarled at the black-eyed monster.

"Life is hell," he replied as he watched his henchmen drag her off the stage and down a flight of stairs.

At the bottom of the stairs was a thick steel door. The henchmen opened it to reveal a cold, empty concrete room, and then they threw Becca inside.

Moments later two more henchmen came down with Markus. They shoved him in after her, slamming the door with a heavy thud and locking it shut.

Chapter 20

FARRELL

When the Graysons arrived home just before midnight, Farrell's parents had insisted that he and Adam go up to their rooms without any discussion of the night's events. For once in his life, Farrell hadn't argued. He needed to be alone.

His brother seemed to disagree, since he quickly appeared at Farrell's door.

"We need to talk," Adam said, his voice strained.

"No thanks. Not in the mood."

"It wasn't just Markus that bastard took with him," Adam said, undeterred. "He took Becca too."

"And . . . ?"

"Don't tell me you don't care. I don't believe that for a second. Please—like you really don't care about either of them?"

It was all Farrell could do to push away Markus's voice, which now competed with Connor's for space in his head. So he definitely couldn't deal with his do-gooder little brother who had a knack for getting himself into deep trouble with forces far beyond his understanding. Farrell knew he wouldn't always be there to bail him out.

"Why don't you leave me alone and go get your beauty sleep, kid," he said, trying to sound calm.

"I saw you with Crys on the dance floor. I'm not an idiot. Don't tell me you feel nothing for her."

"Oh yeah, I feel something for her," he muttered sarcastically. *I feel plenty of things for her*, he thought. *The first that comes to mind is* homicidal. "Get out of here," he said aloud. "Don't make me say it again."

"But Farrell, you need to—"

Farrell brusquely grabbed a graphic novel omnibus from his nightstand—Stephen King's *Dark Tower* series—and threw it, hard, at his brother. Adam managed to dodge it just in time, and it slammed into the wall instead.

Adam narrowed his eyes. "I'm trying to understand what you're going through, Farrell. But sometimes—like now—it's like you're *trying* to make me hate you."

"Good, it's working. Now get the hell away from me."

"Keep insisting like that and I might stop fighting for you for good. Then you really won't have anyone on your side."

"Promise?"

Adam glared at him for one last, lingering moment, disappointment sliding through his eyes, before he finally inched away and closed the door, leaving Farrell alone, with only Markus's murderous command echoing in his head. He pressed his palms against his temples and squeezed.

When that didn't work to dampen the echoes, he put his headphones on and listened to death metal for an hour. A bad choice for trying to stay calm, but at least it worked to block out his thoughts for a little while.

He didn't want to give a damn. Not about anything.

But he did.

Staying under his parents' roof, safely tucked into his king-size bed, wasn't a solution. His arm burned, reminding him that Markus controlled him through his marks, something he'd denied all this time.

He wanted to hate Markus for it.

Instead, what he really wanted was to save him from Damen Winter, a man Farrell knew absolutely nothing about.

But Markus knew him. Perhaps Farrell might be able to find some sort of message or note or journal or . . . *anything* that could help him figure out where Markus had been taken.

If Farrell could find a way to free Markus—and his daughter— it would buy him the right to ask him to remove his marks.

These hyper-evolved senses were great, but not at this price.

At dawn, Farrell left for Markus's. Markus had recently given him a key to the front door—the key that had previously belonged to Daniel Hatcher. He didn't want to ask Sam to drive him to the Hawkspear leader's private home, so he decided instead to take a cab to an address that was a short walk to the mansion.

The cab parked at an out-of-the-way address. Farrell paid and opened the door, accidentally brushing against it while exiting. His forearm yelped in pain, the way it did now whenever it made the slightest bit of contact with anything. He pulled up his sleeve to see that his new mark was now looking much worse than a fading scar; it was bright red and raw, as if it'd just been freshly carved.

"What the hell have you done to me, Markus?" he muttered.

"Kill Crystal and make sure that traitorous bitch knows it was on my order . . ."

The hell he would. Marks or no marks, he wasn't anyone's mindless minion. Crys and Adam were wrong. Farrell did have free will. He'd always had it, and he always would. He and no one else was the master of his destiny.

He made the short walk, checking in all directions to make sure he wasn't seen or followed before turning into Markus's front walk. He let himself in with the key and went directly to Markus's library, where he felt he was most likely to find the answers he needed to his questions about Damen Winter. However, as he stepped inside the room with its vaulted ceiling and wall-to-wall shelves two stories high, holding thousands of books, he found he wasn't quite sure where to begin.

He blinked, forcing himself to concentrate and use his enhanced eyesight to scan books on the top shelves. He made his way across three of the four walls before he let out a frustrated sigh. This was a futile search. He went to Markus's desk and sat down, trying to reclaim his composure. Immediately, his gaze fell on the familiar ornate box that always sat in the right corner of the desktop.

"Did you forget about the dagger?" not-Connor said. *"Best keep that little item close, brother. Markus will want it."*

He hadn't forgotten. He had been momentarily distracted by other matters.

"And what does he want it for, I wonder?" Farrell muttered out loud. "To cut another mark into me? What would a fifth one do? Make me dance on command like a trained monkey?"

"You're lucky he chose you to fill such an important role in his life. Everything has a price, Farrell. The higher the price, the better the reward."

Farrell couldn't stop himself from rolling his eyes, but he had to silently concede that Connor's voice had a point. He tried to ignore his trembling hand as he reached out to lift the lid off the box. For the briefest moment before he opened it, he had a sickening feeling that the dagger was gone.

But there it was, shiny as ever and safe in its black velvet nest. With a sigh of relief, Farrell reached in and wrapped his hand around the hilt. He picked it up and brought the blade so close that he could see his own distorted reflection in it.

"Maybe you can help me find Markus," he told it.

Then he heard a sound: a door opening and closing. He was on his feet and slipping out of the room in an instant to investigate.

He paused in the hallway and concentrated, listening. He heard footsteps—incredibly faint, but definitely footsteps—moving toward him from the front foyer.

As the footsteps drew closer, he slipped into a doorway that led to one of Markus's many sitting rooms. The richly appointed, museum-like den was filled with prewar furniture, including a grandfather clock that told him it was just shy of eight in the morning. He knew that Markus's staff—one maid and one cook—never arrived before noon.

He tightened his grip on the dagger as he pressed his back against the wall next to the door, where he was certain he'd be hidden from whoever was roaming the hallway.

A floorboard creaked nearby. Holding his breath, he edged close enough to the entry to glance out.

Long platinum blond hair pulled into a messy ponytail. A jean jacket unbuttoned to reveal a Wonder Woman T-shirt. Ugly-ass black-framed glasses that some people—Farrell not included—thought were stylish.

Crystal Hatcher, always choosing to be in the worst places at the worst times.

His arm flared with pain at the sight of her, Markus's command now screaming in his head.

Giving her a bit of a head start, he tensely watched her navigate the hallways with purpose. When she was almost out of sight, he began to follow her all the way back to the library.

She entered, gazing up at the bookcases, then further up to the skylight, and then out to the huge windows overlooking the gardens. He watched as she lowered and narrowed her gaze, then went straight for the desk. She opened the box.

And frowned deeply.

"Looking for this?" he asked.

She whipped around to face him as he started dragging the sharp tip of the dagger along the edge of the doorway. It made an unsettling yet satisfying scraping sound.

Her eyes went wide with surprise.

He shook his head. "You really can't stay away from me, can you?"

"I . . ." She scanned the room frantically, as if hunting for an escape, but there was only one entrance, and Farrell was currently blocking it. "I didn't know anyone would be here."

"Obviously," Farrell said drily. "I didn't realize Markus gave you a key. I'm quite positive he would have mentioned something like that to me."

He tried to sound casual and cold, but he felt anything but. The moment he first saw her, the echo of Markus's command had risen to the surface of his consciousness so vividly, so deafeningly, that it was impossible to even attempt to ignore. Every muscle in his body was tense and ready to strike.

"The front door was open," she said quietly.

"*Nice one, little brother,*" said not-Connor, and Farrell had to blink back the rage he felt at his own stupid mistake as he pretended not to be fazed by Crys's news.

"How'd you find this place?"

"It belonged to my great-grandfather. That plus a search engine, and I was in business. Farrell, I really don't have time to explain, but I need that dagger."

"And, what, you just assumed the door would be open and you could waltz right in?" he said, ignoring her demand.

All patience was rapidly fading from her expression. "I was ready to break a window, but luckily I didn't have to."

"Where's your aunt? Your mother?"

"Not here." She hissed out a frustrated sigh. "I know we've had our differences, and you probably trust me as much as I trust you, which is to say not very much, but . . . look, Farrell, I *need* that dagger."

Markus's command rang in his head, loud enough now to block out almost every other sound. His fingers were so tightly wrapped around the hilt of the dagger that they were turning purple. "You say that like you really believe there's a chance I'll give it to you."

"It could be the only way to free everyone from the society marks."

Steadily, angrily, darkness crept into his mind and began to obliterate all other thoughts. Trying to ignore it was a true act of futility.

"Don't you have a sister to rescue?" he asked, his voice suddenly sounding distant and emotionless, even to him. "Shouldn't you be focusing on that right now?"

Her eyes flashed with anger. "How can you be so cold? Don't you give a damn about anything? Are you really that lost?"

Was this what it felt like to be lost? And was he really too weak to fight against these strange compulsions, even when he knew he wanted to?

"*Accept the darkness,*" not-Connor told him. "*Stop fighting it. No one's here to watch, no one has to know. And when it's done, you're going to feel so much better.*"

He blinked back the burning pain in his forearm.

He didn't like pain. Never had. It was a sign that something was wrong.

But in this case, it was something that could be fixed with barely any effort.

Accept the darkness, he thought. *And then I'll feel so much better.*

One command. One dagger. One girl.

Zero choice.

"I'm going to tell you a little secret," Farrell said evenly. "And then I'm going to give you a bit of a head start."

She frowned. "A head start? What are you talking about?"

"You know how you're so fond of telling me that I'm Markus's minion, who'll do anything he commands?"

"What about it?"

"Well, you're right. And I don't think you're going to like what he last commanded me to do."

Crys looked at him, clearly wary. "What did he just command you to do, Farrell?"

He flicked his gaze from the tip of the blade to meet hers. "Guess."

The confusion in her eyes turned to stark understanding in a matter of moments. She began shaking her head. "You wouldn't hurt me."

"Oh, it probably won't hurt for very long." He had to admit, accepting this duty—however much he knew he didn't want to—did make everything easier. Like taking a deep gulp of air after being trapped underwater.

"You won't do it," Crys growled. "You may be a lot of nasty things, Farrell, but you're not a killer."

"You have no idea how wrong you are. You know, up until a few minutes ago I was resisting this compulsion really well. Remember the whole *stay away from me* thing from last night? That's what that was. Me doing my best impression of a Boy Scout. Only I must have forgotten that I got kicked out of Boy Scouts for starting a campfire in the boys' bathroom."

"So you're able to resist this . . . compulsion? You *want* to resist it?"

"I was able to for the short time you listened to me and stayed away. But of all the mansions in all the world, you had to break into this one." He allowed a grin to stretch across his face.

Her eyes were now fixed on the dagger. "So now what?"

"That seems to be the question of the hour. *Now what?* Well, let's see. I don't exactly have a great track record when it comes to impulse control. If I feel lousy, I have a drink. If I'm bored, I have a cigarette. Rinse and repeat. Resisting temptation has never been in my nature."

"Let me leave, and we can pretend this never happened."

"Sorry, but we're about five minutes too late for that. Now, how about that head start I mentioned? Let's make it a game of hide-and-seek. You hide, I'll seek. When I find you, I promise to make it quick and as painless as possible, and you promise to stop being a problem for me for the rest of eternity."

Farrell stepped away from the doorway, leaving it clear and open. He was waiting for her to argue with him or give him a pep talk about how he could fight this thing and come out on the other side happier and healthier for it.

But she didn't. Instead, she just narrowed her eyes at him. "I need that dagger."

"Really? That's what you choose for your famous last words?"

Without another word, she ran past him and out of the room in a flash. He'd forgotten how fast she was when she was running away from him.

He sighed. "This really isn't a healthy relationship we have," he said to himself. "Oh well."

Dagger in hand, he slowly counted to ten.

As he stood there, he tried to remember why he'd been fighting this but found that he couldn't. Crys Hatcher was a problem for him and had been pretty much from the first moment he'd met her, when he'd been trying to charm his way into learning all her secrets about why she was looking into the Hawkspear Society. But when she'd blown him off like he was just some ordinary guy . . .

She'd become an actual challenge.

Farrell liked challenges. For a little while, anyway.

But could you even call it a challenge if she wanted so little to do with him that this whole thing was one-sided? His nagging conscience was trying to remind him that she was out of his league, special in a way he would never be, and that she had every right to curse the moment she met him.

He squashed that little voice inside of him. His conscience had gotten smaller and smaller in recent days, but for now he still carried it around with him, like a sharp pebble in his shoe.

"What are you waiting for?" the much more helpful voice of Connor chimed in. *"Go get her."*

Game on.

Slowly, he left the library and made his way through the halls. Hide-and-seek had been his and his brothers' favorite game ten years ago. Farrell had always won—he was killer at both hiding and seeking.

Killer.

Yes, you're a killer, not-Connor whispered. *No reason to deny it. Embrace it. Your marks make you stronger and better. You know this.*

Farrell tightened his grip on the dagger.

"Come out, come out, wherever you are!" he called. He didn't think she'd go immediately for an exit, considering how much she wanted the dagger. More than likely she was so delusional that right now she was trying to figure out a way to incapacitate him.

Or kill him.

But he was expecting that, and he'd be prepared. His senses were so keen that he could pick out the quiet tick of the grandfather clock in that distant room. He could see the faint prints of Crys's shoes in the hallway rug.

He followed the footprints.

"Hey, Crys, I've changed my mind," he called out. "Let's drop this cat-and-mouse game and order a pizza. What do you say? We could watch a movie, discuss life, the meaning of the universe. It'll be fun!"

Or maybe they could have story time. He'd tell her the one about how he'd watched the life leave Daniel Hatcher's eyes as he'd twisted the knife. About how, at that moment, a part of Farrell had screamed for him to stop, but he didn't. He couldn't.

That he wasn't sure whether or not he believed in souls, but that he was certain he'd lost a very important piece of himself in that moment—a piece that he knew he would never get back.

It didn't matter. Power was all that mattered to him now. Doing whatever Markus commanded was all that mattered.

"*That's right,*" not-Connor urged him on. "*The marks are a good thing, not a bad thing. They make you better. Markus chose you to receive the fourth mark—he saw the greatness in you. He knew you were strong enough to help him.*"

"But not strong enough to resist his command," he muttered.

"*You want this,*" Connor argued. "*Doing this will free you from your weaknesses.*"

Yes, of course he was right. Farrell's weaknesses disgusted him, and he wanted them gone forever. No matter what it took.

The trail of her intoxicating strawberry scent kept leading him on this silent journey through the hallways of Markus's house. Finally, he heard something. A click. Another click, and then a clack.

She'd found the kitchen. And there she hunted for a weapon.

Of course she would fight. Crys had never struck him as the type to wedge herself into a small space and spend her remaining time praying to whatever god might be listening to save her.

He approached the kitchen and watched her riffle through the utensils, her back to him. "Finding anything useful?" he asked, leaning against the doorframe.

She froze. Slowly at first, and then suddenly picking up speed, she turned around and threw something at him. It was headed right for his head, but he deflected it easily.

"Was that a fork?" he asked, frowning as it fell to the ground with a clatter. "Seriously, Crys?"

"You know what?" she said, breathless. "I'll admit it. I did like you in the beginning. More than a little."

"Wow, that's quite a change of subject, isn't it? Go on, though. I'm fascinated."

"What were the chances of me bumping into the infamous Farrell Grayson—twice. *Me*. I thought it was, like, *fate*, the two of us meeting like that."

"Soul mates, did you think?"

"No. I don't believe in soul mates."

"Could have fooled me."

"Especially not when I figured out that there was nothing fateful about those meetings. That you planned them, like some sort of evil stalker."

Farrell rolled his eyes. "What were you saying about liking me?"

"Guys don't usually notice me. Probably because I work really hard at not being noticed."

"Says the girl with the platinum blond hair and obnoxious T-shirts."

"You think those things matter? That they attract any sort of real attention? If anything, they just make it easier for me to play a part: the quirky, artsy girl that you can judge by her appearance and then move on. All the while I hide behind my camera, and I observe. It's way safer there, but I can still pretend like I'm out in the world, experiencing life just like anyone else."

"Someone got bitten by the philosophy bug, huh? Are you trying to distract me? Sorry, but it won't work. We played our game: You hid—poorly—and I sought. Here we are. And now it's time to take this relationship to the next level. For you, that'll be heaven."

"See? You do the same thing. I hide behind my camera, and you hide behind your jokes—which aren't even slightly funny, by the way. We've got that in common. Hiding."

"Wow, Crys, I really appreciate this insight into my inner psyche. But I have to say, I'm getting a little impatient. Where were we?" He took a step closer to her. She backed away until she hit the wall behind her, then pressed her hands back against it as if might give way to an escape route.

"For a few days, though, before I figured out what was really going on, I thought you liked me too. Insane, right? Farrell Grayson pursuing Crys Hatcher, even trying to impress her by taking her to a fancy bar for a fancy cocktail. Buying her a new camera. Making her feel important." She shook her head. "But there was always a small part of me that knew it had to be a lie. And when I found out it was, do you know how I felt?"

"Heartbroken?"

"*Relieved.* And this"—she glanced down at the dagger, and when her eyes met his again, they were void of emotion and cold as ice—

"doesn't surprise me at all. You're scum, Farrell. You could never deserve somebody like me. Somebody *real*. Where would a person like that even fit into your great big fake life? There's no way. It's impossible. And I think you know it."

Ugh. Was she ever going to stop talking? "You've really got a strange idea of what it means to beg for your life."

"I'm not begging. I'm saying what I have to say. You do what you have to do. You loser. You mindless *minion*." She spat at him.

He grimaced and wiped the saliva off his cheek.

Mindless minion.

Nobody spoke to Farrell Grayson like this. And nobody spit on him.

Nobody.

"But you let Mom slap you last night," Connor said. *"I doubt you'd let that happen again."*

"Thanks so much for that, Crys," he said. "That helped more than you might think."

He moved even closer to her, close enough to feel her body heat, as he leaned over her shoulder with his left arm, bracing himself against the wall with his hand. He looked at her, training all five senses onto her. This pissed-off, angry, and totally unafraid thing might just be part of some act, some desperate attempt to fool him.

But he could see it, the fear, bottomless in her ghostly blue eyes.

He was certain he would remember that look for the rest of his life. However long that might be.

"I'm nobody's damn minion," he snarled, and then, with the force of every scrap of strength he had within him, he plunged the blade down, breaking the skin, hitting bone . . .

Impaling his own hand to the wall.

Crys's eyes were squeezed shut. She let out a little shriek, her body cringing as if instinctively from the dagger, but after a few moments she grew silent and still. She blinked, opening her eyes, and then stared up at him. She turned around and saw his hand, pinned to the wall by the golden blade, dripping blood.

She scrambled away from him, ducking down and away from the cage his body had made for her. "What the hell?" she gasped. "What is this? What have you done?"

The pain was exquisite. Exquisitely *horrible*, especially when doubled by the wound on his arm, searing and screaming anew now. But the act had managed to clear his mind just enough to get a little bit of control over Markus's hold on him. "What does it look like? I just stabbed myself in my damn hand."

"Why?"

Because when my mother slapped me, it cleared my head, he thought. *Pain helps me regain control over myself.*

Not-Connor had no immediate response to this realization.

"Would you rather I had stabbed *you*?" Farrell said out loud as he grimaced, watching as his blood trickled down the floral wallpaper. "Because that's what would have happened if I didn't do this to myself."

"I thought that was your plan all along."

"Yeah, me too. But plans change." He glared at her. "Why are you still here? Why aren't you running for the front door as fast as you can like you should have done ten minutes ago? You're still hoping for that dagger, aren't you? Trust me, it's not worth it. You really don't want to be around me right now."

"Oh, I think I got the memo on that. Loud and clear."

"Aw, you're mixing your metaphors. How adorable." He eyed her warily as she moved closer to him. "What are you doing?"

Crys grasped the hilt of the dagger and, grimacing, pulled it out of his hand. Immediately, he clasped his injured hand against his chest, giving her a very dark look. "You know how in horror movies, there are those girls who hear a weird noise and stupidly decide to go down to the basement to check it out, and then they get torn apart by a monster? Welcome to Hollywood, Hatcher."

"You like thinking of yourself as the monster, don't you?" she sneered, grabbing a dishtowel from the counter. Farrell thought she might give it to him, to help his bleeding wound, but instead she just wiped the blood off the dagger's blade. "But you just proved that you're not."

"All I proved was that I had a single moment of doubt. It won't happen again. Look"—he held out his hand to her—"the memory of that little fleeting moment is already fading."

She gasped as she watched the wound begin to heal and close before their eyes. "Holy crap."

"The gift with purchase of my soul. One of the many perks of being a mindless minion."

Suddenly, something hit him hard in the gut. Whatever it was was invisible to him, but it knocked him right to his knees all the same. He cried out in pain, doubling over.

The pain left him in seconds, but so did his strength. He found that he could barely move.

"See this right here?" he mumbled from his prone position. "Another perfect cue for you to start running away."

"What the hell is happening to you?"

He knew exactly what the hell was happening to him, but he wasn't ready to share that with her.

Something had happened to Markus—something bad. The

fourth mark that connected them shared Farrell's energy, his very life, with the Hawkspear leader.

"Having a lousy day so far, that's all," he grunted.

"Looks like more than that to me."

A flash of jagged, fragmented images sliced through his mind, each one fleeting and more painful than the last. A breakfast spread on a long table. Becca's pale, frightened face. Worn wooden floorboards. Bright lights shining down from far overhead. Markus clenching his fists on the table before slumping down on top of it, staring off, dead-eyed, at a sea of red seats.

And then Damen Winter's cold, bottomless eyes burning darkly in his chalk-white face.

"Farrell! Snap out of it!" Crys was yelling at him and nudging him, not all that gently, with her sneaker.

With a painful *snap*, the images in his head disappeared. Now the only pain he felt was concentrated in his burning forearm.

"Has anyone ever told you what great bedside manner you have?" He clutched his head and eyed the dagger in Crys's hands as he tried to sit up. He didn't like that she still had possession of the blade, for too many reasons to count.

"What just happened?" she demanded. "You stared mumbling something about Becca. And Markus. And a dungeon. What was that?"

He paused to work it over in his head, trying to decide if this had been his imagination or an actual vision brought on by the fourth mark. His imagination was usually much kinder to him. "I think I know where they are."

"You know where Markus is?" Crys gasped. "Where Becca is?"

He closed his eyes, trying so hard to focus, to find that strange—if painful—connection again. But it was gone.

Still, he'd seen enough. "I think so." He then let out a very small, very humorless laugh. "Why, you believe that I might have some kind of magical connection to Markus that might help lead the way?"

"I don't know what I believe anymore, to tell you the truth. All I know right now is that, unbelievable or not, it's the best lead we have. Where are they?" Her expression softened. "Please, Farrell. You have to tell me."

"Markus's theater."

She inhaled sharply. "I need to go there."

"Lucky for you, I know where it is."

Crys left the kitchen suddenly. Farrell slowly went after her, feeling the full extent of his exhaustion now, as if someone had just pushed a brick wall on top of him and left him for dead right after he'd finished running a marathon.

He followed Crys back to the library. She was at the desk, fishing around in her purse, which she'd left on top of it. She pulled out a phone.

"What are you doing?" he asked weakly.

She held her finger up to him and began speaking into the phone. "Angus? It's Crys. Jackie was arrested this morning—they came to the penthouse with a warrant. She thinks Markus told them, but I don't know how they knew . . . that's the least of our problems right now. Anyway, it means that you have to deal with me until Dr. Vega can bail her out. I have the dagger. Call me back if you ever want to get your hands on it."

She pressed the red button on her screen and looked at Farrell.

"First," he began, "your aunt's been arrested?"

"Yes." She didn't elaborate.

"Second, who the hell is Angus?"

"A thief. And though he doesn't come right out and say it, I'm pretty sure he's also a hired assassin. He's also Jackie's friend, and he's going to help us get Becca back."

"Us?"

Crys narrowed her eyes a bit. "I'm sorry, I was under the assumption that you wanted to free your lord and master. Especially now that you've got this nifty little magical bond with him."

He hissed out a breath. "Why do . . . *we* need Angus's help?"

"Jackie thinks he's trustworthy and all he wants to do is help. But I know what he wants." She held up the dagger to the light streaming through the window. "Shiny, magical objects that he can sell for big bucks. He's a horse, and this is the carrot he's after. We definitely don't want to go it alone against Damen Winter. And Angus may be petty, but he's also pretty badass from what I can tell, and he's heard of Damen and the kind of magic he can do. I know it's not a lot to go on, but . . . are you in?"

"Markus hasn't taken back that command he gave me last night, you know. It's still right here." He tapped his forehead. "As soon as I regain my strength, all bets are off."

She sighed with what sounded like an edge of impatience. "You're not going to kill me. You stopped yourself already."

"Once. I stopped myself once."

"You didn't answer my question," she said, the impatience in her tone even sharper now. "Are you in?"

Her phone lit up and started to ring, and by the way Crys looked down at the screen, Farrell could tell it was Angus calling her back.

This was going to be a very bad day, even worse than he'd already expected it to be.

He glared at her. "Yeah, I'm in."

Chapter 21

MADDOX

Princess Cassia arranged lodging at the inn on the second floor of the tavern for everyone for the night. She promised that they'd talk more in the morning as she sent Maddox, Barnabas, Liana, and Al off with one of her henchmen to escort them to their rooms.

As soon as he saw the henchmen disappear down the hallway, Maddox turned to Barnabas. "I don't trust her," he whispered.

"Who, her?" he asked absently, his gaze focused on Liana as she slipped down the hall and into her room.

Maddox glared at him. "No. The princess."

"In this life, trust can be earned by very few. Lucky for us, then, that we don't need to trust her. All that matters is that we found her and that we now have a chance to make her see our vision for a better Mytica. I know we can win her over."

Maddox eyed him skeptically but remained silent.

Barnabas gave him a smirk. "Perhaps you should lock your door if you're so nervous. By the way, you get Al tonight." He thrust the canvas sack at him.

"Marvelous," said Al, his voice sounding particularly muffled in the narrow hallway. "I will keep watch over you, young necromancer, and alert you to any dangers that may arise."

Maddox looked down at the bag in his hands and sighed. "Great."

"Good night then," Barnabas said before ducking into his room, and with that, their conversation came to an end. Maddox crept into his room as well, a wave of relief washing over him as soon as he saw his warm, welcoming bed for the night. Despite how uneasy he felt about Princess Cassia and her seven hulking henchmen, all of them sleeping under the very same roof as him, he was pleased to find that sleep claimed him far faster than he ever would have guessed.

———

He dreamed of Becca Hatcher.

"Maddox!" she cried out across a wide chasm that separated them from each other. The ground was black and dry and void of life, the skies dark and swirling with storm clouds. "Maddox, please! Help me!"

Panicked, he tried to find a way across, but the split in the earth was miles wide in every direction and descended down into nothing but darkness. It was a place he'd never seen before, not even in his nightmares.

Another scream drew his attention back to her. Grabbing hold of her was a man with pale white skin and eyes the color of a starless night.

"Does this girl mean something to you?" the man shouted across the abyss to Maddox.

Terror gripped his heart and squeezed. "Yes! She's important to me—*very* important. Please don't hurt my friend!"

"Your magic is too dark for friends. Too dark, too old, and soon it will frighten everyone away, leaving you by yourself. Eternally. We have that in common, witch-boy. We have so very much in common."

"Who are you?" Maddox demanded, fists clenched. He tried to will his magic forth, hoping to render the man unconscious, but no matter how hard he focused, nothing happened.

"Don't you know who I am?" The man smiled as Becca slid, as if boneless, to the ground in front of him.

Suddenly and with horror, Maddox realized that he was looking into a mirror at his own head-to-toe reflection, at his own black eyes. Becca's lifeless body lay at his feet.

He woke, clawing at the bed linens. Sunshine streamed in through the small window to his right. It took him several moments to clear his mind of the chilling nightmare, the first he'd ever had that didn't include dark spirits tormenting him.

"Becca," he said under his breath. "I very much hope that your dreams are more pleasant than mine."

"Becca?" Alcander asked from his perch on the nightstand. "So that's the name of the lass you were dreaming about? You were a sight during the night. So much grunting and groaning and tossing about. But I do not judge, for I was once a young lad like you."

"It's not like that," Maddox grumbled, embarrassed now—and embarrassed that he was embarrassed. But if nothing else, this did help to clear his mind some more.

Still shaken by the dream, he got up and dressed. His shoulders ached from sleeping on the coarse straw mattress in the tiny room, which was far less comfortable than sleeping outside on the ground. With Al in his sack, Maddox descended the rickety stairs to the dark and currently vacant tavern. Shutters were drawn over the windows, and only a few candles and lanterns lit the cavernous room.

Then he saw Liana already sitting across from Cassia at a table behind a wooden pillar. Liana greeted him with a smile.

"Sleep well?" she asked.

"Mostly." He glanced at the princess. "Good morning."

Cassia nodded. "And to you as well."

He swept his gaze over the room. "Where are your large, hulking friends this morning?"

"I asked for some time to speak privately with you all. My friends don't like it very much when they're not close by." She smiled. "They worry about my safety."

"I get the feeling that you can handle yourself quite well," Liana said.

"True enough." Cassia eyed the sack that Maddox carried. "You may free your bodiless friend from his canvas prison. We have this establishment all to ourselves this morning."

After a moment's hesitation, Maddox drew Al out of his sack and gently placed him on the table, then took a seat himself.

"Good morning, Your Highness," Al said cheerily. "I would bow, of course, but, alas, my current condition prohibits that."

"So incredibly fascinating," Cassia whispered. She leaned closer to peer at him. "How do you feel?"

"Surprisingly, I feel fine, princess. But I hope to feel much better very soon."

"Really? How so?"

"Oh, let me tell her, would you, Al?" Everyone except Al turned to watch Barnabas enter the tavern. He approached the table and pulled a chair up to the end of it. "Al was Valoria's scribe for quite some time. We have hope that he'll provide us with some inside information that will help us bring about her swift demise. Should he prove his worth, we will see what we can do about reuniting him with his body."

"I did help you find the princess," Al reminded him curtly.

"True," Barnabas said.

"You can do that?" the princess breathed, now regarding Maddox with unmasked awe.

"My son is incredibly gifted," Barnabas replied before Maddox had a chance to respond, then gestured at the head on the table. "As you can see."

Maddox stared at him with both shock and a sudden sense of warmth. Did Barnabas realize that that was the first time he'd referred to him so openly as his son?

"He certainly is." The princess glanced at Liana. "Are you Barnabas's wife?"

Liana laughed very long and very hard at this. "Hardly," she said once she'd finally recovered. "I like to think I have finer taste in men than that."

Barnabas frowned at her while the rest of the table tried hard to suppress their laughter. "I don't find this quite as humorous as you all."

"Just speaking the truth," Liana said cordially. "Nothing personal. But I can tell you wouldn't make a very good husband. You're too . . . oh, I don't know. Too guarded, perhaps. And much too jaded when it comes to love, obviously."

"Guarded, perhaps, but I am not jaded." Barnabas shook his head, groaning. "And I think we're done discussing this and other things that have no basis in reality." He turned to face Cassia alone. "Princess, thank you for giving us the chance to speak with you. Once again, I am so very glad to see that you are well."

She raised an eyebrow. "Do I seem well to you? Appearances can be deceiving."

"I know you've gone through a great deal in these last several years."

"You've put it extremely mildly, Barnabas. Three years ago my adoptive family was murdered, and I barely escaped with my life." She glanced at Al. "Perhaps, as Valoria's former scribe, you were already aware of this."

Al sighed. "I'm afraid that I was. The goddess made many decisions that I vehemently disagreed with, but I hope you know that I had nothing to do with them, nor was I complicit. Please find it in your heart to forgive me, princess. To argue with the goddess on any subject is to volunteer to face her wrath."

"As you can see," Maddox said. "Al did face her wrath. That's why he's only a head."

"Had I not been aware of the horrible fate of your family," Al continued, ignoring Maddox, "I would not have known where to instruct Barnabas and Maddox to start searching for you."

"I understand," Cassia said. There was no blame or outrage in her eyes, only a faraway look of grief and sadness. "They never kept any secrets from me, you know. My mother, my father, my sister . . . they were so wonderful. For thirteen years they treated me as their own. They raised me, fed me, clothed me, educated me. Kept me safe from harm. All the time telling me stories about my true father, King Thaddeus, and how incredible he was. How brave and kind and that everyone loved him—before Valoria arrived and killed both him and my birth mother." Cassia paused. Maddox worried that she might begin to weep, but instead she took a deep breath and went on. "She is evil."

"She is," Barnabas agreed. "I am so sorry for your losses, princess."

"For so long I wanted to die as well, to join my family in their graves. I sat by those graves day and night, praying that they would come back to me." Her eyes were on Maddox, who was regarding her intently. "You look like you understand how this feels."

He swallowed past the lump in his throat. "I lost my mother. It happened very recently. She too was killed by one of Valoria's men."

Cassia reached across the table and clasped his hand. "I'm so sorry."

"Thank you. Me too."

One of Cassia's henchman approached the table and placed two trays down in front of them. On top of the trays were plates of fried quail eggs, smoked sausage, and ground roots cooked with onions.

Cassia smiled down at the food and then up at the henchman. "Axel is an excellent cook," she said to the table. "He feeds us perhaps a bit too well. I have grown far too large in the time he's been with me."

"You're just a slip of a girl, princess," Axel said with a bow of his head, although his cheeks flushed at the compliment. "It will take much more than a hearty breakfast to put any real fat on your bones."

Again Cassia smiled at him and then turned to the rest of the table. "Axel and the others found me while Valoria's guards were performing yet another sweep of the countryside. I was out by the graves, in danger of being found. They welcomed me into their homes, fed me, kept me safe. They knew who I was—they'd heard the rumors of what had happened to my family. Instead of handing me over to the goddess for a large reward, they chose to offer me a home here. They taught me how to fight, how to protect myself, and how to survive."

"The princess is a fast learner," Axel said proudly. "She's like a sister to us all."

"You know how to fight?" Liana said.

Cassia raised an eyebrow. "You sound surprised."

"Well, it's rare for a girl to learn such things," Liana admitted. "Most men prefer to keep women helpless and reliant on their protection."

Barnabas grumbled. "And you say I'm the jaded one?"

"I agree," Cassia said to Liana. "It is rare, and I am fortunate. My men have treated me like a queen without a throne. I don't deserve them."

"You need no throne to be our queen, Your Highness," Axel said.

She smiled at him again. "Axel was the one who taught me how to use a dagger. From there, I learned how to wield a sword. I can hold my own quite well in hand-to-hand combat. Considering what lies ahead for us all, this knowledge will be an asset."

"You are a true rebel princess," Barnabas said with admiration.

"*A rebel princess*," she repeated, nodding. "I like the sound of that."

The door swung open. Another of Cassia's large henchmen entered the tavern room with purpose and reached the table in a few large strides. He leaned over and whispered something in the princess's ear.

As she listened, her cheerful, composed expression faded and was replaced by something harder, more determined. "I see," she said tightly. "Barnabas, Liana, Maddox . . . Al . . . this is Huck. He has been scouting nearby villages to learn the latest status of Valoria's movements."

"Sorry . . . what?" Maddox asked.

"For days there have been rumors that the goddess has been drawing closer and closer to Central Mytica with a small army at her back. Now those rumors have been confirmed."

"Oh my!" Al exclaimed. "It's me! She's come after me!"

"What?" Liana asked. "After *you*?"

"She must have heard that I'd . . . that my *head* had disappeared. I'm sure Her Radiance has regretted . . . well, what she ordered to be done to me. The guilt must have been tearing her apart, stealing her sleep and haunting her days. She wants to help me, restore me, give me another chance. This is wonderful news!" Al blinked and, in the silence that followed, shifted his eyes from Barnabas to Maddox. "I mean, that evil creature must die, and of course I will help you in any way I can."

Maddox tried to remain calm as he willfully ignored Al's self-centered ramblings.

"She's after us," Barnabas said, giving voice to Maddox's thoughts.

Cassia nodded. "When we first heard the rumors, I assumed she was coming to finish what she'd started with me. But the more I think about it, the more I know—as well as she does—that I'm no competition for her. She doesn't fear me enough to leave her palace to come after me herself. But you . . ." She stared across the table at Maddox. "You are another matter altogether."

"You think the goddess fears *me*?" he asked quietly, his nightmare of the man with eyes like midnight echoing in his mind.

"I think she would be unwise not to," Cassia replied.

"Perhaps it's true," Al said. "Perhaps Maddox is the only key you need to defeat the goddess. His magic—"

"No." Barnabas cut him off. "That's not the answer. I have the answer, princess, and forgive me for laying out my plan in such haste, but it seems our circumstances have changed. The answer to all of our problems lies with the southern goddess."

"Just say the name," Liana said. "*Cleiona*. This is no time for misunderstandings."

Barnabas winced. "That name leaves a rancid taste in my mouth."

Liana rolled her eyes.

"It could work," Maddox said, nodding. He was pleased that Barnabas seemed more open to this idea now. If need be, Maddox would be more than happy to combine his magic with the southern goddess's to destroy Valoria.

If Cleiona didn't destroy them first.

"My plan is for you to join us on our journey south, princess," Barnabas continued. "Together, we can convince Her Goldenness that we are earnest."

Liana shook her head. "I'm less inclined to think this plan will work. Why put the princess in such peril, with only us to protect her?"

"Agreed," Axel said darkly. "The princess will go nowhere without me."

"Or without me," Huck added, his arms crossed over his hulking chest.

Barnabas glared at Liana. "I was hoping I'd have your support on this."

She glared right back at him. "You have decided on this course of action without fully considering all the dangers it presents. What if the goddess refuses to listen to a word you have to say? What if she incinerates you on sight and uses her air magic to blow your ashes away?"

"She won't."

"Oh no? And why not?"

"Because I've met her before. She'll give me a fair audience."

Liana rolled her eyes. "You think you're that memorable of a man?"

"In a word? Yes. Let me handle Her Goldenness. And if you have a problem with that, then you don't have to come any further."

"Perhaps I won't."

"That's fine with me."

"Stop it," Maddox snarled. "Can we focus, please? For just one moment? I'm so sick of the constant fighting between you two."

"Agreed," Al said. "Just kiss each other already!"

Liana looked at Al with shock as Cassia watched them both, a fresh and genuine smile on her face.

"Apologies," Cassia said. "But hearing you all squabble . . . it makes me think of my family. That's what you are, whether you realize it or not. A family."

Barnabas gave her a forced, polite smile as he turned to her again. "Princess, my offer still stands. I would be honored if you would join us as we go to request an audience with the southern goddess. I cannot guarantee we will be received graciously, but I feel that this is a vital step we must take to reclaim your rightful throne. Will you join us?"

Cassia went quiet, regarding each of them in turn as she leaned back in her chair.

"I will agree," she said finally. "On one condition."

Maddox watched Barnabas try to suppress a grin. "Of course, princess. What is it?"

"I need to show you something. Come with me, all of you."

They followed her out of the tavern and down the road until they reached another stone building that looked like a shop but had no sign hanging above the door. She bowed her head quietly as she placed her hand on the door handle. She took a deep breath and glanced over her shoulder at Maddox. "I feel as if my prayers brought you here, and I know now that you can help me. That you're the only one who can."

"If I can help you, princess," Maddox said, incredibly curious now about what was behind the door, "it would be my honor."

Cassia pushed open the door. Maddox followed her inside with the others trailing after him.

"This is my one condition," she said as she stepped aside to give them a view.

In front of them was a large farm-style table, atop of which lay, side by side, three rotting, dirt-covered corpses.

Maddox watched Cassia gaze at the corpses with love in her eyes before she finally looked up and locked gazes with him again.

"You will use your magic to raise my family from the dead."

Chapter 22

BECCA

The shadow was still with her. Becca could see it lingering in the corner to her right in the Hawkspear Society dungeon.

She knew it was ridiculous to feel any sort of comfort in this, but she did anyway. This shadow—whatever it *really* was—made her think of Maddox and the spirit he'd trapped.

This dungeon was nothing like the one she had shared with Maddox in Mytica. That one had been much smaller, with impenetrable stone walls, a dirt floor, an iron door, and not much else. Still, despite how forbidding and bare and foreign that place was, Becca had been there as a spirit who could walk through walls and locked doors. She hadn't felt trapped there—certainly not in the way Maddox had.

And though she'd of course been able to guess how wretched and desperate Maddox felt about being locked away in a place like that, she'd now come to understand those feelings better than ever.

Feelings of being trapped and helpless, with rapidly diminishing hope.

I wish you were here with me, Maddox, she thought. *I need you to give me some hope.*

Thinking about him helped her stay calm—or as calm as she possibly could, given that Markus King sat motionless in the opposite corner. Sweeping her gaze over Markus again to make sure he was still unconscious, she took in more details about the stark space. The room wasn't entirely empty; there was a toilet in the corner. In Maddox's dungeon, she cringed to remember there'd been only a bucket.

Her gaze rested on the door. It didn't even have an inside handle, but that hadn't stopped her from trying to push, pull, and force it open several times when they were first thrown in. Nor did it stop her from getting up now and trying once again.

Of course it didn't budge. Knowing that she was kidding herself, Becca still inspected every wall and every corner, trying to notice anything—even the smallest feature or detail—that might in some way lead to a way out.

"Sit down."

Becca froze at the sound of Markus's weary voice.

"You're going to tire yourself out."

Markus had looked like hell after whatever Damen had done to him. But now, as she dared to look directly at him, she was surprised to see that he didn't look quite so bad anymore. In fact, he looked nearly back to normal. The shadows under his eyes were fading, and his complexion was regaining its healthy color.

"You've practically recovered," she ventured.

"Somewhat."

"So fast? Even after all that Damen did to you?"

"I have ways of recovering that even Damen doesn't know about."

"I thought he knew everything."

"No. Not everything," he said from the floor, one leg crossed on top of the other, gazing up at Becca. "Is there anything you need to tell me?"

She actually laughed at that—just a short, nervous burst of a sound, but a laugh all the same. "Can't think of a thing."

"I'm serious, Becca. A lot happened last night, and I'm sure you're quite upset about these . . . revelations."

"What is this? Are you trying to bond with me?" She hissed out a breath, unable to hold her anger in check any longer. "I don't care about any revelations. I'm not your daughter—I could never be the daughter of a monster."

"It's as much of a shock to me as it is to you."

Becca glanced around the makeshift dungeon, eyes lingering on the as-yet-unexplored area behind the toilet, frantically searching for a way out. "Please tell me there's a secret passageway out of here."

"No passageway." He blinked once. "Tell me about the shadow that follows you, Becca."

She pressed her lips together. The shadow was her secret, one that was directly related to the book Markus wanted so badly. Which meant that telling him about it would be very dangerous. She forced herself not to look at it.

"This is not a time to stay quiet," he said, his tone edged with annoyance. "I saw the shadow with you at the breakfast table, and I can see it now, right there, in the corner. There's no point denying it." He paused, and Becca just stared down, refusing to look at him. "Today isn't the first time I've seen it."

Suddenly she brought her gaze up to his. She couldn't help it—curiosity was burning away some of her fear and anger.

Markus's expression was tense. "The last time I saw it, it was attached to someone with far more power than you could ever dream of possessing. An immortal named Eva—who is also Damen's twin sister. She was a sorceress of the elements, and our leader. And my friend." He narrowed his eyes and watched her as she listened. "You don't look surprised by any of this."

She already knew that Eva was Maddox's birth mother, and in her vision had heard Eva refer to Damen as "brother."

But . . . *twin sister*?

Still, she shook her head, uncertain and fearful.

His eyes narrowed. "What exactly do you know about all of this, Becca Hatcher?"

She thought back on her plan to talk to Markus at the masquerade ball. She'd been so confident that sharing with Markus what she knew about Valoria, about the dagger, was the right course to take. That plan had been destroyed when she'd overheard his and Jackie's conversation.

Now that Damen had entered the picture, it seemed she'd run out of options.

"When I touched the book," she said, her voice hoarse and quiet, "my body fell into a coma, but my spirit visited Mytica."

Markus went silent, his expression steady except for a slight widening of his eyes. "Tell me more."

"Valoria was on the throne. She was hell-bent on finding you and getting the dagger back. Another goddess, Cleiona, ruled in the South, but I didn't see her."

"*Goddess?*" Markus furrowed his brow. "What—how can that be?"

She shook her head. "I don't know. All I know is that I wanted to get back home, and I did."

His eyes shifted back and forth as if he was trying to make sense of all the information Becca had just set before him. "What about Eva? Did you see her? Did you hear anything of her?"

Markus didn't know what had happened.

She forced the words out. "She's dead."

Markus inhaled sharply. He pressed himself back against the wall, regarding Becca with unshielded shock. "No. Impossible."

She swallowed hard. "She was killed by the goddesses."

He continued to stare at her for several moments before he leaped to his feet and let out a roar, a sudden and deafening yell that made her yelp and stumble backward until she hit the wall.

"No! She's not dead, she can't be!"

"I—I'm sorry. I am, but it's true."

Grief shattered Markus's expression. He sat down on the floor again and held his face in his hands.

She hated this creature before her, but she also hated seeing anyone having to endure pain like this. Her mouth had gone too dry to speak, and her heart thundered in her chest.

"It makes sense now," he muttered. "The book . . . the shadow that follows you. It's chosen a new guardian. And that guardian is you."

She swallowed hard, trying to gather her composure as much as possible. "What does *that* mean?"

He was silent, his eyes growing glossy with a distant look.

"*Markus*," she hissed. "What does it mean?"

Markus blinked, bringing his gaze back to the present. "It means," he said slowly, "that we might actually have a chance. That Damen might not succeed in destroying everything I've worked so hard to achieve here." Then he started to laugh, and the hollow, humorless sound chilled Becca right down to her bones.

"What are you talking about?" she forced out. "A shadow isn't going to get us out of this room."

"If it was only a shadow, I'd have to agree." He pushed himself up to his feet again and pointed at the shadow. "But that right there, Becca, is the book's pure and undiluted magic. And it has attached itself to you in particular." He laughed, chillingly, again. "Oh, Damen. You've helped to brew a perfect storm in here, and you have absolutely no idea. Just wait until you see what you've done. I wish I could be there to witness it."

"If it's so important, why can't he see it like you can?"

"Because Damen was never like the rest of us. And this magic—this magic in particular—has been guarded from his eyes."

Becca had never felt more confused, but she wasn't about to push him to explain further. Markus King didn't seem like the type of person who would tolerate being pushed.

"When Damen was draining me of my magic—of my life—he didn't realize that I was attempting to do the same," Markus went on after a pause. His voice sounded far off, as if he wasn't speaking specifically to Becca but perhaps to a small audience. "Damen had a very special kind magic within him before we thought he'd been destroyed forever—special even beyond his ability to influence minds and end lives. He can walk between worlds."

"The book . . ." Becca thought back to what happened behind Camilla's cottage, when they were faced with the goddess and her dark scheme to get to Markus and the dagger. "Valoria used the magic in the book on a stone wheel to create a gateway here."

"Damen didn't need any book, only his own magic. And I stole a trace of that magic without him realizing it. I also have my magic—what little is left of it. We have that," he said, nodding at the shadow. "And then we also have what seems to be the most important secret ingredient in this particular recipe. You."

The final word, especially when directed at Becca, sounded incredibly ominous.

She crossed her arms tightly over her chest. "A recipe for . . . for *what*?"

"For sending you back to Mytica."

She gaped at him, eyes somehow narrowed yet wide with shock at the same time, certain she'd heard him wrong. "Impossible."

"Improbable? Yes. Impossible? No. It's vital that you go there and find an immortal at once—even Valoria, if there is no one else. Find them and tell them that Damen still lives. Tell them where he is, that I'm here too. Only an immortal will be able to save this world."

"Why would they care about *this* world?" Becca said, her mind reeling and her mouth so dry she could barely speak.

"I didn't say they would. But I know they care about Damen. They know how dangerous he is. And they know that if they don't act, he will return one day to seek his vengeance on them. When that happens, everything—I mean *everything*—will be destroyed. They won't want that," he said with a thin, sickly laugh. "It was one of the few common goals that united my people: ridding the universe of Damen."

"Maybe if you'd accepted him instead of treating him like an outcast, he wouldn't be the way he—" Becca said frantically before Markus cut her off.

"You don't understand!" Markus snapped. "Damen can't be any other way. He *is* death and chaos and destruction. He can't ever change, not even if he wanted to."

This was too much for her. All of this unfathomable information was too overwhelming to even begin to digest. She began pacing the small cell, wringing her hands.

"I know you're afraid," Markus said. "I'm not telling you not to be or that you shouldn't be. This is not a mission that ordinary fifteen-year-old girls are asked to take on. But you're not an ordinary fifteen-year-old girl."

"Why can't you go?" she asked, her voice cracking. "If the magic necessary to make a trip like this possible is in this very room, then why not you? This is your world, your immortal friends or enemies, you're talking about. Not mine."

He smiled, but it held no joy. None of his smiles did. "Because to make this work, it's going to take all of my magic. Every last trace of it."

Becca remembered what Crys had said the night she woke from her coma, on the stage of this very theater. She said that if Markus was made of magic, and if that magic was fading, he would die because of it.

"Doing this is going to kill you," she said, stunned yet somehow calmer as one more piece of this puzzle settled into place.

"Yes," he said simply.

She stared at him, shaking her head. "But why? Why would you make a sacrifice like that?"

"Because, Becca, this is my world to save, not Damon's to destroy. For that, I am willing to make this sacrifice." He looked at her solemnly, and for a fraction of a second she could almost forget that the melancholy man before her was the same one who was responsible for so many deaths and ruined lives. "Now, Becca, I can't make you do this, so I need you to agree to follow through with this plan, knowing what's at stake."

She was stunned into such a silence that she wondered if she would ever talk again, let alone answer his question. The thought of going back to Mytica terrified her—even if it meant she might see Maddox again.

But how likely was that? She had no idea how big his world

was. She might get there only to find herself all alone, searching, unseen and unheard. Trapped there forever, possibly unable to ever return . . .

But with Damen here, if no one came to stop him, there might not be a world to return to.

Somehow, unsure whether it was her own will or some other force's doing, she found herself nodding. "Yes," she said quietly. "I agree."

With nothing more than a single nod—not a smile or a pat on the head or some comforting words about how brave she was—Markus got to work. Silently and with intense focus, he held his arms out to either side of him.

Becca watched him and realized she still didn't fully trust that he would do what he said. Was this selfish man actually willing to give up his immortal life for this, even if it was so important?

The idea that he had the ability—the pure desire—to put the future of this borrowed world above his own survival . . . it was a concept so confusing that she could barely steady her mind long enough to think about the journey that lay ahead for her.

Part of her, the fearful part, hoped that Markus would fail at whatever he was trying to do. The other part of her, the brave part, was ready to do whatever she had to in order to stop Damen.

Unfortunately, the brave part of her was much smaller than the fearful part.

Then, seemingly from nowhere, a wind began to swirl around the room, blowing Becca's hair back from her shoulders. Markus's eyes began to glow as the inky shadow, governed by the path of the wind, moved toward him. The swirling funnel of air kept gathering force around Markus, the eye of this particular storm.

He shifted his glowing gaze to her. "Farewell, Becca Hatcher."

All she could do was nod as she grappled to understand what was about to happen to her.

His eyes began to glow brighter. Then he grunted, as if in pain. She watched those dark circles return underneath his eyes, watched his cheeks grow hollow, his skin become sallow and dry, like the skin of a corpse. His chest heaved, as if every breath was a massive undertaking.

And then he cried out. His glowing eyes flashed with blinding light as his body shattered into a thousand pieces . . . and disappeared.

Becca watched, horrified, her hand pressed to her mouth and her eyes burning with the threat of tears.

"Oh my God," she whispered.

He was gone.

In the spot where he was just standing there was now a whirling gateway. Becca recognized it immediately—it looked just like the one that Valoria conjured with the book and Maddox's magic.

"I can't do this!" she said to herself, frantically looking around the cell again, praying that this was all a trick, that Markus had left her a secret passageway after all. "I can't do it," she repeated. "I can't go. Maddox, wherever you are, I need you to give me courage. I need you to be with me for this. I need you to help me. Please."

She heard the unmistakable sound of a key turning in a lock, and her blood ran cold.

Damen. Here to check on his little experiment about the difficult but necessary choices one will make to survive.

Becca watched the door, barely breathing, as it began to creak open.

She closed her eyes, turned, and leaped through the swirling gateway.

Chapter 23

MADDOX

Maddox stood, stunned and speechless, in the room with the princess and her deceased family.

Cassia frowned. "Did you hear what I asked of you?"

"We all did," Barnabas said. "And the answer is no."

"I believe I asked Maddox," Cassia said. Axel and Huck stood on either side of her, their jaws clenched.

"And I believe I have the right to answer for him," Barnabas said, his tone now completely void of both patience and friendliness. "You can't be serious about wanting this."

"I've never been more serious about anything in my life," Cassia said, indignant. "This is my *family*. The only family I've ever known, taken from me by that evil creature that proclaims herself a goddess. I didn't ask to be the heiress, sentenced to a life of hiding from her unrelenting wrath. I was no threat to Valoria. I was content to live my life quietly, as a normal person, but she destroyed all that for me. And my family is dead because of me—they died protecting me!" Her voice broke, and she grew quieter as she went on. "I—I watched as guards cut my sister's throat . . . as they slayed my mother and father while they begged for mercy. Begging mercy not for themselves, but for *me*. They were brave and selfless in the face of their undeserved deaths. It wasn't their time."

"I'm so sorry for your loss, princess," Liana said gently, "but you must realize that what you're asking for—what you think you want—it isn't natural. And it isn't right."

"Oh, isn't it? And *that* is?" Cassia pointed at the sack Liana held. The top was open so that Alcander was visible from the nose up. He blinked.

"Your Highness," Al said, his voice muffled but earnest, "I seem to be an . . . anomaly."

"Not to get into unpleasant details," Barnabas said, his voice strained, "and I certainly don't mean to be flippant or unsavory, but Al was, um, *freshly* dead when he was resurrected. Your family . . . their souls have been separated from their physical forms for three years."

"I don't care how long it's been," Cassia snapped. "Your son is powerful—the most powerful of all the witches. And I request—I *demand*—that he use his magic to bring my family back to me."

Barnabas shook his head. "No. I won't risk it."

Her eyes flashed with anger. "*You* won't?"

"Apologies, princess, but Barnabas is fearful for my *own* soul," Maddox explained, finally finding his voice. "The depth of my power . . . it's vastly unknown, even to me."

"Then let's find out how deep that power goes," she persisted.

Barnabas flicked a glance at Axel and Huck. "How do you feel about your young princess making this request? Do you see, as I do, how horribly troubling it is?"

Axel stayed still, looking straight ahead and not meeting Barnabas's glare, just as any well-trained guard would. "I support any command that Princess Cassia makes. And right now she commands that your son use his magic to bring her family back to life."

"If you do this for me," Cassia said, her voice becoming more pitchy and desperate now, "I will do *anything* for you. I will go to the ends of the world to help you destroy Valoria or any other enemies you have. Please."

"Princess, I'm sorry, but I must agree with Barnabas," Liana said, eyeing the corpses uneasily. "The magic that Maddox possesses . . . it's rare. So incredibly rare and so very dangerous. To use it in this manner, on not one subject but *three* . . . that would be as detrimental to him as taking a mortal life. His soul will almost definitely darken, possibly to the point of no return."

"You say that it's *almost* definite. But you don't know for sure." The princess turned to Maddox once again. "Maddox, I'm speaking to you. Only you. Don't let these two answer for you. I know you understand what it's like to lose someone you love so deeply that their absence hollows out a bottomless hole in your heart. I see it in your eyes."

"I do understand," Maddox said. In fact, he woke up today with memories of Damaris strong in his mind, and he knew there would always be days like this. "I wanted to raise my mother from death. I appealed to Barnabas to let me. But after he put up such a strong fight, I knew that Barnabas was right. Not only would it damage my soul . . . there was no guarantee that she would have been the same as she was before. Not long before she was murdered, I accidentally raised a whole cemetery of skeletons, and that was . . ." He shook his head, grimacing to remember the horror he'd felt that day, doubled by the fact that he'd been the one to draw those creatures from their graves. "I—I cannot do this for you. Princess, please understand that what you're asking for is impossible."

"I see," she said quietly. "Then it seems we've reached an impasse."

"What do you mean by that, princess?" Barnabas said, his glare turning suspicious. "I trust that you're not changing your mind about accompanying us south."

Cassia's eyes flashed with anger. "I don't care about the throne. I never have. All I want is my family back—getting revenge on the monster who did *this* would have only added a little sweetness to the situation. The only reason I would have gone with you to speak with that *other* monster would be to pay Valoria a little vengeful visit. But you refuse to help me, so I refuse to help you."

"Fine," Barnabas spat out. "Liana, Maddox, let's go. We cannot afford to waste any more time in this barren place."

"Good!" Cassia screamed, tears now streaking her cheeks. She picked up a vessel filled with dried flowers from the farm table and threw it at Barnabas, who deflected it with his forearm. "Leave and never come back! I hate you all!"

They left the house of corpses immediately. Maddox found his steps were shaky, his legs weak.

They were leaving behind so much grief in their wake. He felt horribly guilty for not being able to help her.

"Do you both have everything you need from the tavern?" Barnabas asked.

"Yes. There's no need to return there," Liana said tightly.

"Are you sure this is a good idea?" Maddox said, glancing over his shoulder. The furious princess and her two soldiers had exited the home and were now standing in the middle of the road, staring after them. "Leaving without her? I *could* try to do as she wishes . . ."

"Damn it, boy," Barnabas growled. "Didn't you hear me? I said *no*."

Maddox stopped, anger rising within him like a blazing sun.

"I'm getting a little tired of you making all of my decisions for me."

"Is that so?"

"Yes."

"Oh dear," Al said. "Please, stop this fighting. It's beginning to give me a rather severe headache."

"You mean to tell me you would risk your soul to raise the souls of people you've never even met?" Barnabas snapped.

"It's important to the princess. Those *souls* are important to the princess."

"The princess, I'm very sorry to say, has clearly been driven mad with grief. She's unable to see reason."

"My magic is powerful, Barnabas. But I can control it. You've said so yourself."

Barnabas let out a sharp bark of a laugh. "Is that right? All of a sudden, young Maddox Corso can control his magic? This is news to me."

Maddox glared at him, outraged. He was tired of being treated like a silly, misbehaving child.

Liana cleared her throat to get their attention. "Let's leave this village before the princess changes her mind about letting us go freely and sends her men after us. Yes?"

Barnabas scoffed. "A traveling band consisting of a witch and a witch-boy is intimidated by a little girl and her tribe of brainless muscle? How sad for us."

Liana narrowed her eyes at him. "There is no reason to lash out at me."

"Oh no? Tell me, Liana: Why haven't we seen even a glimpse of your magic since the night we met? Not even a single flame to help start one of our campfires? I'm starting to think it wasn't just your fortune-telling abilities that were a ruse. And all your stories about the immortals and their imaginary siblings . . . you'd make a better scribe than Al."

"I resent that," Al huffed. "I am the greatest scribe in Mytica—and *beyond*. I was chosen as such by Her Radiance herself."

"Before she *cut your head off!*" Barnabas yelled right into Al's face. Al flinched and squeezed his eyes shut fearfully. "I am traveling with a pack of fools! Enough of this. I will go to see Cleiona on my own. You all can find somewhere nice and safe to wait it out while I take care of this mess alone."

Barnabas turned away from them, only to be stopped in an instant by a wall of flames leaping up before his feet.

"Still think it's all a ruse?" Liana hissed.

Maddox smiled at the incredible display. "Nicely done."

Liana raised an eyebrow. "Nice enough to burn the prideful attitude right out of your father, don't you think?"

Slowly, Barnabas turned to face them, a small, frozen smile on his lips. "Fair enough. Not a ruse."

Suddenly, as if cowering in response to Liana's show of magic, the sunny village began to grow dark. They looked up to see storm clouds gathering above.

Al furrowed his brow. "I have a funny feeling that there's going to be—"

Then, as if on cue, the skies opened up. Rain began falling in torrents, dousing Liana's fire almost instantly.

"A storm," Al finished.

Barnabas swore under his breath. "We can't travel in this. We'll have to take cover until it passes."

"Fine," Liana said.

But then Maddox interjected. "*We? We* need to take cover? I thought you were going on by yourself from here?"

Barnabas sighed wearily. "Apologies for holding strongly to my beliefs about your magic and what it can do to you, Maddox. But what I saw when you raised Al . . . it unsettled me deeply."

Liana frowned and pushed her long wet hair back from her face. "What exactly did you see?"

"His eyes." Barnabas turned his worried face to her. "Maddox's eyes. They went . . . black. Completely black. It was only for a moment, but I can't begin to describe how chilling it was."

"What?" Maddox shook his head. "You never told me this. I didn't feel anything happening to them at the time. I felt my magic, but it . . . it . . ."

"It felt good," Liana said, her gaze laced with deep worry.

Maddox nodded.

"You must never use your magic to raise someone again," she warned. "And never, *ever* use it to kill anyone."

He regarded her and her deadly serious tone with confusion. "How can you be so certain about that?"

"All that matters is that I am certain," she replied immediately. "Please, promise me you'll never use it again."

"I don't mean to interrupt," Alcander gasped. "But I think I may be drowning."

"Oh! Apologies, Al." Liana adjusted his position in the sack so that he could breathe properly, and Al responded with a sighing smile of thanks.

Maddox found himself staring at the head, his thoughts in turmoil.

Here was Al: nothing more than a head that possessed no lungs, yet still he breathed life.

A severed head that managed to live without a body.

He had done this to Al. And it hadn't even been that difficult.

What *was* this strange magic of his? What were its limits? And if it was so bad, so dangerous and dark, then why did it feel so good whenever he used it?

Suddenly, the earth began to rumble and shake violently, almost knocking Maddox off his feet. He shook his head and braced himself against the trembling.

"What's going on?" he shouted above the din.

"Rain *and* an earthquake," Barnabas said, then swore loudly. "Not good."

"We need to go," Liana replied tightly. "Now."

They heard a shriek from somewhere in the road. *Cassia.* Maddox spun around. All of her men had run out to the princess and were now surrounding her in front of the house.

He watched two new figures approach the huddle. Behind them followed what looked like an army of hundreds of men in red uniforms. As they walked, the rain parted like a stage curtain over their heads, keeping them dry.

Maddox's heart sank as he squinted to get a clear view. It was who he feared: Valoria, in a crimson gown with a long, flowing train, holding her arms out to her sides, her palms revealing the water and earth magic symbols blazing upon them. Her elemental magic swirled around her in fierce golden wisps.

To her right walked Goran.

Maddox clenched his fists. Immediately he felt his death magic rise within him, filling him with cool darkness and clear determination.

"Don't you dare," Barnabas growled. "What did I just say to you?"

"He needs to die. They both do."

"Agreed, but not at your hand. Not with your magic. Maddox, look at me. Damn it. Don't make me do this."

Maddox ignored him. He had no choice: His focus could go no-where except on the pair of murders closing in on Cassia and her men. This was his chance.

Barnabas slapped him, hard, across his face.

The pain stunned him. He turned to stare at his father with wide eyes. No one had hit him since Livius, who'd beaten him regularly to keep him fearful and obedient.

He'd hated Livius right down to the marrow in his bones.

"I'm sorry." Barnabas's voice was twisted with regret. "Really, I am. But I had to."

Maddox just stared at him as the ice-cold desire to destroy and kill began to melt away.

"Don't kill Barnabas," Al yelped at Maddox. "He was only trying to help!"

The serious plea made Maddox's breath catch. Was that what it had looked like? That Maddox would kill Barnabas for striking him?

A flash of the nightmare he'd had about Becca and his own re-flection, his eyes black as night, tore through his mind.

He took a shaky step backward. "I'm not going to kill him."

As his momentary bloodlust dissipated, he knew deep in his heart that he didn't want to kill anyone.

"Good. Then may I make a humble suggestion?" Al asked. "Run. Very fast!"

"I agree," Barnabas replied.

At Liana's nod, they turned and ran along the village street, already muddy with rain, toward a tree line marking the edge of the forest several hundred paces away. Other villagers had emerged from shops and cottages to see what was going on, peering through the rain.

Something shiny fell from Barnabas's pocket, and Barnabas im-mediately stopped dead in his tracks.

"What are you doing?" Liana demanded from up ahead.

"The ring! I can't leave it behind."

Had Barnabas really kept that purple-stone ring in his pocket all this time? Maddox had all but forgotten it, but now all he could think was how foolish his father was to be so careless with an object he valued so much.

"Hurry!" Maddox yelled as Barnabas snatched the silver chain off the ground.

"They've spotted us!" Liana cried.

Maddox whipped around to see that Valoria and Goran had shoved past Cassia and her men and were now in swift pursuit of his group. They were so close that Maddox could see the smile on Valoria's face. As she strode swiftly toward them, she stretched out the hand bearing the earth symbol, and it began to glow. The ground started once more to shake, then it split open in front of him, creating a sizable chasm, reminding Maddox again of his terrible dream. With quick thinking all around, they leaped across the quickly widening expanse.

From the opposite direction, a gust of wind rushed toward Valoria and Goran, picking up strength as it traveled. It hit the goddess and assassin with the force of a hurricane, blowing them back fifty feet before slamming them against the side of a stone building.

"What the hell was that?" Barnabas shouted, loud enough to be heard over the howling wind.

"No idea," Maddox gasped, "but let's not stick around and find out."

As they ran along the muddy road, Maddox was hit anew by how terrible he felt for having to leave Cassia behind. Still, while she might be mad, he could tell she was a survivor—he hoped she'd managed to escape during Valoria's change of heart to go after Maddox instead.

On and on they went, pushing their bodies so hard they could no longer speak, until they finally reached the edge where the village met the forest. But they didn't stop there. They continued, outrunning the storm, Maddox's lungs and legs screaming for relief, their clothes beginning to dry under the reawakening sun. Barnabas led the way in a winding path, purposefully inefficient so as to confuse anyone who tried to follow.

Maddox ran until his legs screamed for mercy, until he couldn't take another step. A creek trickled nearby, and he realized he was desperately thirsty.

"Enough," Maddox said, gasping. "I need to rest for at least a moment."

To Maddox's surprise, Barnabas listened. He slowed to a stop, as did Liana behind him, and then turned around to Maddox. He bent over in a gesture of exhaustion, bracing himself with his hands on his knees. "I thought they had us, Maddox," he choked out. "I thought that was it."

"It wasn't," Maddox said.

"No, it wasn't." Barnabas lunged straight toward him and grabbed him in a tight embrace. "I'm sorry for striking you. I'm so sorry."

Maddox was so stunned by this unexpected embrace that he started to laugh. "I forgive you."

Barnabas leaned back and clasped Maddox's face between his hands, his expression full of pain and relief. "I thought you'd try to kill them."

"I wanted to."

"But you didn't."

"No."

"Good." Barnabas nodded firmly. "That's good."

Maddox shook his head, bemused. "And here I thought that was the goal."

"Not at such a steep price."

Liana watched them silently, a sweet but exhausted smile gracing her face, as she hugged Al's sack against her chest.

Barnabas glanced at her and sighed. "As for you . . . you are far more trouble for me than I predicted."

"Trouble for *you*?" she said indignantly, her smile turning into a fiery scowl. "What does that—?"

Barnabas closed the distance between them in two steps, pulled Liana against him, and kissed her. She gasped with surprise against his lips—but she didn't push him away.

Maddox blinked. He hadn't expected that.

"Erm, excuse me?" Al gasped, currently squished tightly between their torsos. "Can't . . . breathe . . . help!"

Barnabas pulled away and looked at Liana, a certain darkness in his gaze that wasn't there before. Al took several deep, desperate breaths as a shocked Liana stepped back and pressed her fingers to her lips.

"Perhaps you also need to be slapped," she managed.

"Al was the one to suggest that we kiss, if you remember. He put the idea in my head. Blame him."

"Ah," she said, nodding. "So that was all Al's fault."

"Completely," Barnabas said, smiling widely now.

"Wait," Al said. "You kissed her? I can't see anything from in here!"

Barnabas ignored him. "Now let's keep moving. We'll find horses, a wagon. If we make great haste, we'll reach the palace of Her Goldenness in a day and a half. And now that we have those two on our tails, I'd say the hastier we move, the better."

With a small smile from Liana, a strong nod from Maddox, and an exasperated sigh from Al, they set out once again on their way. Barnabas led, and Liana and Maddox had to jog in intervals to keep up with his impressively quick pace. As they went, the relief of reaching the forest and hearing kind words from Barnabas faded as Maddox truly began to feel the darkness of the day. He felt so weary, and immeasurably more anxious and uncertain about their mission. How was he supposed to stay positive about reaching their goal when their success depended entirely upon whether or not one hateful goddess would agree to help them destroy another? On today of all days—when they'd found and lost a princess and became bait once again for the evil Valoria and the brute who'd killed Damaris—it seemed particularly impossible to find any hope.

But then he remembered that today was also the day that Barnabas embraced him and told him he was proud of him.

And that it was also the day that stubborn old Barnabas had gone even further and kissed Liana.

If those two events weren't evidence that there was still hope in the world, then Maddox didn't know what was.

"Well," Al said sadly, "I believe I'm starting to come around to the possibility that Her Radiance didn't come here to apologize for the execution and bring me back to the palace."

Maddox felt a pang in his chest for poor Al, yet strangely his sense of hope was bolstered rather than diminished by the talking head's acceptance of reality.

Barnabas turned to the sack in Liana's hands. "I'm sorry, Al. But you're right. That is not why Valoria came."

Maddox was happy that he managed to say this gently.

Al sniffed. "I see."

"Don't be upset," Liana said, hugging the sack close. "You're with us now. I think that's much better than where you were a few days ago."

"Yes," Al agreed. "Quite true. And I must hold tight to the promise of a brighter future."

Barnabas glanced at Maddox, who got a pang in his chest at the allusion to their agreement to reunite Al with his body. Maddox didn't think he could follow through on it.

Summoning consciousness from the dead was one thing, but fully reuniting Al with his body . . . it was uncertain at best.

"A bright future indeed," Liana said. "Now let's go find some horses so we can continue south, shall we?"

Maddox couldn't agree more, but just as he was about to start moving, he was stopped short by Barnabas's outstretched arm, palm forward in a halting gesture.

"*Shh*," Barnabas hissed.

"What is it?" Maddox whispered.

"I hear something—someone—drawing closer."

All four of them went deadly silent, and Maddox strained to listen. There it was: the sound of branches and twigs snapping, of swift footsteps drawing closer.

His hands clenched to fists as, completely by instinct and with no conscious thought, he summoned his magic. As he drew his powers forth, he once again promised himself he wouldn't use them to kill anyone, though he reminded himself that it was perfectly all right to direct it toward rendering this potential threat unconscious.

The noises grew louder until there was no question in Maddox's mind that they were being made by a person heading straight for them. Barnabas motioned for them all to crouch down behind a dense wall of leafy branches, and there they waited for whatever was about to come. Finally, a figure appeared through the thick foliage. The silhouette was slim, and as it drew closer Maddox saw that it belonged to a girl—a lovely girl with long honey blond hair. She wore a black frock—shockingly short—that bared her knees and lower legs.

Suddenly, as if she sensed she was being watched, she stopped a dozen paces away and turned her head. In a single instant, her gaze locked with his. He couldn't look away from those eyes. They looked darker while she stood under the forest canopy, but he knew their true shade to be a brilliant deep blue.

"Maddox!" the girl gasped.

Eyes widening, fists unclenching, he had to steady himself against a tree so that he wouldn't topple over. His face broke into a smile as he managed to choke out a single word.

"Becca."

Chapter 24

CRYSTAL

Crys waited for Angus outside Markus's mansion. She sat on the front step, hugging her knees to her chest, keeping as much distance between herself and Farrell as she could manage. He had remained inside to "try to clear his head," he'd said, for the twenty minutes since Angus had swiftly returned her call. Just as she'd predicted, the thief was eager to learn more about the dagger.

She looked down at it, clenched in her hand, impressed by how calm she'd managed to be so far. It wasn't every day that she was hunted to within an inch of her life by someone who had been magically commanded to kill her.

Farrell's not a killer, she reminded herself over and over, like some sort of twisted mantra. "He's an asshole, a misogynist, and a spoiled brat," she allowed out loud, "but he's not a killer."

"Aw, come on." The front door clicked shut behind her. "You shouldn't give me so many compliments," Farrell said. "They're going to go to my head."

Her whole body went tense. She turned and gave him a wary glare as he slid on his dark sunglasses, repressing the sudden urge to run. "It's not funny."

"I'm not laughing. You really think I'm a misogynist? I love wom-en! All sorts of women. Young, old, brunettes, redheads . . . platinum blondes." His words were flippant, but his tone was strained and serious. He paused and let his smile fall a little as his eyes rested on the dagger in Crys's hand. "I think it would be best for you keep the dagger in that handbag of yours before you cut yourself."

"Fine." She put the blade away and clutched her handbag to her chest.

"I hope you realize that I'll need that back. It doesn't belong to you."

"It doesn't belong to you either," she countered.

His jaw tightened. "At the ball, Markus told me that Damen Winter made that thing."

Crys hated even thinking of that cold, sick, cruel man with the black eyes. He had taken Becca somewhere, and she didn't even know if her sister was still alive . . .

Dad, she thought, her throat growing thick in seconds, *I wish you were here. So, so badly. You'd know what to do.*

Her eyes burned, but she refused to cry. She couldn't. Which was why it was best not to think about her father at all right now.

Especially while she was with Farrell.

He'd said he didn't know where her father was or when he'd be back. Was that the truth? Or did Farrell know exactly what really happened to him?

She eyed Farrell now, wondering if he was capable of telling her the truth about anything.

"If looks could kill," he said. "What summoned the sudden look of death?"

"Forget it," she muttered. *For now,* she thought.

"Consider it forgotten."

Becca had told Crys that the dagger was from Mytica and that some sort of goddess was looking for it. Now apparently Damen Winter had been thrown into the mix. Crys could barely keep up with it all anymore. "So you're saying it's Damen's dagger? Please tell me you're not thinking about trading it in exchange for getting your lord and master back."

"No. That's not even a possibility."

"Interesting," Crys said. "When I called Markus your lord and master, you didn't correct me."

"No, I didn't, did I?"

"So you're finally agreeing that's what he is?" She braced herself for a witty or cutting reply, but Farrell didn't even smirk. Nor did he answer the question.

"We're not giving it to this Angus person either," he said.

Even when Crys glanced away, she could feel the heat of his gaze on the side of her face. "I made him a bargain."

Farrell let out a chilly scoff. "You bargained with something that's not yours to bargain with."

"He wouldn't have agreed to help if I hadn't. All I did was *say* I would give it to him. See that bridge, Farrell? Let's cross it when we get to it, okay? All I care about right now is saving my sister."

"Right. Pesky little Becca, always getting kidnapped. It's too bad she's so unlike her responsible older sibling who breaks into private homes looking for buried treasure—"

"The door was unlocked," she reminded him.

"—or her aunt, who's currently finding out if orange really *is* the new black. Oh, wait. Not her aunt, her *mother*." Farrell smirked as Crys narrowed her eyes at him. "Just remember something, Crys. Of all the people joining in today's little field trip, you're the only one who doesn't *need* to be involved. I know where Markus and your kid sister are being held, Angus has the greed, skills, and magical knowledge to get us in and out. Say, for instance, you had to call in sick and couldn't bring the dagger. I'm sure Angus and I could agree on a price he'd find fair enough to help me do whatever's necessary to free Markus."

It was only more proof of what had been bothering her all her life. That she wasn't important, wasn't necessary, wasn't . . . special.

Well, screw that, she thought.

"I'm coming. Don't even think about stopping me."

He held up his hands. "Wouldn't dream of it. Just remember: Be careful around me."

"You didn't kill me before when you had the chance. You won't kill me now." At best, it was a guess. A hope. And only out of desperation would she remain anywhere near him today.

"See, it's logic like that that's going to get you killed."

"So you're saying that I shouldn't trust you? At all?"

"Finally we speak the same language. That's right, Crys. Don't trust me, not for one damn minute, while I have these marks on my arm and his command in my head. Got it?"

All she could do was nod. After what he'd done inside the house, both stalking her and saving her, the least she could say was that Farrell Grayson had her extremely confused. Fifty percent of her hated him. Forty percent of her feared him. And the last ten percent . . . well, that was most confusing slice of the pie chart.

That was the part of her that wanted to help him. To trust him.

It was also the ten percent she'd begun to call *the stupid part*.

Angus pulled up in a silver Porsche. Crys watched Farrell eye it appraisingly as Angus rolled down his window. He wore a blue bow tie and had a yellow daisy tucked into his lapel button.

"Here I am, Crystal," he said.

"Good. Let's go."

He shook his head. "Let's see the dagger first, if you please."

Glaring, she reached into her bag and pulled it out by its golden hilt.

Angus's eyes glinted with greed. "Excellent. Now let's go save your sister. Or whatever."

"The 928. Great car," Farrell said as he approached. "I have a Boxster, but I can't drive it at the moment. I'm in serious Porsche withdrawal."

Angus pulled his mirrored aviators down his nose and looked at Farrell. "Who's this guy?"

Crys didn't answer right away; she was in the process of learning that the backseat of a Porsche 928 wasn't exactly luxuriously large. Still, she'd much rather wedge herself into it than sit in the front with her back to Farrell.

"This is Farrell Grayson," she said once she'd managed to get in a seated position. "Farrell, Angus Balthazar."

"Balthazar?" Farrell repeated as he climbed in the front seat and shut the door. "Is that for real?"

"Of course not," Angus said. "Grayson . . . I recognize the name." He nodded. "Yes, I believe I stole a Picasso sketch from your grand-mother—Sophia Grayson, right? Oh, when was it? A decade ago or so. How's the old bat doing now?"

"Not well," Farrell replied, leaning back in the passenger seat. "She died five years ago." He narrowed his eyes. "A Picasso, you say?"

Angus waved his hand. "Don't worry about it. Condolences on your granny. She was a firecracker, that one."

"How's my mother?" Crys asked. "Did you tell her about Becca?"

"No, I thought it best not to. Your mum is safely locked away in her lovely hotel suite with a plethora of snacks and entertainment options to keep her occupied until all is well with the world again."

"What hotel?"

"Jackie wanted it to be a secret."

"Angus, I'm her daughter."

He shrugged. "Sorry. Orders are orders."

"Can I call her? See how she's doing?"

"I think, given the way Mr. King has been manipulating her over the telephone, that would be a bad idea. Besides, her mobile has been confiscated, and she doesn't have a phone in her suite." He glanced over his shoulder. "Try not to worry. She's fine. And now we're going on an adventure to help make that state of fineness permanent."

"This is important, Angus. You don't seem like you're taking it very seriously."

"This is as serious as I get, darling. Any more serious and, trust me, you wouldn't like me very much."

She didn't like him much to start with. "Fine. Farrell will tell you where we need to go. Just . . . go fast."

"This car goes no other way." He pulled away from the mansion and onto the road. He glanced over at Farrell. "You okay, fella?"

"I'm fine," Farrell said tightly. "You'll want to head east once we get to the end of the street."

"East it is. You're sure you're fine? You're sweating all over my full-grain Italian-leather seats."

"I've got it under control."

Small car, tight quarters. Crys knew she was too close to Farrell. Markus's command was working overtime, which was one of the many reasons she'd wanted to bring the dagger with her. She would use it if she had to—not to kill Farrell, of course, but she wasn't above stabbing him in the shoulder or leg in self-defense.

If she got a chance, she'd use it on Damen to do much more damage.

Don't get carried away, she told herself. *In and out. Find Becca and escape.*

"When we spoke on the phone, Crys, you mentioned the name Damen Winter," Angus said as he followed Farrell's directions and went east.

"Yes," Crys said. "We had the displeasure of meeting him at the ball. He killed people just by looking at them."

"That sounds incredibly—"

"Horrifying?" she finished.

"*Fascinating.*"

"Of course it would, to *you.* You're the magic enthusiast. You have the whole Hogwarts library in your penthouse." She bit her bottom lip. "Angus, please tell me you know how to protect us from Damen's magic?"

"I have this." In the rearview mirror, Crys watched Angus pull a necklace out from beneath his shirt. Strung on the silver chain was a silver medallion.

"What's that?" Farrell asked. "Some sort of talisman? Protective rune? What's that symbol on it?"

"It's a four-leaf clover. I got this in a box of Cracker Jacks as a kid, and it's been my lucky charm ever since."

Crys slumped back in her seat. She really hated this guy, but hopefully he'd serve his purpose.

Then, out of nowhere, Angus began to laugh.

"What?" Crys growled.

"Oh, I'm just thinking about your aunt. I stopped by my place before I came to collect you. Dr. Vega has been on the phone all morning trying to figure things out—hire a lawyer, nail down bail hearings, et cetera. She has him so well trained, it's . . . well, it's sad, really. Another man twisted around your aunt's pretty little finger."

Hearing him mock Dr. Vega, who had been nothing but helpful and kind to Crys, made her raise her hackles. "I take it from your tone that you're not in love with her too? Why would you be different from any other man in Jackie's path?"

"Well, she is attractive, but I think my husband would have something to say about me seriously pursuing her." He glanced at Crys in the rearview mirror and winked. "He's the jealous type, you know."

She crossed her arms and fell into silence, but silence wasn't a good idea either. Silence only brought far too many worried, anxious thoughts about her sister, her mother, her aunt.

And her father.

A sob rose in her throat. She tried, and mostly succeeded, to swallow it back down, feeling grateful to be hidden in that tiny backseat. She couldn't fall apart yet. Later, definitely, but not yet.

Farrell continued to give directions to Angus. They drove for another fifteen minutes, the route taking them through the heart of downtown.

"Take the next left," Farrell told him.

Angus nodded. "So, tell me, Farrell. You say you have a Boxster but can't drive it. May I ask why? Forgive me, but I'm horribly curious about other people's business."

"It was in the news, so it's not exactly a secret. Long story short: I got in an accident and was charged with a DUI."

"Ah, I see. Alcohol consumption should be a deadly sin. I haven't touched the poison myself in fifteen years and twenty-six days. Dulls the mind and the soul."

"That's kind of the point," Farrell muttered. "But I know what—"

Suddenly, he let out a loud, pained roar and grabbed the dashboard, his body convulsing.

"What in the hell—?" Angus swerved then righted the car. "What's wrong with you, boy?"

Crys watched, horrified at whatever was happening to Farrell. His shirtsleeves were rolled up to his elbows, and she could see the mark on his forearm: intricate red lines, like words written in a foreign language. Suddenly the angry scar began to glow with golden light. It was just like the light that filled Becca's eyes whenever she touched the Codex.

Farrell swore at the top of his lungs, slamming his fist against the dash.

Angus quickly lurched the car over to the side of the road as Farrell fell back in his seat, chest heaving.

Crys grabbed Farrell's shoulder. "Are you okay?"

"I would be much better if you weren't touching me!"

She yanked her hand back as if it had been burned. "Sorry. But—but what *was* that?"

Angus was inspecting the dashboard for any signs of damage, glaring at Farrell out of the corner of his eye.

"I have no damn idea," Farrell said, breathing hard. "But it felt like I was being torn apart and then slammed back together."

"Does it still feel like that?"

He shook his head. "Whatever it was, it's passed." He looked down at his arm. The glowing had stopped, but the scar was now bleeding. He unrolled his sleeves back down to his wrists and buttoned the cuffs. "Damn it, Markus," he muttered, barely audibly. "What the hell have you done to me?"

"Finished?" Angus asked. "Good. Should we continue, or do you need a quick nip of scotch to dull your pain?"

"You're a serious douchebag, you know that?" Farrell growled.

"Oh yes. I know. Does that kind of convulsion happen all the time? Should I call my car insurance agent right now and upgrade my plan?"

"No. First time ever."

That wasn't normal. The marks on his arm should be healed if they'd been given to him by Markus. But Crys bit her tongue before she asked any questions she knew he wouldn't answer.

But she was worried. Farrell's sudden outburst of pain . . . it had to be due to something other than those marks. Something worse.

"Are we close?" Crys asked instead.

"Yeah, very close," Farrell said, his voice shaky as he looked through the windshield. "Angus, park in the lot two blocks up so nobody spots us. I know a back way in."

—⚫—

Farrell led them to a roped-off and boarded-up staircase that looked like it might lead down to a subway station. He removed four boards that seemed to be secured with what Crys could only guess were some kind of trick nails that he knew to look out for, and then he led them down the stairs.

Her limbs went numb as she realized where they were. "The society tunnels," she said, her voice trembling.

"Oooh," Angus said. "How exciting. I've heard stories but never seen them for myself."

Farrell nodded grimly. "Of course it's completely illegal for you two to come down with me this way without explicit permission, but my capacity for giving a damn about society rules is quickly diminishing. Keep close to me. Less talking, more walking. I have the keys to the castle."

"Divine. Lead the way, young man."

Crys hated these cold, dank tunnels that alternated between narrow, suffocating, and pitch-black, and creepy, cavernous, and fluorescently lit. She had really hoped after her last time in here that she would never have to see them again.

Angus pulled out his phone.

"Don't even think about taking pictures," Farrell growled.

Angus cleared his throat. "Wouldn't dream of it." He tucked the phone back into his jacket pocket.

Finally, they came to a winding metal staircase. They climbed to the top, where they faced an iron door covered in symbols that reminded Crys of the writing in the Codex. Hanging above it was a plaque that read: TODAY, TOMORROW, AND ALWAYS.

"Hawkspear motto," Farrell said. "Catchy, right?"

Crys recognized it all: the tunnels, the staircase, the door. They were at the abandoned theater where the Hawkspear Society held its meetings.

Farrell pulled out a ring of keys from his pocket and unlocked the door. Carefully, he pushed it open a crack and peered inside.

"Let me go first," Angus said, nudging Farrell out of the way.

"Why you?" Farrell said without any friendliness. "I'm the one who knows the way around here."

"Perhaps. But I'm the one who has this." He pulled out a gun from his jacket. The weapon was inlaid with red enamel and had the initials AB on the side in gold letters.

"Ugh, I hate guns," Crys said. "But I guess I'm okay with that one. Just for today."

"Goody," Angus replied. "Any further arguments?"

"I suppose not," Farrell said darkly. "Just be careful where you point that thing."

Farrell crept closely behind Angus. Crys shifted her handbag to her other shoulder, feeling the weight of the dagger at the bottom, and followed Farrell.

They moved into the theater slowly, quietly, keeping to the walls and corners. Crys watched Angus lead the way with coolness and confidence.

The theater was completely empty, its lack of occupants making it seem more cavernous than opulent.

"Are you sure this is the right place?" Crys whispered.

"I thought so," Farrell replied.

Then an unbidden thought ripped through Crys's mind, booming so loudly she was worried someone might hear it:

Don't give up. This is only the auditorium, the tip of the iceberg. There are lots of hiding places in this theater where Becca might be.

She shook her head to try to clear it, succeeding only somewhat as the words kept ringing in her ears.

"We should check backstage," she whispered.

Angus nodded. They moved closer to the stage, slipping through a door to the right of it.

The door led to a hallway. Also deserted.

"You're too close to me," Farrell growled at her. "You're making this much harder than it needs to be."

She couldn't risk an argument now, so she dropped back and put just a little more space between them.

"Should've stayed in the car," he continued.

"You mean *you* should have? I guess you should have thought about that earlier."

They'd reached a corner. Angus put up his hand to silence them. "Wait here, kids. I'll do a quick sweep."

He slipped around the corner while Crys and Farrell stood there in near silence, their shaky breathing the only sound.

Minutes passed. Crys wrung her hands. "How long do we wait?"

"Until now." Farrell turned the corner and Crys followed, scanning the hallway for Angus or any other sign of life.

"Where did he go?"

Suddenly, Farrell grabbed Crys and clamped his hand down over her mouth. Crys tensed up and grabbed his arm as he dragged her into a room to their left. She was about to grab for the dagger when she heard footsteps.

She went very still. Farrell finally dropped his hand from her mouth.

Someone walked past the door, a masked man wearing all black. One of Damen's gunmen from the ball.

A second man joined the first. They were checking rooms along the hallway.

Farrell nodded at a closet in the corner. They swiftly slipped inside of it, pulling the door closed just as one of the gunmen entered room. Crys could see him through the slats on the closet door.

They won't find you. They're not even looking for you. It's all right, don't worry. Everything's fine. You should stay where you are for a few minutes. Wait for him to leave, and make sure he doesn't come back.

The man scanned the room for several long seconds. Satisfied it was empty, he turned and exited to the hallway.

Farrell hissed out a long, shaky breath.

"Let's give it a minute," Crys whispered to him.

"Another minute this close to you might actually kill me," Farrell gritted out.

She looked up at him. Even in the dim light filtering into the slatted door from the hallway, she could see that his forehead was damp, his jaw tight. His arms trembled.

Less than two hours ago he'd been trying to kill her, had to stab his own hand to a wall just to stop himself, and now she was pressed up against him in a tiny closet.

He doesn't want to kill you. He wants to save you. He's a hero, really. Fighting the marks, fighting Markus's orders. For you, Crys. All for you. And you know why? Because he likes you. More than just a little.

What a ridiculous thought.

Or was it?

It seemed to make sense. If she meant nothing to him, why wouldn't he have saved himself the pain and followed through on Markus's orders?

Despite what he was desperate for everyone to believe, Farrell Grayson was a good person. She knew it now—she had the proof. He wasn't a murderer.

He was a hero.

Yes, that's right. And he wants you. Do you see the passion in his eyes? It's all for you, all because of you. It was there when you danced together at the ball. It was there in Markus's kitchen. And it's there now. You know what you want to do, Crystal. Don't be afraid. He wants it too.

Her head felt woozy, foggy, as if her mind were a separate entity sending her thoughts from some faraway space station.

"Farrell . . . I don't know what's happening here, but . . . but I have to do this . . ."

She felt his cool hands at her throat, trembling as they circled her neck. "Me too . . . Crys, this is bad. I really, really don't think I can stop myself from—"

She reached up and grabbed his face between her hands, rose up on the tips of her toes, and crushed her mouth against his.

His hands fell away from her throat. A second later, they were on her arms, gripping tight.

"What are you doing?" he managed to say.

"Kissing you."

"Bad idea," he whispered against her lips. "So very bad. You—you need to stop. We can't do this."

"Sure we can."

Farrell pulled back and stared at her. His eyes were full of torment, but she watched as all that pain faded and was quickly replaced by desire.

He pressed her up against the closet wall and kissed her, his hands sliding down to her waist to pull her closer to him. Now chest to chest, she felt his heartbeat against hers.

She wanted more.

"Crys, you're killing me," he said, breaking away from her with a groan as she started to unbutton his shirt and slide her hands against his chest. "Like, literally. Please, stop. My resistance is . . . futile. Oh God. *Star Trek* quotes. Kill me now."

Suddenly, with tortured effort, he pushed her hands away from him and escaped from the closet.

Slowly, the haze lifted from her mind, and she was struck full force by what had just happened.

She'd kissed Farrell Grayson. In the middle of a mission to rescue her sister.

And if he hadn't stopped her . . .

"What the hell is wrong with me?" she mumbled.

Farrell swore under his breath. "Someone's coming."

Heart racing, she went to the exit and pressed herself up against the wall to the side of it.

"Crys?"

Her eyes widened with shock. "Mom?"

Julia Hatcher appeared at the entrance to the room, nervously looking left and right down the hallway. "I thought I heard you. My God, Crys, honey, what are you doing here?"

"*Me?* What are *you* doing here?"

"I had to come. Dr. Vega found a way to get ahold of me at the hotel, and he told me about Becca. I'm here for the same reason you are: to get her the hell away from Damen Winter."

Crys hugged her mother. "Angus told me there was no way to reach you, but I'm so glad you're here. Thank God for Vega's research skills. Everything's going to be okay."

"Crys . . . ," Farrell said quietly, in a tone that set off an alarm bell in Crys's heart. He was standing behind Julia, facing Crys as she hugged her.

"What?"

"Everything's not going to be okay."

She looked at him, frowning, and he nodded at her mother. Crys pulled back from the embrace and swept a quick glance over Julia. She was dressed all in black, her least favorite color.

She took another step back to see that in Julia's right hand was a gun.

A gun with red enamel and stamped in gold with the initials AB.

Julia looked at them patiently. "It seems we'll have to do this the hard way," she said, then gestured at the doorway with the gun. "Come now. Damen wants a word with you both."

Chapter 25

MADDOX

For a long moment, all Maddox could do was stare at her.

"You," he finally said. "You can't really be here."

"I *am* here." Becca laughed then, and it sounded as stunned as Maddox felt.

"Just like before?"

"Um . . . not exactly." She closed the distance between then and reached out and grabbed his hands. "This time I brought more than just my spirit."

A strange warmth flooded him at her touch. Her soft skin, her delicate fingers . . . this *had* to be a dream. He needed Barnabas to slap him again, to wake him up to reality.

"How?" he asked, unwilling to let go of her just yet.

Becca's smile faltered a bit. "Well, that's the crazy part. I actually don't remember how I got here. I do remember you giving me the magic to get back home . . ." She shook her head and frowned. "And that's where things start to get seriously fuzzy."

"What's happening?" Al whispered, loud enough for all to hear, from his sack. "What am I missing?"

Startled, Becca let go of Maddox's hands and took a shaky step backward, as if noticing for the first time that they weren't alone.

"This is Becca, you said?" Barnabas said, frowning as he came to Maddox's side. Liana approached as well, keeping Al's sack mostly closed. "That was the name of the spirit girl."

Maddox's heart began to overflow—it seemed this wasn't a dream after all, but a wish come true.

"Yes, this is her," Maddox said, unable to keep the smile from his face. "This is Becca Hatcher. Barnabas, you two have already met . . . in a way. Becca, this is our new friend Liana."

"Very pleased to know you," Liana said.

"So you both can see her," Maddox said, half in disbelief.

"Clearly," Barnabas confirmed.

Becca's gaze was fixed fully upon the canvas sack. "Uh, sorry, I don't mean to be rude, but . . . I heard another voice. Coming from"—she pointed—"there."

Liana raised an eyebrow at the girl's flustered expression. "That would be Al."

Maddox touched her arm, drawing her gaze to his again. "Don't be scared. Al—Alcander Verus is his full name, but he likes Al better—is . . . a severed head. I kind of used my magic to bring him back to life."

"And will reunite me with my body very soon!" Al piped up from his hiding place. "Delightful to meet you, young lady!"

Becca's mouth fell open. "Holy crap."

Maddox frowned, uncertain about what that meant. "Erm, yes. Exactly."

Barnabas's mouth was set in a straight, skeptical line. He swept an appraising gaze over Becca. "So she says she doesn't remember how she got here?"

"I can hear you, you know," Becca said with a small, nervous laugh. "You don't have to talk to Maddox like I'm not here. It's good to see you again, Barnabas. Sorry—learning about, uh, *Al* has me a bit frazzled."

"Completely understandable," Al allowed. "It is rather incredible, isn't it?"

"To say the least," she agreed in little more than a squeak.

"Pardon my skepticism, Becca," Barnabas said, "but it's been a most difficult day. We just barely escaped with our lives from Valoria and her army of assassins."

"What?" she gasped, then turned to Maddox. "Are you guys okay?"

Are you guise o-kay. Maddox had nearly forgotten Becca's strange vocabulary, but he found he still understood her meaning.

"Yes, indeed," he assured her. "O-kay."

"Well, we wouldn't be if it hadn't been for that unexpected blast of air magic," Barnabas said suspiciously.

All Maddox could do was stare at Becca, still stunned that she was here, standing before him, as solid and real as anyone he'd ever met.

To be reunited with this girl—the one who visited only briefly before she was sent back to her world, but about whom he hadn't been able to stop thinking ever since—was the happiest and most surprising moment in his entire life.

And yet, he knew it meant something had gone wrong. Something very important.

"Becca, what else do you remember?" Maddox asked urgently. "Why are you here? *How* are you here?"

A shadow crossed her expression, and she furrowed her brow. "I—I remember the book. The book Valoria wanted, which she used to open the gateway. It's in my world because you threw it through the gateway." She gave him a shaky smile. "Kind of ironic, right?"

Maddox gasped. He very clearly remembered the moment he threw the book through the gateway just before it closed. He couldn't believe he'd been the one to send it to Becca's world.

"I—I had no idea," he said, shaking his head.

"Of course you didn't."

"What book are you talking about?" Liana asked.

"The Book of the Immortals," Maddox said shakily. "It's in Becca's world."

"The Book of the—?" Liana shook her head. "That's impossible."

Barnabas eyed the young witch. "It's a long story. I'll explain it in further detail later."

She met his gaze and nodded slowly. "I look forward to it."

"The other day, I touched the book," Becca continued. "The first time I did that, it sent my spirit here. But the second time . . . I saw you, Barnabas, and Camilla at Valoria's palace." Her expression was strained. She bit her bottom lip, making Maddox think she was about to arrive at something crucial, but then she shook her head. "I'm sorry. That's all I remember right now."

"It's . . . o-kay," he said, using her word again and hoping he'd done so correctly. Becca smiled at him. "I'm just thankful that you're safe and that your path quickly crossed with ours."

"Is that what's happened here?" Barnabas asked, this time speaking directly to Becca. "Quite a coincidence, isn't it, that in this entire kingdom, on the day you magically returned to Mytica—body and spirit combined—we were traveling the same route at the same time?"

Becca scowled at him. "I don't know what to tell you, Barnabas. I'm just as confused as you are. I just figure it must be like last time—I, like, *honed in* on Maddox's magic, and it led me to him."

"How positively romantic."

"It is, isn't it?" Al spoke up. "Young love always finds a way."

Maddox shot Barnabas a dark look. "You don't believe a word Becca says, do you?"

Barnabas's face remained stony. "Frankly, I don't believe that *this* Becca is the same Becca whose spirit you remember so clearly. She could be a witch, perhaps the witch who sent that gust of wind into the village, and maybe now she's using the same air magic to look like someone you think you know."

"A common witch wouldn't be able to summon air magic strong enough to change her appearance so drastically that she'd be able to fool someone up close," Al commented. "This is a fact."

"You're wrong," Maddox said bluntly, ignoring Al. "Besides, I'm the one who could see Becca when she was here last. I'm the only one who knows what she looks like."

Why was Barnabas being so combative? This was the best thing that had happened to Maddox in . . . well, ever.

But was it possibly the worst thing as well? Arguing with Barnabas now didn't make him any less excited to see Becca, but it did make him see a simple, strange truth: Becca Hatcher shouldn't be here. Not again, not like this. She was from an entirely different world—a different time altogether, perhaps—and all she'd wanted last time was to go home to her family. Why, after all that, would she return? And in such a . . . *complete* state?

She wouldn't.

Well, not unless she had a very good reason.

The gateway magic that allowed her to pass through these different worlds allegedly did strange things to time and space—and memory, it would seem. He had no idea how long she'd even been back in her world. For him, it had only been a fortnight. For her, it could have been anywhere from two seconds to two hundred years.

But, aside from the clothing she wore, she looked exactly the same today as she did that fortnight ago. When she'd first been to Mytica, she'd worn blue trousers and a soft tunic the color of a rose. This silky black . . . garment—he truly couldn't place it in the same category as any gown he'd ever seen before—was incredibly, shockingly revealing.

But not necessarily in a bad way.

"I hate to be the one to mention this," Maddox said, clearing his throat nervously, "but I believe something may have happened during your travels. It seems you are in your . . . undergarments."

Becca winced, frowned in embarrassment, and looked down at herself. Instantly her serious expression faded, and she laughed. "This is a dress, silly! And a pretty fancy one for me. I definitely prefer jeans."

Jeans. *Jeans.* Perhaps that was the word for the style of tunic she'd worn last time?

"Oh, of course," he said, trying to hide his embarrassment. "It *is* pretty. But you will definitely need different clothing now that you—both your spirit *and* your body—are here."

"Wonderful," Barnabas said, rolling his eyes. "Let's go find a dressmaker. We've nothing important to do at the moment, after all."

"What of continuing our journey to visit the southern goddess?" asked Al.

Barnabas sighed with frustration. "Shut up, Al."

Al said something under his breath that Maddox didn't catch, but it didn't sound friendly.

Becca looked at Maddox, her previously happy expression now

only a memory. "Last time I was here, Barnabas didn't hate me. Or at least that's what I thought."

"I don't hate you now either," Barnabas said. "But do consider me extremely skeptical about the circumstances under which we met today."

"Of course you're skeptical," Maddox growled, annoyed at Barnabas's tone. "When are you not? But whether you like it or not, she's coming with us."

"By all means. She'll be your responsibility."

"Fine."

"Fine."

"Well, wasn't that a riveting debate between father and son?" Liana said good-naturedly. "Now that that's all settled, I'd like to volunteer my services to you, Becca, in helping you find some new clothing. Maddox is right: It would be best for you to fit in a little better around here." Becca smiled gratefully, and then Liana turned to Barnabas. "It won't take long. In fact, while we're doing that, you can find us some horses and a wagon, and then we'll meet up."

Barnabas grumbled but didn't argue, and Maddox felt just as grateful to Liana as Becca seemed to be.

They continued on, swiftly reaching the next village to the south. At the edge of the forest, Barnabas disappeared to search for means of transportation. Liana planned to go to the city center to find Becca a new gown.

"I'd take you with me," Liana said to Becca. "It would be lovely to learn more about you, after all . . . but I do worry about the reaction you'll get in that . . . rather daring ensemble."

Becca laughed. "I understand completely. Thank you for doing this, Liana. It's very nice of you."

Liana nodded and set off in the opposite direction that Barnabas had.

Maddox remained behind with Becca. Alcander stayed too, so that Liana could have full use of her arms at the dressmaker's.

Maddox held the sack beneath his arm, keeping it open so that Al could breathe easily, as he stared at Becca.

"What is it?" Becca said, twisting a piece of her hair. "You're making me more nervous than I already am!"

"I'm sorry. I just can't believe you're really here."

"I know." She furrowed her brow. "Me neither. I hate that I can't remember what happened. It's like when there's a word on the tip of your tongue but you just can't think of it, no matter how hard you try. It's there—the memory, the reason I'm here—and I know it's really important, but I . . . it's just not coming to me."

A word on the tip of your tongue. Maddox quite liked that strange expression.

"Was that the way it was last time? When you—your spirit— first arrived here in Mytica?"

She shook her head. "No. I mean, when I was all of a sudden in the garden at that lord's house—where I met you—I was *seriously* freaked out. And I knew exactly why. One second I was in my family's bookstore and the next I was here, but there was no doubt in my mind that it was the book that did it."

"*Seriously . . . freaked . . . out?*" said Al. "She speaks in coded riddles! Are you able to decipher them, Maddox?"

"I understand her meaning, yes."

"Loosen up this sack a bit more, young man. I want to see this creature with my own eyes."

Maddox shrugged and looked to Becca. "Would that be . . . *o-kay* with you?"

She nodded.

Maddox folded the edge of the canvas sack down so that Al was fully exposed from the mouth up.

Becca's face paled. "Um, hi there."

His eyes widened. "Oh yes. That's better. She *is* beautiful."

"Very," Maddox agreed, then felt a bolt of heat reach his cheeks.

They'd been through so much together. Why did he revert to being so bashful around her?

But it seemed that Becca either didn't notice the embarrassing way he was acting or didn't care. Instead, she just kept staring at Al and then at Maddox. "Wow. Maddox, I still can't believe you did *this* with your magic."

"Well, don't say too much about it to Barnabas," he said. She looked at him curiously. "He's absolutely certain that if I do something like this again, my soul will go dark. I'm not sure he's right, but I have no way to know if he's wrong."

"Well, he's given his blessing for you to work your magic at least one more time," Al said. "And then, once you've reunited me with my body and made me whole, you will never delve into such dark magic again."

"You really think you can do something like that?" Becca asked with surprise.

"He can and he will!" Al replied before Maddox had a chance to sidestep the question. After all, Maddox still didn't know if he could, let alone whether he should, and the guilt was eating at him.

Al had helped them find the princess. It hadn't been his fault that Cassia chose to ruin everything with her unreasonable demands. Whether or not Al would be of further help in defeating Valoria, Maddox felt as if the scribe had already fulfilled his end of the bargain.

The trouble that lay ahead was with Barnabas. Maddox knew that at no point did Barnabas have any intention of allowing Maddox to attempt to use his magic for this.

Perhaps he'd try anyway.

Suddenly, Becca reached out and touched Maddox's arm. He jumped a little, surprised at her touch, and then met her blue eyes.

"Thank you for believing me back there," she said. "And for believing *in* me. Again."

He nodded. "Of course. I know it's really you."

She raised her brows. "So you didn't even want to quiz me? Ask me questions only I would know? I mean, it's a shock for me too that I'm here fully this time, not just in spirit."

"I don't need to *quiz* you." *Whatever that means*, he thought. "I can look in your eyes and know it's you." He smiled at her. "I missed you a lot."

She leaned closer to him. "Me too."

All he could see then were her beautiful eyes, her soft lips . . .

Al sneezed. Becca released her hold on Maddox's arm.

"Apologies!" the head exclaimed. "Just a bit of pollen, I think."

Stupid head. Maddox couldn't say for sure that Becca had been about to kiss him, but he'd like to think it was a possibility.

"Bless you," Becca said.

Al looked at her quizzically. "My goddess, child. *Bless* me? For such a trivial act as sneezing? What an odd thing to say!"

Maddox flipped the top of the sack back over Al's head and discreetly placed him on the ground.

"Would you mind telling me more about your visions, Becca?" he said. "Like the one in the palace square—if you can remember."

She nodded, then paused. Suddenly, her eyes lit up. "I *do* remember! I remember another one now! Maybe it is like you said: The longer I'm here, the more I'll remember. Okay, so the square out-side Valoria's palace was the second vision I had. The first one came to me as a dream. You were in some sort of tavern with Barnabas. No Al or Liana, but there was a woman. I'm pretty sure it was your mother . . ." As soon as she said it, the light in her eyes dimmed. She looked up at him nervously. "Oh, Maddox. I'm so sorry."

His breath caught in his chest. "You . . . saw that? My mother's death?"

Becca nodded, her eyes glossy.

He nodded stiffly. "I loved her very much. I still love her. She'd only just found out that I knew the truth about Barnabas . . . about Eva . . ."

"Wait . . . ," she said, frowning. "Eva . . . something about Eva. I feel like—oh God, I'm sorry. I can't believe I just interrupted when you were talking about your mother."

"It's all right, you need to remember. It's over now, and I'm do-ing the best I can," Maddox paused, allowing a measure of fire to burn in his gaze. "But I wanted to kill him—Goran, the man who did it. I still want to."

She shook her head. "You're not a killer."

"Perhaps that was true of me the last time you were here."

"No." Becca touched his face, and he went very still, barely breathing. "You're the same as before. Perhaps you're a bit sad-der, a bit more mature. I hear grief can do that to a person. But your heart is good, and nothing can change that." She hesitated. "Besides, I'm sure Barnabas would be happy to kill that disgusting piece of garbage for you."

"You're right, he is."

"Well, good. Better him than you."

He almost smiled. "What was it you remember about Eva?"

Becca sighed. "I wish I knew. I just had a flash of something, but the whole memory isn't coming back to me just yet—except for the vision I had of you at the palace."

"That's the only one you remember?"

She frowned. "I feel like there was another . . . or more than a couple, even. *What was it?* Oh!" Her eyes widened. "I remember watching you wash your clothes. In a river. And . . . it sounds crazy, but in that one"—her frown deepened—"I . . . I think I was a *hawk*."

"The hawk," he said, his eyes widening. "Yes, I saw a hawk that day. I remember. Of course I do—she was beautiful, with dark blue eyes. I had the strangest feeling it was you, and I thought I was going mad!"

She gasped. "Oh my God, I remember! *Liana* was there too. She was following you, and she had a knife! Maddox, she's dangerous!" She stood up, alarmed, looking everywhere for a sign of Liana heading back to the edge of the forest.

Maddox stood up and put his arm around her. "It's okay, it's okay. I know that part of the story too. She explained herself. It's all right now."

She relaxed and sat back down with him. "Oh. Well, good." She paused, looking exhausted. "I think that's all I remember for now."

"That's quite a bit." Maddox wanted to tell her that he'd dreamed of her only last night, but the nightmare had been so disturbing that he didn't want to conjure up the memory now, let alone share it with Becca. Luckily, that had only been a nightmare and not a vision.

They turned and stood up at the sound of someone approaching, and Maddox smiled to see Barnabas striding toward them, two brown workhorses and a rickety wooden cart following behind. "This was the best I could do," he said grumpily.

Maddox snatched Al's sack off the ground just in time to save it from being trod on by one of the horses. "Well, it looks perfect to me," he said.

Barnabas ignored him and turned directly to Becca, his hands on his hips, his eyes narrowed.

"Where did you say you are from?" he asked—or, rather, demanded.

She took a step back from him. "Uh . . .Toronto."

Barnabas scoffed, as if Becca had just told him she came from a land made entirely of sugar lumps and biscuits. "Why are you dressed in that strange frock?"

"It's not strange where I'm from. It's the kind of thing people—girls and women—normally wear to . . . um . . ." She frowned. "Well, I don't remember exactly why *I'm* wearing this. But in general, people wear something like this when they're going out to dinner at a nice restaurant or to the theater."

"What is a . . . *res-trawnt*?" he snapped.

"Uh, you're asking me what a restaurant is? Okay . . . it's like a . . . a tavern. A place where you sit, and people bring you food, and you pay for it?"

"What's your mother's name?" Barnabas asked, not taking the restaurant discussion any further.

"Julia. Julia Hatcher. Her maiden name was Kendall."

"Hmm."

Becca exchanged a worried look with Maddox.

"Satisfied?" Maddox asked, annoyed now.

"Not even close," Barnabas replied. "She could be making everything up."

"How about this to make you absolutely, one hundred percent sure?" Becca said. "You're Maddox's father. You hooked up with an immortal named Eva." She frowned again at the name, and Maddox wondered if she remembered something new, but then she went on. "I think you said you were eighteen at the time?"

"*Hooked up?*" Barnabas repeated.

Maddox shrugged. "This is how she speaks. How everyone speaks in her world, I assume."

"Hmm," Barnabas said again.

"I have more," Becca said. "When the guards threw you in the dungeon with Maddox, they called you Crazy Barney. And you went along with it—you liked eating human bone marrow or something like that. Maddox was scared of you."

"I was not," Maddox grumbled.

"You told me to find the room in Valoria's palace where the Bronze Codex—uh, that's what we call the Book of the Immortals back home—was hidden." Becca pointed at Maddox. "Valoria's gigantic cobra killed his abusive jerk of a stepdad, and then later, Barnabas, *you* killed the cobra. Valoria didn't like that very much. He was her favorite pet."

Maddox smiled. "Are you going to say *hmm* again, Barnabas? Or are you finally satisfied?"

"*Hmm*," Barnabas said. Maddox rolled his eyes as his father's hard gaze moved beyond Maddox's shoulder and softened. "Ah, good—here comes Liana. We don't know how much of a lead we have on Valoria and her army so let's concentrate now on putting more space between us."

Liana approached, gown in hand. Becca jumped up and hugged her, clearly catching Liana off guard, but the witch smiled anyway and handed her the new garment.

"Turn around, boys," Liana said.

Barnabas and Maddox turned their backs so Liana could help Becca change into the gown. "There," Liana said.

"You can turn around now," Becca said.

Maddox did so and his breath caught in his chest.

The gown covered every inch of Becca's legs—which was a bit disappointing, he had to admit—and though it wasn't fancy, it made her look like a royal princess. The simple, elegant silhouette allowed her figure to be the focus of attention, and the soft-looking fabric was a shade of dark blue that matched her eyes almost exactly.

"Is it okay?" she asked, pulling at the skirt.

"More than *o-kay*," he confirmed.

By her smile, this was the right thing to say.

"Ah—I almost forgot!" said Liana. She reached into the burlap sack that the gown had been wrapped in and pulled out a small parcel. "These are also for you, Becca."

Becca opened the parcel. Inside was a pair of shoes—a sensible brown leather pair, but nice all the same. Maddox thought Becca looked even more thrilled to see those than she had been to see the gown.

"Oh my gosh—you have no idea how happy I am to see these!" she said, tearing off the torturous-looking shoes she'd worn with her old dress. "My feet were *killing* me in these things. Thank you, Liana!"

"Yes," Barnabas echoed, his gaze again drawn to the young witch—currently the only one in their group upon whom he looked without ire. "Much gratitude."

She met his gaze. "I'm happy to help."

Barnabas finally tore his attention away from her and cleared his throat. "All right," Barnabas grumbled as he made for the horses and cart. "Enough with this little show. Let's move. We should have already been on our way by now."

Maddox sent him one more annoyed glare and then helped Becca gather up her old dress and shoes and escorted her toward the cart. They all climbed inside, and Barnabas sat up front to steer.

"You know the way?" Liana asked from the back as Barnabas took hold of the reins.

"Well enough," he replied. "I'll keep heading south until I see a palace fit for the vainest goddess in the land. Off we go."

He guided the horses away from the village and along a dirt road leading south, while Maddox, Becca, Liana, and Al endured the shaky ride in the cart that was normally meant to transport things like bales of straw or bags of grains to and from the village market.

They rode hard and fast for the rest of the day, until they were finally approaching the official border of Southern Mytica: a massive wall of a forest that stretched from the jagged black mountains in the east to the edge of the sea in the west.

"This is the forest that Her Radiance created with her earth magic," Al explained as it came into view. "It was her way of telling the southern goddess to remain separate and apart from her and her territory, lest she wished to face the northern goddess's wrath."

Liana snorted. "Is *that* what Valoria told you to write in her official record? Is the whole *thing* filled up with fantasy tales?"

"I believe it is the truth."

"This forest has been here since the beginning of time," Liana said. "No goddess made this. There is a legend about this place and how it came to be that gives it its unofficial name: the Forest of Demons."

"Lies!" Al piped up. "Her Radiance created it. She said so!"

Maddox pressed his lips together so as not to argue with the head. It seemed pointless when discussing Valoria.

Becca turned to Liana, her expression etched with worry. "Is that true?"

Liana shook her head. "Don't worry, there is no true magic or demons to be found here."

"Plenty of magic here," Al scoffed, clearly offended. "*Earth* magic."

"Still so loyal," Liana replied. "I wonder when that will finally fade."

"I wouldn't call myself loyal so much as respectful of the goddess's incredible magic."

"What about the other goddess's magic?"

"Bah. She is no match—in either beauty or strength."

"I certainly hope you're wrong," Barnabas growled from up front. "Since that would make this journey we're on completely futile, wouldn't it? Besides, even if this place *were* full of wild fanged beasts and evil demons, we'd still be going through it. It would take far too long to go around it."

"Really?" Maddox said. "You mean to say that if a fanged beast were to greet us at the edge of the forest, you wouldn't change your mind?"

"Not for a moment."

Al cleared his throat. "Whether or not I believe this, I request to remain safely inside my sack for the rest of our journey."

"Fine by me," Barnabas replied.

Maddox and Becca exchanged furtive smiles, but Liana looked off in the distance, strangely contemplative.

Barnabas looked up at the sky, which held only about a minute or two's worth of daylight. "We'll make camp for the night here. This is the perfect place—the forest will give camouflage."

Barnabas and Maddox gathered wood for the campfire.

"You look far too pleased with yourself," Barnabas said.

"Do I?"

"I don't think I need to ask why."

Maddox rolled his eyes. "It's really her." He was sick to death of arguing about it.

"I know."

"Oh." Maddox blinked. "Well, good."

"*Not* good. Not at all, actually. Why is she here?"

"She doesn't remember."

"Perhaps that's true. But it's clear that something happened to her in her world—something important, Maddox. I hate to be the one to tell you this, but she didn't make the long trip back here just to give you a big kiss."

"I know that." Of course he did. But why did Barnabas have to pull the joy out of absolutely everything?

"Pleased to hear it." But he didn't look pleased; he looked troubled.

They returned to the campsite, and Barnabas got to work at once on building a fire with the wood they'd brought back. Maddox tied up the two rabbits his father had caught and prepared them to be cooked. Becca eyed them uneasily as they worked.

"I suppose this isn't a good time to tell you I'm a vegetarian, right?" she said.

"A vege-*what*?" Maddox asked.

"Never mind. I can deal."

"The riddle-maker never rests!" Al said happily. He'd been so enchanted by the warm fire that he changed his mind about staying in his sack. "It's a delight to listen to you talk, lovely Becca. It's as if you speak a completely different language."

"You say *tomato*, and I say *toh-mah-to*." She frowned. "Only I don't actually ever say it like that."

"Exactly!"

When the rabbit was finished cooking, Barnabas gave them all their portions. Becca eyed the meat with trepidation.

"It's good," Maddox told her.

"I'm sure it is."

"I wish I too could partake in this meal," Al said glancing downward, where his stomach would have been. "It smells delicious!"

Maddox watched as Becca tentatively took a small bite of the meat, grimacing.

"It's fuel," she said sadly. "I have to remember that. Sorry bunny."

After they'd finished eating, Barnabas cleared his throat and poked at the fire with his dagger. "Perhaps we can take a moment to discuss what happened during our little visit from Valoria and Goran earlier today."

"What about it?" Maddox asked.

"They had us. Even if I hadn't stopped to retrieve this"—he held out the ring, which he now wore around his neck—"they would have easily taken us. If not for the air magic that swept through the village at exactly the right moment, we would have been at their mercy."

"You truly think it was air magic?" Maddox asked. "Liana? What do you think?"

The witch nodded. "Yes. I'm as sure of it as I am that the rainstorm and the earthquake were caused by water and earth magic."

"Given the sequence of events," Barnabas said, "I first thought that Becca might have had something to do with it. But now I know she didn't."

"Then what caused it?" Liana asked.

"Not *what. Who.*" He looked directly at the witch, and this time his gaze wasn't soft, as it had been ever since he kissed her. "*Who* caused it? And I think we both know the answer to that question."

Liana frowned. "I don't understand. I told you I possess fire magic, not air magic."

"Yes, your fire magic is incredible. I've never seen another witch create a wall of fire like yours with only her inner magic. Light a candle? Yes. But a fierce barrier of flames?" Barnabas stopped to give a little scoff of disbelief. "At the time I was simply impressed by it and . . . by *you*. But the more I think about it, all I have are questions."

Maddox found that he was holding his breath as watched these two discuss Liana's magic calmly—which was strange, because there was something about this situation that was very *not* calm.

He glanced at Becca. She met his gaze, and judging by the guarded and uneasy look in her eyes, she felt this strangeness too.

"Questions?" Liana asked. "What questions?"

"Who are you really? Where are you from? What is your family name? All of the questions you've been unwilling to answer so far."

"The answers to those questions are so inconsequential that they would be a waste of breath and good hearing to say aloud. Are there any others?"

"One comes to mind. Do you possess air magic?"

Liana let out a sharp laugh. "I think I'd have shared that with you if I did."

He studied her for a silent moment. "A witch who possesses air magic can use it to change her appearance. I've witnessed my friend Camilla do this before. But since she is merely a common witch—no disrespect to her intended—she is only able to effect subtle changes, and even then you can still see the shimmering and shifting of the air magic on her changed features. I assumed that the stronger the witch, the better and more impenetrable the disguise. Originally, I suspected that Becca was such a witch, but not anymore."

As Barnabas had been speaking, he'd made his way over to Liana. Liana now stood to face him. She raised her chin, glaring at him defiantly.

"Get to your point, Barnabas."

"How long did you think you could fool me?" Barnabas asked, his voice soft but dangerous-sounding.

"After you kissed me, I assumed I finally had you completely fooled into thinking that I was nothing more than I said I was: a young woman looking for something or *someone* to believe in. A young woman who might follow that someone to the very edge of the world."

Barnabas's jaw tightened.

"What's going on?" Maddox demanded.

"Apologies, Maddox," Liana said. She turned to him, a sad smile on her face. "It seems that our strange little family will be broken up much sooner than I would have liked. But it was inevitable, I suppose."

"What are you talking about?" He shook his head. "Who are you? Who is she, Barnabas?"

"It's all right," Liana replied. "I've nothing to hide anymore. I'll show you myself."

She straightened her shoulders and stood as tall as her petite frame would let her. Then something very strange began to happen.

Golden wisps formed, born from nothing at all, and began to float and wind around her. Maddox was unsettled to find that the wisps reminded him of the magic Valoria had used as she'd entered Cassia's village.

He watched, gaping, as that golden magic spun around Liana, encircling her face, her hair, her body.

Within the tornado of gold, she began to change.

Her dark blond hair grew lighter and longer, until it became bright gold and flowed past her waist. Her muted eye color shifted to an intense blue. Her freckled skin turned glowing and flawless. Her plain traveling dress transformed into a gown of glittering orange and gold, like a sunset.

In a matter of moments, Liana had transformed from a pretty witch into a young woman so ethereally beautiful that she was fearsome.

So beautiful and fearsome that she was worthy of being called a goddess.

And all Maddox could do was gape at her, mouth open and eyes wide.

"It's true what they say about me, Maddox." Even her voice sounded more powerful now, traveling across sound waves and penetrating his very body, holding his rapt attention. "When people speak my name, I can hear it, carried on the wind—thousands upon thousands of times a day. It's one of the reasons why I've come to loathe my true name. It's maddening."

"*Cleiona*," Maddox whispered.

Becca reached down to clutch his hand.

"Oh my goddess!" Al exclaimed.

The goddess swept her gaze around the campsite. "I recognized Barnabas immediately. After that, it didn't take long to realize who you are, Maddox, and why Valoria is so desperate to get her talons on you. I needed to know your motivations, your heart. Why you wished to seek me out. I needed to know about your magic and how dangerous you might be."

"Stay the hell away from him," Barnabas growled. He gripped his dagger and pointed it at her, but she merely glanced at the blade and then met his gaze.

"Really, Barnabas? Do you really think that tiny weapon will have any effect on me? You of all people should know better than that."

She flicked her wrist. The dagger flew out of his hand and embedded itself into a nearby tree.

"You hateful bitch," he snarled, his hands now clenched at his sides. "You deceived me!"

"And this from someone who is desperate for my help?" Cleiona shook her head. "I'd suggest starting with honey rather than venom."

"I despise you."

"Of course you do. And this is exactly why I chose to conceal my identity from you."

Maddox stared at them, knowing that to get in the way of this fight would only amplify it. This was the woman that, just a short time ago, Barnabas had kissed very passionately, and, to his recollection, she hadn't tried to stop him.

Now his father looked at her as if he wished her dead every bit as much as the other goddess.

Becca remained at his side, holding tightly to his hand.

He would protect her. If Cleiona tried anything, he swore he would use his dangerous magic to protect her.

"I needed to learn more about you—about both of you," the goddess said. "And I knew that, in my true form, you wouldn't allow it. So I chose another. One that wasn't so familiar to you."

"I didn't come to know *you*," Barnabas snarled. "I came to know a secretive young witch named Liana."

"This conversation is over," she spat. Slowly, she stretched her arms out to her sides, revealing two marks—the fire-magic triangle and the air-magic spiral—one on each of her palms. The symbols began to glow. "If you wish to continue this journey, make haste. You must arrive at my palace before my sister catches up to you. I will consider speaking with you again at that time."

Cleiona swept her gaze over them all. Maddox saw both pride and regret in her eyes as she regarded them.

Their color may have changed, but they were still Liana's eyes.

A sudden wind picked up, swirling around the goddess until it gathered into a tornado. It disappeared just as quickly as it had appeared, and so did she.

Barnabas remained standing in the same spot, his expression fierce, his body trembling.

Maddox had no idea what to say.

"Incredible," Al breathed. "Absolutely incredible!"

"Oh no!" Becca cried. She clapped her free hand over her mouth.

"What?" Maddox turned to her with alarm.

She pointed at the spot where Cleiona had been standing. "That was . . . oh crap! I just remembered! It's all rushing back to me now. And she was here, right in front of me the whole time!" She grabbed the front of Maddox's tunic. "We have to go after her. I need to speak to an immortal!"

"What? An immortal? But why?"

"I—I can't explain it all now. There's no time. My world is in danger. I was sent here—Markus sent me here."

"Who's Markus?"

"He gave his life, all of his magic, for this! So that I could come here and deliver a message to an immortal. I hate the man with everything I have, but for him to do something like that . . . Oh, Maddox, I need to talk to Cleiona. It's so important!"

"All right, all right." He gripped her shoulders. "We will. Everything's going to be all right." He glanced over his shoulder at his father. "Barnabas, we need to—"

"We need to do nothing of the sort," Barnabas said through gritted teeth. "We'll not chase after that evil creature. That's exactly what she wants us to do. There we were, traveling with her all these days, and she said nothing. She knew what was at risk, what we wanted. And yet she stayed silent."

"Barnabas, I'm sorry, but I have to go," Becca told him. "Just point me in the right direction, and I'll go on my own."

"Now you're speaking nonsense," Barnabas replied.

Becca stiffened. *"Nonsense?* Are you saying that me trying to save my world is *nonsense?"*

"Your world is of no concern to me. Maddox, gather your belongings. We're going back to the North to make a new plan."

"No," Maddox said flatly.

Barnabas raised his brow. "No?"

"That's right, *no.* We're going south, to the palace, to talk to Cleiona."

"Maddox . . . ," he growled.

"My decision is final." Maddox turned his back on the stubborn man and took Becca's hand in his. "We're going to see Cleiona, with or without you."

Chapter 26

FARRELL

The first three marks had made Farrell feel like a billion dollars. They had increased his strength, his senses, his ego.

Now it seemed the fourth mark had taken all of that away.

Markus had been dishonest, to say the least, about its side effects, which so far included debilitating weakness and random bursts of massive pain.

And now that Markus had once again drained him of his strength, this time rendering him all but feeble, most of his new skills and sensory advantages had also been dampened.

Terrible timing, really. As Julia Hatcher marched him and Crys out of the dressing room, all he wanted was to be able to overtake her, to use his formerly quick reflexes to come up with a plan to free themselves. But he couldn't do anything except follow her.

Silently too—it seemed that even his gift for conversation was currently lacking. Perhaps he had Crys and not Markus to blame for that—he wouldn't be surprised if she'd stolen his tongue entirely when she'd kissed him in the closet—a handful of moments that had perfectly defined the words *torture* and *bliss* for him.

He glanced at Crys out of the corner of his eye as they walked down the hall in front of Julia, who had Angus's gun trained on them. Crys's face was flushed, her pale blond hair covering half of it.

As he looked at her, two polar opposite compulsions raced through his mind:

Kill her.

Kiss her.

And then a third compulsion butted in:

Save her.

"Mom, don't do this," Crys said, her voice strained. *"Fight this. Becca needs us. Both of us."*

She laughed lightly. "Damen speaks, and I obey, Crys. His power is without equal in this or any universe."

Crys's face blanched. "Mom, you have to break free of this."

"Aw, sweetheart. Quite honestly? I don't want to. This is how it has to be."

"Oh, little brother," imaginary Connor suddenly piped up. *"You are so screwed. All because of this incompetent blonde."*

"Shut up," he growled.

Julia poked him in the back with her gun. "Keep moving."

He narrowed his eyes but kept shuffling forward until they reached the end of the hallway, which opened up to the backstage area. He was half expecting to see Markus waiting for him at their destination. It was his theater after all, his stage. His domain.

The stage lights were on. Farrell looked out at the audience, and the brightness blinded him. He shielded his eyes and scanned the stage, then looked out at the familiar sea of red seats.

No sign of Markus. No sign of Crys's kid sister.

Suddenly, a memory of his Hawkspear initiation three years ago washed over him. Markus himself—an enigma, a god—had called a sixteen-year-old Farrell up in front of the whole society.

Farrell, whose flesh was still free of any marks, agreed to abide by society rules. He swore to honor their code and keep the society's secrets safe from the rest of the world—especially the details of what happened at their quarterly meetings.

Soon after Farrell had made these promises, Markus called a stranger to the stage. It became clear that Markus had brought this man to the stage to be tried for the crime of murdering a society member's cousin and husband.

The jury of society members swiftly found him guilty, and just as swiftly Markus's dagger found his heart.

Afterward, Markus had turned to Farrell and reemphasized the purpose of these criminal hearings: Hawkspear members had been called to perform the duty of ridding the world of evildoers and thus evil things. He then asked Farrell if he was still prepared to pledge his support, and Farrell had responded with a quiet but resolute *yes*.

Though he'd said yes almost immediately, he foggily remembered feeling a large measure of reluctance to join in the horror that he'd just witnessed.

But all of his doubt and fear faded as soon as Markus sliced the dagger through his skin to create his first mark.

"Crystal and Farrell," echoed a voice from the audience. Farrell squinted again until he could just make out Damen Winter, the man who'd made that very dagger. "Welcome to my stage."

"This isn't your stage," Farrell said, forcing himself to sound much stronger than he currently felt. "Where's Markus?"

"Odd," Damen eerily cooed. "I was going to ask you the very same question."

Farrell tried very hard not to react, to make himself look as calm and collected as he possibly could. Was Damen no longer keeping Markus here? If not, where was he?

Suddenly, stumbling in from stage left was Angus, pushed along by one of Damen's masked men. Angus glared at the man, then dusted off his sleeve.

"Hi, kids," he said. "Hello again, Julia. What a fine gun you have there."

"Angus Balthazar," Damen said. "It's certainly a pleasure to meet you."

Angus frowned out at the audience, straining to see past the blinding lights. "From the little I've heard about you, I'm sure I'm quite pleased to meet you too. What can I tell you that might prevent my swift and untimely death?"

Farrell shot the thief a dark look. From the moment they'd met, Farrell could tell by Angus's tacky, faux-sophisticated demeanor that he was an opportunist who'd sell out his own grandmother—or steal from someone else's—to save his own neck.

"You got a plan, little brother?" not-Connor asked. *"Or are you going to stand here like a victim in waiting? Then again, so many of Markus's victims have lost their lives here on this stage. Why should you be any different?"*

He'd thought he and Markus had been growing closer, that they were becoming friends, but all this time Markus had been grooming him to become the victim of the mysterious fourth mark.

Did you get one too, Connor? he wondered, but this time his imaginary brother chose to remain silent.

"Hold on to that thought, Mr. Balthazar," Damen said. "I very well may need some information that only you can provide."

"Please, call me Angus."

"Very well, Angus. Now stop talking."

Angus made a strange little squeaking sound. He kept opening his mouth, but no words came out.

Damen turned his hollow black eyes to Crys. "Crystal, how are you feeling?" he asked. "I know it's been a difficult couple of days for you."

She was trembling. Farrell was expecting her face to fill with fear at this sudden confrontation with Damen, but as his eyes adjusted to the glare of the bright stage lights, all he saw in her was fury.

"Let my sister and my mother go," she said.

"Did you have a pleasant tour of the dressing rooms?" he said, ignoring her request completely. "Of course I noticed the moment you three snuck in. You were quite quiet little mice, but not nearly quiet enough."

Crys frowned. "The Whisperer . . . that's what Angus said some people are calling you, right? I didn't understand that nickname before. What you did at the ball, it . . . it was the opposite of a whisper . . . when you killed those people . . ."

"I didn't kill *you*," he pointed out.

Angus squeaked again.

"But . . . but it's you I've been hearing in my head. Whispering. At the ball and here too. I thought it was me, my own thoughts, my own voice in my head telling me what to do, what to believe. It was impossible to ignore." She pressed her hands against her temples. "It was *you*, wasn't it?"

Damen smiled coldly, his mouth set in a grim line. "Have I really *told* you what to do? I didn't tell you to kiss Farrell. Not specifically, at least. But all it took was a gentle nudge to make you take action. Imagine what I could make you do if I actually tried."

Wait, Farrell thought. That kiss had been a result of Damen's magical persuasion?

Of course it had been. Why should this come as even the slightest surprise? Crys would never have kissed him of her own free will.

He was surprised to find himself disappointed at the truth.

He forced himself to focus again on Damen, hate rising within him. He'd never felt loathing like he did for this creature—this monster who had appeared from nowhere to destroy everything that crossed his path.

He was far more powerful than Markus—that much was clear. Farrell had to admit how truly frightening that fact was.

Markus, where the hell are you? he thought.

Crys stared at Damen, her expression a mix of shame and shock. Julia watched her watching him, her brow furrowed slightly but her expression otherwise blank. Crys blinked a few times, as if willing any distracting feelings away, and then stood up straighter.

"Do you do this with everyone you meet?" Crys asked. "Force them to do things because you're just that terrible at face-to-face communication? And I thought Markus was evil."

Damen laughed lightly. "Oh, you mortals. Always hearing only what you want to hear, believing what you want to believe. Watching you all is so fascinating . . . and so very tiresome. Now I'm going to repeat myself, and you see if you can listen carefully and understand this time. For some mortals—mortals like you, Crystal—no force is necessary to push them where I need them to go. When it comes to their basest desires, all mortals can be manipulated with only the quietest of whispers. Rarely does anyone even attempt to fight these kinds of suggestions. Crystal certainly didn't, did she, Farrell?"

Again, he was rubbing the fake kiss in Farrell's face. Damen seemed to know that would bother him, even before Farrell himself did.

"No," Farrell replied, still fighting to appear calm. "She certainly didn't. Best kiss I've had all week, so I guess I should thank you."

"What *are* you?" Crys managed, her voice breaking.

Damen turned his icy gaze on Crys. "I'm the whisper in your ear encouraging you to take the first step. To be brave. To follow your heart and kiss the boy. Or to listen to your fear and run away and hide. Or to recognize a loss and give up, jump off the ledge." Damen paused, turning back to Farrell now. He waited, just staring at him with that evil, grimacing grin that set Farrell's chest on fire with dread. "Or even," he finally continued, "to slit your wrists."

It took a moment for his words to sink in.

But then they did. Farrell turned to ice.

"It was you," Farrell said, his voice now raw and brittle. "You got into Connor's head. You told him to kill himself."

"Did I?" Damen's tone was casual as he let his chilling question hang in the air. He just sat back and watched them, lurking like a black-eyed predator in the shadows of the auditorium.

Silence hung in the air as Farrell began to tremble with rage and a fresh, stomach-churning dose of grief.

Not-Connor remained quiet, offering no commentary.

"My—my great-grandmother committed suicide too," Crys said, glancing at her mother, who stood stiff like a soldier on the stage. "She jumped off a building."

"Pushed," Julia said under her breath, shaking her head. "She was pushed by Markus."

"Ah, yes, Rebecca Kendall," Damen said. "She was such a single-minded woman. Always so determined to protect her family yet failing at every turn."

Julia's frown deepened. Crys tore her gaze from her mother's to look accusingly at Damen. "So you just decided she should take her own life?" she asked.

Damen shrugged slightly. "She was already old, sick. She didn't have much time left. In a way, I did her a favor."

"Connor was young. He had his whole life in front of him," Farrell growled. "I knew it. I knew my brother would never kill himself, no matter how bad things got."

Not-Connor was silent inside Farrell's head. It was the first time since he'd taken up residence there that he hadn't piped in to comment on the topic of his own death.

"You look at me and you see a monster," Damen said. "But your eyes deceive you. The real monster is the mutual friend Rebecca and Connor shared. *Markus King.* Markus needed Connor, so I took Connor away. Markus needed Jackie, but he lost her the moment Rebecca died and she was led to believe that Markus pushed her. And what a fool he's been, completely unaware that I've been here the whole time. Watching. Waiting. Manipulating the world around him until it was the perfect time for me to come forward to destroy it completely."

It took every last scrap of control for Farrell not to make a suicide leap into the audience and tear Damen into small, bloody pieces with his bare hands. He seethed, his body blazing with hatred for this dark creature.

"Did my great-grandmother's death also have to do with you wanting the book too?" Crys asked. Farrell could tell she was fighting tears.

Damen frowned. In the loaded silence that followed Crys's question, Farrell could tell that Damen had no idea what she was talking about.

Farrell went very still. He hoped that Crys would notice this too and know to close her mouth, not to say another word. Damen seemingly knew everything, was omnipotent, and could control the fate of this and any other world. But if he didn't know about the Bronze Codex . . .

Maybe there was still hope.

He almost laughed. *Hope.* What a strange word to come to his mind. Until just now he'd thought that word had been dropped from his vocabulary altogether.

Maybe Crys felt that same hope: She didn't say another word after Damen failed to acknowledge her question, and Farrell knew she noticed his confusion too. But now it was too silent in the theater.

"You know, the book?" he said. "The one that Rebecca Kendall owned for years and refused to sell to him? It needs to be translated from some ancient language and he's still looking for where it went after all these years."

"Markus and his books," Damen said, shaking his head. "His first love."

"Where is he?" Farrell demanded. Thanks to the bizarre bonding and visionary magic of his fourth mark, he knew Markus had been here earlier. "I know you're keeping him here somewhere. Markus and Becca."

Damen nodded shallowly, his eyes narrowing. "They were here."

Crys gasped, and her gaze turned frantic. "Mom," she turned to Julia, "what happened? Where's Becca?"

Julia remained as still as a statue, her gaze resolutely forward, but her jaw was tight.

"It's all right, Julia," Damen said. "Tell your daughter what happened."

"Yes, Damen." Julia turned toward Farrell and Crys. "Earlier this morning, Damen placed Markus in a locked room, alone, with Becca."

Crys let out a desperate gasp. "Oh God. Did he hurt Becca? Is she all right?"

"We don't know. When we returned less than an hour later, the room was empty."

Crys's eyes widened. "They escaped."

Julia shook her head. "Impossible. That room is impenetrable."

"Which, as a Hawkspear Society member, Farrell should be well aware of," Damen said. "So my question to you is: Where did they go?"

"I don't know," Farrell replied. "I honestly don't."

"Tell me the truth."

"I am telling you the truth. I don't know where they are. I suppose they did escape." He paused, frowning at his own words. "No, they couldn't have. If you're talking about the prison room, it's completely sealed: only one way in and only one way out."

Farrell couldn't believe his own words. Why had he answered so truthfully? And so quickly too?

It was Damen. He was using his magic to get him to tell to the truth.

"Did you know that when an immortal dies, he leaves no corpse?" Damen said, his voice an intrusion on Markus's thoughts. "In death, an immortal's body returns to the magic of which it's composed."

Farrell stared out at him, in denial of what Damen was suggesting.

"If Markus didn't escape from that room," the monster continued, "then my belief is that he is dead."

Oh my God, Farrell thought.

The pain—that wrenching moment of pain in Angus's car when he'd felt as if something vital was being torn from his very soul . . .

Markus . . .

"But what that theory doesn't explain," Damen continued, "is where young Becca is. Perhaps Becca has more magic within her than I suspected. What do you think, Crystal?"

Crys shook her head. "I don't think so. She would have told me."

Damen was using his magical influence on her too. He was drawing the truth from both of their lips with barely any effort.

"You have a question for me, Crys," Damen said. "Please, go ahead and ask it."

"Did you kill my father?" she said immediately. And though there was no hesitation in her response time, she still choked out the words as if they caused her pain.

Farrell tensed.

"Your father also worked closely with Markus in the Hawkspear Society, didn't he?" Damen went on.

"Yes," Crys said quietly.

"How long has it been since you last saw him?"

"A week and a half." She sniffled, and a tear slid down her cheek.

Panic building, Farrell darted his gaze around until it fell on Crys's pink handbag, which she still held tightly to her side. Inside was the dagger.

Could a magical dagger affect a magical being?

He needed to say something, needed to diffuse this situation. To force this interrogation in a different direction.

But his mouth was too dry to speak.

"A week and a half, my goodness. We have a classic Hawkspear mystery on our hands, it would seem," Damen said. "Perhaps Mr. Grayson can help us solve it. Farrell, do you know where Crys's father is?"

"Yes," Farrell answered automatically.

Damn it. This couldn't be happening. He couldn't allow Damen to force him to say these things to Crys. Farrell was a powerful and important member of the society. He wasn't a puppet. He wasn't a victim.

He and he alone controlled his own fate.

She couldn't ever know the truth of what he'd done—*please, no.*

"Ah! And where is he?" Damen taunted.

"He's . . . nowhere," Farrell said through gritted teeth, each word like a shard of glass slicing his throat. "He's dead."

Crys inhaled sharply as Farrell grappled to find some sort of foothold that could help him fight back against Damen's influence.

"Did Markus kill him?" Damen asked.

Farrell tried to clamp his mouth shut, fighting to keep his tongue glued to its bottom. But it was useless. "N-no," he spat out.

"Who did?"

No. No, no, no. Don't say it. Fight this!

"I did." The words were out before he even had a chance to stop them. They echoed loudly in his ears.

Standing next to her mother, Crys stared at him in shock, her pale blue eyes wide and glossy.

Farrell's fists were clenched so tightly now that his short fingernails bit into his skin. He tried to focus on the pain, hoped it would clear his head enough to crawl his way out of this. But that was the problem. His head was already clear. Damen's magic made Markus look like an ant wielding a grape stem and calling it a wand. He couldn't remember a time with Markus when he didn't have at least a *chance* to resist his power. But Damen . . . Damen didn't give him a choice.

"Look at Crystal," Damen said, his tone still humming in that constant flat monotone. "Tell her what happened. Tell her when you killed her father."

As if at the mercy of a sadistic puppeteer, Farrell turned and met Crys's stunned gaze.

"It was the night you and Becca escaped from here. Markus knew Daniel was a traitor. That's an offense punishable by death."

"No." Crys's eyes welled with tears. She started to sob, releasing her pain in heaving gasps.

He watched her, helpless, as a sudden wedge of pressure built up in his chest. It went deeper than the reach of his marks, past the darkness, and lodged there in his heart. He knew it wasn't the effect of dredging up the memory of killing Daniel. It was the expression on Crys's face as she finally learned the truth. Her sorrow found its way inside of him, burrowing into his soul so deeply that he knew it would be changed forever.

"Tell her how you killed him," Damen said.

"I used Markus's dagger," he said, grimacing. "I stuck it in your father's heart, twisted it, and watched the life fade from his eyes."

"Tell her how it made you feel."

"Incredible," he said, hating himself. "Powerful. Worthy." He drew in a shaky breath. "Terrible. Guilty. Horrified. But then those feelings went away, and soon I felt powerful again. I . . . I'm sorry, Crys." How could someone apologize for doing something so heinous? Only a fool would try to use simple, empty words to explain away something so unspeakable. "I'm so sorry. I really am."

She was shaking from head to foot. Her face was a tortured portrait of denial, fear, grief, and hate. Quickly, with a fierceness that made Farrell wince, she whipped her fiery stare over to him.

"You're *sorry*?" she snarled, her voice cracking before she broke out into a scream. "You murdered my father!"

Suddenly, she was upon him, fists flying. She was beating him, throwing punches to his face, his arms, his chest. She didn't hold back, and he didn't try to stop her.

Farrell tasted blood and invited in the sting and hatred of each and every strike.

Angus hurried up behind her. He hugged his arms around her waist as he tried to pull her off of Farrell, silently and clearly still under Damen's order to remain mute. He glared at Farrell, a tome's worth of words behind his dark look.

"You may speak again, Mr. Balthazar," Damen said.

"You bloody *idiot*," Angus snarled.

"P-puppet," Crys managed. "Farrell is a puppet—a slave. His marks make him Markus's slave."

"That doesn't excuse what I did," Farrell said, the truth of it sticking in his throat like poisoned syrup.

"No," Julia Hatcher said. "It doesn't excuse it at all."

Slowly, Farrell turned toward the calm yet vengeful voice.

Angus's gun was in her hand, pointed right at him.

The world around him slowed, and he watched her pull the trigger. He heard the muted crack of the gun.

Farrell staggered back a step as Julia fired again.

And again. And again.

Crys screamed.

Farrell looked down: Four black marks blossomed on his chest. Then came the blood, seeping out and soaking his favorite shirt.

"Yeah," he whispered, as the delayed pain finally slammed into him. "I guess I kind of deserved that."

He fell hard to his knees, then collapsed onto his side. He lay there, neck limp and head heavy on the floor, and watched as his warm red blood formed a pool beside him.

He heard Crys screaming and the clatter of a gun hitting the hard floor. How many other people had died on this stage over the last sixty years, had lain in this very spot and watched their blood soak into the very fibers of this old wooden floor?

His world grew darker and darker, until finally it went black and quiet and cold.

—⚬—

Farrell blinked. He coughed, over and over, smacking his hand down against the slippery blood in a desperate attempt for leverage. He kept blinking away at the blur in front of him until he could see Angus kneeling next to him, his fingers at Farrell's throat.

"No, no," Angus said hoarsely, shaking his head. "No pulse means you're dead. Good God, boy, why are you trying to get up if you're dead?"

Farrell ignored him and somehow managed to push himself into a sitting position. Dazed, he scanned the stage. Crys stood across from him, staring, her hand clapped against her mouth.

He looked down at his ruined shirt. He tore it open and wiped at the blood.

The bullet wounds were closing. All four bullets had gone straight through his chest and come out the other side. He reached over his own left shoulder to feel that the exit wounds were also healing. He wiped at the blood with confusion, so stunned he could barely think. Nothing was clear to him right now—except for the fact that there was something distinctly different about himself.

In the center of his chest he saw a mark that hadn't been there before. It was a gray spiral, about four inches in diameter, that looked like a very old, very faded tattoo.

"Check his skin," called Damen from the audience. "Check his arms. Show me."

Two of his masked gunmen pulled Farrell up like a rag doll. They removed his jacket and what remained of his shirt.

Farrell looked down at his forearm.

His fourth mark was no longer red and raw. It was black.

"Oh, Markus," Damen breathed. "How very clever. I never would have guessed."

"What?" Angus said. "What the hell just happened? What the hell is this?"

"Eva must have shared some of her greatest secrets with him. She was the only one who knew that there is a way for beings made of pure magic to cheat death. The immortal must find a vessel perfect enough to hold his magical essence until he is strong enough to return. Connor Grayson was originally supposed to be that vessel. But then he found that you, Farrell, would be just as perfect."

Farrell couldn't speak. He knew what Damen said was true.

The massive pain he'd felt when Markus had died . . .

No, he hadn't died. He'd merely faded. He'd shed his physical form and transcended into pure magic.

"That's right, Farrell," Damen said evenly, a sinister smile stretching his pale cheeks. "You are the flesh and blood vessel for Markus's immortal magic. Whatever shall I do with you now?"

Chapter 27

BECCA

And just like that, Becca remembered everything. It all came hurtling back to her the instant Liana, a normal girl only a few years older than Becca herself, transformed into a golden goddess.

In a moment of desperation, she tried to find humor in the fact that the very person she was sent here to seek help from had been standing right next to her all day. But the moment quickly faded as the severity of her mistake settled in.

Barnabas finally, grudgingly, agreed to accompany her and Maddox—and Al—to Cleiona's palace, which was another day's journey from where they'd made camp. They set off, and though Becca was overwhelmed and exhausted by what her failure might have caused, she knew she had a very important message to deliver.

Becca sat with Maddox in the back of the wagon only a short time after Liana left. She hugged her knees to her chest, trying to keep herself calm.

"Tell me everything you remember," Maddox urged.

And she did.

He gave her his full attention. With Barnabas listening from the front of the wagon, she told them all that had happened in her world while she was away, right up to her clash with Damen Winter.

Maddox sat, completely rapt and clearly stunned, as Becca told him that Damen was Eva's twin brother. The dark one. The evil one. Eva had been full of light and life and the magic of creation, while Damen was death itself.

She told him how Eva had siphoned the death magic out of Damen in an attempt to weaken him enough to kill him and save what was left of their world.

She finished catching him up, but she left out the dire conclusion she'd drawn from all of this: that when Eva became pregnant, the magic she'd stolen from Damen had been transferred to her child, Maddox.

Of course this was only a guess, but it made so much sense. Still, she didn't feel she could share this with him. Not yet.

She had to talk to Cleiona.

She had to be brave.

As soon as she'd remembered her mission and how she'd gotten here, she thought of the inky shadow of magic. She searched everywhere for it, but the strange shadow that had followed her for days back in Toronto was nowhere to be found now. All she could think was that one of two things had happened: The energy of that dark magic had been used up in transporting her to Mytica, or it was still right where she'd left it, back in that dungeon in the Hawkspear Society headquarters.

How am I supposed to get back home? she wondered, an uneasy feeling settling deep in her gut.

Thunder rumbled up above. Becca turned around to see a dark and distant rainstorm traveling toward them from the north—the same storm that had been following them ever since they left camp. It was the only sign they'd seen that Valoria and her army were still tracking them, but Becca thought it was a pretty convincing one.

To help distract her from the unsettling weather, Maddox told her the story of how they found Princess Cassia and what she'd asked of him. Hearing that he'd denied Cassia's chilling request helped to ease Becca's mind, if only a little.

"You did the right thing," she told him.

"I know," he replied, but he didn't sound completely convinced.

"This day is dark enough without dwelling on such unpleasantness," Al said. He was sitting next to Becca, less than an arm's reach away from her. "Why don't we converse about some more lighthearted topics?"

"What else should we be talking about, Al?" Maddox asked.

She regarded Maddox now as he responded so patiently to Al's interruption. Becca had almost forgotten how cute he was, with his messy dark hair and chocolate brown eyes. His quirky nose that had a slight slant to it, as if it had been broken once. And that shy smile of his that shot straight to her heart every time she saw it.

"I know," Al said. "I'll tell you a story I wrote many years ago, long before Valoria chose me as her personal scribe. It's about a handsome prince and a beautiful sorceress who lived atop a tall mountain. One day, a cruel sea witch put a curse on the handsome prince that turned him into an immortal merman. He grew fins where his legs once were, and he was cast out to live in the sea. Then the beautiful sorceress started to dream about the handsome prince, and he started to dream about her. They would dream about each other every night, and in these dreams they fell in love. They began to search for each other by day, but the searches were never fruitful, because the prince could not leave the sea. The sorceress called out his name over and over until she lost her voice. When she grew too old to continue searching, she died, and her body was swept away by the tide. The sea people drew her down to their kingdom, where her remains were transformed into a young mermaid. Finally, she found the prince, they were wed, and they lived together forever in bliss."

When Al finished, Becca looked to Maddox for his reaction. His mouth had dropped open, and he stared at Al, shocked. "I've read that tale before," he said excitedly. "It was in a collection of my favorite stories . . ."

"*The Teller's Tales*," both Maddox and Al said in unison.

"Oh!" Al exclaimed. "You've read my stories! How wonderful!"

"I had no idea you were the scribe behind those tales!"

"I certainly was. And I still have many such tales within me, but, alas, thanks to the goddess's new laws, I will need to keep them within me."

"Or you can share them with us."

"I would be happy to do that!"

Despite all the stress of the day and the urgency of reaching the goddess, Becca had to smile. Al had managed to find his most ardent fan right in this very wagon.

"What did you think of my tale, Becca?" Al asked.

"I thought it was well told," she said, deciding not to point out the problems so glaring that any creative writing class would have sniffed them out in no time.

"Yes. Yes it was," he agreed.

"There are no such things as sea people," Barnabas said from the front as he guided the horses along the narrow winding road. According to him, they weren't very far from the goddess's palace.

"That is why it's a tale of *fantasy*," Al said.

"I don't have time for fantasy. There's far too much reality to deal with."

Becca shared a tense look with Maddox. Barnabas had been in an extremely unpleasant mood ever since Liana had revealed her true identity, but they hadn't dared pry him about it yet. Still, after spending so many days observing him as a spirit, Becca was fairly certain that Barnabas wasn't someone who would let a personal grievance stand in his way of making a difference in this kingdom.

Cleiona could be an ally. And Becca believed the goddess could help him make that difference.

"There it is," Barnabas said. "And it looks just as loathsome as I've always heard."

"The palace?" Al cried. "Let me see the horror with my own eyes."

Maddox picked Al up and held him aloft so they could look ahead together. Beyond rolling green meadows and hills, past patches of lush farmland, beneath the sunny sky, and at the edge of a river, sat a palace. It shone like gold and sprawled out for what seemed like miles. The tops of its tall spires were inset with sparkling gems so that each one resembled a point in a jewel-encrusted crown.

"Horrifying," Becca said under her breath as the country road transformed into a pathway through a large village. As they rode through, each cottage and shop was nicer and newer than the next. "Yes, I've never been so horrified by anything in my entire life."

Al frowned. "This can't be. Her Radiance told me that all of Southern Mytica is in smoldering ruins, for whenever the goddess has a temper tantrum, she breathes fire through her nostrils."

Barnabas eyed him. "Is that really what Valoria told you?"

"Yes. She also told me that the southern goddess herself is the size of a large cow. All she does is eat lard and ham hocks and sit upon her massive throne all day while jesters entertain her."

"You saw her yourself," Maddox said. "Definitely not like any lard-eating cow I've ever seen."

"I assumed that was more air magic at work."

Maddox furtively rolled his eyes as they moved swiftly through the village. As they drove, citizens going about in the village greeted them with waves and smiles.

"Supposedly the place is populated by cruel, horrible, overworked, and angry people," Al whispered.

"They look rather happy to me," Becca said, waving back at an old lady whose smile revealed sparkling diamonds in her teeth.

"Teeming with fire," Al said, his voice getting quieter and quieter. "Flames and screaming and misery."

"Only in my soul," Barnabas growled. "Now do me a favor and shut up for a moment."

Al pressed his lips together, but his frown remained.

Gradually the buildings became sparse as the village gave way to a grassy field and then the riverbank. They crossed a bridge over the river and were greeted on the other side by the sight of the tall, ornate golden gates leading to the palace grounds.

A guard wearing a blue-and-gold uniform approached and halted them.

"What is your business here?" he asked.

Barnabas stopped the horses but didn't reply.

Maddox sighed and stood up from the back of the wagon. "We're here to see the goddess."

The guard scoffed. "You assume you can simply drive up to the palace and be granted audience with Her Goldenness?"

Barnabas shot a cold look at the man. "Apologies, but did you just refer to that . . . *being* in there as Her Goldenness?"

The guard nodded. "That's what we're to call Her Goldenness.

She commanded it herself only this morning. It is the title with which she now wishes to be addressed, and of course we obey."

"Of course," Barnabas replied flatly.

"She'll see us," Maddox persisted. "Tell her who we are: Barnabas, Maddox, Becca, and Alcander. She knows us."

The guard swept an appraising gaze over the cart. "Yes, she mentioned you. She said you might be arriving today." Frowning, he turned and signaled to another guard, who opened the gates. "Go right in. Kostas will take your horses and vehicle to the stables."

—⁂—

Kostas took the horses away, and another guard swept them up to take them inside the palace. Becca tried her best to remain calm, to remember everything she needed to say as quickly as she could possibly say it.

Several more guards joined them as they were ushered in, and suddenly Becca's gaze was pulled in every direction as she took in the incredible beauty the palace had to offer. Everything gleamed—the mosaic stone floors inlaid with the swirling patterns of red, orange, and yellow flames; the immaculate ivory-colored stone walls adorned with beautiful paintings evoking different aspects of this part of Mytica. And of course there were also several portraits of Cleiona to greet them at every turn as they made their way down a main hallway.

"Vain," Barnabas grumbled, gazing up at a particularly massive depiction of the goddess. "No surprise there."

"I can't see anything," Al complained from the sack Barnabas held.

Becca looked out the multipaned windows and admired the palace grounds, which featured perfectly manicured gardens filled with sculpted hedges and trees. Colorful flowers bloomed everywhere, and now Becca knew where all of the fragrant bouquets set in vases throughout the palace had been gathered.

They stopped at a set of doors that had to be about thirty feet tall. Two of the guards pulled them open to reveal a gorgeous throne room, and a third guard gestured for them to go inside.

This was the second Mytican throne room Becca had seen, and this one—easily the size of a football field—was just as massive as Valoria's had been. The main difference between the two was that Valoria's was beset with earth and water magic to make it resemble a tropical jungle, while Cleiona's was much simpler and more streamlined—but still beautiful.

Yet another mosaic gleamed on the floor of Cleiona's throne room, this one composed of colorful, intricate landscapes. Thick golden pillars reached up from the floor to the gilded ceiling, and the walls were decorated with tapestries and more paintings. In the back of the huge room sat a golden throne, mounted at the top of a dozen steps.

And standing before the throne was the goddess, watching them as they approached. She wore a gown that looked to Becca like it was made from millions of threads of real gold. Woven into her hair—a shade of blond so brilliant it made Becca feel that hers was as dull as dishwater—were dozens of diamonds and sapphires. A hawk was perched on the arm of her throne.

Becca's heart was pounding so fast that she found her steps had slowed down. The weight of her responsibilities felt like a two-ton elephant perched on her shoulders.

"Hey," Maddox said, taking her hand in his. "You can do this."

"I hope you're right."

"I believe in you." He squeezed her hand. "That's what you once said to me. It helped more than you'll ever know."

She met his gaze and gave him a small smile. "Thank you."

"Well, well," Cleiona said, gazing down at them as they reached the bottom of the golden dais. "Look who's arrived. Part of me didn't think I'd ever see you again, Barnabas."

"Trust me," he said tightly. "That would have been my preference."

"The young ones talked some sense into you."

"I wouldn't exactly describe it as *sense*."

After some struggling, Becca finally found her voice. "Excuse me," she said meekly, "but I need to—"

Cleiona raised her hand, silencing Becca, her attention remaining entirely on Barnabas. "Sixteen years. It's been sixteen years, and you hate me today just as much as you did then."

"More, if that's possible."

"I know you think I killed Eva. I didn't. I understand your desire for vengeance, but it is misplaced. Your hatred for me would be put to better use elsewhere."

Barnabas's jaw was clenched so tight it looked painful. "You and Valoria and all the others—you conspired against her. She told me her fears—fears that came to pass."

"You weren't there on that horrible day. You didn't see what happened."

"No, I did not. But what I do see are two goddesses seated upon the thrones of two grand palaces, while mortals kneel at their feet and worship their names. I see what you stole from Eva—the very things you were supposed to stand by her side and protect— burned into your palms. That is all the proof of your guilt I need."

"And yet you still come before me today to ask for my assistance in destroying my sister."

"I know you hate her."

"You're wrong. I don't hate Valoria." She frowned as she glanced at the hawk. "She *is* a bully, granted. And she sees no true value in mortal life. That's how she's always been. But down deep, her heart isn't nearly as black as you think it is."

Barnabas scoffed. "Then you must be referring to a place down *very* deep. Far too deep for a mere mortal like me to ever see."

"I can make a request for you to have an open forum with Valoria and me, so that we might right any grievances you feel you have with either of us. We do have a longstanding agreement to keep to our separate ends of this kingdom, but seeing as how she's recently taken up some extensive travel and a new obsession with Maddox, it would seem that the rules have changed."

"Oh yes. The rules have most certainly changed."

The goddess paused and fixed a small, sad smile on her face.

"You've such loathing in your eyes, Barnabas. You never looked at Liana with such venom."

"Liana was a lie."

"No, she wasn't. Liana and I are the same in every way that counts." She raised her chin. "In fact, you may continue to call me Liana if you wish."

"I believe you prefer Your Goldenness now, don't you? How interesting that you chose the moniker I hurled at you, especially considering that I didn't mean it as a term of respect."

"I found it amusing. Very few things in this world amuse me anymore." She hesitated. "I want you to call me Liana."

"No, I don't think I will. Liana is dead to me, every bit as dead as Eva is. And I pray that the moment I leave here will be the last time I ever see you."

The goddess flinched. "Very well."

Becca was stunned by the boldness with which Barnabas spoke to the goddess, as if he had no fear that she might lash out at him with magic. But Cleiona absorbed it all, her beautiful face beset with grim lines, her vivid sapphire eyes filled with sadness.

Maddox squeezed Becca's hand. "Go on, have your say," he whispered. "You must be aggressive or you'll never get a word in between these two."

"Liana," Becca said, and the goddess shifted her steady gaze toward her. "Barnabas came here because I insisted. You see, after you left, I remembered why I was sent here."

"Is that so?"

Becca gathered all the courage she could so her voice wouldn't tremble. She took a deep breath, then launched right in. "It was Markus who sent me here. With a message. Damen has returned."

Cleiona blinked. She drew in a sharp breath, then sat down on her throne heavily. "Impossible." Suddenly, her eyes blazed with fire as she narrowed them at Becca. "You would dare to come to me with such heinous lies?"

Oh crap. "N-no, not lies," Becca pleaded as calmly as she could. "It's the truth!"

"It can't be. Markus is gone, exiled. By now his magic will have faded away to nothing. And Damen . . . Damen is long dead."

She couldn't back down now. It didn't matter how kind Liana had seemed; Becca had no doubt that if Cleiona thought she was a liar only here to try to manipulate her, she'd react with the exact opposite of kindness. She needed to convince Cleiona she was for real—and fast.

"Damen possesses death magic—he can kill someone with a thought," she said, and she had to brush off Maddox's look of shock in order to continue. "I've seen it myself. I also know that he was Eva's twin brother. In a vision I saw Eva siphon his magic and stab him with a golden dagger—the same dagger Markus stole from the immortals before he was exiled. Just before I came here, Damen imprisoned Markus and me. We were in the same cell together, and Markus used the last of his magic to send me here to give you this message."

The goddess stared at her, her expression shifting from fury to a mix of emotions that were ultimately unreadable. Flames still danced in her eyes. "And just who are you that you're able to have such visions? Who are you that you can travel between worlds?"

Becca swallowed hard. "I am Markus's daughter."

Cleiona went deadly silent. Becca felt a cold trickle of perspiration slide down her spine. She didn't look at Maddox or Barnabas, trying to keep her attention fixed on the goddess.

Cleiona stood up, descended the stairs, and stood before Becca. She reached out and grasped Becca's chin tightly, lifting it up.

Staring deeply back at the goddess, she could feel the heat from the goddess's eyes singeing her skin. Becca wasn't sure which was more horrifying: fire-filled eyes or fully black ones.

The goddess inspected Becca closely, sweeping her gaze over her features and hair, then appraising her entire body from head to foot. By her stern expression, Becca could tell she didn't like what she saw.

"Markus told you to find *me* specifically?" she asked. "How strange. I was never one of his favorites."

The hawk, still perched on the arm of the throne, squawked.

"Well . . . ," Becca started, "he told me that the important thing was for me to find *any* immortal. Valoria had already shown that she wouldn't listen to reason, but I thought you would. I *hoped* you would."

"Damen cannot be alive," she said, her voice breaking midway through.

Cleiona squeezed her eyes shut for a long while. When she opened them, they had returned to their jewel-like blue shade.

Barnabas cocked his head. "Are you . . . crying?"

The goddess blinked her glistening eyes. "Of course not."

"You're terrified," he said so quietly it was almost a whisper. Concern slid through his gaze, and he took a step closer to her, reaching for the goddess before his hand dropped to his side. "Not that it's of any concern to me, of course. Just, don't cry. It's not a becoming habit for a goddess."

"Thank you so much for your interest in what I should and should not do." Cleiona inhaled shakily and turned back to Becca. "What else can you tell me, Becca? What else did Markus say to tell me about this situation?"

"Nothing more," Becca said, giving a helpless shrug. "I assumed you'd know what to do next."

"You assumed, did you?" She laughed, and it sounded pained and humorless. "Damen nearly destroyed my entire world. He reduced it to a gaping hole of nothingness. My closest allies and confidantes are now trapped in a small fragment of what was spared. And because of *this* horrible mistake"—she held out her palms to show the elemental symbols—"they are trapped there, just as I am trapped here."

"*Mistake?*" Barnabas repeated. "You stole the Kindred so you and Valoria could become goddesses."

"Wrong," she snapped. "Another example of your mortal ignorance. We merely touched the crystals and they burned themselves into our very souls, changing us forever. Valoria may have you fooled, but this"—she gestured with her palms again—"is a burden, a daily torture that I have barely been able to withstand all these years. And I'm very sorry, Becca, but there is little that I can do about Damen. Even now, I don't have the power to stop him."

"But Markus said—"

"I don't care what Markus said. He's a liar," she hissed. "You say he sacrificed all of his magic to send you here? Even if it were to relate such vital information, I don't believe Markus would so readily forsake his immortal life. No, he's not truly dead. I don't believe it for a moment."

"I *saw* him disappear—he, like, exploded in a flash of light! Nothing was left behind."

Cleiona scoffed. "You abide by the rules of a mortal's life and death. We are different." She crossed her arms over her magnificent golden gown and began pacing back and forth.

"Her Radiance could help," Al piped up from his sack. "Imagine: two great minds working together with all of your magic combined. You *did* just deny that you hate her."

"It's difficult for Valoria and me to be in close proximity for very long."

"And why is that?" Barnabas asked.

Cleiona flicked her impatient gaze to him but didn't reply to his question. Then she looked to Maddox. "I have been searching for you all these years, believing you were a girl. And now here you are." She shook her head, her gaze solemn and pensive. "You look so much like your father, but I do see your mother in you too."

While Becca was somewhat relieved to see Cleiona soften now, she was also growing increasingly impatient for the goddess to make some sort of decision, to come up with some masterful plan for how to save her world from Damen. She desperately tried to hold her tongue.

The goddess furrowed her brow. "I have something to share with you, Maddox," she said. "This is clearly the right time to do so. But . . . I find that I'm not quite ready yet. I will arrange accommodations for you all so you can rest and eat, and then we will speak again, when I decide that it's time."

Becca couldn't hold in her growing anger for a moment longer. "You want us to just wait around until you're ready to deal with this? My world is in horrible danger! The other night, I watched as Damen killed *five people* without even blinking an eye. And you want to dismiss us so we can rest and eat?"

Cleiona's brows drew together. "I understand your urgency—"

"No, I don't think you do!"

"—but this is my decision and mine alone."

"Fine," Barnabas said, clearly trying to avoid angering the goddess any further. "We'll stay, but for a short time only. But if you keep a harem of men for your personal pleasure, I'd like to know which wing of the palace to avoid, if you please."

"There is no harem here," she said coolly.

"Good." He cleared his throat somewhat awkwardly.

"I need to think by myself," Cleiona said. "I will send for you all when I'm ready to speak again." She gestured to a pair of guards, who approached her at once. "My friends need living quarters and sustenance. Please take very good care of them for me."

The guards bowed. "Yes, Your Goldenness."

—⧓—

Sitting in her sleeping chambers, which were larger and more opulent than the entire second floor of Angus's lavish apartment, Becca couldn't relax. How could she? Even in these accommodations fit for a princess, all she did was pace.

Did her family know she was gone? Were they safe? What had Damen done when he realized that she and Markus had disappeared from the dungeon?

Would Cleiona find a way to stop Damen? Or had the journey here been nothing but a horrible mistake?

And without her shadow with her, how was she ever supposed to get back home?

Too many questions and not nearly enough answers.

She barely picked at the trays and platters of food—fruit, cheese, small delectable-looking pastries—that were brought to her room. She felt too ill, too worried, to even think about eating, but she forced herself to nibble on some of it to maintain her strength.

Becca stood on the balcony and stared out at the beautiful green landscape and the bright blue sky. The sun had been high when they'd arrived, and now it was only a short time before dusk.

There was a knock at the door. She opened it slowly and peered outside.

Maddox stood in front of her, a lopsided smile on his face. "Did you rest?"

She shook her head. "I can't sleep."

He frowned. "But the bed is so soft! I've never felt anything like it." He shook his head. "Never mind that. Cleiona's summoned us back to the throne room. It seems she's finished thinking about . . . whatever she's been thinking about."

Relief washed through her. "Thank God. I was worried she'd take days."

Together they slipped out of the room and navigated the maze of hallways leading to the throne room. She was glad Maddox seemed to know the way, since she definitely didn't.

"Everything will be fine," Maddox assured her. "I know you're worried, but Cleiona and Valoria will figure it out."

"You're willing to trust them?"

"Uh, definitely not."

"Then what makes you think everything will be okay?" She grabbed his hand, stopping him there in the corridor. She searched his face. She really wanted to know the answer to her question. If he felt confident, then maybe she could too.

"Honestly?" He studied the floor and shifted his stance as he spoke. "When you went back to your home, I never thought I'd see you again. But you came back. I know it wasn't because of me, but in that moment, when I first saw you in the forest, I knew with all certainty that anything is possible."

How had this boy managed to work his way into her heart so deeply and so permanently in such a short time? She'd never met anyone like him. There was no one else in the entire universe like Maddox Corso.

"I have to confess something kind of dumb," she said, chewing her bottom lip for a moment before she continued. "But when you kissed me just before I left . . . that was my first kiss. Ever."

He laughed a bit nervously. "It was mine too."

He looked up from the floor. Their gazes locked, and they held them there.

The sound of footsteps ruffled Becca's concentration, but neither of them looked away. From the corner of her eye, she could

404

see Barnabas carrying Al's sack, strolling down the hallway to-ward them. "Are you two coming to meet with Her Goldenness or what?"

Becca finally tore her gaze away from Maddox's, her cheeks warm.

Maddox grumbled something Becca couldn't hear.

"Apologies, was I interrupting something?" Barnabas said.

"Of course not," Maddox hissed.

"I am starting to hate this sack," Al complained. "I can't see a thing! Plus, it itches. I can't wait to have my body back."

Becca repressed a smile as they all continued down the hallway toward the throne room. Becca kept her pace a bit slower than Maddox's and Barnabas's, since she wanted to make sure she could take in all of the amazing details of the palace while she was here.

The men rounded the corner ahead of her. Becca was about to do the same when an iron bar of an arm came around her from behind. A hand clamped against her mouth to silence her scream.

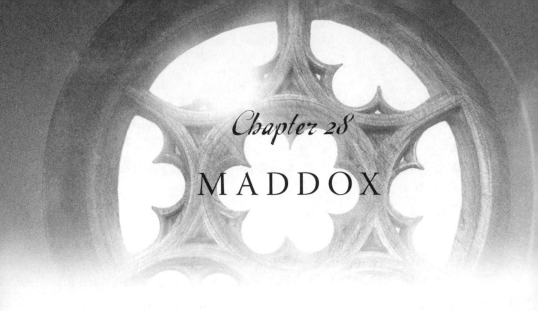

Chapter 28

MADDOX

Becca had disappeared.

Frantic, Maddox searched the halls for her, retracing his steps all the way back to her chambers.

"Where is she?" he asked, his throat tight.

"I don't know." Barnabas helped with the search, bringing Al out of his sack so they'd have another pair of eyes.

"Perhaps she's returned to her world," Al suggested.

"Just like that? Without any warning?" Maddox said. He hated to think it might be true, but it did seem to be the most likely explanation.

Just the thought of it—that she was gone, and he might never see her again—overwhelmed him. In the face of so much pain and trouble, Becca's arrival had given him new hope for the future.

Had that hope been ripped away from him so soon after it had been delivered?

He stopped walking. Feeling weak and lightheaded, he bent over and braced himself with his hands on his thighs, trying to breathe.

Barnabas laid his hand on Maddox's back. "It'll be all right, son."

"No, it won't."

"She delivered her message. That was why she was here in the first place. The only reason. I know it's painful, but if she's gone, then we know that this is the way it needs to be."

"I am loath to remind you," Al said nervously, "but the goddess is waiting. In my experience, an endless amount of patience is one thing goddesses do not possess."

Barnabas nodded and looked at Maddox with both sympathy and urgency. With heavy steps and a heavier heart, Maddox followed his father to the throne room. On the way, they passed a crystal-paned window that looked out to the gardens.

"The sky," Barnabas said warily. It took effort, but Maddox focused his bleary gaze and saw that the heavens were suddenly dark with storm clouds, blotting out any sunset.

The sight of it chilled Maddox. "Valoria."

Barnabas nodded. "We need to hurry."

The guards quickly escorted them into the throne room, where Cleiona was already seated on the dais. She wore her hair loose, in a long cascade of golden waves, and her deep blue, crystal-covered dress matched her eyes. Maddox saw a subtle hint of confusion settle upon her face as she watched the two of them—and Al— make their way forward.

"Where's the girl?" she asked.

Before Maddox could say a word, the tall golden doors behind them were thrust open. A bevy of guards entered, escorting a man into the throne room at sword point. Maddox expected to see a look of fear on his face, but as the man approached, all that was there was smugness.

But the most alarming thing about him was that he wore the brown uniform and red cape of Valoria's guards.

"What is this?" Cleiona asked sharply.

"There is a problem, Your Goldenness," one of her guards said. "A troop from the northern army is at the palace gates."

"Are you attempting to tell me that an entire army managed to travel all the way to my gates without anyone noticing and stopping them?"

"I'm sorry, Your Goldenness. I believe magic was involved," the guard said. He jabbed the enemy soldier with his sword. "Tell her."

"I am here representing Her Radiance, Valoria, the goddess of earth and water," the man said, and his tone was just as smug as his expression. "We have traveled here a thousand strong to demand that you turn Maddox Corso over to the goddess immediately. Do so without argument or organized resistance and the goddess promises that no blood will spill today."

Cleiona regarded him with disdain. "Guards, step back."

In an instant, they did as they were told.

Cleiona kept her gaze on the soldier as suddenly a ring of fire leaped up around him, trapping him within the flames.

"I am only the messenger," he explained, the flames licking at him all the way up to his chest.

"I'm sure you are well aware of the terrible trend of messengers having to pay for the unwelcome news they deliver." The fire rose up, sparking and hissing, to the man's shoulders. "A thousand strong, her army is? Does she really think that has a real chance against me?"

"She wanted you to know that, uh"—he eyed the flames fearfully—"that she, with her own hand, has marked all of her soldiers with special symbols. She said that the time and vast amounts of energy it required of her were well worth it in the end. Because though she sent only one thousand men, those thousand now possess the strength of a hundred thousand."

Barnabas and Maddox shared a worried look. If Valoria had given each soldier the same mark she'd given Goran, would it even be possible to defeat them?

"Valoria, Valoria," Cleiona said under her breath. "You have lost your way, my sister." She turned again to the soldier in red. "And you. Are you marked as well?"

He nodded.

"Show me." With the shifting of her eyes she lowered the flames around him, giving her a clear view as he rolled up his sleeves and showed her the black marks on his forearms. A moment later, the flames were back, roiling down his flesh. He shrieked, but when the flames subsided again, his skin wasn't burned, just raw and pink. The marks were completely gone.

He looked up at Cleiona, deep worry in his eyes. He kneeled before her immediately. "I beg for your forgiveness, Your Greatness."

"She prefers *Her Goldenness*," Barnabas said drily.

"What else can you tell me?" Cleiona asked.

The soldier looked up at her. In the span of a few moments, his face had gone completely pale. "Valoria has taken someone captive. A girl whom she believes means something to Maddox Corso. She is willing to make a trade."

Maddox gasped.

"So she's kidnapped some poor girl, that's it? She thinks that will be enough to make us do as she wishes?" Barnabas scoffed.

"Becca," Maddox managed. Barnabas shot him a look of shock, which quickly shifted to one of understanding.

"Apologies," the frightened soldier cut in, "but she says you have a very short time before she orders the girl's throat cut."

In a flash, without thinking for another second, Maddox was storming out of the throne room. Barnabas caught up to him in the outer corridor, and four guards also emerged from the throne room but made no move to stop him.

"No, you can't go out there," Barnabas said firmly as he stepped in front of Maddox to block his path.

"Get out of my way."

"You're not sacrificing yourself for her. You can't."

"Becca's helpless out there!" Maddox jabbed his index finger in the direction of the gates. "Valoria's after *me*, not her. She won't kill me—and she won't kill Becca if she sees me."

"I'm not willing to take that chance." Barnabas reached into the sack he held and pulled Al out by his hair. Al blinked several times, looking scared and scandalized all at once. "Al, listen to me. We need you. More than we ever have. Please, tell us something, anything, about Valoria that might help us handle this situation. What is her greatest weakness? Is there anything you can think of that might convince her to release Becca without any bloodshed today?"

Al was silent for a long moment, not even complaining about being dangled by a clump of his hair—something Maddox knew he hated. "Apologies, Barnabas. But I cannot."

Barnabas growled and gripped Al's hair even tighter. "Your delusional loyalty toward Valoria is maddening!"

"No, please don't misunderstand me. I am no longer loyal to her, I promise you that. She had me executed for treason—for a treasonous crime I'd yet to commit, and that I never would have committed. She had me killed because she had a bad dream. She was wrong to have me killed. And I've slowly come to see that she has been wrong about so many things and has made so many bad decisions over the course of her reign. That's why she needed me—a scribe specializing in fantasy tales who could tell her story the way she wanted others to hear it. She didn't want to relate the truth. Which is why, Barnabas, I'm sorry to say that all I know about that dark creature are the falsehoods she's told me. The lies meant to cast her in a better light—in any light at all. And if the price I pay for this admission is you hurling me into a fire because I haven't proved my worth to you, then so be it."

Barnabas hissed out a long sigh. "Don't worry, Al. You're not going in any damn fire."

"Oh, thank the goddess! Er, I mean, thank *you*. Thank you, my friend."

"Enough," Maddox growled, shoving past Barnabas. "Get out of my way. I'm going."

"Didn't you hear me?" Barnabas snapped, grabbing the back of his tunic. "I said no. *No*, Maddox!"

"Let go of me." Maddox clenched his fists, channeling his magic with all the rage he felt.

He released one of his fists, and Barnabas went skidding backward, clutching his throat and gasping for breath. Then, without a pause or a glance to make sure his father was all right, Maddox continued down the corridor.

Suddenly, Cleiona was walking next to him, a group of her guards trailing several paces behind.

Maddox eyed her but didn't slow down. "If you want to stop me—"

"I don't. I'm coming with you. I need to speak to Valoria."

"I thought you said you couldn't get too close to her."

"I'll have to make an exception today. It seems she's given me no choice."

Together they exited the palace and entered the darkened day. Storm clouds still gathered, but no rain had fallen yet. A strong wind from behind them blew Maddox's hair over the front of his forehead, forcing him to slick it back again and again so he could see what lay ahead.

Cleiona had gathered her army, which was at least double the size of Valoria's troop, which awaited them on the other side of the gate. They stood at attention behind her.

And there, standing before her red-and-brown-uniformed army, was Valoria. She wore a black gown, its massive skirt embroidered with a gruesome pattern of intertwined silver cobras. Maddox took a deep breath. He tried to look for Becca without compromising the fierce expression on his face as he and Cleiona kept walking toward the northern goddess.

"Well," Valoria said as the two approached. "This is a surprise. Greetings, sister."

"It was a mistake for you to come here today," Cleiona said.

"Come no closer."

Cleiona stopped, her expression growing ever tenser. They were about ten feet away from the main gates.

Maddox watched Cleiona carefully before casting a dark look at the other goddess. Despite her flippant words, it seemed to him that Valoria was greatly perturbed by the sight of her sister, the goddess of fire and air.

A sudden bright light directed Maddox's gaze downward. The goddesses' hands had begun to glow, brilliant light emanating from the elemental symbols branded on their palms.

Cleiona noticed his curious look before turning her narrowed gaze back to her sister. "It seems that our magic doesn't want us so close to each other."

"Or perhaps it does. Perhaps we're the ones who stand in its way," Valoria said, grimacing.

"It gives both of you great pain to be near each other," Maddox said. "I can see it."

Cleiona nodded, her expression pinched. "This is the closest we've been in well over fifteen years."

There it was, the solution to one of the great mysteries he'd always wondered about: One goddess lived in the North, while the other, her sister, stayed in the South, leaving a wide stretch of un-claimed land between them.

He wondered now what might happen if they accidentally touched each other.

"Let's move this along as swiftly as possible," Valoria said tightly, then nodded at Maddox. "I assume you're here to exchange yourself for the girl?"

Maddox met her gaze. "I want to see her first."

Valoria turned to her sea of soldiers and gestured with a jerk of her chin.

There was a rustle among the men, and then Goran appeared, holding Becca tightly by her upper arm.

"Maddox!" she called out.

Maddox swept his gaze over her, checking if Becca was wound-ed. He only breathed once he saw that she was unharmed, only frightened. But he could not feel true relief—not while the man who murdered his mother had Becca in his filthy grasp.

"Are you all right?" he asked.

She nodded stiffly. "For now."

"Perhaps you'd prefer that she come along with us as well?" Valoria said, keeping a keen eye on Maddox as he stared at Becca. "It's always a delight to witness the power of young love."

"Is it?" Maddox asked sharply. "And how would you know how delightful it is? Have you ever loved anything—ever truly felt warmth or kinship or passion with anyone—in your long, wretched, selfish life?"

Valoria's lips curled into a cruel, unforgiving smile. "Barbed words can't injure me today, my dear boy. Not when I'm feeling so victorious. Now, shut that running mouth of yours and come with me. This won't be as bad as you think. You'll be happy to know that I've had time to think, and I've decided to forgive you for your crimes." She glanced away from Maddox, her attention now fixed on something behind him. "I will even spare your father's life if you come along without any further difficulty."

Maddox turned. There was Barnabas, carrying Al's sack and pushing his way past Cleiona's soldiers. Maddox was relieved that he seemed to be uninjured.

"Don't interfere," Maddox growled at him as he came to stand on Maddox's other side.

"I'm not interfering," Barnabas replied. "I'm observing. You've made it clear that you don't need my advice. That you know what path is best."

"Is that what that was? Advice? It sounded to me like an order."

"Your father cares about you, boy," Al said quietly.

Maddox turned to Cleiona. "Open the gates."

Al drew in a breath. "Cover me, Barnabas. I don't want her to see me like this."

Barnabas did as requested and pulled the canvas material completely over Alcander's head.

Cleiona hesitated a moment before nodding at the pair of guards stationed at the gate. Maddox watched as the gates opened up before him.

There was no longer any barrier between the two armies. Motionless, silent, they stared at one another from across a divide of a mere twenty paces.

Maddox took one step forward.

"Valoria!" Cleiona called out. Maddox froze. "Damen is alive."

Valoria snapped her gaze to Cleiona. "What did you say?"

"You heard me."

Valoria smiled her wicked grin again and scoffed. "That can't be. He's dead. I saw him die with my own eyes."

Cleiona shook her head. "The girl you've taken captive? She was sent here by Markus to bring me this information. Damen is in her world. He's there to play with it, like a cat toys with an injured bird before tearing off its head."

"*Markus?*" A sliver of fear slid through Valoria's green eyes. She shook her head. "No. I don't believe it. I can't."

"Are you sure? Are you so sure that you're willing to risk everything? You know what's at stake if you're wrong."

Valoria turned to Becca. "Is this true?" she snarled.

Becca nodded. "Yes."

"You came here from another world, the same world in which Markus lives in exile?"

"Yes. That's right."

"Becca is Markus's daughter," Cleiona explained.

Stunned now, Valoria's eyes grew wider. "Tell me more. I need to know more! Where is the golden dagger? Where is the book that the witch-boy and his father stole from me?"

Cleiona laughed, deeply and without humor. "I've just told you that the greatest evil of our world is back from the dead, and you want to know where you can find a dagger and a book? Your obsession with power continues to disgust me."

Valoria glared with narrowed eyes as the ground began to rumble. In mere moments, the earth cracked and splintered, dividing both armies as it spread between the goddesses.

"Be careful with your words, sister," Valoria hissed. "Or today will not end well for you."

Cleiona narrowed her gaze and flames suddenly shot up from the crack in the ground before disappearing just as quickly. "Do not be vain in your display of magic today, or you will be the one cowering at the end of it."

Valoria scowled before turning to regard Becca again.

"What does Damen want?" she demanded. "Is he coming here to seek vengeance?"

"I—I don't know."

"Have his powers subsided? Is he still a threat? Is he still capable of destroying worlds, breaking them apart and crumbling them to dust as if they were clumps of dirt in his fist? How did he manage to survive? There were witnesses to his death; he couldn't have fooled us. Eva wouldn't have let him live, knowing what he was capable of."

Becca shook her head, her face pale. "I . . . let me answer as much as I can. I want to help, but I confess I don't know everything."

"Worthless girl," Valoria hissed. "It's obvious that Cleiona has trained you, taught you how to respond to me so that you might manipulate me. I refuse to listen to another valueless word that comes out of your lying throat."

"You hear that, little girl?" Goran spoke into Becca's ear, making sure he did so loudly enough for Maddox to hear. "Her Radiance says you're worthless."

She shook her head. "But wait. I said I can—"

With a sharp twist, Goran snapped Becca's neck. He let go, and her lifeless body fell to the ground in front of him.

In an instant, everything in Maddox's world went dark. Everything—the goddesses, his father, the murderer, the dueling armies standing atop the cracked earth waiting to do battle—except Becca. She was all he could see. Everything else became meaningless.

"Becca," he found himself whispering. "Get up. Please, get up."

But he knew it was in vain. Becca Hatcher didn't move. Didn't breathe. Her eyes were open, glossy, and staring directly at him.

She'd come here to help. To try to save her world from evil, despite how frightened she must have been when Markus proposed that plan to her. And now she was dead because of Maddox. Because of Goran. Because of Valoria.

His mind was blank of everything except those few simple truths.

"Maddox!"

He could hear someone shouting his name as if from underwater. The shouting kept on, over and over, until finally he made out Barnabas's voice. He kept calling out, his voice pitchy and filled with panic. "Don't get any closer to them. Whatever you want to do right now—don't! Please, don't do it!"

But it was far too late for that warning.

Once again the edges of his world darkened to black. Ice flowed through his veins, his limbs, penetrating every inch of his body until he was certain he'd never feel warm again.

In a violent flash of rage, Maddox tore his gaze away from Becca's broken body to look directly at Goran. The assassin stared right back at him, foolish defiance in his eyes, the marks Valoria had given him visible on his arms and throat.

This man killed his mother. And now he'd killed Becca. He'd broken a young girl's neck as if taking her life was no different than swatting a fly.

He narrowed his gaze, channeling all that icy rage into a single, cold-blooded thought.

Die.

And with that, Maddox crushed his heart.

Without a sound, without a single gasp for breath, Goran dropped to the ground.

Maddox had a moment of regret that it had been far too kind a death for such a demon. He should have concentrated harder, made him really suffer. To have heard Goran scream for mercy, to have watched him squirm with unspeakable pain before taking his final, torturous breath—that would have been much more satisfying.

"Maddox!" Barnabas's shouting managed to penetrate Maddox's shield of anger and death magic.

But Maddox could still barely hear him.

Valoria looked down at her fallen assassin. Her face was ghostly pale as she turned to her army, raising her hands. They took the gesture as a command to charge. They drew their weapons and, with a rising battle cry, stormed toward the gates.

Maddox cast out the bottomless darkness within him. Like a shroud of shadows, it hurtled up into the air to cover all of the men who dared take any steps toward him. They were all his enemies. Every single one, by their very presence on the other side of Cleiona's gate, had a hand in Becca's death.

As the shroud of shadows enclosed them, the army froze in place, swords and battle-axes in hand.

One by one, every last soldier dropped to the ground, kneeling for a moment before making their final fall, as if showing allegiance to a new leader.

Maddox shifted his gaze to Valoria, the only one left standing beyond the gates. The only one who still lived.

"I didn't want this," Valoria said, shaking her head. "I didn't command him to kill her. I didn't know—I had no idea that you were this powerful. Please, Maddox. Spare me."

Was the goddess admitting that his magic was strong enough to kill her?

Did she truly fear him?

The thought was incredibly intriguing.

"Maddox, please, spare her . . ." Cleiona's soothing voice came from behind him. "I know quite well how many wrongs she's committed in her life. I do. But she's my sister."

Maddox turned his gaze away from both of them and looked out at the field of dead before him. He searched the bodies calmly, stopping when he found her. He walked past the gates and went to kneel at her side, where he found his mind utterly blank of rational thought. His world was now completely shrouded in shadows, even the part of the world where Becca lay.

Her lifeless eyes stared up at him as he took her limp hand in his.

He could feel how much magic he had left inside of him. It truly seemed to have no end. He focused this magic on her, and the effort it took—the sheer will it took to concentrate—was much greater than it had been when he'd unleashed that darkness upon the soldiers.

It took far more effort to coax life out of hiding than it did death.

And then Becca gasped the first breath of her second life.

Chapter 29

BECCA

Becca opened her eyes. She smiled and tried to focus on Maddox. On his handsome face, his crooked nose, his messy hair. And his . . .

And his jet black eyes.

Jet black, just like Damen's.

Becca scrambled away from him. "Maddox! What happened?"

"Good. It worked," he said, his voice strangely cold.

"What have you done?"

"Let me help you up." He offered her his hand. She stared at it, frozen, for several moments until, not knowing what else to do, she took it. He pulled her to her feet.

On her way up, she saw the bodies. She winced and shut her eyes against the image, but then forced herself to open them and look around. A wave of sheer horror washed over her as she took in the sight of a thousand men lying on the ground around her, not moving, not breathing.

Maddox sent a dark look toward Valoria, whose hands flew to her throat as she began to sputter and gasp.

"No," Becca gasped. She clutched his arm, her frantic thoughts swirling in her mind. "Don't. No more, Maddox. You've done enough."

Maddox regarded her with disbelief, as if she'd committed some terrible betrayal. "You'd protect someone like her? Someone who'd stand by and watch as that monster Goran snapped your neck?"

She touched her throat. The twist, the crunch, the darkness . . . She remembered now.

Oh God. Dead—I was dead! He killed me!

Her heart thundered painfully in her chest as shock threatened to silence her.

She forced herself to speak, to put her thoughts of what had happened aside for now. "Maddox . . ." She tightened her grip on him. "I don't give a damn about her. I'm trying to protect you. Stop it! Please!"

Finally, her frantic pleadings got through to him. He looked at her with a somewhat calmer expression. "Very well."

Valoria wheezed. Becca watched her stagger back from the gate, nearly tripping over a fallen soldier. She turned again to Maddox.

His eyes were still black. "I killed them all, and it was so easy. Too easy."

Becca touched his face, forcing herself not to be afraid of him. "It's all right. I'm all right now and . . . and you are too, right?"

Cleiona stepped forward until she was face to face with Valoria. The two sisters stood about a dozen paces away from Becca and Maddox. "You know what this means," Cleiona said, her expression grim and pained at being so close to her sister.

Valoria nodded stiffly. "I suppose I do."

"It's the sign we've been waiting for."

"That *you've* been waiting for, you mean."

Becca strained to listen to their quiet conversation. What had they been waiting for what? For what Maddox just did?

Had they known the truth about his magic? How it was connected to Damen's?

Barnabas stood only a few feet away from her and Maddox, still holding on to Al's canvas sack. His body was rigid. His jaw was tight. He'd said nothing since Becca was brought back, and now his attention was not on the two goddesses but fully on Maddox.

Cleiona's guards remained behind the gates, their swords sheathed. They stood at attention but made no move to cross the threshold before them.

"You honestly don't care that Damen is alive?" Cleiona asked. "That he's out there, wreaking havoc somewhere? He could return to Mytica and exact revenge on all of us. Consider *that* before you go back to your throne and try to pretend this never happened."

Valoria said nothing, though her brow was deeply furrowed. Cleiona scowled impatiently, then turned her back on her sister. She flicked her pained gaze to Barnabas for only a moment before she regarded Maddox.

"I need to show you something. Will you come with me?"

After a moment's hesitation, he nodded.

Becca took his hand in hers as the goddess led them past the somber fleet of her guards and soldiers and back inside the golden palace. She turned to look at Barnabas as he silently trailed after them along a golden corridor. Their eyes met for a moment, but then Barnabas looked away.

"I had to do it," Maddox told his father softly, glancing over his shoulder at the man. "All of it."

Barnabas nodded. "I know," he said sadly.

He glanced again at Becca, and she could see the bottomless worry in his eyes. And fear. Fear she knew was meant for Maddox.

They followed Cleiona deeper into her palace, and in the silence of their procession, Becca fell into a daze. Was this all really happening? Or was this merely the first stop on her journey to the afterlife?

No. No, it was too soon. She wasn't as strong as she pretended to be, especially not now. She was the same scared little girl now that she'd been at Damen's mercy, tongue-tied and uncertain.

She'd been dead.

Dead.

She slid her hand over her throat—the same throat Goran had crushed. She stumbled, and Maddox caught her arm to keep her steady.

"Are you all right?" he asked.

She tried to find her breath, her composure, but they both slipped away from her grasp. "No."

His expression tightened. "I'm sorry."

She shook her head back and forth until she felt dizzy. "Don't be sorry."

A piece of art on the corridor wall caught her eye: a tapestry depicting a golden hawk that she'd noticed when they'd first arrived at the palace. She stared at the beautiful details and the texture of the fabric.

She tried desperately to concentrate on something real, something concrete. Anything to keep her from giving in to the panic swirling inside of her that made her want to run away from this place, as far as she needed to go to forget what had just happened.

Her chest fluttered wildly, as if there were a frantic bird trapped inside. *My heartbeat*, she thought, pressing her palm to her chest in an effort to steady it. She made a point of deeply drawing air into her lungs and exhaling it out, just like she did thousands of times a day without thinking about it. She had never been more conscious of the simple tasks she needed to perform to stay alive.

"It's not much farther," Cleiona said as she unlocked a door that lead to a long flight of stairs that took them deeper into the palace. A series of torches magically caught fire to help light their way in the darkness.

"You're trembling," Maddox said as they carefully descended the staircase.

Becca forced herself to meet his eyes—still pitch-black. "How are you feeling right now?"

He shook his head. "I don't know. I feel . . . strange. As if there's this . . . hollowness inside of me. I don't know how to describe it. I feel like all my blood has turned to ice."

"Does it hurt?" Barnabas asked, his voice raspy. He'd folded back the canvas on Al's sack so that the solemn, serious-looking head could observe as Barnabas carried him.

"No." Maddox shook his head. "Nothing hurts."

Becca shivered and glanced at Barnabas, who looked back at her with a deeply pained expression. What exactly had Maddox sacrificed when he'd killed all those men and brought her back to life?

Becca had a lot to learn about magic, she knew, but it didn't take a sorceress to know that there had to be a steep price for practicing magic this dark.

Cleiona stopped at a stern-looking iron door and turned to face Maddox, Becca, and Barnabas. "Valoria and I are the only ones who know what lies beyond this door."

"What is it then?" Barnabas asked, his tone a combination of weary and determined.

"A secret."

Barnabas sighed. "This is not the time for games, Liana." He frowned. "I mean, *Cleiona*."

"I've told you: Please do call me Liana."

"It's not your name."

Cleiona searched Barnabas's face with reverence, as if she expected to find a lost treasure somewhere inside of it. After a long moment, she placed her hand against the door. "For a multitude of reasons, Valoria and I have spent many years searching for Eva's daughter. But Eva didn't have a daughter. She had a son, and now that son is here inside my palace. Maddox, you've proven the incredible depth of the magic that flows within you. I only hope it will be enough."

"Show us this secret of yours," Barnabas growled.

She cast him a wary, almost fearful look. "I hope that one day soon you will come to understand that it had to be this way, Barnabas. That it has been necessary for us to guard this secret."

"Open the door," he said.

"Very well." She reached for a small golden key that she wore on a long golden chain around her neck. She slid it into the lock and pushed the door open.

Becca braced herself for whatever horrible truth they were about to confront, but as Cleiona opened the door and gestured inside, all she did was frown. She blinked to be sure she hadn't missed anything, and she took one step closer, stopping just before the threshold but not crossing it. Behind the door was a small room. In the center of it was a canopy bed made up with pale linens. Otherwise, the room was empty. Becca narrowed her eyes—this couldn't be the secret Cleiona was talking about. And then she saw it: a figure, a woman, tucked underneath the covers and sleeping soundly.

Barnabas hesitated at the threshold before taking a step inside. He approached the bed, inspecting the sleeping woman. Suddenly, his ruddy face went completely pale.

"Who is it?" Al finally spoke.

Maddox frowned. "Barnabas, what's wrong?"

Barnabas attempted to reply, but his voice was too choked and raspy.

Alarmed by Barnabas's reaction, Becca drew closer to the bed. "Who is this?" she said, staring down at a beautiful young woman with long dark hair. Then she knew. She recognized her from her vision about Damen. "Oh my God. It's Eva," Becca said.

Maddox gasped and stared down at the woman with unguarded shock.

"Yes, that's right." Cleiona came forward and sat on the edge of the bed. "Eva is the only one who can save our worlds. Both yours and ours, Becca." She paused to let a profound wave of sadness flood her gaze as she looked up at Maddox. "And your magic is the only way to wake her."

THIS THRILLING SAGA OF MAGIC, MYSTERY, AND

MORTALS WILL CONTINUE IN BOOK THREE OF

THE *Spirits* AND *Thieves* TRILOGY....

ACKNOWLEDGMENTS

Thank you to my amazing editor, Liz Tingue, for sticking with me on this one, for encouraging me, for being patient, and for wielding her magical, sparkly editing wand (it is a magical, sparkly wand, right?) like a fairy godmother to help this book fully live up to its potential. You are truly the awesomest of awesome.

Thank you to my agent, Jim McCarthy, for the pep talks and cheerleading and unfailing confidence in my writing. I could almost imagine the pom-poms. Sometimes we all need pom-poms.

Thank you to Amber Curtis for winning my contest to rename the character formerly known as "Bob the Scribe" who is now named Alcander Verus. Huzzah!

Thank you to my readers. I adore you all and your most excellent taste in books.

Thank you to my fabulous friends and family who have put up with all my writer's angst over the last, oh, decade or so.

Thank you to my Keurig coffee maker.

Thank you to chocolate.

Thank you to Netflix.

And thank you to Ian Somerhalder. I don't know him personally, but I just wanted the chance to thank him.